The
Abandoned
Heart

ALSO BY LAURA BENEDICT

NOVELS

Charlotte's Story

Bliss House

Devil's Oven

Calling Mr. Lonely Hearts

Isabella Moon

ANTHOLOGIES

Surreal South '11

Surreal South '09

Surreal South: An Anthology of Short Fiction

The Abandoned Heart

A BLISS HOUSE NOVEL

LAURA BENEDICT

PEGASUS CRIME
NEW YORK LONDON

THE ABANDONED HEART

Pegasus Books Ltd.
148 West 37th Street, 13th Floor
New York, NY 10018

First Pegasus Books cloth edition October 2016

Interior design by Maria Fernandez

ISBN: 978-1-68177-229-5

10 9 8 7 6 5 4 3 2 1

Printed in the United States of America
Distributed by W. W. Norton & Company, Inc.

For Nora

beloved beyond words

Prologue

It was the spring of 1876, and the first families of Old Gate, Virginia, were putting on quite a show for the man from New York who meant to be their new neighbor. The world was not such a large place that someone from a good Virginia family did not have connections in New York who could make *inquiries* about such a man. So everyone in the county already knew that Randolph Hasbrouck Bliss was about thirty years old, the son of a man who was reputed to have made an enormous fortune buying cotton from farmers in the Confederate States (sometimes from the government itself) for resale to the Northern textile mills, and then selling arms and ammunition back to the Confederacy. That he had a wife who was, interestingly, several years older than he, and a young daughter who, it was said, wasn't quite right in the head. That he had been educated at the College of New Jersey, and, after having shown some skill in managing one of his father's import operations (French wines, and more textiles), had decided to try his hand at farming apples and peaches in central Virginia. Those who had made the *inquiries* hadn't been able to find out exactly why he had decided to change careers, but there were whispers that he had *habits* of a nature that embarrassed and displeased his mother, who was from old Dutch New York stock. It was believed that those *habits* involved women. Often much younger women, and women of ill repute.

But the dinner guests at Maplewood, the gracious, pillar-fronted home of Katharine "Pinky" Archer and her husband, Robert, found their prejudices undermined as soon as they met Randolph.

He wasn't a man whom any woman would particularly call handsome, with features that were heavy and decidedly non-patrician: a prominent nose and thick, dark brows. But his jaw was strong and his brown eyes alert and lively. He wore his clothes well, despite having a waist that did not taper much from his broad shoulders, and an overall frame that was more like that of a laborer than of a man who spent his days giving orders to others. Like every other man in the room, he was dressed in a double-breasted evening coat of black, with matching trousers. His silk waistcoat was a rich shade of peacock blue that was at once daring and elegant. They could see that everything he wore was of superior quality, and though his face was rather common, he inhabited his expensive clothes with an easy, animal grace.

After a dinner that included expected delights like smoked oysters, turtle soup, bison, and a French cream tart, the Reverend Edward M. Searle and a couple of the other men of Old Gate watched Randolph with interest as he stood, smiling, surrounded by women. The women, including Edward's wife, Selina, and their hostess, Pinky Archer, preened under Randolph's gaze. His compliments were easy and witty. Was it that gaze that attracted them? As he looked at each woman, he seemed to give her his undivided attention, and when he looked elsewhere, she would wilt a bit. The women's attraction to Randolph was puzzling to all of the men, and, if they had spoken to one another about it, they might have agreed that it had something to do with the juxtaposition of his wealth and his common appearance. Or was it the uneasy sense that he was capable of doing the unpredictable?

When Pinky sat down at the piano, she asked who would be willing to sing "Silver Threads Among the Gold," as she had recently learned it, and Randolph volunteered readily. He sang confidently in a bold, baritone voice, but showed a strong degree of modesty when the group—particularly the women—applauded enthusiastically at the song's end. One of the older women, Pinky's mother, dabbed discreetly at her eye with a handkerchief.

When the singing was done, the party broke into smaller groups. Some played cards, others gathered around the enormous book of drawings of New York scenery that Randolph had sent as a gift to his hostess. With most of the women occupied, Edward, who was the priest at St. Anselm's Episcopal Church, saw his opportunity to speak to Randolph alone.

A servant had brought Randolph a glass of water, and he was finishing it when Edward approached. He spoke quietly. "Randolph, won't you walk outside with me for a moment? The evening is fine, and I like to take a small stroll after a large meal. Maplewood's garden is quite fragrant in the evening."

Randolph smiled, his dark eyes full of mischief. "Are you sure you wouldn't rather take a turn with one of these beautiful ladies, Edward? Your wife looks very becoming. In fact all the women I've met since I arrived in Old Gate are possessed of charms unseen where I come from in New York. And I warn you. I won't sit still if you try to kiss me beneath a rose bower."

Robert Archer, their host, was passing and chanced to hear Randolph's response. He stopped, chuckling. "You can trust Edward. I've known him since we were boys, and he never tried to kiss me once."

A slight look of irritation passed over Edward's face, but he banished it quickly and, with feigned gruffness, said, "But you haven't Randolph's exotic Yankee charm, Robert. Familiarity breeds contempt, as I'm sure you'll agree."

"Scoundrel. Don't be long with your stroll, gentlemen. I fear the ladies will not tolerate Randolph being away from them much longer." He laid his hand on Randolph's broad back in a gesture of camaraderie that was not quite a slap. "You've become quite the favorite already. You'll have to tell me your secret sometime. My Pinky and I have only been married five years, yet sometimes I think that since I've passed the age of thirty she sees me as ready for the ash heap. Beware, Randolph. The young women of the county are a flirtatious set, but we love them dearly, don't we, Edward?"

Edward nodded sagely and guided Randolph to the door.

Outside, the evening was indeed fine, and the cloudless sky above Maplewood was a brocade of countless stars.

"You can't see the sky like this in New York, in the city." Randolph stopped on the garden's path and looked up. "Too many factories, too many lights. My wife, Amelia, will like it here very much. She is reluctant to leave Long Island, but I think she and my daughter will be happy in the end. I have a working design for Bliss House, though it is sure to take more than a year to build."

Edward cleared his throat. "Some would say Old Gate is a bit rough around the edges, but I was happy to come back here after the war and seminary."

"I can't think of a better place to build new traditions for myself and my family. Sometimes a man needs to escape the bonds of family tradition, don't you agree?"

"Then I would say you will find its isolation to your liking. Old Gate is not like other Virginia towns. We are an insular place. The people who settled here, rather than in larger places like Lynchburg or Charlottesville, came here—or come here—because they were either not wanted in those larger societies or had reasons of their own for absenting themselves." He looked closely at Randolph. "What are your reasons for wanting to come to a place as remote as Old Gate?"

Randolph smiled and gave a small laugh. "I suppose I want a change. Nothing wrong with that, is there? As I said, sometimes the bonds of family can become too tight."

Rather than pressing him further, Edward glanced over his shoulder to see if they were being followed and continued walking. "This way, please." When he was satisfied that they were far enough away from the house, he stopped again. He was several inches taller than Randolph, and the moonlight sharpened his patrician profile: a high, Grecian nose, tall forehead, and chiseled chin. His prominent height intimidated many people.

Randolph looked up at him without any sign of anxiety. "Is something troubling you? I'll be of assistance if I can."

"My friends would not thank me for speaking with you. While I am of their society, they hold somewhat more jaundiced views than I on many things." He shook his head. "I would never accuse them of a lack of integrity, but I fear that the trio of individuals who own the property you are about to purchase for your home has not been completely honest with you."

Randolph laughed. "It is business. No business can be conducted in complete honesty. Nothing would ever be settled. Do you think the price they ask is too dear? It seems quite reasonable to me. It's a prime bit of land. Perfect for orchards, and an excellent home site."

"If it is so excellent, is it credible to you that it should be so close to town and as yet undeveloped? We have undergone much improvement since the war."

"Is there some defect I should know of? I have found none. Monsieur Hulot, my architect, has approved the surveyor's report, and will depart with his assistant from France at my telegram. I have spent much time at the site. I am satisfied. What is this, Edward?" Randolph assumed a joshing tone. "Is there some other bidder you want it for? I'm not afraid of paying a bit more to ensure that I have it. Or—" He seemed to consider for a moment. "Is it that my erstwhile neighbors are disturbed because they've learned that the distinguished Monsieur Hulot happens to be a Negro?"

Edward gave a little cough. "I'm sure that has never come up."

"Then just tell me what it is you have to tell me."

"Very well," Edward said. "A lot of the old families struggle to keep up their homes. The ones farming tobacco are just recovering. They need the money. Your money."

"Seems a fair trade."

"That particular farm was never planted with tobacco. It was part of an early land grant, and the owners leased different parts of it to many tenants over the years. When I was a boy, it was home to the Doyle family, a family with Quaker sympathies."

"Quakers? Here?"

"The Doyles were friendly with the Quaker group down in Lynchburg. And as you probably know, the Quakers had no sympathy for slaveholding and subverted it in every way they could. Old Gate was on the route from Lynchburg to Culpeper County, which was a kind of gathering point for runaway slaves headed north."

"Is there anywhere here that isn't touched by that kind of history? We must move past the war, man. It's our duty."

"Please, listen. We need to go back inside soon." Now Edward was brusque. "There was a house and a barn on the property, and the house had a shed attached to it. Sometime in 1847 or '48, the Doyles began to hide runaway slaves who were on their way north, in that shed. It became a kind of open secret among certain people in Old Gate."

Randolph nodded. "That sounds like it was virtuous, but dangerous."

"There are people in this house tonight whose parents didn't like what the Doyles and the Quakers were doing. People who didn't want to lose their own slaves because of such subversion close to home. Randolph, a group of Old Gate men surrounded the property one night and set fire to both the house and shed. When the family and, it's said, two female slaves and their children tried to escape, the men held them at gunpoint until they went back inside the buildings. If they didn't, they shot them dead, right there."

In their own momentary silence, they heard a woman's laughter from the house.

"It's a terrible story, but it has nothing to do with me. I thank you for telling me, Edward. Was anyone prosecuted?"

"Of course not. It was done at night, and there were no witnesses left. No one is really even sure how many were killed. Eight, maybe ten people."

"I see."

"No, I don't think you do. A few years later, another house was built there, on that same site. But no one was able to live in it for more than a few months at a time. Everyone who lived in that house suffered some tragedy, and they were forced to leave. Suicides. Madness. A murder."

Randolph scoffed. "That's bald superstition, and quite ridiculous. You're an educated man. Surely you don't believe in such things. Superstition is the stuff of old women and parlor games. To be honest, I'm amused by the superstitious aspects of the old pagan rites. Why, the Romans were a noble bunch, and the Celtics, too. But ghosts? That's nonsense."

Edward stiffened. "You would put your family at risk?"

"Of course not. There *is* no risk. There's nothing left of any buildings there except traces of a foundation. And that will be dug up before any building begins. I dare any curse to try to cling to me. It would find that I am not so easily cowed."

"I wish you would listen. There are other farms to be had."

"We should go back inside, Edward. It's growing late."

Edward's shoulders fell, and he shook his head. They started back to the house.

Not wanting to leave his new friend dispirited, Randolph made an effort to acknowledge his obviously genuine concern. "As a priest, perhaps you could perform some sort of blessing on the land. Might that not help obviate any curse, or whatever seems to be going on?"

Edward stopped. "I dislike that the Old Gate parties involved in this sale have not been frank with you. They seem to take it as rather a joke that someone like you—someone from a part of the country that they revile—is paying good money for the site of such an atrocity. You do not have true friends here, I'm afraid, Randolph. I don't know that they will ever be different if you choose to build your house here."

The light from the salon touched Randolph, illuminating his not quite handsome face. When Edward looked down into those eyes, he wasn't sure if the sincerity he saw there was true or skillful manipulation. There was something else, too, something harder, that he hadn't seen when they were in the house.

"I hope I may consider *you* my friend." Randolph rested his hand on the taller man's back, just as Robert Archer had touched *him* in friendship, and Edward felt an unpleasant sensation of cold spread over his body.

An hour later, the party broke up with many promises for future invitations. Randolph was heartily enjoined to write to his new friends just as soon as he knew when he would be returning to Old Gate to begin building his new home.

As he settled into the coach that would take him back to Missus Green's Inn and Boardinghouse near the center of town, Randolph felt in the left pocket of his waistcoat for his matches. The matches were there, but there was something else: a small, folded note, which, when opened and held close to the flame of a lighted match, was revealed to be an invitation of a particularly intimate sort, written in a delicate, well-formed hand. He smiled. It was an invitation he would gladly accept.

He blew out the match and settled back in the seat. Yes. He was very much looking forward to settling in Old Gate.

Chapter 1

LUCY

Walpurgisnacht 1924

Lucy Bliss ran blindly through the moonlit rose garden, thorns grabbing at her as though they would keep her from leaving. As she reached the break in the garden wall that would lead her to the woods, her robe tangled on the last bush, so she tore it from her body with a cry and left it behind. Was someone following? Surely Randolph, who was as frail as a man risen from a grave of five years, could not capture her.

My husband risen from his grave! So much is explained. The voices in the night. The light near the springhouse. How did I not see?

Above the trees the distant lights of Old Gate shone silver on the scattered clouds. Only twenty-five years earlier, before she had married Randolph in 1899, there had been but a dozen gas streetlamps in town, and the night sky had looked endless and cluttered with stars. How different it had been. Walking with her friends to the little theater, or home from a party, her laughing voice louder than she knew was proper. But she hadn't cared. She had been cheerfully rebellious, happy to disregard her mother's constant instructions about minding her behavior, and her father's lectures from both his Episcopal pulpit and the dinner table. Though they were rigid people, and difficult to love, she had loved them both, and had obeyed—to a point. Few things were ever serious to her in those days. It had all been in fun.

Bright. Her life had been so wonderfully bright.

Now she was well into her forties, and her life had dimmed. Her feet were bare, tender from running over the crushed shells on the winding garden paths beside Bliss House, and her breath came in bursts. From moment to moment she wasn't sure if she were dreaming or not. Before she'd gone to bed, Terrance, who had run Bliss House for her these past few years, and was no older than she, had given her the medicine that helped her feel calm, helped her forget. But she had terrible dreams and often woke to find that she had chewed the knuckle of her finger until it bled and there were tears on her cheeks. Now, dreaming or awake, she had fled the house, running, running. For months she had been loath to walk outside. Loath to leave her room. How she had run when she was a child! And when her son, Michael Searle, was young, they had run through the orchards together, playing and racing, far from Randolph's critical gaze.

Michael Searle, my son. But more than a son. A gift.

This very night he was on his way home from North Carolina, where he had been visiting the woman he would marry. She had to get somewhere safe, to warn him—before he arrived—never to return to Bliss House.

Your father is alive! He will steal your happiness, my sweet child.

The path into the woods was crowded with brush and newly red switches of wild blackberry whose thorns were even more ambitious and brutal than those of the roses. She slowed. Her thin, torn gown was no protection from the cool night, and a layer of sweat caused her to shiver violently. Craving the former safety of her own bed within her flower-covered bedroom walls, she thought of sinking to the ground, nesting in the brambles like an animal. Still, she pushed deeper into the woods, even though no one seemed to be coming after her.

Do they think I am weak, that I will come crawling back?

As a girl, she had thought of Bliss House as a mysterious, magical place, all the more fascinating because her parents had told her to stay away. Now she knew every inch of its shining wood floors and paneled walls. She had danced in the ballroom dozens of times, and hurried up and down the staircases twenty times a day, and aired the rooms, and watered flowers and written letters at her desk in the morning room, and rocked her son to sleep, and wiped his brow, and entertained friends, and listened to the bees drowsing over the roses, and watched her husband, the man who had built Bliss House, go slowly mad. And she had lived in the presence of ghosts, and had even ceased to be afraid of them.

But if Randolph were alive—truly alive—she would have to live in fear.

Again. It didn't matter if she were awake or dreaming. She would rather die than live with Randolph. Again.

Ahead, in the trees, there was a quivering light where there should not have been a light. Lucy glanced again over her shoulder to make sure she hadn't gotten turned around, but there was Bliss House rising tall and threatening behind her, its windows glowing warmly as though it were still a safe place. A place where, sometimes, she was happy.

Thank God Michael Searle is away. I will keep him safe.

Yes. Ahead of her was a light where there was supposed to be nothing, and desperation carried her toward it.

Chapter 2

LUCY

Walpurgisnacht 1899

Lucy Searle was breathless, but more from excitement than exertion as she and her best friend, Faye Archer, rode their bicycles up the dark and silent dirt road that led to the woods on the western side of Bliss House. It was ten o'clock in the evening, and no one knew where they were except, perhaps, Josiah Beard, the young physician who was Faye's beau. Or, as Faye called him, giggling, her *lover*.

The Searle and Archer families were among twelve families in the county that made up what Selina Searle, Lucy's mother, called the "first families of the county." Only three of Virginia's true first families—the Blands, the Carys, and the Archers—lived in the area. But given the esteem in which Selina Searle held the Archers, she never questioned Lucy's desire to spend even a few days at a time at Maplewood, her friend's home. The information that Mister and Missus Archer were in Charlottesville for a few days, visiting friends, had not been shared with Selina. Lucy was desperate to cut the suffocating bonds she had to her parents. Each time she thought she might be free of them, her parents pulled her back, treated her like a child. But tonight she was *truly* free.

Faye had gone to finishing school in Europe, while Lucy had had to be content to spend eighteen months in Boston society with an aunt who kept a very close eye on her. Not because her parents couldn't afford to send her to Europe, but because her father, who was also Old Gate's Episcopal priest, didn't trust "those damned spoiled continental jackanapes" around his pretty daughter. He had noted, too, that on Faye's return, she didn't come as often to church.

Faye had attached a small basket to the handlebars of her new English bicycle, and in it were the two elaborately decorated half-masks that she had sent for from a costumer in Philadelphia: a black-and-silver one for herself, and a white, feathered one for Lucy. Both had matching veils attached so that their faces would be further hidden, and the girls had traded dresses so that they might confuse anyone trying to guess who they were. It was to be a masquerade ball.

Earlier that evening, Faye had pressed a white-and-gold beaded gown into Lucy's arms. "Nobody is wearing these enormous sleeves in New York anymore, and it's one of Josiah's favorites. No one will know you're not me. Especially not Josiah." When Faye had first suggested that they might fool Josiah in particular, Lucy had thought it very daring, if a little mean. But as they approached the woods, and she could see hints of light from Bliss House peeking through the trees, her excitement grew. She had waited much of her life to get inside Bliss House, and tonight she would go as a mysterious guest. If it meant that Josiah would be the victim of a little joke, then it would be that much more enjoyable.

When they reached the end of the dirt road, they hid the bicycles among the trees and kept their voices at a whisper despite the absence of any dwelling or people nearby. The house was still a five- or ten-minute walk away.

"Are you sure Josiah said it was tonight?" Lucy, her hands shaking, stayed Faye's arm as she took the masks from the basket. "What if they don't let us inside?"

Faye smiled. The moonlight smoothed the already soft features of her face—her apple cheeks and dimpled chin, and generously long eyelashes—and picked up the light in her dark blond hair. Like Lucy's, it was wound into a loose Grecian braid that sat like a crown on her head. Lucy's hair was blond but sometimes had a hint of strawberry in it in the strong sunlight, and her eyes were a vibrant heather blue. The veil would hide the fact that her face was more heart-shaped and petite than Faye's, and her nose rather tipped up at the end. "A sweetheart's face" was how Faye had described it once, "like a woman on a box of fancy chocolates." Lucy had never been sure that Faye meant it as a compliment. She had always been jealous of Faye's combination of blond hair and large, round brown eyes, thinking it very romantic.

"Darling Lucy, don't worry. One holiday we spent the whole night and most of the next morning at a stranger's villa in Venice. No one came home with anything worse than a pounding head from all the wine we drank. And we're here, not a mile from your very own house. What could possibly happen? Of course they'll let us in. I'm *expected*, and I'm supposed to bring a guest."

Lucy felt the warmth of Faye's lips as she kissed her cheek. "Let's be sure not to lose each other," Lucy said. "I don't want to be there on my own."

They passed through the trees, grateful for the moonlight guiding their way. When they reached the garden, they put on their masks and hurried around to the front of the house. Lucy took Faye's hand, as though they were children on some great adventure.

The house glowed with warmth and light. In the twenty years of her life, Lucy had only seen Bliss House at a distance through winter-bare trees. Randolph Bliss was several years younger than her father and had long been a member of her father's church, which was the largest and oldest church in Old Gate. He had moved to Old Gate from New York and built the house for his wife, Amelia. But after Amelia and his young daughter died, just before Lucy was born, he spent almost two decades away from Bliss House, living up east and traveling in Europe. Since Lucy had returned from Boston a month earlier, she had only seen him twice: once in his private pew at church and once on the street. He had been back in residence at the house for almost a year, but her parents never accepted his invitations. Faye had met Randolph through Josiah, because he and Josiah's father, Doctor Cyrus Beard, were good friends, but Randolph was still a mystery to Lucy.

Bliss House had been forbidden to her. Edward Searle, her father, had hinted that, since Randolph's return, he had filled the house with bacchanals and unsavory foreign company, and had enticed many of the locals to sins he deigned too appalling for Lucy's ears. But nothing about the enormous three-story house of yellow brick that was as pale as mother-of-pearl in the moonlight seemed threatening to Lucy. Its tall windows glowed gold, and strains of music floated from somewhere deep inside. Could there be a more welcoming, more pleasant house? Carrie, her mother's housemaid, had told Lucy that no one had wanted to work there and caretake it during the years that Mister Bliss had been away, that there were spirits who ran along the galleries that surrounded the hall that would touch you if you were alone and laugh if you ran from them. Lucy didn't particularly believe in ghosts, and Carrie herself said she didn't know if the stories were really true.

Tonight I may find out if Carrie was right. Won't she be surprised when I tell her I've been inside?

A smooth-faced young man of about Lucy's age opened the front door.

"Hello, Terrance." Faye lifted the hem of her skirt and sailed past him. He returned the greeting with a nod that only Lucy saw.

Despite the fact that she had just entered a place she had wanted to visit since she was a girl, Lucy found herself staring at Terrance. She was certain that they had never met before, but he seemed very familiar. He was taller than either girl, and awkwardly thin, which was why, she suspected, he looked ill at ease in his too-large jacket. His dark brown hair was badly cut. Not only was it oddly short, cropped close to his scalp, but it wasn't slicked back with hair oil following the fashion of both servants and gentlemen alike. He had large ears and a number of moles on his neck and face, but was otherwise not unpleasant looking. His eyes were as dark as Faye's, deep set, and held a look of confidence that Lucy didn't see often in butlers—if that's what he was. When she realized that he was staring frankly back at her, Lucy blushed and turned away. Why did she have both the sense that he was a foreigner, and that she was supposed to know him?

Looking up, Lucy was immediately overwhelmed with the height of the room and the sparkling chandelier and dome far above their heads. She had been to beautiful homes and public buildings in Boston, Philadelphia, and New York, but she had never seen a sky of stars inside any of them. The music was louder, now that they were inside, and the hall was full of candlelight and the scent of a hundred lilies. The effect left her full of wonder.

"How lovely. Surely nothing is frightening here."

"What?" Faye turned back to her and laughed. "Why would anyone be afraid here? Surely you don't believe those silly stories."

Lucy was surprised to find that she had actually spoken aloud.

"Close your mouth, Lucy. I can see it's open even through the veil." Faye pinched her arm. "You look like a rube," she teased.

Mortified, Lucy closed her mouth.

A few masked people sat quietly in a long, dimly lighted salon to her right, but the dining room to her left was empty. To the rear of the hall were doorways and other rooms, but everything appeared to be happening on the upper floors. A broad staircase with a single landing rose to the second floor, but there didn't seem to be any way to reach the third floor, whose gallery railings ran, unbroken, all around the great hall. She guessed that the stairway to it was simply hidden from sight. The music was no doubt coming from the ballroom, which Faye had told her was on the topmost floor. The paneled walls were covered with paintings: portraits and fantastic landscapes that made her want to get closer to examine them. But unlike the overstuffed rooms of her mother's and friends' houses, the interior of Bliss House felt open and uncluttered. Lucy felt like she could breathe here.

"We should go upstairs." Faye started toward the staircase, and Lucy hurried to follow.

Though she recognized no one in their elaborate masks, it seemed that the entire population of the county was either loitering in the galleries or in the crowded ballroom. She had the thrilling sense that she had been transported far, far away.

At the far end of the ballroom, there was a small orchestra, and a dozen couples were dancing. On entering the room, Lucy and Faye were given cordial glasses filled with bright green liquid by a veiled woman in a gossamer harem costume. Lucy had wanted to refuse, but it was pressed on her so quickly that she would have had to force the woman to take it back.

Faye slipped her glass beneath her veil and drank the stuff in one long swallow. Lucy followed suit but was unsettled by the bittersweet taste. It was strange to see Faye in Lucy's own dear emerald velvet-trimmed chiffon dress, and wearing two of Lucy's rings and favorite jet-and-diamond bracelet. She felt as though she were looking at a ghost of herself.

The ballroom was beautiful. Windowless, but beautiful. Burning wall sconces cast a gentle glow over the crowd, which was flush with dancing and laughter and the heat from the fire blazing in the enormous fireplace. The mostly empty chairs along the walls were red enamel with gold cushions. Her mother would have been horrified, but they looked well with the crimson wallpaper that was covered with oriental motifs: men, with beautiful women in kimonos, pagodas, and blossoming trees. But in the very center of the ceiling hung two large metal circles, like the eyes of giant bolts. Inwardly, Lucy recoiled. They spoiled the civilized effect of the room. How strange they were.

She and Faye weren't on their own for long.

"Finally, you're here. Where have you been?"

Josiah Beard didn't wait for an answer, but nodded quickly to Faye, and took Lucy's elbow to lead her to the dance floor. Lucy almost told him that he was mistaken, but then she smiled beneath her veil, pleased and a bit excited that their plan had worked so completely.

"I thought you'd never arrive. What took you so long? Did Lucy take too long to dress?"

At the mention of her own name, Lucy felt butterflies in her stomach and wondered if Faye and Josiah often talked about her. But the thought came with a worry that she might hear something about herself that she didn't like.

How would Faye respond? "Yes. Of course. Silly Lucy."

As he swept her into a waltz, she noticed a woman whose bare shoulders looked very like her mother's, but the color of her hair was wrong, and she didn't recognize the dress. But certainly, either could be easily changed. Wasn't she herself with a man who thought she was her best friend? As they danced, a flush came over her.

She stole a glance at her partner, who was looking down at her, a happy smile on his lips. He was handsomer than his gray, curmudgeonly father, with chestnut eyes and russet hair that tended to unruliness. He kept it fashionably long about his ears, but wore it only lightly oiled. Where the hair of the servant, Terrance, had simply looked untidy, she thought that the styling of Josiah's hair showed an admirable independence. A few years older than she and Faye were, he was nearly finished with his studies and would soon join his father's medical practice. Faye was fortunate. There was no man, yet, who had taken Lucy so firmly in his arms, his hand possessively on her waist. She had danced with Josiah before, but he had never held her just so.

They glided past Faye, who was surrounded by a group of men and was fluttering an old-fashioned fan that Lucy had never seen before against the heat of the room.

"You're distracted. Are you not well? Are you not glad to see me?"

Lucy regretted the hurt in Josiah's voice, but quickly looked away. She wasn't playing her part very well, but Faye had reminded her to not let him see her eyes too closely as they were so different from hers in color.

"It's warm in here. So many people."

The number of people had, indeed, seemed to increase since they'd started dancing. Was that the same song that had been playing when she first arrived? This was a waltz, but perhaps a different one. Now she noticed that the faces of some of the other guests were very dark below their half-masks. A dark woman speaking with two men who were not. A dark man dancing with a woman with skin even paler than her own. Was that her cousin, Becky, with the man in the turban and jeweled mask?

While Lucy's father was quite liberal about people of different races mixing socially, his brother, Becky's father, was not. But when they danced close to the couple again, she wasn't sure it was Becky at all.

She looked around for Randolph Bliss. It was his house, his party, and yet he hadn't greeted them as they arrived in the ballroom. But, of course, he had no wife to act as hostess to mind such things. When she finally saw him, she noticed that he was alone, standing at the edge of the fireplace. He looked relaxed, a half-smile of pleasure on his face below the mask. Lucy admired the elegant cut of his evening clothes; though he wasn't a particularly tall man, he had a substantial presence, an air of self-possession about him. Even with a half-mask on (or perhaps because of it?) he looked much younger than his fifty-something years. Catching her looking at him, he stared back at her and nodded with an appreciative smile. For a moment she forgot who she was and was flattered.

But he doesn't even know who I am. How fascinating.

She turned her attention back to Josiah. "It *is* far too crowded in here."

Before she knew what was happening, Josiah was leading her by the hand, and they were leaving the ballroom. She looked back, for Faye. What would Faye think they were doing?

She protested, almost saying Faye's name, but caught herself. "Won't Lucy be worried?"

Josiah laughed.

In the hall, the chandelier shimmered just below them, and people and shadows moved along the lower gallery. They went down the back stairway to the second floor, and as they came out of the dimly lighted hall, she blinked. The gallery was crowded, and as Josiah pulled her along, she looked across the expanse of hall to see that a woman had stripped naked to her waist, the silky satin jacket of her evening suit trailing down over her skirt; a man, his mask pushed back on his head so that it stared at Lucy with blank-eyed menace, was fondling and licking the woman's breasts. The woman's own mask—that of the whiskered face of a white rabbit—was still in place, but the sensual movement of her shoulders and the tilt of her head told Lucy that she found plea-sure in it. Lucy gasped, but Josiah was pulling her away. When he turned back to her, he didn't look like himself, but some other man, with sharper features below the half-mask, his mouth firm with intent. But she could not bring herself to pull away from him. Why, if they were out of the ballroom, was she still so beastly warm? She thought of the man at the woman's breasts, but would not let herself look again.

Josiah stopped at a door at the end of the gallery, and as he tried the knob, she caught their reflections in a window. Was she Faye, or was she herself? She felt strange, yet happy, animated by some welcome enchantment. Her hand felt warm and secure and pulsing with life in Josiah's.

Did Randolph see us leave? Is he thinking of what Josiah and I were hurrying toward?

Rectangular shafts of moonlight lay on the floor beneath the tall windows and turned jagged as they climbed over the room's furnishings. She saw a child's bed and cabinets and shelves lined with dolls: twenty or thirty dolls of all sizes in old-fashioned dresses, glass eyes shining. But not just dolls. Animals as well. Birds and chipmunks. Mice, an opossum, and a small owl. Two dolls and two fur creatures—one a nearly bald squirrel—sat in small chairs around a child's table that had been set for tea. She strained to get a closer look, but Josiah pulled her along toward one of the windows.

"We shouldn't be in here," she whispered, forgetting that Faye wouldn't have hesitated to come to this place with her lover. "What if someone comes in?"

"My Faye, why do you tease me so tonight? I'm desperate for you."

Josiah slipped one of his hot hands around the back of her neck, which had turned damp with her nervousness. Her excitement had drained away. Some note in his voice sounded like a warning.

"I haven't. I'm not—" She wanted to finish, but he had lifted the veil and his mouth was on hers, easing her lips apart, and she didn't resist. His tongue tasted clean and slightly sweet, or perhaps it was the remnant of the cordial in her mouth. Was it that the kiss was so forbidden that made her want it all the more?

The kiss seemed to last for hours, but at last he pulled away, only to kiss her neck, seeming to delight in devouring it, the evening growth of his beard rough against her skin. Every so often he whispered Faye's name: "Oh, my Faye." She didn't resist when he took one of her hands and guided it to the front of his trousers. There was no thought of her friend or the house outside the closed door of the room.

Lost in what they were doing, she heard the faint sound of her own name coming to her from a far, far distance. It wasn't just one voice, but a kind of mocking chorus.

Lucy. Oh, my Lucy. Lucy!

She froze in Josiah's arms.

"What is it?"

"Don't you hear it?"

When the first object hit her in the back, she shrank against Josiah, and he laughed. "Are you afraid of the dark? Is that what's going on, my poor dear Faye?"

The second came: a doll from one of the shelves, bent in half, tumbled in the air as it approached, and its porcelain head struck her bare arm. Some piece of decoration on its dress caught her skin and she cried out.

The voices were buoyant, pleased with the game. *Lucy! Lucy!*

"Stop!" Lucy covered her ears and turned to run from the room. Two more dolls came, but they missed her, seeming to be focused on the spot where she'd been standing with Josiah.

Lucy! Lucy! Lucy!

But Josiah called Faye's name after her. *How does he not know? Doesn't he hear?*

As she hurried, she tripped over one of the small chairs, knocking it over. She reached for a second chair to catch herself, and her hand closed on a rough, fur-covered head. The door to the hallway opened slowly, of its own accord, spilling light into the room, and she saw that the animal she'd touched was a whistle pig, once alive, now dead and stuffed, with glass eyes fitted into its blunt head where the real ones used to be. Its mouth was open in a death cry, its teeth sharp and threatening,

14

yet its clawed front feet were set close together as though it were about to pray or applaud.

"Faye, come back!" Josiah's voice was followed by the sound of crashing furniture and cursing, and she knew that he had fallen as well.

Lucy had made it through the door and into the hall. There were fewer people now along the gallery. Most everyone was upstairs. She couldn't stay with Josiah, yet she couldn't bear the thought of going back up to the ballroom. It was indecorous to run, but run she did toward the back of the house. Instead of going up the stairs to the ballroom, she hurried down the back stairway, which was much narrower than the one in the great hall. There was a window facing the stairs for light in the day, but now there was only the light from the wall sconces, which cast flickering shadows as she ran.

When she reached the first floor, she wasn't sure which way to go. Did she want to get out of the house? She imagined running through the woods on her own, in the darkness, and riding the bicycle through the back roads and into the sleeping town. No. Though she knew it marked her as a coward, she knew she couldn't do it.

She really just wanted to hide somewhere and catch her breath. The first room she came to was dark, but there was a glow coming from the next room, and its door was partially open. Her sigh of relief as she pushed the door open was unconscious.

The paneled room was smaller than the other rooms that she'd been in inside the house, but there was a substantial fire roaring away in the stone-manteled fireplace. Along with several comfortable-looking chairs and a few tables, the room was furnished with bookshelves filled with books, most bound in the same rich, red-brown leather. There were portraits, too, including one of Randolph himself looking quite young, perhaps only fifteen or so, his face dignified and a bit severe. His hair was long and rakish.

One hand rested on the edge of a painstakingly detailed model ship, and she wondered if he had built it himself.

The moment's contemplation helped her calm down. Whatever had happened in the nursery seemed far, far away.

"I almost didn't bring that portrait with me here, but my mother wanted it out of her house."

Lucy startled. Randolph, still wearing his mask, stood in the doorway behind her.

"Now I've spoiled it. You know who I am." He stepped into the room. "Or perhaps you knew already?"

"I'm so sorry. I've disturbed your privacy. I'll go." Lucy wasn't quite sure what to do. She was too embarrassed to try to walk past him. It occurred to her that he didn't know who was apologizing. She started to untie her mask, but he stopped her.

"Please don't. I enjoy the mystery."

Beneath her veil, Lucy smiled.

"Won't you sit down for a few moments?" Randolph indicated a chair. "Let me pour you some water. Or wait. Maybe something stronger?"

Lucy sat, slightly nervous. "Yes. Thank you."

"There is champagne upstairs, and there will be more at supper in an hour or so, but I only have cognac and whiskey here in the library. I think cognac would be a good choice for you right now." He poured drinks for them both and sat down. The liquor stung her tongue, but she welcomed its warmth as it moved down her throat.

"You're very kind," she said.

"I was concerned that you were in distress, but you seem to be better now."

Lucy looked away at the fire.

"An argument with your young man?"

The suggestion was such a surprise that she let out a nervous laugh. But of course it must have seemed that way to him, or to anyone else watching. Wasn't that what young women like her were always supposed to be upset about?

He looked a bit taken aback by her laughter, and she hurried to explain. "I was—again—somewhere I shouldn't have been, and something fell from a shelf. It was all very foolish. Then I got lost. You must think me a terrible ninny. And a snoop. My mother would be mortified if she knew. I can't apologize enough."

He got up to pour them both more cognac. "I'm rather glad to hear you say that. That it was not some young man who had caused you to be sad. Now I don't have to find him and take him to task for spoiling your evening. I want you to have a memorable time. If you do, perhaps you'll return to Bliss House."

"Oh, I would like that very much." Her voice sounded too enthusiastic to her own ears.

Why do I feel so giddy, like a young girl?

"When I returned to Old Gate, I learned that this house had garnered a bit of a reputation for strange occurrences. I worried that no one would come here again, even though I know the house to be perfectly safe." His gaze, through his mask, was intent on her, as though he were waiting for her to share her own impressions.

"The house does have a sense of *being alive* to it," she said cautiously. Whatever had thrown the dolls—*I know very well what threw the dolls, but I cannot say it*—had seemed more playful than dangerous. The strange *occurrence* also felt slightly less unseemly than what she had been doing in the room with Josiah. "But perhaps it is just because it's full of people."

Randolph relaxed. "Yes, I'm very glad. I've had good success these past months with my little parties. It makes *me* feel alive to have people in the house. I'm afraid that when Bliss House was first built, I didn't have much of a chance to make an impression on the neighborhood. You may already know that my wife and daughter died shortly after they arrived. And then I was gone for many years."

"I'm very sorry." Lucy was not ready to admit to gossip. But it had occurred to her that, if there were indeed ghosts in Bliss House, they would probably be those of his family. The voice that had called her had definitely been feminine.

"It's an old wound, and I am well healed. Though they won't be forgotten."

They sat in silence for a few moments, the sounds of the party drifting through the open door.

"I confess that I would very much enjoy spending the rest of the evening here by the fire. Talking," Randolph said. "But I must see how the ball is progressing. We'll be serving supper in the theater in a while. I hope you will stay."

"Supper sounds wonderful." The room had become a bit warm, or perhaps it was Randolph's proximity to her. She took her time getting up. When was the last time she had sat in a lonely room with a man like Randolph?

What sort of man are you really, Randolph? I feel I must know.

As they walked to the door, Lucy's ankle felt stiff, and she hesitated. Randolph stopped before they reached the hall. "I know it's not any of my business, but did you hurt yourself? You seemed to be limping just the slightest bit as you came in here. And now—" He rested a gentle, avuncular hand on her arm.

"It's just a little bruise, I think. It's nothing."

You are touching me. My ankle doesn't matter at all. I am happy that you are touching me, but I don't for the life of me know why.

"Good. Because although I don't even know your name—yet, that is—I have planned a surprise for after supper that I think you'll particularly like. Also, when we meet in the ballroom, I hope you will save me a dance. Or two."

Lucy smiled again behind her veil.

Chapter 3

LUCY

May Day 1899

Lucy discovered Faye and Josiah dancing together in the ballroom. The cognac had made her feel ever so much better, and she had taken a glass of champagne from one of the gloved servers. Randolph had said that he wished to dance with her, and she found herself eager for his appearance. When Faye spotted her, she made Josiah stop dancing and they cut through the crowd to where Lucy stood with her champagne.

"You were wonderful, Lucy," Faye whispered close to Lucy's ear, then turned to Josiah. "You were a perfect beast, dragging her off like that."

Josiah appeared chastened. A different young man from the one who had kissed her so boldly. But Lucy also heard irritation in his voice. "It wasn't a very good joke, either of you. You put me in a very awkward position."

Lucy recalled what his position had been in the nursery. Yes, it had been awkward for both of them. Faye appeared to be the only one who had gotten any fun out of it.

"Darling, Josiah said that you tripped on your way out of the nursery. I hope you didn't hurt yourself. I was just telling Sir Galahad that we should find you. I was so afraid that you had decided to go home without me."

Josiah had mentioned that she had tripped, but what else had he said? Was he pretending that he hadn't heard anything, hadn't seen the dolls and animals flying through the air to hit her? He had admitted to Faye that he had taken Lucy into the nursery, and Faye was no fool. It had been Faye's intention to tease him, to push him into doing what he had done, and she was obviously pleased with the result. If he *had* realized what was happening to Lucy, it was odd that he would not say so, if only to deflect his rather amorous actions. But he said nothing more.

"I twisted my ankle a bit in the dark. I'm fine. All is well." Lucy glanced up at Josiah. "Friends?"

Josiah relented, and smiled. "I'm glad you're not hurt. I was sorry when I didn't find you." He bent down to say quietly, "Then Faye made me even sorrier."

Faye pushed at him playfully. "Now you're being silly. You've made up, so now we can dance some more."

Randolph did not appear in the next half hour, and Lucy was disappointed. She danced several songs with two other men, both of whom were rather forward with their compliments. The older man she did not know, but she was certain that the other was Josiah's cousin, James, from Richmond, but they pretended not to recognize each other, and she excused herself from dancing with him again, saying she was weary. Still no Randolph.

Supper was announced at two A.M., and Faye and Josiah came to collect her so that they could sit together at one of the dozen tables set up in the theater. Their table filled quickly, and when Lucy looked around for Randolph, she saw him take a seat near the stage at the front of the room. Again, she was disappointed. She picked at her food: a cold strawberry soup, scallops, cheese biscuits, and roasted pork that smelled heavenly of rosemary. As they ate, acrobats dressed in wintry Cossack hats, ballooning black pants, and vests that sparkled with rhinestones over their hairy chests tumbled and raced across the stage. As they jumped, and made pyramids, and tossed each other back and forth, they called, "Hup! Hup!" The crowd laughed and applauded. Most, including Lucy, had never seen such strange entertainment at a party. She was diverted for a while, but she remembered that Randolph had promised a surprise. Had the acrobats been it?

No. After a dessert of delicate French-style pastries, Randolph stood and requested that those who wished to stay until dawn join him on the lawn at the end of thirty minutes.

Most of the guests readied themselves to depart, still wearing their masks. As she and Faye and Josiah went downstairs, Lucy noticed—without wanting to look too closely—several couples, and, shockingly, a small group of men and women entering the bedrooms along the gallery with glasses and open bottles of cham-pagne, and disappearing behind the closed doors. Where once the thought of such goings-on might have excited her, or at least piqued her interest, the memory of what had happened behind the closed door of the nursery kept her from being too curious. She suspected that theirs would be a very different experience from hers—one of pleasure rather than fear.

The three of them sipped after-dinner cordials in the salon with a lively dozen of the remaining guests. When the thirty minutes had passed, they heard music—this time coming from outside the house. As Lucy followed the others in search of the haunting violins playing somewhere in the predawn twilight, she looked up to the second-floor gallery to see that the nursery door was open, the room unchosen, unoccupied.

There is something there, and it knows my name.

She was only too happy to get outside.

On the lawn at the eastern side of the house, two violinists stood silhouetted in front of a massive bonfire. A Maypole towered beyond the bonfire, a tall, straight shadow against the sky.

"Oh, Josiah, look!" Faye hurried ahead to the Maypole, and Josiah quickly followed. Lucy hung back a bit, savoring the sight.

There had been a Maypole on the commons in Old Gate every year since she could remember. This one was majestic in the fire-light, elaborately decorated and crowned with a lush, woven array of tulips and daffodils and clutches of wildflowers. When she reached it, and saw the colorful circle of red and white ribbons stretched out twice the length of the pole, she felt an unexpected sense of release. Of happiness. She laughed and clapped her hands like a happy child.

Randolph touched her arm, and she turned to him. Behind him, the other guests were hurrying out of the house.

"Oh, it's wonderful. It's even taller than the one on the green. Look at all the flowers."

"I thought that it would please you," he said.

Her father had never allowed her to dance around the town's Maypole as a girl, calling it pagan nonsense. What would he say to her if he could see her now? In truth, he could not say anything. The freedom she felt at that moment was as intoxicating as the champagne she had been drinking all evening.

"It's the perfect surprise."

"Is your ankle better? Are you up to dancing?"

Lucy was about to answer when a tall, raven-haired woman wearing a mask crowned with a fan of peacock feathers, and a wine-colored cloak she held close and closed, walked out of the darkness beyond the Maypole and joined the crowd. People moved away a bit—not in fear, but with an instinct that told them that they should all be watching her. When she had her audience, she untied her cloak, letting it fall to the ground. First there were startled gasps, then a few appreciative chuckles from the men. The woman was nude beneath the cloak, her body sheathed in some glimmering paint like an unearthly goddess. Her painted nipples stood erect with cold, despite the fire. She stood looking back at the crowd with daring stillness. The man nearest her began to disrobe as well, and after him, another man, and another woman.

Lucy glanced around for Faye. Sure enough, there she was, Josiah helping her out of Lucy's own gown. There was no hesitation. No shame. Lucy knew she would have to make a decision.

If Faye can do it, then so shall I!

Unlike the others, Randolph was not yet disrobing. His eyes, which had held such pleasure when she had exclaimed over the Maypole, now held a question.

Seeing the fun in it, the pure joy of acting as freely as children, Lucy nodded to him and moved closer to the fire. As she peeled off her gloves, she was still a bit nervous, and would not let herself look at Randolph's masked face again until the dancing began.

The sparkling, dark-haired woman led them to the Maypole, signaling the women to take the red ribbons. Lucy's was a sensuous red velvet that ended in a rich fringe like a woman's sash. It was so soft that she couldn't help but touch it to her cheek. She closed her eyes and breathed deeply.

Yes, I will do this.

When she opened her eyes again, the violins leapt into a dancing tune, and the painted woman beckoned to the men to take the white ribbons. She smiled to see Josiah hurry to Faye's side like a well-trained dog. In his nakedness, he was as well shaped as Faye. Deeply in love, they were like a masked Adam and Eve. But Lucy was not at all jealous. Randolph was beside her, now turned to face her, and as they looked into each other's eyes, she felt an unbidden sense of pleasure.

The painted woman danced, her long black hair sliding wantonly over her shoulders to tease over her breasts. Lucy thought she heard her chanting, but the music quickly swallowed her words. As the woman raised her arm with the ribbon in her hand, the first man facing her walked his ribbon under hers. Randolph walked beneath Lucy's ribbon, and he was gone.

Her reserve was quickly lost in her concentration and the quickness of the dance that made her ankle ache just a bit. After a few minutes, she glanced up at the pole to see that the ribbons had wrapped the pole in color, the red bleeding over the white like blood flowing over the palest of skin.

The fire burned hot, and her heart pounded with exertion as it had when she had ridden her bike from Faye's house.

How long ago that seems. As though we are stopped in time.

Finally the music began to slow, and the sky lightened with jagged lengths of murky blue. The pole was nearly wrapped, the dancers coming closer and closer together, their bodies touching, skin against skin, arm against breast. They glistened with sweat, and though their faces were covered by masks, Lucy could see the sharpness of their eyes, alive and hungry. She could feel that hunger and, suddenly feeling vulnerable, she found herself shifting her body so she could avoid the searching touch of the others. By the time the gay wreath fell down the pole to shoulder height, several of the dancers dropped their ribbons and drifted from the Maypole toward the fire and their clothes. Lucy followed, grateful, limping the slightest bit because of her ankle.

There she found Randolph nearly dressed. She turned her back to the fire to put on her own clothes and saw that the dozen people left at the Maypole had finished the dance and were now engaged only in touching and fondling one another. Faye and Josiah were among the group, and though Lucy sensed she would be welcome even without a partner, dawn was quickly approaching, and it was not the way she wanted to spend the rest of her time at Bliss House.

As though by mutual agreement, she and Randolph fell in beside each other as they walked back to the house, each carrying their shoes.

Terrance stood by the open door, waiting. Was that a smile hiding behind his thin lips? There were circles beneath his eyes.

How many of these sorts of parties have you seen, Terrance?

"Bring a warm towel, Terrance. And some . . ." Randolph looked at Lucy. "Chocolate or coffee, my dear?"

"I would very much like some chocolate, Randolph."

I have used his name. Randolph. Because I am a woman, and not a child.

"Chocolate, then, Terrance. For both of us. I assume coffee and chocolate are set up in the dining room, as we planned."

Terrance didn't reply, but Randolph didn't appear to take it for insolence.

He led her to the large salon off the front hall. Several lamps inside were still lighted, but dawn played at the windows and the French doors that opened onto the garden. At first she thought the room was empty, but then she noticed that there were two women and a man, asleep (and clothed, for the most part) on a sofa in a distant part of the room.

"Let's sit by the fire."

Lucy put down her gloves and shoes and sank into a deep-cushioned chair, exhausted. The champagne had worn off, and she found herself sober, yet consumed by a strange feeling of contentment.

"Shall we?" Lucy asked. "Our masks?"

"Wait just a moment. It is the anticipation of a pleasure that I enjoy the most. Do you find that is true for you, as well?" Randolph's rugged face bore a healthy flush, and he looked happy, if a little anxious.

Lucy tilted her head in thought. Finally she said, "No. I don't think so. If there's something that I think will please me, I want it right away. I haven't always been that way, but it seems I'm guided by different stars now. I have no patience at all."

Her answer pleased him. "Then I would not dare to stop you. I fear you will have no surprises with me, once my mask is removed." He untied the mask with one hand and let it fall with theatrical flourish into the other. The mask had made small vertical impressions on either side of his face, but otherwise, he was familiar to her. They had nodded to each other in town, and at church, but had never been formally introduced. Her impression from earlier in the evening that he looked younger than his fifty-something years was still true. His features were strong and definite, particularly his jaw and the pronounced shape of his nose—not overly large, but assertive. His brown eyes regarded her without trepidation. She smiled, and it was returned.

"My turn." Lucy put her hands back to untie the velvet ribbons of the mask, but the ribbons had caught in her hair.

"Here. Let me help you." As Randolph came to stand behind her, he touched her shoulder for the second time that evening, and Lucy had to stop herself from reaching up for his hand.

"I'm afraid Faye tied it up with my hair. It was very dark outside."

"Faye? Josiah's Faye?"

Lucy laughed. "Oh, yes. We've been friends since we were children. Though we've been apart much of the last two years. We've both been away. Like you."

Randolph silently disengaged the ties from the twist of her blond hair. She shivered as one velvet ribbon trailed over the back of her neck.

"I hope that *you* won't be disappointed." Lucy found herself unaccountably nervous. She took the mask away and waited for him to come around the chair. When he did, she looked up at him. "Hello."

He looked genuinely surprised and did not speak for a few moments—a long enough time that she began to get uncomfortable.

"Why, you're Lucy. Selina and Edward's daughter. I didn't know."

She looked for some sign of delight in his face, but she found only a strange sort of curious wonder.

"I *have* disappointed you."

"I didn't know. Josiah told me that Faye was bringing a pretty friend, but I never put the two of you together."

Lucy tried to rally from her disappointment in his reaction. "I wonder who you were expecting, then. Faye has any number of friends, but I have always wanted to come here."

"I think your father and mother would not like it at all that you're here." Despite his words, there was no censure in his voice.

"But I'm not a child, Randolph. I'm twenty years old, and it's the dawn of a new century. I can't live like a child in a . . ." She found the word *nursery* hard to say, given the monstrosity in the hall above them. "I am not like my parents."

"Oh, but you're so like your mother. You look like her. As I recall, she liked to dance as well."

Lucy blushed with irritation and just a little pleasure. Her mother was beautiful. "Shall I go? I know my parents have been unpleasant to you. I would not want to deepen the wound." She watched his eyes as he contemplated the alternatives.

I have ruined it. I can never come here again.

He looked away from her for a moment, and shook his head, disagreeing with some internal voice. There were sounds of people speaking in hushed voices in the hallway, as though the coming dawn had illuminated the events of the evening, and made them reluctant to acknowledge them. Perhaps Randolph was having a similar revelation.

His face changed. "I've been ridiculous, Lucy. I've striven to live my life without worrying about the judgment of others. But when I saw who you were, I was momentarily overcome. Your father would judge me. He has judged me from the day of our first meeting. That has nothing to do with you. I hope you'll forgive me."

The relief that it had not been something that she had done, or some way she looked, flooded over her, and she thought for a moment that she might begin to weep.

What will he make of that? Weeping like a little girl.

She breathed deeply. The air smelled of flowers and wood smoke. Safe, happy smells. "There's nothing to forgive. I have lived with my father a long time. I understand judgment."

"I'm so glad, Lucy. Very relieved."

Terrance arrived with the chocolate, set it down on the table, and left again without speaking. Randolph poured, and they were very careful and quiet with each other.

After a while she suggested that she and Faye should be getting home. "It's late. Or perhaps just very early." She hadn't seen Faye come inside, but hoped that, somehow, evoking her name would bring her into the great hall, dressed and ready to leave. The truth of where Faye was, and what she was doing, hung in the air between them.

Randolph sat back in his chair.

"It's been a long time since a woman like you has sat in front of this fireplace with me."

Was he talking about Amelia? Her portrait hung above them. She was older than Lucy had expected, but beautifully dressed in an off-the-shoulder evening gown of the type popular a quarter century earlier. Despite her feminine appearance, there was an almost masculine aloofness in her fair face. She might have been described as handsome, for she was not lovely. Her waist was thick and her blond hair was worn close to her cheeks, making her face look overly narrow. She did not look unkind, but only unhappy.

Is it you, Amelia, who calls my name in this place?

28

Surely there had been other women close to him in the, what? Twenty years since she had died? There were plenty of rumors about Randolph. That he had little discretion when it came to women, and sometimes even married women. It was one of the reasons her parents declared that they would not accept his invitations.

"It wouldn't *do*," her mother had said. "It's bad enough that he dares to occasionally come to church. What sort of example would it set if the priest was entertained by an adulterer?"

"I only note it because it's such a pleasure to have you here." Randolph smiled. "I wonder, though, what your esteemed father will think of your being here until dawn. I have invited them here, you know. Though they are probably beginning to suspect that my invitations are a jest on them."

Yes. That is exactly it. I can see your wit in your eyes. How clever you are, Randolph Bliss!

"Let's just say that it's been arranged so they won't worry."

Randolph threw back his head and laughed, startling one of the women on the distant sofa to wakefulness. Lucy had even forgotten that they were there. The woman gave a little cry and said, "Thomas. We've fallen asleep!"

The trio roused themselves and, straightening their clothes, crossed the room unsteadily. They didn't look at Randolph and Lucy, but when they'd passed, Randolph called out to them.

"Coffee is in the dining room, ladies. You may freshen yourselves upstairs when the time comes." He turned his attention back to Lucy. "So you're not only independent, but a mite devious as well."

"Not devious. Perhaps just cautious?"

"Cautious. An excellent word."

She knew she and Faye really would have to leave soon. The Archers' housekeeper had a habit of sleeping late when Faye's parents were gone, but Faye said she could not be trusted if she found they had been out all night. But it was pleasant in front of the fire,

29

and Randolph was so companionable. She wished it might go on forever.

"I loved seeing the tumblers. I had never seen any before. Do tell me about the theater. I've never seen a house with a theater in it. What made you think of such an unusual thing? It's terribly original." Lucy leaned forward, the firelight shining in her eyes.

"Now you're just flattering an old man." But she could tell Randolph was truly pleased.

"Well, if you say that you're old, then *I* must accuse *you* of fishing for compliments, mustn't I?"

Now Randolph laughed heartily. "*Touché*, dear Lucy. You are absolutely correct." He finished his cup of chocolate and offered her brandy, which she took. It was delicious after the chocolate.

"My parents were somber people. My mother's parents were Dutch, and she was very much raised in the old ways. Religious, protected from society. The poor woman didn't have a bit of fun in her, and my father was much the same way. Always with his head in his business. I might have been that way, too, except I had particularly good preparatory school experience in Massachusetts. A wonderful old don and his wife there helped me see that there was more to life than lessons and taking over the family business. My parents wouldn't have liked it, but I got involved in amateur theatricals without their knowledge."

"Ah. You like to play roles, then?" She lightly touched her mask, which lay nearby.

"I do. Well, I did. I never got the romantic roles, always Tybalt, but never Romeo; Claudius, but not Hamlet."

"Heroes are often dull. And Hamlet—he was simply mad."

"You have me thinking like a youngster, Lucy. Remembering careless days." He shook his head. "Amelia thought our theater even more frivolous than the ballroom." Here, he looked up at his wife's portrait. "I think she imagined that I saw myself up on my own stage, but in truth I think it's a more joyous, playful room for dinner parties like tonight, and the occasional entertainment for the neighborhood. Concerts and speakers."

"Old Gate needs that kind of stimulation. I fear we are a little dull."

"*Walpurgisnacht* has many bold traditions, particularly in Europe, but I'm afraid that you're correct. Old Gate has been difficult to persuade to cast off its outdated prudishness, but it is coming around. You enjoyed the Maypole, I hope?"

Lucy blushed, her voice almost a whisper. "I enjoyed it very much."

He leaned forward and closed both of his cool hands around one of her hands with a gentle pressure, and she felt the chill make its way up her arm.

What is this? I feel I may be going mad, as though I am bewitched. If he were to ask me to join him in one of the upstairs rooms right this moment, I would not hesitate.

"I am so glad, dear Lucy."

He asked her nothing more.

⁓

Faye and Josiah were saying farewell to each other in the far end of the salon where the trio had been. Both were unmasked, dressed, and still giddy from their adventures outdoors. They had each drunk warming cups of coffee before preparing to leave. Faye carried both her and Lucy's masks in a small velvet bag that Terrance had brought at Randolph's request.

Lucy stood in front of Randolph, now a little awkward. He took her hand and lifted it to his lips.

"Your company is such a pleasure, Lucy. If I send you an invitation, will you please come? Or will you need to be your parents' daughter?"

She saw in his eyes that he already knew the answer.

"I'll always be my parents' daughter, but I can't forever be their little girl."

In the hall, Randolph offered them the use of his carriage.

"No. On bicycles we arrived, and on bicycles we'll depart!" Faye smiled at Randolph. "Thank you for a lovely party."

"You are most welcome." Randolph kissed Faye's hand.

Faye nodded sweetly, as if she had her hand kissed every day, and gave a quick smile to Josiah, who looked charmingly forlorn, as though he feared he might never see her again. She and Lucy started for the door.

Lucy! You will return to us, Lucy. Clever Lucy!

Hearing her name, Lucy paused, but the rest of the group continued on. She looked up at the two figures standing at the gallery railing.

It was the tall, blond woman from the portrait: Amelia. The dour little girl beside her was surely Randolph's dead daughter.

Lucy caught her breath, and the figures disappeared.

"Are you all right?" Randolph touched her elbow, concerned.

"Of course," she said, with more conviction than she felt. She hurried after Faye.

Chapter 4

KIKU

August 1878

Kiku was fifteen years old, and though it was 1878, and she had traveled halfway across the world in her young life, she had never been on a train until that morning. The luxurious sleeping car in which they sat was no longer moving, having been unhooked from the train that had brought them to Philadelphia, but she was nervous, and her stomach was upset. She could never let the man sitting beside her know how she was feeling. As his Japanese concubine, her temporary discomfort was not his concern.

"If someone sees you're a girl, they'll think you're a witch. Or a freak. You don't know what these country people are like. They'll put you in a menagerie." Randolph Bliss laughed, squeezing Kiku's knee as though expecting her to laugh along with him. "It's a neat

33

trick in the first place for anyone who's seen you to think you're a servant boy. But I should probably have put you in a second-class carriage. Goddamn New York conductor looked at me like he thought I might bugger you right there on the platform."

Kiku smiled automatically. At the brothel in New York City, Madame Jewel had trained her in appropriate responses. She spoke enough English to understand what he had just said, but she didn't actually see anything funny in it. When he had said the word *menagerie*, she thought of the animals in their cages in Central Park. Virginia—the place they were going—was foreign enough to her that she could believe the people there might put *her* in a cage.

The air in the train car was close, and she wanted to ask him to open more windows. But she hadn't yet asked him for anything, and wanted to spend her requests carefully.

The stiff, masculine collar abraded her neck, and the wool vest and breeches were making her sweat. He'd let her take off the itchy cap the minute the porter had closed the door of the private car behind them, but told her she needed to keep the clothes on until it was time for bed, in case they were disturbed. She fingered the bottom edge of her black, blunt-trimmed hair, and imagined how sad the strands must be, with the rest of themselves back at Madame Jewel's. She had wept—silently—as Madame Jewel cut them away, careful to band the hanks together and not let them get lost on the floor. Kiku (whom Madame Jewel called "Jade") knew better than to ask if she might keep it. The other girls had told her that Madame Jewel cut off as much hair as she dared from the girls, saying it kept the head lice under control. But they all knew that she sold it to the wigmaker, and told Kiku that she would get a very good price for Kiku's fine black hair.

"Stop crying." Madame Jewel had spoken quietly so that Randolph, sitting at the other end of the room, wouldn't hear. "You don't know how lucky you are."

Kiku had been at Madame Jewel's for almost six months—long enough to understand that not so many of the men asked for her the way they asked for the other girls. Ruby, whose real name was Edith, and who had never really warmed to Kiku, had told her that Madame Jewel had been about to put her out on the street with the older whores.

"You don't *try*. You think you're better than the rest of us girls, when you're only just different."

There were men who wanted her, though. Three months earlier, Randolph Bliss had come to the house in the company of one such man, especially to see her.

The other man, who called himself Mister Jackson, always talked about money when he took her into the opulent Red Room, which Madame Jewel had decorated with some silk hangings and pillows and two bowls she said were Oriental. The figures on them were unfamiliar to Kiku, and she guessed that they might be Chinese or Korean. But she wasn't sure. She had never learned even to recognize more than a few Japanese characters. There had been no money for school when she was a little girl in her village.

Mister Jackson—who cried out the names of currencies: pounds sterling and dollars and drachmas and dinars and francs and lire, as he stabbed into her with his small, frantic penis—had introduced Randolph to her in Madame Jewel's parlor, as though they were at a party, and Kiku had bowed, knowing a lot of the men thought it charming. It had charmed Randolph Bliss. After another week, Mister Jackson had stopped asking for her, and soon Randolph Bliss requested that Kiku be reserved for him, and him alone, telling Madame Jewel that the money involved didn't matter.

Madame Jewel had cheated him, making Kiku lie, and had let other men have her. But now Kiku was on the train, and Randolph had told her that they were going to Virginia, where—the other girls had told her—there were still secret slaves and everyone was poor. Randolph Bliss wasn't poor, though, and because he had bought her, she believed them about the slaves.

～

"Does the boy speak English so you can understand him?"

Kiku took the heavy food hamper from the porter, who addressed Randolph as though Kiku weren't standing right in front of him. At Madame Jewel's there had been a pair of sculleries who brought the food to and from the table in the basement kitchen where the girls ate, but Kiku at least knew enough to lay everything out on the train car's small dining table. Outside, the Philadelphia siding where the car waited to be picked up by a southbound train was bleak and dusty. She would have liked to have seen Philadelphia, or any city besides New York, which had stunned her with its noise and grit and horses and stench. People had stared at her the way the porter had stared at her, as though she were the captive golden eagle in the park's menagerie.

I am more like a swallow than an eagle. What harm can I do, what prey can I take?

"What time in the morning will the company hook up the car? It took them far too long to detach us when we got in today." Randolph had no patience. Everyone was beneath him, as though he considered himself a lord and the rest of the world his vassals.

"Six forty-five A.M., Mister Bliss."

As Kiku unpacked the hamper, she felt the porter's eyes on her. Could he see that she was not really a boy? She wished she had her hat on again. Madame Jewel had warned that there might be questions if Randolph was found traveling with a young, foreign-looking girl who was obviously not his daughter. The shirt she wore was big, and Madame Jewel had tied Kiku's corset so that it was tighter at the top, though her breasts were small, especially compared to those of the other girls at the house. While she was used to stares, the porter was not the kind of man who would have been welcome at Madame Jewel's. He was more like one of the Portuguese sailors on the boats that had brought her from Japan to New York. When he'd given her the hamper, his breath had smelled familiarly of gin. She narrowed her eyes at him the slightest bit and he gave a little start.

Randolph gave him several coins.

"I won't be needing anything else tonight."

The porter touched his cap. "Yes, sir." He backed out of the door, then stopped.

"Be sure to have your boy pull the shades down for you when it gets dark, sir, if you'll be burning the lamps. There will be two other cars on the sidings and there are trains all night. You won't want to be disturbed."

Randolph had already turned away, but Kiku saw the corners of the porter's mouth turn up in a sly smile.

⁓

They dined early, before it was time to light the lamps. The carriage smelled of sausage and strong cheese and smoked fish and cider and wine. During the months she had traveled on the ocean, Kiku's teeth had suffered, and while she had lost only one, far back in her mouth, her mouth remained tender so that she had to soak her bread in wine or water and stay away from overcooked meat. There were pickles, too, and slices of pale green sugar melon and grapes. The fresh fruit was a miracle to her, and she ate the grapes and melon as quickly as she dared while trying to remain ladylike, as Madame Jewel had taught her.

"You may be a heathen, Jade, but there's no reason why a man can't expect you to eat like a Christian girl." The lessons had intensified after Randolph had requested to see her exclusively, and Madame Jewel began to suspect he would take her away. "You might become a great lady down there in Virginia. He may even want you to serve at table." The other girls had snickered, and Kiku had colored with embarrassment. She would not miss any of them. But she did understand that Madame Jewel was wrong about what Randolph Bliss wanted from her. She would not be a favored courtesan, but only a concubine to satisfy him when he was away from his wife, who lived on Long Island. Randolph Bliss had been the least handsome of the men who had come to her at Madame Jewel's, and the things he did to her, and had her do for him, were often ugly.

Randolph ate quickly and fully, as though he had better things to do. And she was quickly learning that when he was done, she was done.

"Enough food. Bring me my humidor."

Kiku brought him the carved wooden box containing the odious cigars and, when he was ready, lit one of the safety matches he kept in another small box.

She had laughed a rare, natural laugh the first time he had shown her how to strike a match on the box, and he had smiled, surprised. She would have liked to sit down with the entire box, lighting match after match, watching them burn down until just before they reached her fingertips. At fifteen years old (though Madame Jewel had told everyone, Randolph Bliss included, that she was only thirteen), she was still like a child in many ways, particularly when she was alone.

After she cleaned up the hamper and pulled down the car's many window shades, he excused her to the tiny servant's room behind the car's kitchen and water closet.

The porter in New York had carried in the pair of dull gray canvas portmanteaux that Madame Jewel had purchased for her with Randolph Bliss's money. She had followed, giving a little gasp when she saw that the room would belong to her and her alone. The porter had turned around to look at her strangely, and she'd caught a glimpse of herself in the mirror over the small, rimmed shelf on the other side of the bed. She looked like an excited young girl, and she was supposed to be a servant boy. Composing herself, she had coughed into her hand.

For two days she would have a room of her own.

Kiku sat on the cot, listening to the rumble and clanging of the trainyard around them, wishing that they had gone to a hotel for the night as Madame Jewel had said they surely would. She was alone. At Madame Jewel's she had never even been alone to bathe, which they were required to do once a week. On the ships—both the one from her home in Japan to Hawaii, and from Hawaii to New York—she had been hidden in the second mate's cabin with the English girl, Christiana. And at home? She had had to leave the house to be by herself. At night she slept on the tatami mat in the corner she shared with her sister Hanako, their bodies often warm against each other. Her grandmother and her other younger sister and brother slept nearby. Her mother and father slept on the other side of the room, and sometimes she lay awake and listened to them make the sounds of love, and wondered what it would be like when she was married and her husband made those sounds over her. Would she lie quietly, like her mother? She had wanted to ask her mother what it was like, but she never had the nerve.

Did her mother know that she had been kidnapped from their village and hadn't run away? Kiku tried to imagine her mother's face if she told her that she had had many husbands of her own now. That the first had been the second mate on the steamer to Hawaii, while the other girl, Christiana, lay humming to herself on the floor. Another girl who hadn't run quickly enough.

No. She didn't want to imagine her mother's face.

Now she was going to a place called Virginia, and she had a room of her own, if only for a few hours.

She slowly took off the tight, stiff collar that made it hurt when she swallowed, and the shirt, and the itchy wool pants, as well as her undergarments. Folding them neatly and laying them on the dresser that, like the bed, was bolted to the floor, she was hopeful that she might be allowed to sleep on the bed at least for a while. It had a pillow in a crisp white cover at its head, and the coverlet was deep blue, with the railroad's insignia stitched across the middle. How she longed to fold back the snowy white edge of the sheet peeking from beneath the pillow, and slip into the perfect whiteness and sleep. A long sigh escaped her lips. She was naked because he didn't like her to wear clothes, or even pretty nightdresses, like some of the other girls at Madame Jewel's wore. Her eyes lingered on the perfection of the bed for a moment. What were her sisters doing now? They would never see a bed such as this. Were they on the other side of the world, sleeping in each other's arms?

"Kiku."

She quickly fitted one of the several sponges that Madame Jewel had given her far up inside her body, careful to make sure the thin bit of yellow ribbon she had sewn on wouldn't be felt by him. She hadn't had her monthly in several months, but she didn't want to think about that now.

Entering the car's state bedroom, she found Randolph, also naked, waiting at the end of the bed. He had turned down the lamp, so that he sat in shadow. His shallow breath emerged with a faint wheeze, and it was the first of many times she imagined him ill or dying.

His chest was almost three times the breadth of her own, and though he was not as tall as the skinny second mate had been, she felt herself disappear when he wrapped his arms around her. There was no sense of shelter or safety. It was like disappearing into a cave where a capricious tiger lived. Sometimes she would emerge broken and shaking, sometimes certain that he would never be cruel again.

The plane of his forehead was broad and unlined, and his cheeks were like high ledges on either side of his broad, strong nose. She had heard Madame Jewel flatter him about his handsomeness, but

Kiku saw nothing handsome in him. Even though he might smile, she never saw pleasure in his eyes unless he was hurting her, and she had only seen that pleasure by chance, once, when she had dared to open her eyes and look at him. She had no guess as to how old he might be, but she didn't think he was more than forty. So many of the men she had been with after she arrived in New York had been as old as fathers or grandfathers.

He beckoned her over with a benign smile.

Tonight he held out a hairbrush that she had never seen before. The ivory handle and back were of a single piece and carved to look like a plaited rope. She thought of the elephant named Cuyo that a rich country cousin of her father's had imported for farm work. The cousin had planned to work Cuyo until he died, then make his fortune selling his tusks. But Cuyo arrived with only small stubs where the tusks were supposed to be. Kiku had been glad when, after a year of the cousin's harsh treatment, someone had unchained the elephant, and it ran away. His body had never been found, and she imagined that he had walked into the ocean and died peacefully in the waves.

"Take it."

Outside the car, the brakes of an approaching train squealed like a dying animal.

"Come now. Take it," he repeated, just as calmly.

She walked over to him, trying to smile as Madame Jewel had constantly reminded her.

"Smile, but don't show your teeth, Kiku. You're much prettier when you don't show your teeth. Always let him know how glad you are to be with him."

The bedroom's carpet was soft beneath her bare feet. How much happier she would have been if she could simply have lain down on it and felt the vibration of the railyard pass through her body. The motion might carry her away from this place. Not to unknown Virginia, but somewhere else. Somewhere safe.

She took the hairbrush from him. When he touched his own hair, she understood that he wanted her to brush it.

He was vain about his hair. In the time since she had met him, he had let it grow longer, past his high, stiff collars. It was thick and wavy, and if he had not kept it lightly oiled, it would have been as hard to brush as Emerald's stubborn, knotted red hair, or the thick hair of the pretty Negro girl, Jet, who had slept in the bedroom with her at Madame Jewel's.

Kiku knelt on the bed behind Randolph to reach his head better, and, as tenderly as she knew how (she hated for someone else to brush *her* hair), she ran the bristles through the soft, twisted strands. They smelled of lemons and bergamot, like the tea that Madame Jewel was fond of. There was none of the hideous smell of animal fat of the inexpensive pomades that Madame Jewel gave to Jet and some of the other girls. Though Kiku had often shared the little presents of perfume that Randolph gave her with Jet because Jet couldn't stomach meat or see harm to come to any animal, and it made her cry to smell of it.

As she brushed, Randolph reached behind and touched her knee, her thigh. His hand slipped to the inside of her thigh and upward. She made herself relax as he began to touch her in the hidden place, and adjusted her body so he could reach her more easily. His breath quickened as she stroked him with the brush, and she knew she wouldn't be brushing his hair for very much longer.

There was a movement at the window, but Randolph didn't notice. She suspected that his eyes were closed. The shade was pulled down, but perhaps there was an inch revealed. How much could someone see with the lamp burning low?

She was certain it was the porter, standing on some steps or a tall box, come back to spy on them. For a moment she was angry, thinking of his sly, ugly smile, thinking he knew what she was.

But what did it matter to him, or even to her, what she was? The time for shame had passed a long time ago. She felt old, like the peddler woman who came to the kitchen door of Madame Jewel's with her boxes of fancy buttons and trims. Sapphire had told her that the woman bought her wares from the undertaker, who snipped them from the clothes of dead before they were buried.

"Don't stop." Randolph's voice was strangled in his throat, and his hand was busy in her hidden place.

She had been distracted, imagining she could feel the porter's breath on the window.

Leaning forward, she flicked her tongue like a butterfly's wing on the edge of Randolph's ear, and he moaned. Let the porter see what he had come to see. She only wished that she were truly a boy, because wouldn't that have scandalized the nasty little man!

Randolph took his hand away and quickly rose to stand over her, surprising her (and no doubt the man at the window, as well). Despite the dim light, she saw that there was no pleasure in his eyes. Only blind lust. It was a look that all the men wore, and Madame Jewel had explained many times that the girls were lucky because they were so desired, that it was a calling that not every woman could answer.

Kiku did not believe her. The other girls did not believe her. Kiku was certain that Madame Jewel didn't believe it, either, that it was perhaps a story that she had once told herself, before she had turned wrinkled and ugly and had to dye her hair a beastly orange to hide the streaks of gray.

Randolph roughly pushed her farther up onto the bed, so that her head was against, but not resting on, the pile of snowy white pillows. She smiled her pleasure smile, the one that said, *Oh, what fun we'll have now*, and languidly turned her head to look at the window. A light had come on somewhere nearby, outlining the porter's now-hatless head. It was perfectly still.

When she turned back to Randolph and saw that he still had the beautiful hairbrush in his hand, she knew what sort of tiger dwelled in the cave of his arms tonight.

The porter would get all he had hoped to see.

Chapter 5

KIKU

August 1878

It was dusk the next evening when the train, to which their car had been noisily joined that morning, stopped at an unlighted station, and a porter and conductor came to help them with their luggage. Kiku kept her hat on and her face down, as Randolph had instructed her, but she stole a glance at the tiny station that was no more than a leaning wooden booth with a sagging lintel and broken window, set on a long wooden platform. A porter—not the one from the day before—set her bags down a few feet away from the booth and gave her a curt, disinterested nod before retrieving Randolph's bags.

Randolph had awakened her only fifteen minutes earlier, and despite the cool of the evening, she wanted to sink onto her bags and go back to sleep. There was enough light that she could see the

44

outlines of a few buildings well beyond the station, but when the train pulled away again, she looked across the tracks into an impenetrable mass of trees, whose jagged tops stood in relief against the gloomy sky.

Randolph stood a few feet away, his own bags at his feet, peering at his vest watch, which he had checked ten times since awakening her.

The nighttime sounds were different here. In the city, even during the darkest hours there had been the sound of horses and cabs, laughter, a policeman's whistle. People, loud and brash. But here were sounds that came from her memory: The rustle of the trees in the night breeze. Crickets. A night bird. But no sound of the sea, or smell of a rotting seabird or fish, or salt on the air. She hadn't been magically transported back home, but the sounds made her feel less afraid, less needful of the softness of the nearly shapeless rag doll in her bag, the one that Randolph had seen on her bed when he had looked into her tiny room on the train. He had picked it up and stared at it for a moment, and his skin had flushed and he had dropped it as though it had burned him.

After many minutes she wearied of standing and, without asking his permission, she sank onto her bags and rested her arms and head on her knees. She was hungry, but they had eaten everything packed in the food hamper and left the hamper in the train car. At Madame Jewel's, the food hadn't been plentiful, but there had always been food when she was hungry.

"No man wants a skeleton in bed." Madame Jewel seemed to delight in dabbing the cook's lumpy mashed potatoes onto the girls' plates. "If they do, they can go to the city morgue and find some poor thing wasted from opium. And don't think there aren't those who won't!"

When would they eat again? Randolph had told her little about where they were going except that it was a town called Old Gate. Madame Jewel had talked of a great house, but he had only talked of the town.

"Full of the most godawful, sanctimonious sticks you've ever met," he had said. "But they mind their own business down there. They were taught a lesson in the war."

Kiku had no idea what the word *sanctimonious* might mean, but she understood being taught a lesson. It was what people said when they thought you had done something wrong, or that you didn't know better.

"Goddammit, it's about time."

Kiku turned her head to follow his gaze. She noticed the matching blazes of white on the two horses' faces first, and then the large man seated at the front of the carriage they pulled. His skin was so dark that he took shape from the night like a spectre.

⌒

Settled inside the carriage beneath a thick woolen blanket, Kiku stifled a sneeze. Outside, a woman was making a fuss over Randolph, and Randolph was replying in the same formal but condescending tones he used with Madame Jewel. The woman was certainly welcoming him, but she didn't know that Kiku was inside the carriage. When Mason Goodbody, the man driving the carriage, unloaded Randolph's luggage and boxes, the carriage shook, and Kiku squeezed one of her own rough portmanteaux to reassure herself it was still there.

At the station, Randolph had roughly introduced her to Mason. "Mason, this is Kiku. Take her to the cottage and make sure she gets some food." Mason didn't stare at her as so many people did, but only nodded and said, "Yes, Mister Bliss."

Randolph turned to her. "I'll see you in a day or two. Behave yourself. Mason will make sure you have everything you need."

She had wanted, just in that moment, to cling to him. He had told her nothing about where she was to go or what she was to do. Only that this Mason would be somehow responsible for her and that she was supposed to be a good girl. She knew what the men at Madame Jewel's meant when they told her to behave. Would this Mason take her into his bed? Alone, without the protection of Madame Jewel, was she to become the property of any man Randolph wished?

Madame Jewel had told her that she was not owned by Randolph Bliss, but obligated. Standing in the rising moonlight, watching as Mason helped Randolph into the carriage, Kiku saw no difference between ownership and obligation. With Randolph inside, Mason startled her by putting a gentle hand on her arm and whispering, "Get on in. We'll get you home soon."

Mason had helped her into the carriage, and as he indicated that she should cover herself with the blanket, he said, "I'll tell you when we get out of town and you can sit up."

As Randolph's and the woman's voices receded, Mason told the horses to "get on," and the carriage began to move. A few minutes later, just as Kiku felt she could no longer bear the suffocating blanket, he told her that she could come out. "There's nobody out on the road to see you."

She shook off the blanket, feeling her hair fly up, stretching after the wool, and when she was free, she breathed deeply. The air smelled of horse, but it was clear air, and chilly. As her eyes adjusted, she looked out the window to see that the sky had become a star-meadow. Not since she'd last been on ship's deck at night had she seen so many stars. Could a place that let her be this close to the stars be a bad place?

She knew she was being foolish. Anything could happen to her. Anything had.

Randolph had talked of the town, but she was being driven away from the town.

For a while, the land on either side of the wagon seemed to be cleared. Perhaps farmland. But finally the trees thickened, and when Mason nickered at the horses, they slowed and turned onto a narrow road. Kiku watched as the trees and darkness closed behind them.

It was peaceful with the slow thuds of the horses' hooves on the dirt road, and the creaking of the wheels. But Kiku's heart started to pound in her small chest and she began to have trouble breathing. Were the woods enchanted? She had never in her life been in so desolate a place. Empty yet not empty. It was the place of nightmares, of the stories her grandmother had told her of cottages, even whole villages, hidden in the woods, where *kitsune-tuskai* lived, witches who could charm foxes and have them do their evil work. Or the witches who ate children who wandered from their villages.

Oh, Oba, how true those stories were. Do you know how true? Are you dead now, dear Oba? Or do you miss me still?

Kiku wiped her tears on her sleeve. How she hated these stiff boys' clothes. She was not herself anymore. No one knew who she was. She hardly knew herself.

"Ho!"

The horses stopped in a small clearing, but the absence of a few trees didn't make the place any less frightening. She could see the outline of a cottage.

Mason climbed down from the front seat and spoke to the horses. Then the clearing was suddenly brighter with the spark of lantern light, and then another lantern. The lights jerked along as he climbed the porch stairs and hung one of the lanterns on a hook jutting out from the wall. She wanted to ask him if he limped because he'd been injured or if he'd been born that way. There had been a baby boy in her father's family who had been born with twisted legs—it was supposed to be a secret, but she had heard that it was because of some curse in the family. It was said that the baby hadn't been allowed to take a breath, but her mother told her that was gossip the neighbors had made up, that the baby had been born too weak to live. Kiku wasn't sure what the truth was, but she knew she could never kill her own child, no matter the circumstances of its birth.

Mason came back and opened the carriage door. "You all might as well get out. This is it."

This was what? Mason's home? Randolph's home?

Randolph was staying at an inn that was a townhouse, which made sense to her because it was a house, and it was in a town, like the houses in New York. Here, there were no other houses in sight. Only trees, darkness, and the smell of earth.

"It's only getting later. I'm going to have to get up in the morning, and that's about three hours from now, girl. You *are* a girl?"

Kiku took his hand and climbed out.

Mason will take care of me. I am to be a good girl.

She followed Mason up the porch stairs. There was no light on inside, and she had the sense that the cottage had been empty for a long time. The air smelled of paint and wood smoke.

Mason's lantern made shadows of the few furnishings: a sofa and a pair of big chairs near the cold fireplace, a large trunk, a smoking stand, and a side table. A round dining table with two chairs.

"Bedroom's in there. You've got a lamp in there, too, and there's a little kitchen. The sun gets through on a clear day. Necessary's out the back door from the kitchen."

Kiku glanced around, but her eyes kept coming back to Mason. He was tall, but his shoulders had the slightest of stoops, as though he were ashamed of something. In the lamplight, his curled brown hair was tinged with red. He looked older than Randolph.

"There's some ham and beans that my wife, Odette, made, in a dish in the kitchen, and I pumped some water into a pitcher for you."

Now he seemed awkward. Still, Kiku said nothing. What was she supposed to do?

"Here's the bedroom."

She followed him. The bed was larger than any bed at Madame Jewel's, even the bed that was reserved for the men who liked to have more than one girl at a time. A small armoire and vanity table were pushed up against one wall, and two windows reflected the lamplight back to them and brightened when he lighted the lamp on the bedside table.

Mason set her bags on the bed.

Kiku stared down at the floor, uncertain. Was it time? She sat quickly down beside the bags and wrestled off the tight shoes. Then she undid the suspenders from her wool pants so that they loosened quickly and slipped from her, onto the floor, as she stood again. She was wearing no underwear—which was what Randolph preferred, but the long shirt covered her front.

Mason gasped. She looked up.

"Good Lord, girl. Stop! What are you doing?" He had turned his face to the wall, his hands in front of him as though to ward off some terrible thing. "Do you want to get me shot?"

His footsteps pounded the floor, shaking it, as he hurried from the room, leaving her alone. Confused and frightened, she pulled the pants back on, struggling with the suspenders. If he were to leave, she would be alone in the cottage, surrounded by the dark and whatever spirits lived in the walls or in the woods outside. "Wait. Please wait." She wanted to cry out, but found she could not raise her voice above a whisper. "Don't leave me."

When she reached the parlor, she found Mason standing near the open doorway of the cottage, looking out. Hearing her, he turned around.

"It's not like that. Don't do that for anybody but Mister Bliss, do you hear me? You won't if you want to live . . ." He shook his head. "Not if you want to live here."

It hadn't taken Kiku long to learn some English from the girl, Christiana, on the ship, and she had learned plenty more in her months at Madame Jewel's. She knew exactly what he meant. She shivered in the cool air coming from the open door.

"I'm sorry for you, but I can't do nothing about it. I'll be back to check on you when I can. Nobody will bother you. The workmen aren't allowed in the woods on this side of the big house." He nodded and closed the door behind him.

Kiku stood, listening, as the carriage moved slowly away from the cottage, leaving her alone in the wavering lamplight with her own thin shadow.

Chapter 6

KIKU

August 1878

Kiku didn't remember sleeping.

She had been paralyzed for a long time after Mason left, afraid to move beyond the soft glow cast by the parlor lamp he'd lighted for her. After a few frozen moments, she heard an owl calling out in the woods, and found herself waiting, anxious for an answering call. But there was none. Only the same owl calling again and again. It was all alone, as she was. For a moment, she had fantasized that she might open the door so that it might come inside: *Fukurou* meant good fortune, a sign for a hopeful future. The rug in front of the cold fireplace was thick sheepskin, and she sank to her knees, exhausted, yet listening, listening as hard as she could, not wanting the owl to stop calling.

She had seen only one owl in the city: a black shadow that had swooped from the steel-gray sky as she walked one early evening with Emerald, hours before the busy time at Madame Jewel's. The air had trembled with a rush of wings, and a rat that neither of them had noticed in the gutter shrieked as the owl sank its claws into its back and carried it up, up into the shadowed rooftops on the other side of the street. Kiku had stared after them, but Emerald had grabbed her arm and hidden her face against Kiku's shoulder, terrified.

There had been brown water rats that lived near the shore of her village, and her family kept their food baskets and jars covered to keep them out. But the rats of New York were gray, with pointed noses, and they ate the noses and fingertips off of infants living in the tenements. It had gladdened her heart to see one murdered by an owl.

When she opened her eyes to weak sunlight, half of her face was buried in the sheep's fleece, and she pulled a bit of wool from her dry lips.

She was still alone, and nothing had murdered her in the night. Though she knew that it was just superstition—something her father told her was for old women and fools—she couldn't help but think that it had been the owl that had protected her. The thought brought a smile to her face. An unforced smile of the kind she hadn't felt in a very long time.

After drinking most of the water from the pitcher Mason had left, and eating a ravenous, cold breakfast (cold, because she had no idea how to light or use the stove) of beans and thankfully tender chunks of ham, she opened the front windows of the cottage. The sashes lifted easily, unlike the greasy windows at Madame Jewel's, and let in the brown scent of the woods. She looked about for some sign of Mason, but saw only the expanse of flattened dirt in front of the cottage. Beyond were the trees—not so thick or forbidding in the daylight—and the roof of a house. Closer, the brighter edges of the canopy floor were scattered here and there with stems of wildflowers whose petals hung in graceful rows of bright pink.

Alone as she was, she forgot to be afraid.

She had no guess as to when Randolph might come. While she had very few notions of keeping an American house, she did have a fair understanding of what Randolph was eventually going to want of her, and she knew that she should make some effort to be ready. But it was early yet. Randolph was not a man of morning appetites. Always, he had come to her in the late afternoon or evening, after his important business was done. On the train he had not wanted her in the morning, but had attended to his own shaving and toilette and then had written letters and read a book for most of the day.

Taking her shoes, two dresses, two hats, and a nightshift from her bags, she laid one dress and her petticoats on the bed, and hung the other dress, along with the nightshift, in the wardrobe. Her hairbrush and pins and few cosmetics she arranged on the dressing table and tucked the sponges, her clean, dry monthly rags, and the special things Madame Jewel had given her for a man's pleasure into the vanity drawers. At the bottom of one bag, she discovered the peacock feather that she had found near the park's menagerie soon after she had met Randolph. She had been shy about picking it up from the path, afraid that someone might accuse her of stealing it from the peacock who strutted up and down the small enclosure, but she couldn't resist it, and quickly tucked it into a fold of her dress. After she had it for a few weeks, she sometimes wore it behind her ear when she met with a gentleman. Randolph had found it particularly charming. Now she laid it on the vanity.

The mirror set into an ornate frame on top of the vanity made her shy, and she wouldn't look directly into it. The other girls at

Madame Jewel's had been silly for mirrors, but Kiku preferred not to look at her own face except to apply makeup. She had long ago decided that she looked how she looked. It would have to be good enough.

Her sister had always teased that her nose was too broad, like a peasant's, and her lips too thin. Her eyes were like her mother's eyes: small and brown and deep-set within her oval face. But there was always kindness in her mother's eyes. Kiku felt no kindness in her own. Only resignation.

She set the rag doll on the vanity's top, its head resting against the mirror, so it could watch everything she did.

Standing in the dust in front of the cottage, she wondered where she might take a walk. It was hotter here than in New York, and her plum-colored dress, with its lace-trimmed white bib and black bows set along the edges of the overskirt, was tighter than it had been just four days earlier. There was the dirt road that curved around the cottage that must somehow lead to a larger road, and that was all, except for the hint of a path angling away from the cottage in the opposite direction. It was so faint that it might have been a deer's path, or—to her sudden worry—one made by the wild hogs Madame Jewel had warned her about.

"I hear that Virginia and the Carolinas are beset with them. In the war, they attacked soldiers and ate runaway slaves and children!" She had said this with a kind of glimmer in her eyes that made Kiku wonder if she was going mad. "But I'm sure you'll be fine with Mister Bliss." Kiku would ask Mason about the wild hogs. Surely he would know.

Then she heard the voices. Sharp voices and orders given. The sound of men. When she had gone out to the necessary at the edge of the cottage's small backyard, she hadn't heard any sounds coming from the woods except for the fluttering of birds and their songs. The voices came from the other side of the cottage, from the direction of the big house.

The men aren't allowed on this side of the woods.

⁓

Kiku knelt beside a clump of pink flowers that were like the ones she'd seen from the cottage window, mindful of her skirts among the dirt on the ground. She was just inside the line of trees, but far enough away from the men that she could watch them, unobserved, as they went in and out of the house that rose from the middle of a field like a tall, yellow giant. They weren't gentlemen, but workmen carrying tools and pieces of paneling and other bits she didn't recognize. Many wore neatly trimmed beards, dungarees, and tidy caps, but she was far enough away that she couldn't see the details of their faces. Watching them, she was surprised that she had even heard their voices. They were not the boisterous journeymen of New York. These voices weren't raised and were more furtive than good-natured. The men's faces were grim, their gazes downcast unless they were speaking directly to one another. They didn't seem to notice the beauty of the day, the perfect sunlight.

The sun shone on the house's warm yellow brick, and construction activity around the house spoke of beauties to come: a garden with trees and flowers, and the beginnings of a garden wall. A secret garden, perhaps, like the ones she'd heard of hidden behind the walls of the great houses of Nagasaki, and the temples outside the city. She saw herself walking in such a garden, kneeling by the water, watching fish, the way she had as a child.

Though Randolph had told her that the house wasn't quite ready to move into, that it would take another couple of months, to Kiku the house looked finished. Finished and forbidding. Its black-framed windows were like rows of watching eyes, and the strange gray roof that hung over the house's top floor reminded her of the protective *shikoro* of a samurai's helmet. A set of stairs clung to the garden side of the house and led all the way to the topmost floor. Just the thought of climbing them made her feel dizzy. Who would use such stairs? Was Randolph so unfriendly that he would make visitors come in that way? She felt a strong, disturbing presence when she looked at the house, and she saw that the workmen, with their hunched shoulders and purposeful movements, sensed it as well.

In fact, the house itself looked unfriendly, the way it stood alone against the sky. Madame Jewel had told her that Randolph's second name, Bliss, meant "happy." But this was not a happy house. She was glad now that she most likely would not be living inside it, and would be sure to watch it very carefully.

Despite the sunshine, a film of gray gathered and descended over the scene of the workmen and the big house. At first she thought she was about to faint, the way she had the first time Madame Jewel had laced her into a corset. But the gray wasn't in her head. It was a living thing, resting on the house and the men like a silvery shroud that moved with them like gossamer silk. Like a clinging, suffocating death.

The tiny, heart-shaped flower she had been unconsciously fingering broke away from its stem, and she held it to her face to see that the petal had bruised and darkened like wounded flesh. Sickened and ashamed, she flung the ruined blossom away and rose from the ground to hurry back to the cottage.

Chapter 7

KIKU

August 1878

"You don't look like much. Mason says you don't talk."

Kiku had arrived back at the cottage, breathless with hurrying, her mind filled with death. Her own? She knew that with Randolph, someday she might actually be praying for her own death.

The dark-skinned woman in the cottage kitchen came forward to examine Kiku more closely, her arms crossed below her bosom. Her simple yellow cotton dress, which was covered with small blue blossoms, hung neatly from her shapely hips, its waist nipped in as pointedly as Kiku's own. She moved without hesitation, and though her clunky boots were loud on the cottage floor, she moved with grace. For the briefest of moments Kiku wondered if this might be Randolph's wife, but Madame Jewel had led her to believe that Randolph's wife was a grand lady who wore jewels and furs (but perhaps not in summer, not in Virginia?) and rode everywhere in a carriage drawn by four enormous horses. And she had seen many dark-skinned women in New York walking with white men, but when she glanced at this woman's hands, she saw that they were rough. She did not seem like the sort of woman Randolph would marry.

Catching her glance, the woman grimaced and slipped her hands beneath her folded arms so that Kiku could no longer see them.

"Is that true? Don't you talk? Maybe you just don't speak English." She took a step back, narrowing her alert brown eyes. "Maybe you just fuck."

Kiku understood that the woman meant to insult her. She stared back, saying nothing. It didn't seem unreasonable to her. She hadn't come here expecting friends. She hadn't dared to hope that she would find kindness in this forsaken wilderness. Once she had been good at catching gray crabs on the beach and keeping her younger brother and sisters from trouble while her mother did her work. But now she had learned new things. Distasteful things that she sometimes watched herself do from another part of the room, as though it were another girl doing them.

She held her breath, waiting for the woman to begin berating her. Instead, the woman shrugged and turned away, so that Kiku could see the sprig of tiny yellow flowers tucked into her low chignon.

"Makes no difference to me whether you talk, but I'd hoped for better. Mason's too quiet, like living with a ghost some days, those days when he gets home before I go to bed. That's not often." Kiku caught a glimpse of the mannish boots beneath her dress as she moved to the stove, on which sat another towel-covered bowl, like the one that had been there the night before. "Mister Bliss . . ."

The terse, unpleasant way she said his name—as though she could not say it quickly enough, as though she didn't want it on her tongue—made Kiku look at her retreating back more closely. Again she appraised the woman's figure. Randolph had preferred Kiku over all the other girls, dark-skinned or light, at Madame Jewel's, but maybe she'd been wrong in thinking Randolph wouldn't have lain with this woman. Mason's wife.

"He likes his people to be available to him night and day." She turned to look at Kiku again, and this time Kiku thought she saw a glimmer of pity in her eyes.

"Yes." Kiku's voice stayed at a whisper.

The woman smiled.

"You are a strange little thing. How old are you? Who cut your hair like that?"

Kiku put her hand to her shortened hair. As she had dressed, not an hour before, she had tried to pin her hair into some kind of shape, but it was too short. Looking in the mirror, she felt she looked like a boy wearing women's clothes.

"Do you know how to use the stove? Can you cook?"

Kiku shook her head.

They both turned at the sound of a carriage and horses coming around the front of the house. Kiku felt the blood rush from her face and felt once again that she might faint. She had never gotten the water she had come to the kitchen for. The pitcher was still empty because she hadn't filled it.

Why this fear? Why this feeling of death?

"Did you know he was coming here this morning?"

"No."

The woman didn't look afraid, but only perturbed.

"Looks like Mason's with him." She paused and added, "Thank God. I can't stand that man on my own too early in the morning." She spoke hurriedly about the food on the stove, but before she could finish, Kiku heard Randolph's heavy tread on the porch stairs.

"Kiku! Where are you?"

Randolph looked larger here in the small cottage, larger even than he had that first night he'd come to her in the Red Room at Madame Jewel's. His skin had been tinged with yellow, as though he had been ill for a long time. Now his cheeks were ruddy with sunshine. If he had been another man, she might have thought him handsome.

But Randolph Bliss was not handsome, and try as she might to imagine him as Madame Jewel had told her to imagine him, she couldn't. She could only see the cruelty and shrewdness in his eyes. *Greedy eyes.*

"I am here." She bowed so that her shorn black hair hung about her cheeks. "Sir," she added. This for the benefit of the woman. *See*, she seemed to say. *This is why I am here. This will keep me alive. What will keep you alive?*

"You're dressed, I see. Settled?" He didn't wait for her to answer. "Please see to this, Kiku." As he handed her a low brown hat that she'd never seen him wear before, he nodded to the woman as though it were the most natural thing in the world to see her there. "Odette! Mason said you were available to help my young ward acclimate herself to her new home, and for that you have my great thanks."

Kiku was glad to hear the woman's name. Mason had, perhaps, told her, but she had forgotten.

Odette nodded, her voice subdued. "Yes, Mister Bliss. I'll see that she fares well as best I'm able."

"Fine. That's just fine." He inclined his head toward the kitchen door. "Please assist Mason with the provisions. There's a good girl." He beamed on her, and Kiku found his unusually broad smile chilling. His teeth were perfect. He was as vain about them as he was his hair.

Kiku held the hat in both hands, uncertain exactly where to put it. Odette slipped past her, her boots less noisy on the floor now; she seemed shy in Randolph's presence, which surprised Kiku. Perhaps it was not so surprising. Although Odette had seemed bold when they were alone, Kiku had yet to meet the person who did not seem to feel uncomfortable, or at least somewhat diminished, in his presence.

When the front door closed behind her, Randolph sighed. "Stupid woman. She should know better than to come and go through the front door. You're the mistress here, my dear." He pointed at her. "You will need to admonish her."

Kiku almost laughed, but quickly covered her mouth. He was telling her that she should give orders to Odette? She had never given orders to anyone, except to her younger brother and sisters.

"Put the hat on the table beside the door. Stop standing there like you don't have a brain in your head. You're not the employee of that shrew, Bernadette Jewel, anymore."

What am I to be now, Randolph?

She hurried to set the hat on the table. Niall, the Irish boy at Madame Jewel's, had always seen to the gentlemen's hats and coats, brushing and cleaning them if required. He kept them in a little room beside the hall, hidden away, so that the gentlemen who visited would not see the belongings of some friend, acquaintance, or even family member. Madame Jewel was very discreet.

"The Virginia air suits you." When she returned to him, Randolph took her chin in his hand and turned her head side to side. "What's this in your hair?" He touched the locks of hair covering her ear and she froze. His face changed, and he flung something away with his hand.

Kiku looked down to see a silver and blue dragonfly casting about the floor, trying to right itself.

Randolph mashed the thing under his boot. "Filthy bugs." He looked back down at her. She held his gaze for just a moment, but could only think of the poor crushed dragonfly. Dragonflies were good luck. It was the only one she had seen since leaving the village, and now it was dead.

"You've been outside."

Kiku nodded, taken off her guard. He had said nothing to her about not leaving the cottage, but perhaps she should have known. Still, she tested him. "It is a fine day. Am I not allowed?"

He threw his head back and laughed, again showing his perfect teeth. "Not allowed? As long as you stay within shouting distance, roam as you like. But stay away from the house." He lowered his voice. "And the men. You're not for them. Old habits, eh?" His grin was wry and suggestive.

Then I will not be used by all the men.

The idea that she might be given at some point to the men had flitted through her mind when she had first seen them outside the big house, but the idea had been so terrible that she hadn't followed it far.

⁓

The front door opened, and Odette started in with a stack of boxes that reached her chin. Mason stood just outside.

"Tell her." Randolph didn't bother to lower his voice. "You are mistress of this house."

It occurred to Kiku to say that if she was the mistress, then she, like her mother in the house in which she had grown up, or like Madame Jewel, had say as to who could come and go and through what doors. But she was not really the house's mistress. It was only Randolph's game.

Kiku gathered herself and crossed to the front door. Her instinct was to help Odette with the boxes, but she checked her actions.

"You must come in the back door. Please."

Odette glanced from Kiku to Randolph and back.

"I will next time. Let me just put these down."

Randolph gave a little cough.

"You must go out now, and come in the back." Kiku felt her voice waver, but the heat of Randolph's cruelty was like a great beast at her back. At least for now, obeying him was what would keep her alive.

Odette's lips parted, and Kiku was sure she was going to argue. *Please, please don't.*

Then Odette closed her mouth and turned without a word. Beyond her, Mason looked angry, his kind eyes no longer kind as he watched his wife cross the porch. Kiku shut the door, her heart pounding. She could hear Mason grumbling at his wife.

"What are you trying to do, woman? What did I tell you?"

Kiku couldn't hear Odette's retort, but only the irritated tone. When she turned back to Randolph, he was nodding. "Well done."

Chapter 8

LUCY

June 1899

The arrival of Hannah Tanner, the infamous female preacher and daughter of famed Pennsylvania abolitionist E. L. Tanner, wasn't announced with posters or handbills in Old Gate, but word quickly spread that the meeting would happen on Thursday, and Lucy knew she would go to hear her. Hannah and her followers, the Tannerites, were zealous Christians, but were better known for their spontaneous demonstrations for the rights of working women and children. Lucy had thought a lot about the travails of the poor and prayed for them often. But she also knew that her father would forbid her if he caught wind of her plan, which made it all the more likely that she would find a way to go. He could not be allowed to persist at running her life.

Though the national church had quieted its criticism of women who had the temerity to preach the gospel, they didn't interfere with the local priest's preferences. Her father very much believed Paul's admonition from 1 Timothy: "But I suffer not a woman to teach, nor to usurp authority over the man, but to be in silence." Her mother, of course, maintained her own neutral silence on the subject. Lucy didn't see why a woman shouldn't preach, though female preachers had the reputation of being as dull as nuns and sometimes were even known to wear pants (Hannah Tanner was said to smoke, but not wear mannish clothing). Lucy had visited the country home of a friend near Boston, and as a lark they had attended a camp meeting that featured two woman preachers. She had been struck by the energy of the crowd of faithful, and if she had flirted with a boy from the next county over, and let him kiss her in the darkness as a simple late night supper of bread and soup dished from a large kettle over the fire was served inside the tent, it didn't mean that she was not still a good Episcopalian. So she had spent all of Wednesday excited about Hannah Tanner's appearance. But the biggest attraction was, of course, that Hannah Tanner would be speaking in the theater at Bliss House.

⌒

Faye complained that nothing bored her more than preaching, and that women preachers were always worse than men.

"Most of them are so ugly, they only preach because they couldn't get someone to marry them. But I know why *you* want to go. You can't fool me, Lucy Valentine Searle!" A month had passed since the *Walpurgisnacht* party, and though Faye's parents were perfectly happy to have Josiah as a guest at their house, or for Faye to dine at Bliss House with him, Lucy had no such permission or excuse to go to the big house outside town.

The passage of weeks since she had been to Bliss House hadn't dimmed her thoughts of that night. At any given moment, she found herself remembering the touch of Randolph's hands on her skin. No man had touched her before with such solicitude. She had felt like a woman, and no longer a child. He hadn't shown up in church the following Sunday, but he had in later weeks, and they had greeted each other no differently than they had before they had danced, naked, around the Maypole.

Even now the thought of that dance, of the nakedness of people she saw clothed on the street in Old Gate, caused her to flush so that her mother would ask her if she felt ill.

Ill! In fact, she felt something that was quite the opposite of ill. She felt alive. She felt as though that aliveness might flow out of her, covering all that she touched. She felt she could live forever in the memory of that night, even though she knew her parents would have her be ashamed.

In the pure light of Sunday morning services, she saw that Randolph definitely was not a young man. Yet when she thought of him, she did not think of him in church, but in Bliss House. With a certainty and boldness she didn't recognize in herself, she saw herself sitting at the long Chippendale table in the dining room with him, walking in Bliss House's beautiful, well-kept gardens. Saw herself in one of the bedrooms she had seen others enter so carelessly, eager to touch each other, to taste, to breathe in the very scent of each other.

"You don't even mind that he's old, do you? You're so strange, Lucy. Josiah says I'm being silly, but I do believe you very much want to spend time again with Randolph."

When Lucy flushed, Faye laughed and clapped her hands. "You're delicious. Oh, your father is going to want to lock you up in a nunnery!"

After they had left Bliss House together, Faye had commented that Lucy and Randolph had looked very *cozy* when she and Josiah had come into the salon. Lucy had been reticent, but Faye knew her well enough to push further. Lucy told her that she wasn't quite sure how she felt about Randolph. It was a lie. She knew very well that she couldn't wait to see him again. Within two days, Josiah reported to Faye that Randolph had hinted that *he* would very much like to see Lucy again.

"It's just a visiting preacher, Faye. Stop it. You don't know what you're talking about."

"I've half a mind to go so I can watch you. What would you say to that?"

Lucy shook her head. "I'd say I don't care. Do as you please." Inside, though, she was hoping against hope that Faye wouldn't come. She was self-conscious, and she felt like she couldn't bear to have Faye watching her, making assumptions. It wasn't even as though she had a desire to go to Bliss House. It felt like a need. It felt like there was some special sort of air there that she, and she alone, should breathe. Faye couldn't be expected to understand.

⁓

Guests arriving at the front of Bliss House were directed to the garden, where the tall stairs built against the house led straight up to the theater. Terrance nodded to Lucy and Carrie, whom Lucy's mother had required her to take calling with her for the day. (Lucy worried, at first, that her mother suspected where she was planning to go, but, no, she was irritated with Carrie over some small matter and wanted her out of the house.)

Terrance's eyes were half-closed against the June sunshine as though he were unused to being outside. But as he gave her a hand to ascend the first step, he spoke. "Good afternoon, Miss Searle. Mister Bliss has been expecting you. He has asked if you would take a seat in the back row, near the aisle."

The request made her stomach flutter. So he really had been thinking of her. She nodded to Terrance.

"Thank you. I will."

The brilliance of the day and the lively air of the small groups of men and women ascending the stairs were a contrast to the *Walpurgisnacht* ball. Bliss House sat calm and stately in the sunshine, and row after row of luscious white roses bloomed in the garden, soaking the air in perfect fragrance. She and Carrie were climbing up, up toward the clear blue sky as if she were on a staircase to heaven. The joy she felt swept away any disturbing memories she had of her adventures with Josiah in the nursery. Her nerves had been in such a high state that she supposed that she might even have imagined the animals and dolls flying about the room. Perhaps they had simply fallen from the very old shelves. Randolph had told her that though he knew it might seem odd, he wished to keep the nursery as a sort of memorial to his daughter, Tamora. It seemed right to her, given that she had seen mother and daughter standing right outside its door. Bliss House did not like change. Is that why the ghosts had noticed her? They knew something that she did not. Or at least wasn't ready to fully admit to herself: that she would do just about anything to be with Randolph in Bliss House.

"Carrie, you'll sit somewhere else, please."

"Are you sure?" Carrie gave her a questioning look, her green eyes wide. She was a pretty woman, with her red hair and neat, if ample, figure. Though she was a decent enough housemaid, Lucy imagined that she would make an excellent nanny.

Now why does that come to mind?

Lucy had told Carrie about coming to Bliss House with Faye, but when Carrie asked her about ghosts, she had lied, and said that the house was impressive, but decidedly unhaunted.

"Yes, if you would. I'm sure you'll find someone you know. Half the town is here."

Inside the theater door at the top of the staircase, a teenage girl in a drab brown dress handed them printed programs. A line drawing of Hannah Tanner's face encircled with a laurel wreath addressed the top. The face was youthful, with a dignified profile and strong nose. The phrase "United for Christ and Justice" curved over the top of the wreath. Lucy took the program, thanking the girl.

"We serve The Word and Justice." The girl spoke with such vehemence that Lucy couldn't help but look at her face. Her dark eyes burned with ferocious passion of a kind that Lucy would have imagined was impossible in someone so young. Would that she herself could feel so strongly about something important. Already she felt inadequate to the afternoon.

A masculine version of the girl at the door was busy seating guests in the front rows, and Lucy prompted Carrie to sit. Several of the faces in the theater belonged to familiar members of her father's church. Edward Searle was a harsh spiritual leader and was unlikely to be forgiving of their transgression if he learned they had been there. By their shy smiles, she knew that her secret was safe with them, if she would return the favor.

Slipping around the small line of people, Lucy took a seat in the back row. No one followed her or attempted to sit anywhere near her, as though there were an invisible wall around her, protecting her. At once she felt special, yet isolated, like some rare object that could be seen, but not touched.

⁓

Randolph approached the podium. He welcomed his guests with what Lucy saw was genuine warmth.

"I know you all have many other things to do today, and I thank you for coming. Miss Tanner has many important things to say about justice in our state, and in our time. So I will happily cede the floor to her, and ask only that you listen with your hearts. Her words could not have a lovelier, more urgent messenger. Please welcome Miss Hannah Tanner."

In person, Hannah Tanner was a delicate beauty not more than five feet tall. Coming to the podium to enthusiastic applause, she inclined her head to Randolph, smiling, and offered him her hand, which he took. When Lucy saw their hands meet, she felt a twinge of jealousy. But when they parted, Hannah Tanner approached the lectern, and Randolph caught Lucy's eye and made his way to the seat beside her. As he got closer, she nervously clasped one gloved hand in the other.

She smiled up at him, noticing how clean-shaven he was and how the summer sun had lightened sections of his thick brown hair and slightly bronzed his skin. This was not a man who confined himself to stuffy rooms and stale talk. Like her, he was alive. In addition, he had a sensitive heart.

I think my parents simply refuse to know him. I will help them know him better, or I will live without their affection.

There it was. Madness, but truth. She would be with Randolph no matter what. She felt it as a kind of fever.

As Hannah Tanner thanked Randolph from the lectern, Lucy moved over one chair, and he sat down beside her. He whispered in her ear, his breath warm on her earlobe, and she imagined him kissing it ever so gently. "I very much wanted you to come, but I dared not hope."

Her answering smile was radiant.

"There is nothing on this earth that belongs to you!" Hannah Tanner's polite words about feeling welcomed at Bliss House and by the crowd were gone as if she'd never spoken them, replaced by her angry admonition.

Lucy was startled from her pleasant reverie with Randolph. They both looked forward.

"Ladies and gentlemen, we are killing our fellow man. Fellow women. Our children! Our greed and desire for fine things is paid for with the blood of innocents who work until their fingers bleed, or their limbs are crushed in the machinery that produces the useless detritus with which you stuff your drawing rooms and great grand houses and decorate your ridiculous hats. Christ will not stand for it!" She looked around the room as though daring someone to contradict her, but there was only stunned silence. "Would you have Him, who was hanged on the tree, excuse the wanton way we dispose of the weakest among us? Remember Matthew 19:14. 'But Jesus said, Suffer little children, and forbid them not, to come unto me: for of such is the kingdom of heaven.' Did you imagine that he meant for you to send him their broken bodies? Picture the degraded body of one of their shambling mothers. A woman who only sees her children for a few hours a week, if and only if some foreman allows her to leave the factory after she has worked for twelve hours and then spent a quick ten minutes on her back for his pleasure. That she would be allowed to leave at all is by no means certain."

Lucy was riveted. Ahead of her, a significant sample of the people of Old Gate shifted in their seats. Uncomfortable. Who would dare talk to these people so boldly and with such accusation?

"Who will stop that foreman? His master? Who will tell this woman that what she is being forced to do is wrong? That it is inhuman to demand from her the only thing that is hers to give: her dignity. Even that dignity is a gift from the Lord above, but she does without it because that is the only way she can keep her body and soul in one place. How can she mind her own soul if her child is in a factory half a mile away, working the same tortured hours that she does?"

As Hannah Tanner told the story of a boy named James and his sister, Polly, who were employed in a Richmond cotton mill (not even in faraway New York or Boston, but in their own Richmond!), Lucy felt tears gathering in her eyes. The pair arrived at work one day together, their dinner pails nearly empty but for a chunk of bread and fatback, all their ailing mother could find for them, but only Polly came home that night. James had been hurrying across the workroom floor with a sample of dye for a foreman to inspect. He'd been told that if he didn't hurry they would find some other boy to do his job, and he would be on the street. "Can you imagine such a threat, to a boy of eleven? A boy whose own mother had been worked nearly to death herself, and now could hardly leave her bed?"

Lucy *could* imagine such a threat. She could see the boy and his pretty sister hurrying through the dark Richmond streets so they wouldn't be shut out of the mill's tall, clanging gates.

"Thirty feet that boy fell. Because he was hurrying to do his job." Hannah Tanner's voice quieted and she was silent so they could all imagine the boy, broken. Dead.

A woman near the front of the room sobbed.

"Yes, cry for James. But, my friend, spare some tears for his older sister, Polly." Hannah Tanner shook her head. "Polly didn't learn until the end of the day that her brother had died because workers weren't allowed to speak to one another in that awful place. She had to walk home through the streets, in the dark, to tell her mother the news."

Lucy felt a tear fall onto her cheek, and she hurriedly dabbed at it with her handkerchief. When she put her hand back to her lap, Randolph gently covered it with his. She glanced down and then turned her eyes to him. He won her in that moment. Such understanding in his eyes, the way his brow was knitted together. Concern for her. Concern for the two tragic children.

"Like the good daughter that she was, Polly stayed home with her mother until they buried her brother. Did the local church help? No. James was buried on credit. Buried in a churchyard for the grand sum of thirty dollars. Thirty dollars that the family didn't have. And because Polly did not return to work the next day, or the day of her brother's funeral, they gave her job to another girl." Hannah Tanner pointed to a woman in the front row. "Do you *know* what poor Polly was forced to do?"

Lucy held her breath.

Hannah Tanner spoke slowly, her voice lowered as though she were sharing a confidence. "She was forced to sell her body to feed herself and her mother."

"Shame!" Someone near the front called out, but Lucy couldn't see who it was.

"It *is* a shame to see that happen here, in a Christian nation. God's own children. Neglected by their fellow countrymen. Unhelped by the so-called faithful of Richmond or Philadelphia or Atlanta or Boston. Ignored by the hypocrites in the pulpits whose kingly robes or fine suits—"

Lucy had been too focused on Hannah Tanner to notice the tall man standing in the hallway entry to the theater, his body framed in the opening of the huge pocket doors. But now he strode forward into the room, his face pink with agitation above his white clerical collar and somber black frock coat. She slid reflexively down in her chair an inch, wanting to disappear. Her father didn't speak, but stood surveying the crowd. When his eyes lighted on Lucy, she felt the sting of his anger from twenty feet away.

"Would you care to take a seat, brother?" Hannah Tanner addressed him from the lectern, her voice calm. Smooth.

"No. I most certainly would not like to take a seat. Thank you."

She looked away and continued speaking, but much of the crowd turned in their chairs to watch Edward Searle seek out his daughter, who happened to be sitting beside their host. Lucy no longer heard Hannah Tanner's words. Summer sunlight poured through the theater's tall windows, but it might as well have been pitch black outside, because she felt as though she were living in a nightmare.

Beside her, Randolph rose, extending his hand. He whispered. "Edward."

"You'll be kind enough to step out of my way, Randolph. I've come to fetch my daughter home."

Her father had never been a cruel man. Opinionated and sometimes bigoted against people of a different political stripe, but never cruel. How had he known she would be here? He was supposed to be in Lynchburg until evening, meeting with his bishop.

"Let's go downstairs and have a sherry. I know you're not a fan of female preaching."

"Lucy. We're leaving."

Lucy knew she was supposed to meekly rise and follow him, but he was treating her like a child, and a stupid child at that. If she did not, he would be furious with her, not just because of her disobedience, but because she had embarrassed him in front of several parishioners.

"Please sit down, Father. People are staring."

"Yes, Edward. You're welcome to my seat."

Edward Searle towered over Randolph by a full six inches and, to Lucy, seemed to be growing taller. Out of the corner of her eye, she saw Terrance make his way around the edge of the room. He stood near the wall, a dozen feet behind Randolph. Waiting.

Her father gave a wry smile. "Will you have your bastard throw me out, Randolph?"

"Father!" Now other heads turned. Hannah Tanner stopped speaking.

"Lucy, you're breaking your mother's heart. Come home with me now. We don't belong in this godforsaken place."

Realizing that everyone was staring at them now, Lucy looked back at him with hate in her heart.

"I will not."

He stared at her a moment as though she were a stranger who had slapped him. She held his gaze, even though she felt her face grow warm, felt the eyes of the entire room on them.

Randolph addressed Hannah Tanner in a loud, direct voice. "Pray continue, Miss Tanner."

The woman nodded, and resumed at a somewhat less impassioned volume, and the heads that had turned to stare at them returned to watching the diminutive woman at the front of the room.

Randolph got closer to her father and said something that no one but her father could hear.

The color drained from her father's face, turning it a ghastly white, and Lucy feared he might faint. He opened his mouth to speak, but closed it again. Lucy pitied him in that moment and almost got up from her chair.

Even though she could only see his back, Lucy saw that Randolph was facing him with the calm defiance that she wished that she herself had been able to manage. In this case, she would let him defend her. It was one of the hardest decisions she had ever made, and she prayed it was the correct one.

Edward Searle looked past Randolph and into Lucy's eyes. It was *his* eyes that held pity. Then he turned without another word and walked out the way he came. Terrance followed a few yards behind.

When Randolph sat back down beside her, she saw that his usually clear forehead was beaded with perspiration, and his nose and cheeks were reddened with heat.

She couldn't help herself. "What did you say? How did you get him to leave?" she whispered.

Randolph dabbed at his forehead with his handkerchief. At the front of the room, Hannah Tanner had become impassioned again. He put the handkerchief away and beckoned for Lucy to lean closer.

"Only the truth, my dear. That you were no longer his little girl, but a woman."

Chapter 9

LUCY

June 1899

"You're like some Brontë character, darling. They're always so spunky right up until they have some setback in love, and then they take to their bed with consumption. What did you expect your father to do?" Faye picked up the pink rose the cook had put on Lucy's lunch tray and held it to her nose. It was the color of the interior of a seashell, transparent as French porcelain. "I don't think you're sick at all. I think you're just pouting."

Lucy's younger sister, sixteen-year-old Juliet, had been reading *Wuthering Heights* to Lucy all morning, and the book lay on the chair where Faye was about to settle herself.

In truth, Lucy did feel ill. As soon as she had walked out of Bliss House the previous week, her head had begun to pound and the strength left her body. Her mother had made a dreadful scene when she arrived home. Her father sat at his desk, silently staring at her, his hands tented in front of him. But Lucy could barely attend to her mother's words because of the pain in her head.

If her malaise had come from being in Bliss House, why did she feel so certain that, if she could only return there, she would feel much better?

Faye dropped the rose back on the tray. "You do look awful, though. And it's beastly hot in here. Are they trying to sweat it out of you? These windows should be open." She went to the closest window and pushed it ajar. June wasn't much for breezes, but the air that flowed in smelled of grass and horse manure that hadn't yet been cleared from the road.

"Am I a scandal? Mother says I'm a scandal."

"I think she rather wishes you were a scandal, but no one is really talking about it because they're all too considerate of your father. But there's one thing I wanted to ask you: Did he really try to drag you out of there by your hair?"

Lucy's smile was effortful. "Of course not, silly. Who told you that?"

"Josiah says that Randolph is furious. That he's going to stop giving money to the church and give up his pew. What kind of spell have you put on him, you little witch?"

Lucy closed her eyes, feeling a small bit of satisfaction that Randolph had defended her. Her father had been ridiculous and deserved to lose Randolph's patronage. Both he and her mother were treating her like a child. She was twenty years old, and her father's religious politics didn't have to be hers. The lecture from her mother had included mention of the inappropriateness of women like Hannah Tanner: immodest and presumptuous bleeding hearts who had no business inserting themselves into polite society. Blackmailing good Christians by using Christ's name for political ends. She called Hannah Tanner a perversion, and said that by forcing, *forcing* her father to come and rescue her from such a scandalous event, Lucy had put the entire family's reputation at risk.

Faye leaned over Lucy's couch and touched her forehead. "They should have a doctor for you. I don't know what's wrong with your parents."

Before Faye could move away, Lucy grabbed her wrist.

"I have to leave here. I feel like if I stay here, I might die."

Faye gave a little laugh, but there was genuine concern in her eyes.

"Darling, you're not going to die." She disengaged Lucy's hand and took it in both of hers. "It's just one of those things that will have to blow over."

"No! I have to get away from here. You have to help me. What if they send me away? Far away? I dreamed that I was on an island, and I couldn't swim off of it because there were sharks and those awful stinging rays in the water everywhere. Do you remember when we tried to picnic on that island in the James? And there was that nest of snakes, and we got scared and had to leave? It was like that, only I had no boat."

Faye sat on the edge of the couch. "Sharks? You dreamed of sharks in the James? I don't understand." She shook her head. "Listen, darling. Why don't you come stay at my house? At least until your mother's birthday party on Friday. If you like we'll get Josiah's father to look at you. Really, Lucy. You're not yourself at all. I wish I hadn't let you go on your own to that foolish lecture. Then your parents could have blamed me, instead of you, for all of this. I know they think I'm some kind of Satan's spawn, despite Mummy and Daddy being in their set." She lowered her voice. "Thank goodness they didn't see us on May Day. You *would* be in a nunnery by now."

There was a polite knock on the door, and Carrie came in with tea and slices of lemon cake.

After arranging things on the table beside the couch, she picked up the breakfast tray. But before leaving the room, she addressed

Faye. "I beg your pardon, Miss Archer. Missus Searle told me to ask you to encourage Miss Lucy to have a bit of cake."

Faye nodded. "Oh, I will."

Carrie cast a glance at Lucy that said, *I'm just acting as the messenger*. But Carrie was also the only one in her parents' house that she could trust. As she left she closed the door softly behind her.

"I told them I don't want to come to the party. I don't feel like a party."

"We'll go to the river house for a few days. Mummy won't go down unless Daddy's there, and he's in Richmond until the end of the week. You'll feel so much better if you get out of here. I'll have Mummy send the invitation. You know your mother can't say no to her."

"But I'll still have to come back for the party."

"You'll probably feel like it by then. You'll see."

Even as Faye pressed a plate with a slice of lemon cake on her, Lucy was thinking about how she might get to Bliss House from the Archers' river house. Faye would certainly forgive her if she left for just a short visit.

The urge to get back to Bliss House had begun to feel like a desperate need. It was as though she had left some unknown part of herself in its vast hall. A part of her that she hadn't realized up to now was inside her, like a secret part of her soul. If she couldn't get back there, and, perhaps, back to Randolph, she truly felt as though she would fade and die.

Chapter 10

LUCY

June 1899

"Would you like anything before I go to bed, Miss Lucy?" Carrie stood in the doorway with a lamp. The river house was cool, so much cooler than the house in town, and Carrie wore a shawl over her shoulders. A hint of a smile played at her lips as she related that "Miss Faye" had told her she wouldn't need anything more this evening.

It had been a happy compromise for Carrie to come along to the river house. Selina hadn't wanted Lucy to go to the house unaccompanied, and Pinky Archer had told Faye that they could use the house, but that she couldn't spare a maid. Lucy's father had been uncertain about the plan, but Selina had, indeed, been unable to say no where her friend Pinky was concerned. Lucy wondered what the mothers would say if they knew that now, just down the hall, in the parlor at the front of the house, Josiah Beard was furiously making love to Faye. After dinner Lucy had politely excused herself, and Faye and Josiah had made equally polite protestations, but Lucy suspected that Josiah would still be in the house when morning came.

After dismissing Carrie, Lucy lay listening to the sounds outside her open window. There were no voices as there sometimes were in town in the early evening, only the peepers and the frogs living near the river's edge croaking at one another. In the far distance coyotes yipped and howled.

There was a softer sound: the whicker of the mare, Nutmeg, that had brought her with Carrie to the house. The river house had a small barn with a paddock, and they had left Nutmeg loose to come and go from the barn as she pleased. It would be nothing to hook her up to the trap, or even to saddle her with one of the saddles from the barn's tack room. They could be at Bliss House before eleven. In one more day they had to return to town, and while she felt much better, she knew she lacked the boldness it would take to carry her to the barn, then onto the dark roads that would lead her to Bliss House.

Was she even wanted there? Randolph had never written her or invited her back. She turned in her bed and threw off the blankets and got up to stand at the window. Perhaps the big chandelier was lighted, and Bliss House was full of people. Maybe there was a party to which she hadn't been invited. Perhaps Randolph was in one of the darkened bedrooms with some other woman. How had she ever imagined that she might be mistress of Bliss House? She was just a silly girl. She had nothing to offer. Surely his wife Amelia had had money and position, and there were plenty of other older, wealthier, and more beautiful women—if not here, then in the places he traveled—who could be mistress of his house, and of his bed.

She flushed to think of how shy she had felt at the Maypole dance. So virginal!

Hearing footsteps and quiet laughter in the hallway, she hurried back to bed, feeling miserable. She envied Faye and couldn't help but hear the hushed tones of Josiah's deep voice as they entered the bedroom beside hers and closed the door.

There was quiet laughter, and then the voices stopped. She closed her eyes and was in the room with Faye and Josiah.

Josiah unhooking Faye's corset, hungrily putting his mouth to her breast. And Faye pulling at his snowy white summer shirt, laughing as a button falls to the floor. There is no worry because Faye is handy with a needle, and if she chooses, Carrie can be trusted to sew it back on.

A scrape of furniture on the uncarpeted floor. Josiah is in Faye's bed, and they are naked as they were at the Maypole. As he lowers himself to Faye, Lucy remembers the taste of his warm lips on her own, and the bulge of him against her hand.

But as Lucy touched herself in her own bed, it was Randolph's face she imagined, Randolph's broader shoulders outlined against the ceiling above her. Randolph who entered her as Faye cried out in the next room. Randolph was hers and she was his and they were together in his house, *their house*, and the moon outside was full and shining, and the only cries heard in the house were their own as they were united, body and soul.

⁀

Josiah was gone when Lucy came out of her room in the morning.

The sunshine of the day before had turned to rain, and Faye slept until noon. When she emerged, dressed and famished, they ate a meal of bread and cheese and strawberries, then sat together on the gliding swing on the front porch, watching the river.

"Your parents won't know you. You look so much better."

"Well, *you* look like the cat who swallowed the canary."

Faye laughed. "I know what's good for me. Plenty of fresh air, yes?"

"I'm sure that's what did it. The fresh air." Lucy's voice was teasing.

"It's not all a game, you know." Faye was suddenly serious. "He's going to ask for my hand, and then we'll have to play by all the stupid rules that everyone has to play by. I hope he doesn't turn into a stick like his father after we're married."

"I hope some part of him stays like a stick, anyway."

"Lucy Searle! I can't believe you'd say that."

"But I did, didn't I?" Lucy was still somewhat giddy with the sense of pleasure she had felt the night before. She suspected that she should feel ashamed that Faye and Josiah's activities in Faye's room had played a part in it, but she could not. There would be plenty of time for shame when she returned to her parents' house.

Her secret pleasure helped her feel less hopeless than she had the day before. She and Carrie would go back home, and she would somehow find a way to see Randolph, if, indeed, she learned that he wanted to see her. Her parents couldn't stop her. If they threatened to throw her out, she would make her own way: teaching piano or giving singing lessons. She had enough money to buy a small cottage from a legacy her grandmother had left her. She would not starve.

"If I were poor, would you still be my friend?"

Faye laughed. "You're not going to be poor, you goose. So what does it matter?"

"If I left my parents' house, I might be. What then?"

Faye looked out at the river, her fingers tracing the floral design inlaid into the arm of the glider. "When you leave your parents' house, you're not going to be poor. I promise."

⌣

A few hours later, Lucy awoke from a nap to find Faye standing in her doorway.

"Put something pretty on, and come help me do my hair, then I'll do yours. I have a surprise." She shut the door and was gone.

At six-fifteen they were sitting in the parlor, Faye looking as though she would burst with excitement. They heard heavy footsteps on the porch, and Carrie hurried to answer the knock that followed. Josiah removed his hat and stepped inside, smiling broadly when he saw Faye. Lucy was disappointed, thinking that he wasn't much of a surprise. Faye hadn't said he was coming, but Lucy had half expected him.

She hadn't expected that he would not be alone.

Randolph.

Chapter 11

KIKU

September 1878

Kiku had never met anyone like Odette, so forward and yet so sensitive. She was protective of her husband, Mason, but also expected him to do all the things she wished him to do without complaint. If Odette reminded Kiku of anyone at all, it was her own mother.

For those first few weeks, Odette came every day, but never when Randolph was there. Kiku didn't understand how Odette knew when he was there and when he wasn't, as he never announced that he was coming. When Kiku noticed the pattern, she gathered her nerve and asked her about it.

"Why, I see if his walking stick is on the porch. How did you think I knew? Did you think I asked the birds sitting in the trees or something? How would you have known?"

Kiku thought for a moment, and said that she would probably have looked in the bedroom window to see if they were in bed together, because whenever Randolph came to the house, he was likely to bed her.

Odette pursed her lips, then broke into a smile that illuminated her whole face. "Oh, you're playing with me now."

Kiku looked puzzled.

"You mean you would look in people's windows to see if they were shaking the sheets to see if they were home?"

Kiku nodded.

"They must do things a lot differently in Japan, or even in New York, if you think that's the way people should behave. That's just rude, Kiku. People don't like to be spied on."

There had been a special room at Madame Jewel's that all the girls knew had a hole drilled into the wall with a covering on the other side to hide the light. Certain types of men preferred to watch rather than participate. If they were to watch another paying customer, with or without his knowledge (some men had actually enjoyed being watched by other men, to Kiku's amusement), it cost less than it did for him to watch two of the girls in the room together. Kiku herself had only been asked to participate with another girl once, and the girl had been Emerald, so it hadn't been too alarming. The hardest part had been trying not to laugh when it was her turn to pretend to be the man. Emerald had whispered that she needed not to act silly, that if they did a very good job, the man who was paying would make sure that Madame Jewel gave them each a tip of two dollars, which was an enormous sum as a tip for forty-five minutes' work that wasn't really work at all.

Kiku didn't tell Odette this story, suspecting that it would make her frown. Maybe someday, when they knew each other better.

Today, Odette was teaching her to make cornbread.

"Did you put in the baking powder? You can make it without, but it's better with it. Or else it lies flat in the pan."

Kiku looked around for the small crock of white powder that Odette had given her and saw that she had never opened it. She asked Odette to tell her again how much to put in. When she was done mixing, Odette helped her pour the mixture into the hot, buttered, heavy pan that would go in the oven.

The stove was identical to the one in Odette and Mason's kitchen, and burned wood rather than coal, as the stove in Madame Jewel's kitchen had. Mason brought Kiku to their house, which was near the newly planted orchards, on evenings when he knew Randolph would be away from Bliss House overnight. At first she had been reluctant to go, fearful that Randolph would return unexpectedly. But she'd been excited, too, to see where Odette and Mason lived.

"I don't like to make cornbread on top of the stove like some do, so you're just going to learn it my way."

So far Odette's ways had been working well. Kiku had been in the cottage for a month and had gained a small amount of weight, which had pleased Randolph.

"Now no one could mistake you for a goddamn boy, except for that hair," he had told her.

There was another reason she was gaining weight. For several months in a row, she had missed her monthly cycle. In the two months before leaving New York, she had lied to Madame Jewel, stealing one of Jet's bloody rags to show as evidence of her menstruation. If a girl missed more than two months of her cycle, she was sent to the abortionist who lived in the next block. Abortions were expensive, and Madame Jewel took the cost out of their wages, even though none of them wanted to be pregnant on purpose. There were surely also abortionists in Virginia, but she was afraid of them.

For almost the entire month since she had arrived at the cottage, she had had to run outside to the privy to throw up. What would Randolph do when he learned of the child? He already had a daughter, Tamora, but Odette said there was something badly wrong with her. Perhaps Randolph's wife could not give him more children, and he would be pleased about her bearing him one. The idea of having a child was strange to her, but at least with a child, she would never be lonely. Whatever the case, she would not be able to hide it much longer.

When the cornbread was in the oven, Odette followed Kiku outside to watch her fill a bucket of water at the pump.

"So where exactly did you meet Mister Bliss, Kiku? You've never said."

Kiku considered for a moment, letting the icy water run over her hands, cooling them. It was still hot. Hotter than it had ever gotten in the fishing village she had grown up in. She missed her family very much, but she wasn't sorry to be away from the ocean. The journey from Japan to New York had taken six months, and she had come to hate the sight of it. The ocean had taken her life away from her, and if she ever saw it again, she would turn her back on it in defiance. Refuse to bathe in it. Refuse to eat the fish that swam in it. She didn't care if it meant that she starved to death.

"Where do you imagine we met?" She turned the question back on the taller woman, but Odette was not the least bit piqued.

"I think he met you in a whorehouse is what I think. No one but fancy girls wear dresses like the ones you came with. Those aren't ladies' dresses."

Randolph had sent Odette to Lynchburg to buy Kiku some dresses more suitable for wearing in Virginia, as well as some fabric to make more. But he hadn't allowed Kiku to go along.

"Can't have you getting lost in the fleshpots of Lynchburg, my dear." He had picked up his cane before heading down the porch stairs. "A rare flower like you is sure to be noticed and snapped up by someone who knows a treasure when he sees it. Odette is formidable, but she'd be no protection for you, and I can't spare Mason." That Kiku was not allowed to go along had been further confirmation that she was a kind of prisoner at the cottage, despite not being locked in or chained inside, as she had been afraid she might be.

The news that dresses like the ones she had brought with her were only worn by prostitutes took her by surprise. She had always thought them beautiful.

Odette saw Kiku's surprise, but she pressed on.

"And why shouldn't they have been fancy, if that's what you were? Or—" She stopped, but to Kiku's ears, she might have well have finished her sentence by saying, "are."

Up to that day, Kiku hadn't worried much about being what everyone called a *whore* or *prostitute*. It was a fact of her life, a fact over which she had no control. At home, she had heard of prostitutes. Prostitutes were made for sex, and they were licensed by the government for pleasure. Her father's brother spoke often of his favorite prostitute outside the gates of the city. There was not so much shame at home as there seemed to be in the United States.

"I was doing work in Madame Jewel's house, and for that I was paid. Randolph was one of the men who came to the house, and soon he reserved me for himself."

Odette regarded her, her arms folded. "Well, that sounds like the truth. Sounds like something Mister Bliss would do, keep his favorite toy away from the other children. He's greedy like that."

Kiku carefully carried the full bucket to the steps of the cottage's back porch.

"I will tell you how I came here. Will you sit with me?"

She held out her hand to Odette, who looked at her curiously.

"Out here? We can't forget about the cornbread. It only cooks for twenty minutes or so."

"It is hot inside. When I am inside the house, surrounded by walls, I cannot think of how I came here without feeling like the walls will close, becoming smaller and smaller, until I cannot breathe anymore. Then there will be no more air, and I will die."

"Sometimes the way you talk, I think you don't live in the same world the rest of us do, Kiku."

They sat on the stairs. There were no chairs on the porch, as there were on Mason and Odette's porch. Mason had made their chairs—rocking chairs that were so solid that they did not even creak. Both were amazed that Kiku had never seen a rocking chair, let alone sat in one, and had laughed as she rocked, also laughing, like the child she still was.

"I was walking home from the next village, where my mother had sent me to get incense because the incense seller said it was too much trouble to get to the fishing village where we lived, even though we always gave him a nice welcome. My mother is fond of sandalwood incense, though my father says it is too expensive and that our family's prayers are not illustrious enough to require an expensive fragrance. But he does not mean it when he says such things. He likes to tease her, the way Mason teases you. But I think you don't know, sometimes, that he is teasing."

Kiku had been looking out at the trees as she spoke, but now turned her eyes to Odette, who looked for a moment as though she might be angry.

"You say he's teasing. I say he's just a rude man." She smiled in spite of her words, and Kiku smiled as well. Mason was a good man.

"I thought they were robbers at first. Or monsters. My father had told me of the Europeans and the Indians who came to the port in ships. But the port is almost a day's walk from my village, and when I had gone there, I never saw these people. I knew that's who they were when I saw their faces. At first I thought they would rob me for the incense, and I told them they could have it, but they did not listen to me. One of the men spoke a little of my language, but he was not very good, and called me a burning house when I would not walk fast enough for them. I still don't know what he was trying to say."

She told Odette the rest: of being gagged and taken into the port city at night, and smuggled onboard the ship in a large basket that smelled of sea grass and rotted persimmons and mold. What she could not tell her was of the panic that had filled her body when she realized that the ship was moving and no one had come to rescue her. That she understood, but couldn't admit to herself for days, that she would never see her home again. That her body was no longer her own.

No, despite having heard her parents make the sounds of love during her whole life, she could not connect them to what the second mate (who always referred to himself as "Tommy" as though he were talking about somebody else) did to her within hours after the ship had set sail from the port.

She was not alone. The other girl in the second mate's cabin was Christiana, who, Kiku eventually learned, was English, but had been kidnapped from a country called Australia, where her family had settled, and brought to Japan on a different ship, by different men. At first she and Christiana communicated little, except when obeying the often strange and repellent commands of the second mate. But they were forced to spend long hours together in the grubby cabins of the ships in which they traveled, only being allowed topside when the sea was very calm and it was dark and the watchmen appeared to be asleep or occupied. They had been topside only a handful of times before he told them that they had just gone around the end of the world and were headed toward New York.

Two weeks before they reached New York, Christiana died of a fever in her sleep.

Kiku had awakened, shivering, beside her in the bunk. Christiana's body was cold, and the blanket soaked with sweat and urine.

Her eyes were open and staring, no longer glazed with fever. Having seen her grandfather die, and the dead bodies of children who had died in her village, Kiku was not afraid. Her only worry had been that Christiana's spirit might become confused being on a ship and not be able to leave it.

When the second mate came in from his watch, he had seemed almost unconcerned, telling Kiku, "English whores are probably a dime a dozen in New York. I'm glad you're not the one who died." Christiana had taught her enough English that she understood what he was saying, and she thought him very cruel. She did not say another word until after they reached New York.

Sometimes Randolph asked her to tell him about the ship and what the second mate had done to her. She was used to Randolph asking such questions, and she answered, embellishing where she knew it would excite him and leaving out the mundane. The truth was that, after Christiana died, the second mate hadn't used her much, and she spent the days kneeling on his bunk, staring out the tiny window at the endless, rolling ocean, and telling stories to Christiana's rag doll that she had kept hidden so he couldn't throw it into the ocean with the rest of Christiana's things.

She paused, and Odette looked up from the step at which she had been staring, and turned her gaze to the woods.

"Shall I tell you about Madame Jewel's, where Randolph found me?"

Odette didn't answer for a moment, then shook her head. "No."

"Very well."

Odette stood, and Kiku could feel her looking down on her. Finally, without speaking, Odette went into the kitchen.

The air smelled of burned cornbread. It was the last time Odette would ask her anything about her past.

For the first time Kiku noticed that some of the leaves on the trees had begun to change color. Only a few leaves here and there had begun to turn, as though the rest were shy, waiting for the others to go first. She had arrived in New York in the early spring and so had only seen the trees budding out with new leaves, but hadn't seen them fall. At home the trees were mostly shaggy pine trees whose powerful scent in the spring made tears of happiness come to her eyes. In the coldest months, they kept their needles, but didn't look quite so green. Kiku wasn't sure that she could bear to live where so many trees, save a few pines that reminded her of home, lost their leaves. No longer would there be shelter for her beneath them.

Chapter 12

KIKU

October 1878

Kiku woke to a light tapping on her window, and in her dream she imagined that a giant bird was trying to open an acorn or sunflower seed on a platform high above her head. The bird was getting more and more frustrated and banged louder until she finally woke and sat up, perplexed. The knocking continued and she looked through sleepy eyes to see Odette jumping up to hit at the window with her hand, *taptaptap*, before she dropped to the ground again. Kiku hit once on the window back at her to let her know she was awake. Once she was out of bed, she pulled on her robe. She thought of the day when the child inside her would be much larger, and wondered if the robe would still wrap around her.

Odette began talking as soon as Kiku opened the front door.

"Why isn't your bedroom window open? Do you want to roast to death? I guess nobody ever told you how to keep your windows open so the cool air comes in at night. Then you can close them during the day to keep the cool air in. If you're not baking, that is."

"Good Lord, Odette. Do you have to tell everyone how to live their lives? Kiku might want to do things different. You can boss me, but you're not married to everyone else. It was only fifty degrees last night. She's so skinny she'd freeze to death." Mason stood beside Odette, who was giving him a look.

Odette shook her head. "She still has a lot to learn, and somebody has to teach her."

"You know how to lay a fire. You should put some of that wood I had cut for you in the fireplace tonight before it gets dark." Mason gestured to the fireplace directly behind Kiku.

"Now who's being bossy?" Odette put a gentle hand on Kiku's shoulder and eased her out of the way as she came inside. "Get dressed while I get you some breakfast. You do sleep later than a body should, don't you? We've already been to church and back."

Kiku knew Odette wasn't looking for an answer and so said nothing. Odette continued to the kitchen. Mason just shook his head and gave Kiku one of his shy, appealing grins.

"We got a surprise. Mister Bliss has gone out of town, and none of the workmen are at the house today. It's safe for you to see inside."

The news did come as a surprise to Kiku. She had dreamed about the house, trying to make sense of all that Mason and Odette had told her about it. But in her dreams it was always a confusing, dark place, with narrow hallways, and mirrors that seemed to come out of nowhere and turned to mist, beckoning her to step into other, darker rooms. She wasn't sure she wanted to go inside the real house.

Yet she watched from behind a boulder just inside the edge of the woods almost every day. There were still people coming and going, but the garden and grass had been planted (which made the house look less stark, though no less unfriendly), and the visitors were of a different sort—drapers and decorators who arrived in carriages and traps. A pair of women dressed in severe but elegant dresses arrived several days in a row, remaining until the late afternoon. At first she had wondered if they were also Randolph's lovers, but Randolph showed them no special attention and in fact was not always there when they arrived.

Kiku knew she would go with Odette and Mason. But what if she found that it was such a terrible place that she could no longer bear to live in its shadow?

⁓

"Why aren't we going through the woods?" It seemed to Kiku that they were going in exactly the wrong direction to get inside the house. She could see the front drive plainly from just inside the woods. The trees had hung onto their leaves, but most had turned a bright red or gold or a brilliant yellow-orange.

Odette smiled. "Because that's part of the surprise."

"I didn't think we should tell you about it, you being so young and all. But Odette here says she doesn't think you'll be afraid."

Kiku's apprehension grew with the expectation that she would be brave. As they got farther away from the cottage, she wanted to run quickly back, telling them that she didn't need to see. Didn't want to see. But she remained quiet and only followed, hoping that she was really as brave as they believed her to be.

They emerged from the trees well behind Bliss House, closer to Mason and Odette's house than they were to the big house. In the near distance she could see a small, roofed structure with stone walls beside a creek. When they reached the creek, Mason held out a hand to help her jump across.

"Is that where we're going?" She pointed to the springhouse.

Odette nodded. "Be ready."

"I don't know that it's something you can be ready for. It's not like anything I've ever seen in my life. Mister Bliss is a man unto himself." Kiku wasn't sure if it was admiration in Mason's voice, or criticism, or perhaps a fearful kind of respect.

⌒

Outside it was a warm, sunny Sunday afternoon, but as soon as they entered the springhouse, Kiku began to shiver. And when, in the light from the single high window in the springhouse, Mason indicated the wall with a second, barely distinguishable door, she wanted to run back into the light. She had never been in a cave or any underground room, and she didn't understand what this forsaken place had to do with the house many, many yards away. But she made herself stand beside Odette and not move until *she* did. Odette was not afraid, and she would not be afraid.

"At least I don't have to tell you to watch your head." Mason held the door to the passageway open for the women and told them to wait a moment while he went ahead and lighted the lamps.

"When he told me about this, I didn't believe him." Odette was whispering, and Kiku knew it was not because she didn't want Mason to hear. "I told him that I wanted to see it for myself. Mister Bliss doesn't even know that Mason knows about it. One of the foreigners who worked on the grand staircase in the hall got drunk and wandered away from their camp. Mason found him, and he started shooting his mouth out about a secret passage. Thank goodness Mason's a good listener. He got every detail he could."

Of course Randolph would have a secret place. The cottage was a secret hiding in plain sight, but he would want a place that was truly secret. A place where his soul could meet the darkness without interference from the light of day.

"Close the door." Mason's voice sounded hollow as he called from a distance down the passage. "Come on down this way."

Kiku flinched as the door closed and the sunlight disappeared. By the lantern light, she could see that it was not a cave but a kind of rude hallway. Short beams crossed the ceiling, holding up the dirt roof. The walls were dirt as well but when she touched them, they were smooth, as though built from some finer material.

"The workman said the walls were done some special way by a man who learned it in Russia. Some queen there had tunnels built underground so she wouldn't have to go outside in the winter at all if she didn't want to."

At some point Kiku had unconsciously taken Odette's hand, and Odette hadn't rejected it. Her palm against Odette's was the only warm part of her body.

Something about the passageway demanded that they whisper. Kiku had the sense that someone was listening to them. Odette had told her a terrifying story: that the big house had been built on the place where a family and some slaves that they had been helping to run away had been murdered, burned alive in a house. The story had confirmed for Kiku that this was a bad place. A dangerous place. What if those spirits were waiting for someone like her, someone small and weak, to take their revenge? As they walked, the floor sloped downward. Truly they might be going into the underworld itself.

"Mason, the child is freezing to death. Why didn't you say it would be so cold down here?"

"If I had been here before I would've known it, wouldn't I?" When they reached Mason, he took off his jacket and put it around Kiku's shoulders. She tried to protest, but Odette told her to be quiet and to get warm, and that she hoped there wouldn't be much to see, and maybe they would be out quickly.

Odette's face glowed a rich warm brown in the lamplight. Mason was tense, but looked at his wife with approval in his eyes.

His love for her was always obvious, even when they argued. Kiku had once asked Odette how she had met Mason, how they had fallen in love, and she had told her that she and her father had worked with him in an orchard operation in Pennsylvania. Mason was several years older than she, and she had agreed to marry him when he was promoted to manager. They had been together six years when Randolph hired him as his orchard keeper and brought them to Virginia.

They continued to walk. It seemed a very long way, and Mason went ahead to light another lantern. Kiku felt the faintest touch of air moving over her face. Later, Mason said that there were hidden vents in the ceiling where it joined the walls.

"Look out on your right. The man said there's a staircase up to the house. But we don't want to go up it just yet."

They didn't see a staircase, but there was a door ahead. As they got closer Kiku felt her throat constrict.

"I don't want to go in there." She squeezed Odette's hand, and Odette squeezed back.

"Maybe it's not open." Odette sounded hopeful. "I don't much want to go in there, either. Let's just go on up into the house."

Mason spoke. "There's no one or nothing down here. The man said Mister Bliss was going to use it for storage, but there's nothing inside yet."

Odette shook her head as though to say it didn't sound right to her, but Kiku was the only one who saw. Still, Odette continued to follow Mason, and even when they found that the stairway was immediately to the right of the open door, she didn't turn to go up it.

The wooden door was heavy and thick and looked as though it had been made to withstand a battering ram. There were no locks on the front of it, but there was a bolt on one edge and a place for it to rest in the door's heavy frame.

"Never seen anything like that." Mason shook his head.

Kiku hadn't, either.

He lighted one more lamp on the other side of the door.

"What is this place?" Odette's voice was quiet now, as though they were in a church, but there was nothing the least bit holy about the hallway or the rooms off of it. There were two rooms in the vicinity of the wall lamp, and another open door separating them from the rest of the hall. "I want to look in here." Odette put her head into the first room. She let go of Kiku's hand and leaned inside.

Kiku wanted to pull Odette back, but instead she pressed herself against the wall beneath the burning lamp.

Mason came forward with his lantern, and he and Odette went inside together while Kiku watched from the hallway.

The room was slightly larger than the parlor of the cottage, and a bit deeper than it was wide. When Mason held up his light, they could see a large crack in the far wall where it was buckling. Kiku had a momentary vision of the wall crumbling and bringing down the ceiling, and then the entire tunnel. She felt the feathery brush of the dirt as it covered her face. Closing her eyes briefly in a shudder, she opened them to find that she could no longer see Odette.

"What's this here?" Odette asked Mason to hold up the light.

Even though she couldn't bear to go inside the room, Kiku stepped forward quickly to stand in the doorway so she could keep her friends in sight.

The room was empty except for two lamps on the wall, and a single faucet that led to a rude basin on a stand. A pipe led away from the stand and into a hole in the wall.

"I wonder why he would want running water down here?" Mason seemed genuinely perplexed, but Odette looked at him with her *you should know better* look.

"He's obviously planning to have somebody using water down here. And, see? There's one of those vents way up near the ceiling."

Kiku could not rid herself of the idea that the wall would crumble and they would be killed. "I want to go up into the house now. Please, Mason. I want to leave this place." Hearing the tears in her voice, Odette came to put a comforting arm around her.

"That's fine. We don't need to stay another minute."

Odette waited with her while Mason opened the hallway's second door and briefly explored the pair of rooms beyond. They were unfinished and contained only some tools and pallets of bricks.

"Looks like more of the same. You two go on out and wait for me by the steps. I'm going to walk down to the end and put out the lights as I come back. I don't think any of us wants to come back here once we're in the house. Or am I wrong about that?"

Kiku laughed nervously, although she would have said that she had never felt less like laughing.

Chapter 13

KIKU

October 1878

Mason had told them that if they really wanted to, they could start up the stairway without him and he would see them up in the house. He gave Odette the lantern.

"And have you try to find your way in the dark? We'll wait."

Mason looked relieved, and turned to limp hurriedly to the beginning of the passageway to start putting out the lights.

"He loves you very much." Kiku watched after Mason.

Odette sighed. "That's his curse, I guess. Though I really don't know why I thought it was a good idea for us all to come here today. I thought it would be a kind of lark." Her voice fell away.

Kiku nodded. "Why would Randolph want a place like this? Do you think he will have women here?"

"Now why would you say that? That's peculiar of you."

Kiku didn't answer. Men liked strange things, and they didn't always make sense to women.

Ascending the staircase, which was narrow and turned suddenly, again and again, Kiku felt like they were climbing to the top of a mountain. Nearly breathless, she managed to ask how high they were going. Mason, who was behind her, said they were going from underground, past the house's cellar and up to the third floor.

"The foreign man said the staircase comes out beside the fireplace in the ballroom. I've seen the fireplace, but I didn't see anything that looked like a door. No windows in the ballroom."

Kiku didn't want to think about another room without windows. The image of the one she had just seen had been enough to last a lifetime. Even the second mate's tiny cabin on the ship had had a window the size of a man's head, which made it seem less coffinlike. All of the rooms in Madame Jewel's house had had at least one window, though they were all heavily curtained and had window shades so that no one could look inside.

"You can bet that if Madame Jewel thought there was a way to make a penny off of people looking in the windows from the next house or across the street, she would've figured it out." Opal, an elfin English girl whose incongruously large, melon-shaped breasts seemed to have been made for someone twice her size, had been particularly fierce in her criticism of Madame Jewel's stinginess. "I know what she gets from the men who come here. She whines about keeping us then charges us back for every tiddle and wink and how d'you do. Dead cheap that woman is." Some of the other girls thought that having a little pocket money outside of the few dollars a month they sent to their mothers and, sometimes, children was a blessing. But most resented the work and frequently claimed they would leave just as soon as they paid Madame Jewel off for their keep and clothes. Opal had told Kiku she was "damned lucky" that she looked as exotic as she did and had all her teeth. She said she would have gladly stuck Kiku with the bone-handled knife she kept in her purse if she thought that Randolph would pay off *her* debt and take *her* away to "Virginny." She had smiled, revealing that she, at least, was missing at least one molar, and Kiku hadn't doubted she'd told her the truth.

Knowing that the room they were about to enter had no windows, Kiku had anticipated coming out of the stairway into more darkness. But when they reached the top, Mason squeezed around them and easily pushed open the door to reveal a room that glowed a deep, sensuous red. She gasped, and Odette turned to her, obviously afraid that she might faint.

It was the red of Randolph's favorite room in Madame Jewel's house. The first time she had been taken to that particular room, it had frightened her because it was the color of blood. The girls had talked of stabbings in the streets and the occasional violence of their customers (though Madame Jewel protested with a dignified air that *any* man who was ungentlemanly enough to injure one of her *dear* girls was not fit to be one of her callers). So when Kiku was told to take a man she had never met before into the room (the more delicate details of her instruction had been at the adept hands of Ivory, the oldest, most experienced girl), she had begun shaking in fear. Madame Jewel had impressed on him that Kiku was indeed a virgin, and he thought her fear was most pleasing.

Seeing she was all right, Odette pushed her gently through the narrow doorway.

"Good Lord." Odette went to the middle of the room and spun around, first this way, then that. "I've never seen the like. There must be ten acres of painted paper on those walls. Look, Kiku. Look what's painted on it."

Kiku had looked above Odette's head to see two metal circles mounted firmly into the ceiling. They looked like something from which a man might be hanged. They frightened her, but Odette had already sounded worried when she had suggested that the rooms underground might be where Randolph intended to meet with (or keep, perhaps?) women. She didn't want to alarm Odette further.

She crossed the room to where muted sunlight from the hall illuminated the images on the wall.

They were women. Young Japanese women among blooming cherry trees and pagodas. Each woman carried a parasol and was accompanied by a much older Japanese man, who was kneeling. But the man did not seem to be kneeling in supplication. He was kneeling because he could kneel and still be feared. Kiku didn't know how she knew this, but she felt it in her stomach.

"Do you see? It's you! All the women look like you!" Odette put her hand to her mouth, trying to stifle her shock. She laughed nervously. "Did you know? Mason, did you know about this?"

Mason had gone to stand between the sliding pocket doors at the entrance to the ballroom. "I did not." Then he looked at Kiku, and she knew he was lying. He looked away.

Surely Mason had not wanted to hurt her. He had simply wanted her to *know*.

"Why, it is me, isn't it?" She touched the face of the nearest figure. The paper was delicately drawn, but didn't look as though it had been drawn by a Japanese hand. She did not think that anything like it would be found in even the grandest of Japanese houses. It was Americans and Europeans who enjoyed repeating patterns: on curtains, on dresses, on walls. She had no experience of grand things in her childhood, but she understood the concept of simplicity and the value of the unique. Even careful copies of things were unique because it was an artist executing the copy. But these images looked as though they were truly identical. It was odd, though, that the old men and the pagodas seemed to be slightly different from one another.

Randolph, what do you mean by this?

Randolph had put her image in this house, but had he really never meant to have her here? It made her feel unreal, as though she were some *thing*, and not a person at all.

"It's a ballroom, so let's dance!" Odette took Kiku's hand, and Kiku was startled out of her dark thoughts. "Do you waltz? All the quality people waltz. Mason has a hard time of it, but he taught me."

Kiku wondered at all the things Mason could do. She laughingly let Odette guide her around the floor, counting *one two three, one two three, one two three*. Odette's boots were noisy on the patterned wood floor, but Kiku's softer shoes were almost silent.

"Come and dance with us, Mason!" Odette seemed giddy now. They were finally free of the oppressive air of the passageway and silent, airless rooms.

Mason crossed the floor to them. He was agitated. "You've seen the ballroom. You need to see the rest of the house. Stop, Odette. We need to keep moving." He tried to put a hand on Odette's arm, but she slipped away, still leading Kiku.

"One more minute. Remember when we went to that barn dance, with all your people, down by the river? You couldn't keep your hands off of me then. But you haven't danced with me since."

"Odette, please."

Kiku heard the pleading note in his voice. She stopped, and Odette had to stop as well.

"Mister Fauquier." Mason sounded alarmed.

The man standing in the doorway was framed in light, so that Kiku could not see the details of his face. He was a big man, taller and broader than Randolph. "I didn't think anyone was here, Mister Goodbody," he said. "I see that perhaps you were under that impression as well." As he entered the ballroom, Kiku shrank back a step toward Odette.

"My wife wanted to see the ballroom. I thought it would be a good time to show it to her." Mason's voice faltered but recovered. "While we wouldn't get in anyone's way."

As the man walked toward Odette and Kiku, Kiku saw his eyes cut briefly to the open door beside the fireplace, and then back to them. He could see that they had been inside the stairway, but what would he do? If Randolph had gone to the trouble of making the staircase secret, Kiku knew he would be unhappy to have had it discovered by Odette and Mason. And how much worse was it that *she* was there as well? Randolph would be furious. She had never made him truly angry before. What would he do to her? To Odette and Mason?

Odette, who was rarely at a loss for words, remained silent. The man stopped in front of her and bowed ever so slightly.

"Missus Goodbody. It's a pleasure to see you."

The smile he gave Odette was warm and friendly, lighting his fair, whiskered face. His hair was styled in auburn waves, and he had no beard, but his cheeks were framed by long, closely trimmed sideburns. Kiku had seen him many times before, coming and going from Bliss House.

Odette recovered herself and held out her hand for him to shake. "Mister Fauquier."

After shaking Odette's hand, he turned to Kiku and inclined his head to her as well. But he spoke to Odette.

"Missus Goodbody, would you be so kind as to introduce me to your companion?"

"Mister Fauquier, this is our friend, Kiku, who lives near us. She is from Japan, but she speaks English."

Again, he bowed. "I am happy to make your acquaintance, Kiku. My name is Aaron Fauquier."

Kiku bowed in return, then offered her hand. When he took it, he held it for a moment with a firm, gentle pressure. Along with the kindness in his eyes, she saw a hint of satisfaction, as though she were the answer to some question that had been in his mind. She couldn't help but wonder if he desired her. Aside from Mason, he was one of the very few men she had met outside of Madame Jewel's house since she had come to the United States. She saw no lust in his eyes. It was curious, but refreshing.

"I am happy to meet you, Aaron Fauquier. Are you a friend of Randolph's—I'm sorry, I mean Mister Bliss?"

"I worked as an assistant to Monsieur Hulot, the Frenchman who designed Bliss House. When he went back to France, I decided to remain here in Virginia, where I was born. Randolph has asked me to help him with some other projects, and invited me to stay here until my own house in town can be completed in the spring. But, yes, you could say that I'm a friend."

"It is a beautiful house."

"I thank you," Aaron said. "Perhaps I could show you some more of it, beyond the ballroom."

Mason came near. "We can go out the kitchen door, Mister Fauquier. Or through the servants' quarters. I wouldn't want Mister Bliss to think we were taking advantage."

"But isn't that what you were all doing?" Aaron raised his rather full auburn eyebrows inquisitively. Mason looked stricken.

"No, Mister Fauquier. As I said, Odette wanted to see the ballroom, and Kiku—"

But instead of appearing angry, Aaron smiled. "Relax, Mister Goodbody. I won't mention that you and the ladies were here. Of course they would be curious."

Odette and Mason exchanged one of their looks. It wasn't lost on either of them that Aaron Fauquier obviously knew who Kiku was and where she lived and what connection she had to his employer.

"If you'll give me a moment, I'll show you as much of the rest of the house as you like."

When Mason started to demur, Aaron put his hand up. "Mister Bliss needn't know, Mister Goodbody. All I would ask is your discretion in not sharing what you've already seen with anyone else. I think Mister Bliss would require that of you. I'll speak to the artist working in the dining room if he's still there when we go downstairs. He is a discreet man and doesn't speak much English, anyway. Mister Bliss has only spoken to him once." With that, he walked over to the fireplace and closed the open panel that acted as a door, then he pressed it with both hands to make certain that it was secure.

The rest of the house was much simpler and less dramatic than the ballroom. Aaron set the pace, which was not quick or abrupt. He had taken Kiku's arm to lead them out of the room, and so she stayed beside him. Mason and Odette hung a little behind. Kiku wasn't sure why she felt immediately comfortable walking beside this auburn-haired man, but she felt as though she could spend hours with him, getting to know him better. It was something she hadn't felt in a long time. She thought of a boy from the next village named Mitsue, whom she had known. He had teased her when they were young children, but before she had been taken away, he had become shy with her, and she with him. She had very much wanted him to kiss her. Randolph did not often kiss her. Glancing at Aaron Fauquier's lips, she wondered what it would feel like to kiss them.

She had never been inside a building so large outside of New York. And there, the only truly grand place she had visited had been a department store.

Everywhere they walked, she felt the presence of the house itself, as though it were keeping track of them. But the house's spirit did not feel vengeful or cruel, as she had thought it might.

They paused at the gallery railing so she could look up at the dome. It was like a window to the heavens themselves. A window surrounded by windows. Christiana had encouraged her to wish on a star when they were taken topside, and though she had seen many stars since then, she felt the urge to wish on one of the painted, glowing stars now.

"The stars are arranged as they were on the day that Mister Bliss's daughter, Tamora, was born seven years ago. He had it painted as a gift for his wife. Amelia." Aaron looked down at Kiku, and she looked back at him for a moment, unblinking.

Was he passing some kind of judgment on her by mentioning Randolph's wife? He might not know that she had had no say in coming to live with Randolph. Behind them, Odette gave a little cough.

"May we see the theater before we go downstairs? Are there other rooms up here?"

He showed them the other, much smaller third-floor rooms and the stairway to the roof before opening the doors to the theater. Kiku had only ever been inside one real theater before. Emerald had taken her to see a line of women dance a silly dance called the "cancan" before another woman came onstage to sing sad Irish songs that made Kiku weary.

Aaron let Kiku walk up the short set of stage stairs and peek behind the tall, partially open red velvet curtains. The backstage was empty as far as Kiku could see, and she felt a small thrill as she imagined getting ready to perform. At home she had frequently engaged her younger siblings in small dramas that they then performed for her parents. But they inevitably ended with the youngest ones wandering off or forgetting what they were supposed to say. Kiku had tried her best to remain serious, but the dramas often collapsed in gales of laughter.

She went to stand in one of the tall windows. In the distance, she could just see a ridge of mountains. Mason had told her that he had heard of mountains in the West that were much taller, and to Kiku the mountains on the horizon looked like hunched, stalking beasts. Coming down to Virginia on the train she had seen similar mountains drawn in sharp relief, but they were small compared to the mountains that had towered beyond her village. As a child she had dreamed of climbing those mountains, but looking out this window, from this house, she knew she would never see them again, let alone walk on them. She was suddenly overcome with sadness.

"Did you live near mountains back in Japan?" Aaron had come to stand beside her.

Kiku nodded. "There are mountains everywhere, but we lived beside the sea. My father was a fisherman."

"Ah. My father was a bricklayer in Richmond before the war. But my mother wanted me to go to school and do something else. What I'm doing now isn't so different. Do you miss Japan?"

"Look at the trees." She pointed to the woods. "You can just see the cottage."

He didn't press her on the question of missing her home. "I hope you like it. Mister Bliss had me supervise its construction. He was very particular about its design and furnishing."

So this man had not only been inside the cottage, but had built it. Yet Randolph had told her nothing of him. Knowing that he had touched the walls of her home, and that Randolph would never know that they had met, deepened the strange sense of intimacy she felt with him. But would he really not tell Randolph?

Looking up into his eyes, she knew he would not.

"I am very happy in the cottage. What girl would not be very happy to have her own little house?"

"A lot of girls would rather have a house like this one." He spread one arm to indicate the grandeur of Bliss House. "Would you not want to live somewhere like this?"

"But I am a *little* girl. I only need a little house."

Aaron laughed, drawing the attention of Odette and Mason, who had gone up on the stage to see behind the curtains for themselves.

"Mister Fauquier, could we go down to the kitchen?" Odette came to the front of the stage with Mason following.

Aaron turned away from Kiku. "Of course. And I hope we can be less formal. Will you all call me Aaron?"

No one answered him, but Kiku smiled. Mason and Odette relaxed a bit.

When they left the theater, Kiku was confused when she saw no break in the gallery railing for the stairs. Aaron led them to the back of the house. "Two stairways back here. One for the family, the other for the servants and the servants' quarters."

There were no paintings on the walls, and no furniture. But there were draperies on most of the windows, and wallpaper in nearly every bedroom. No other wallpaper was like what they had seen in the ballroom. In the bedrooms, there were abundant floral designs. Flowers and birds and trellises. Leaves and trees. Most of the bedrooms had full bathrooms or water closets with toilets with flush tanks above them, as there had been in Madame Jewel's house.

"There are two large water tanks in the attic that are fed by the spring."

When they reached the *salon*, the enormous empty room that would serve as the house's main parlor, Kiku asked where everyone would sit. "There are no mats or chairs or even rugs."

"Everything will be shipping in over the next month. Missus Bliss is coming in November."

There was a moment of silence as though Missus Bliss, Randolph's wife, had actually come into the room. Odette broke the silence and again asked to see the kitchen.

Aaron took them out into the hall. "You'll like this, Kiku." He felt along the seemingly empty wall, and the paneling moved, opening in the shape of a door. Rather than immediately liking it, Kiku was afraid that this panel must lead to another dark passage, and so she dropped back.

"Oh, it's an entrance to the kitchen!" Odette went in first, exclaiming over the kitchen's size.

Kiku, embarrassed that she'd been afraid, hurried after her. They entered a long washing-up area that had deep sinks and fancy metal faucets protruding from the walls. Beyond was the main kitchen, with a butler's pantry full of empty, glass-fronted cabinets, and a brand-new stove and oven that seemed big enough to Odette to roast an entire small pig. There was an oak icebox as well, with shining brass handles, and a spigot on the side that Aaron said would let water out when the ice melted. He opened one of the doors. "Look. It's lined with zinc."

Kiku had no idea what "zinc" might be, but Odette and Mason seemed duly impressed, so when it was her turn to look inside, she nodded enthusiastically. She thought it looked like nothing more than dull gray metal.

They passed through the main part of the kitchen, directly into the dining room. Aaron looked around for the artist he'd said would be there working, but there was no one. But what was there astonished Kiku and Odette. Mason had seen the nearly completed mural before, but the other two had not.

The sunlight from the windows and the double French doors leading to the patio illuminated the hundreds, perhaps thousands, of peacock feather eyes painted on the wall. It was a kaleidoscope of greens and blues and just a hint of gold. In one unfinished corner was the scaffolding the artist had rigged so he could work comfortably near the ceiling.

"Mercy." Odette put a hand to her throat. "Why would anyone want such an evil, evil thing in their house?"

"Why do you say that?" Kiku touched a nearby eye with her fingertips, feeling the faintly raised texture of the paint. "It's beautiful."

"It's the evil eye. Bad luck. Mason told me what Mister Bliss was putting in here, but I didn't believe that he would really do it. Everyone knows you can't have peacock feathers in the house. Didn't anyone ever teach you that?"

Kiku shook her head. "There are peacocks in Japan. Wild peacocks. I only ever saw one pair of them there, but I saw another in the menagerie in New York. A male and a hen. In Japan, peacocks are very special. It is believed that they bring happiness and good fortune."

The other three looked surprised.

"I've never heard that." Aaron looked around the room as though seeing it anew. "They are rather beautiful."

Odette scoffed. "I wouldn't even want to work in this house, with this here."

"You're not going to have much choice about that," Mason said. "We will be called on plenty to come to the house. You'll have to leave your superstition at the doorstep."

Kiku wasn't sure what the word *superstition* meant. But she understood that Odette had very different ideas about things from her own. "I have a peacock feather that I found in New York. It is very special to me."

Odette raised an eyebrow. Her look said that she thought Kiku had just proved her point that peacock feathers brought bad luck. If they didn't, she might still be safe in her village, rather than halfway across the world, in Virginia.

"We should go home now," Mason said.

Odette was only too happy to agree. "Aaron, would you like to join us for our Sunday meal before we go back to church? I have a chicken in a pot on the stove, and Kiku has learned to make a decent dumpling."

Kiku blushed. The idea of Aaron coming to supper unnerved but pleased her.

Aaron seemed equally flustered. "While I'm grateful for the invitation, I'm expected back for Sunday supper at Missus Green's boardinghouse. Thank you."

They thanked him for the tour of the house, and he again reassured them that he would not mention their presence. But he did caution them about returning, whether Mister Bliss was there or not. "I'm afraid that it really should be at his request."

Kiku suspected there would be no future request for her, and while her curiosity was satisfied, she was still shaken by the ballroom's wallpaper and the tunnel and the strange rooms far underground. A thought was growing in the back of her mind. What if Randolph were going to make her live there after his wife arrived? He could do that. He would no doubt want to hide her so that his wife would not have to look out a bedroom window and see her cottage in the woods. Surely no man would do such a thing to his own wife.

As they left the garden and walked toward Mason and Odette's house, Kiku glanced back to see if, perhaps, Aaron were watching them from a window. But he was not.

"What are you looking for?" Odette was at her elbow, whispering. Mason had gone a little ahead. "Don't get any ideas about Aaron, honey. I saw the way you were looking at him. He certainly had eyes for you. But Mister Bliss will put a bullet in both your heads if you so much as think of seeing him again. Don't you think he won't."

Kiku opened her mouth to protest, but she knew it would be useless to argue. Randolph would certainly make her suffer if he thought she had even looked at another man. Now she had to think of her child as well as herself. She would put Aaron Fauquier out of her mind.

Chapter 14

KIKU

October 1878

When Randolph arrived back in town, he sent a message through Mason that he would have dinner with her that night. It was only a few days after Aaron had shown them the house, and while Kiku had taken up her post behind the boulder each day before lunchtime, she hadn't seen Aaron again. She was disappointed.

At dinner, Randolph picked the last meat from the bones of the rabbit carefully, using his knife and fork as though they were surgical instruments. Fat from the rabbit flesh glistened on his lower lip. He ate delicately for so powerful and intimidating a man. Almost gently. So different from the way he was with people. Kiku knew he was used to getting his way, and he brooked no argument. She watched as he put down his knife and fork and, to her surprise, picked up a tiny leg bone and sucked the end of it. As his wet lips smoothed their way over the bone, her stomach turned, and she looked away, holding her napkin to her mouth. Inside her, she felt the baby move, as though reminding her it was there.

It had begun moving the month before, and she'd been afraid that Randolph might feel it when he was against her. He had been gone much of the end of September and early October, and was only just returned.

"That rabbit was excellently done, my dear. You've become quite the cook." He raised his wineglass to toast her. She bowed her head to acknowledge his praise. "The cornbread, too, was perfect. Odette has taught you very well. Beyond my expectations."

Kiku excused herself and went to get the apple tart she'd made for dessert. It pleased her to have something to do. Cooking gave her a sense of purpose, and Odette had found her an eager student. She had struggled with the crust for the tart, but it had finally come out right.

Randolph's eyes shone with delight as she placed the tart in front of him on the neat round dining table sitting in the corner where the kitchen and front parlor met. "I could weep with happiness, Kiku. I have suffered from the overwrought gastronomy of too many famed chefs. Simple food is best. Simple food from simple hands." As though to emphasize his words, he unexpectedly took her hand and kissed it.

She served him the tart and watched him eat.

"You're not having any? You've hardly eaten a thing."

"I'm not hungry this evening, thank you."

Randolph eyed her closely, then smiled. "You've put on weight. But it is not unbecoming. When I brought you here, you were too thin. That slag, Bernadette Jewel, certainly managed to save her pennies on what she didn't feed you and the other girls."

"Yes, Randolph."

Odette had been clear. "You have to tell him soon. Don't think you're going to be able to go along like nothing is different." Odette had let out the dresses that she had made, and did her best to alter the ones that she'd bought in Lynchburg. She had guessed at the pregnancy when Kiku had become ill at the smell of milk that was slightly off. "I thought girls who knew what was what understood about how not to have a baby."

Kiku had confessed, explaining that all the girls knew that nothing could truly prevent a baby, and that was why Madame Jewel sent any girl who missed her monthly menses two months in a row to the abortionist. "Every other month some girl would have to go. Some girls were not careful. One of the girls, Ivory, died while I was there. She came back to the house, but she bled to death in her bed. Another left the house for her appointment and never came back. It was said that she went back to her family in New Jersey. Madame Jewel told us that she broke into the cook's box and took the money that she kept there for the fish seller."

Odette's mouth stayed firmly closed, and Kiku suspected that she was working hard to hold her tongue. She looked unhappy. Kiku shrugged. "It is the way of things."

After a moment, Odette said, "There is a woman on the other side of the James."

Kiku shook her head. "No. I will not harm my child."

"Think about it. You might as well do it now, because I don't believe Mister Bliss will let it live once it's born."

⁓

Kiku did not want to test Randolph, and she knew she should speak to him before he took her to bed. But before she was able to amass the courage, he put his napkin on the table and pushed his chair back.

"Amelia and Tamora will be arriving in a matter of weeks."

119

Kiku's heart began to pound. He would surely want to hide her away from his wife. She imagined the rooms at the end of the underground passage. What if she were never to see the sunlight again? She would beg him not to send her there.

Her voice was timid. "Must I go somewhere else?"

"What gives you that idea? It would be extremely inconvenient for me to visit you in some other place."

"I'm sorry." She bowed her head, secretly relieved. She didn't want him to see her fear or her relief.

"Amelia will be satisfied with the arrangement. Her duty is to please me as a husband, and you please me. But there may be others who come around to visit her. The ladies of the county will want to pay their respects, and women are a nosy lot."

He paused a moment as though expecting her to answer. She had nothing to say.

"Amelia will no doubt make friends. There will be parties and such. But you're not to concern yourself with the goings-on. Stay away from the house. You are far too noticeable. If anyone comes here, pretend that you do not speak English, and that you cannot understand them. You're to tell me if someone comes, and if I'm not here, you should tell Mason, and he will get me word. I won't have strangers coming here." He leaned forward to look hard at her before getting up from his chair. "You haven't had anyone here, have you? No one besides Mason and Odette?"

She reddened slightly, nervous, unable to put Aaron's face out of her mind. As soon as he'd mentioned the prohibition of strangers, Aaron's image had come to her. But she could truthfully say that he hadn't been to the cottage to see her.

"No man has been to the cottage except Mason. I heard the men working near the house, and sometimes I watched from the woods, but I did not go near and they did not see me."

He regarded her with amusement in his eyes. "You watch the men?"

"I only like to see other people. Odette and Mason are very good to me. But I have little to do during the day, Randolph."

"Sometimes I forget that you are so young, but see that you stay out of sight. I do not need questions from strangers, and you will be punished if you are seen. You understand that, of course. Keeping you elsewhere would indeed be inconvenient to me." He pursed his lips, thinking a moment. "Though it's true that there would certainly be no strangers there."

Kiku nodded, thinking again of the underground rooms. Where else could he mean that there would be no strangers? Aaron had not been a true stranger. He had known about her, had, perhaps, even known her name. What had Randolph told him about *her*?

"It's cold in here. Go and fortify the fire, then go into the bedroom and prepare. I have need of you tonight. It has been too long, my dear."

"Yes, Randolph. It has been many days." She rose and did as she was told.

Squatting in front of the fire, she could feel the slight heaviness of her womb on the tops of her thighs. It had, indeed, been many days since Randolph had been inside her. He was likely not to be gentle. She worried for the child but told herself it would be safe, that she had heard her mother and father together late into each of her mother's pregnancies. The child was probably no larger than her own fist right now, safe in the waters of her womb.

As she disrobed in the chilly bedroom, carefully placing her dress back in her closet and her undergarments on their hook inside the armoire, she was all too conscious of the gentle roundness of her belly. It was far more likely that she would be the one to be injured, rather than her child, when Randolph discovered her secret. She lighted a single candle and slipped into bed. Perhaps this one time he would not notice, and both she and the child would be safe.

Darkness was, indeed, her friend. Randolph, well fed and weary, did not bother her for long, and did not seem to want anything more than to finally exhaust himself inside her. She was only a receptacle this night. He fell asleep quickly after, and she turned over and gathered the blankets to her. In the morning he was gone.

Each night for a fortnight, he returned to have dinner with her and to sleep. He had never been so consistent, so faithful. But with each night he grew quieter after dinner, before finally telling her to tend the fire and go into the bedroom. After the first few days of this, she told Odette that she was afraid.

"He knows. He has seen me, and I have seen him looking at me, and he has touched my stomach, but he won't say anything."

Odette agreed that it was disturbing, but now advised her not to say anything. That it was too late. "You come to us if he does anything to you. But I'm sure he won't, Kiku."

To Kiku's ears, Odette's assurances rang false. No, he had never really hurt her. His favorite abuses were humiliations. Never had he left her with more than slight bruising and aches. This time, though, might be different. Despite Odette's suggestion that she go running to them, she knew that was not possible. She could not run away from Randolph, and he would certainly find her if she remained on the estate. He knew that Odette and Mason were her only friends because he had planned it that way.

On the fourteenth night, he pushed back his chair and stood. She got up as well, assuming that she should tend the fire, then go to the bedroom, but he told her instead to stay where she was and get on her knees.

Her heart quickened, and she was suddenly afraid. There was some relief, too, that he had stopped being so mysterious.

Using the flat of his powerful hand, he slammed her head against the oak table. Her skull made a thudding sound that rang through the room and exploded in her brain. When her body recoiled, still upright, he hit her again. Again her head struck the oak, and when she began to crumple, moaning, to the floor, he bent to take her by the arm.

"Sit up, you filthy whore. Sit up."

Kiku struggled to find her balance on her knees. When she opened her eyes, all was hazy, and there seemed to be two Randolphs in front of her. She started to sink again, and again he jerked her to a kneeling position.

Then Randolph's pants were around his feet, and then his undergarments.

"Open your mouth, filth."

At first the words made no sense to her, but he slapped her face and told her again.

Her head seemed to be made of pain. But she opened her mouth and received him. Several times he thrust himself into her so that she nearly choked. The tricks that the other girls had taught her were far from her mind; pain fought it for control. All she wanted to do was to crawl into a corner and die.

"*This* is all you're good for."

She heard him, and knew it was true. She had been safe for too long, thinking that she could have a life as a woman here. As a mother with a child. The pain renewed her understanding of her purpose. She could go nowhere because he owned her. And he would own her child.

"Pay attention." He cuffed her more carefully, given that he was inside her mouth and didn't want to be hurt himself.

After a few moments, he began to talk again. Quietly this time. She was doing her job. Her only job. And he was enjoying it.

"When I leave here, you'd better pray. Yes, you'd better pray to your heathen gods, my girl. That child had better be a girl, Kiku."

What is he saying? What does he mean? Goddess Kishimojin please make this a boy child, a strong and healthy boy child that

Randolph will be proud of. A boy that I can protect until he is old enough to protect me.

"You need to pray that she's as good a whore as her mother, because I will have need of her."

Hearing those words, she regretted not listening to Odette. How could she watch him do these things to a daughter? A girl she had doomed long before her birth.

When he was finished, she fumbled for the edge of the table and for her napkin to wipe her mouth the way he had done as he had eaten the rabbit. But she had to hold onto the table to keep from falling over. Still, nothing looked quite right to her eyes. Hot tears pressed against her eyelids when she closed them.

Randolph, his pants secured, squatted down. Even squatting, he towered over her.

"I'm disappointed in you, Kiku. I don't even know if the bastard you're carrying belongs to me. For the sake of propriety, I'm going to say it's probably not. I know that cunt Jewel was whoring you out to other men even when I was paying her not to. But just so you understand, I own that child in the same way I own you." He stood again, but she would not look at him, and so did not see his boot lift from the floor. The kick landed on her rib cage, and now she fell onto her side with an anguished cry. She gathered her knees to her chest and lay there, weeping, on the cold floor.

In another few minutes, he was gone, his footsteps pounding down the porch stairs. But he hadn't closed the front door, and when she finally opened her eyes, feeling the rush of cold across the floor, she saw that a tiny brown screech owl had flown in and landed silently in the middle of the parlor. It kneaded the carpet gingerly with its talons. Kiku gasped, drawing its attention, and its tufted ears twitched before its head slowly turned to face her. Its eyes were black disks surrounded by thick circles of gold.

"Hello." Kiku whispered to it in Japanese, certain it would like hearing Japanese rather than English, a language that sounded sharp in her own ears. Staring, it took a single step as though it might come to her, but, hearing a sound that made its ears turn suddenly, it took off again into the night just as silently as it had arrived.

With its departure, the pain in Kiku's heart eased as well.

Chapter 15

AMELIA

November 1878

Tamora's nurse, Harriet, came out of the train car's larger bedroom carrying a bottle of medicine.

"She took it like a lamb. Much better than last night."

"She'll sleep then." It was a statement, not a question. Amelia liked to have all questions concerning Tamora answered before they became questions in anyone else's mind. She had to. If it weren't for her constant vigilance, Tamora would have spent the last three years of her young life in an institution, rather than under her care and that of whatever nurse they had managed to retain.

"I daresay the motion of the train will also help her sleep. May I ask how long it will be before we arrive in Virginia?"

"Not more than six or seven hours, I should think."

The train car was chilly, and Amelia kept on her gloves as well as the jacket of her brown tweed traveling suit. They had brought extra blankets and Tamora was cozy in the bedroom's small bed. Outside the narrow train windows, the northern Virginia country-side rolled by, green and amber in the failing November sunlight. Patches of pale gold flashed through the mostly barren woods, oak trees, perhaps, that lost their leaves so much later than the others. Back home, on Long Island, the leaves were long gone, and the winter winds had settled in. Amelia had never been to Virginia, though friends had told her that it wasn't nearly as pleasant in the winter as, say, South Carolina. And certainly not particularly warm in the part of the state where Randolph had built their house.

"Our country house," he had called it. Though in their world, country houses were usually in Connecticut or even—among the more adventurous of society—the Catskills. No one in their right minds had houses many hundreds of miles away in Virginia. And if they did venture so far, they built within a few miles of the Atlantic. Even now that the war had been over for more than a decade, the idea of living in central Virginia seemed savage. It had been such a wild idea that Amelia had asked him, with a light tone that would maintain their mutual air of civility, why he didn't just take them somewhere truly uncivilized like Ohio. Or Tennessee. Perhaps even Indiana, all their worldly goods in one of those covered wagons she'd read about.

He had laughed, treating her sarcasm as the wittiest of jokes, then smiled with his perfect teeth. It was a sympathetic smile that had once unexpectedly charmed her, and certainly had captivated the rest of her family (it was a story she told herself that his smile had captivated them; it had been only his money that had charmed them).

"Because that is where so many of my investments are, my dear. The investments that keep your mother's carriage and your father in good odor with the suppliers of his taxidermy needs, and his friends, the bookies. It will be good for all of us."

All of us.

Here was reality. She was old enough and, unlike many of her friends, savvy enough to be aware of the financial requirements of her parents, but she could also see that he was speaking more significantly of Tamora. Amelia had been stunned when he agreed with her, against all the protestations of her family, that when Tamora, at age four, had been definitively pronounced by several doctors to be "mentally deficient," the child should not be institutionalized but kept at home. She would stay at the house they shared on Long Island (though never at the apartment in New York City if it could be helped; this was simply understood). Her family had protested that it was unseemly for Amelia to have *such ideas*. *Ideas* were never appreciated by her family. Particularly her mother. Oh, how her mother's behavior toward Tamora had changed for the worse after the diagnosis. A diagnosis that hadn't seemed to Amelia to be a diagnosis at all, but a kind of unavoidable resignation to uncomfortable facts.

It didn't matter to her so much that Tamora was not a winning child, that she refused to speak even though the doctors had said there was nothing physically wrong with her throat or mouth. Despite all of Amelia's efforts, she could not get the child to look her in the eye or into the eyes of anyone around her. When Tamora was unhappy or uncomfortable, she screamed, alarming everyone. Their Long Island house was large enough, and the nursery distant enough, that Amelia and Randolph (when he was home, which wasn't all that much because he often stayed in the city, or was in Virginia) could sometimes pretend it wasn't happening. But they found they could rarely entertain, and Amelia stopped inviting her friends for tea or lunch, mindful of the screams from the nursery.

Unless Tamora was dressed in the simplest of cotton undergarments and dresses, she screamed and removed all her clothes. Amelia had been particularly grateful to Gretna, the nurse who had stayed with them for nearly the whole year that Tamora was three, who had suggested they try putting only very soft clothes on her.

"Willful" was how Amelia's mother described Tamora, and she had recently spent an entire hour trying to get her to use a spoon with her soup instead of picking up the bowl to drink from it directly. The experiment had ended with Tamora throwing a fork (she was never given them, but had filched one from another place setting) at her grandmother's head.

Amelia suspected that her mother was secretly glad that Randolph had planned the house in Virginia. Far away from everyone they knew, and too difficult to travel to very often.

Now it was November and Randolph had sent for them. She hadn't seen him in two months. He had left from the city, letting her know by letter what belongings of his she should have shipped to Bliss House, Old Gate, Virginia.

Bliss House. How preposterous it sounded! No respectable people would name their house after themselves.

But Randolph had little pretense to respectability.

Randolph had had money that her parents needed. They had given up on her being married, and her mother, at least, had resigned herself to decorative penury: the sale of the occasional piece of D'Jarnette silver she'd inherited or one of the few decent landscapes they owned. When so many of her mother's friends were planning to donate their Turners and Edwardses to one of the newly sub-scribed museums that were springing up in cities like New York and Boston, her mother was busy inviting discreet art dealers to dinner. Randolph had changed that. She was keeping both her Turner and her Edwards.

Amelia had been thirty-two when she met Randolph at a dinner party given by the Martin-Joneses. The Martin-Joneses weren't upper tier people, but she liked Dolly Martin-Jones, and they enjoyed laughing over their dancing school days together. And Dolly and her husband, Treadwell, were among the Long Island families who didn't hold the Jewish lineage of Amelia's paternal grandmother against her.

Randolph was younger than Amelia by seven years, and his mother was a Hasbrouck of old Dutch stock. Amelia had never asked Dolly if she had seated them beside each other at dinner on purpose. Randolph had been introduced as a business associate of Treadwell's, which meant Randolph was probably also a customer of the bank of which Treadwell was president. That meant he was wealthy. The knowledge that Randolph's father was notorious— well, as notorious as a wealthy man married to a grimly respectable Dutch heiress could be—for trading with and selling arms to the Confederacy came to her later. After Randolph had seduced her, shocking her out of her well-aged maiden virginity. And well after she realized that he appealed to a baseness in her character that she hadn't known she possessed. For Randolph Bliss was a man who had his father's *raconteur* business sense, but also an overt charm that she found at once irresistible and repellant. Randolph was not a talkative man, but as he bowed his head over his soup, she had noticed that his profile was strong yet appealing. He had been flattering and attentive, and she had, indeed, thought his smile attractive and sincere. The truth was that his earnest attentions made *her* feel attractive, when she knew very well she was not. Her nose was too large, her lips too thin, her waist no longer girlish, and she had a tendency to scowl.

"You always look unapproachable. No man wants a woman who looks perpetually unhappy. Are you so unhappy?" Her mother's critiques had begun when Amelia was only a girl of ten. She never understood her mother's obsession with happiness and knew from her Bible that no one was promised happiness in this world. Yet she could find no reason to call herself unhappy. She had friends whose company she enjoyed, and she had her books and needlework. As she grew older she had taken up some of the household management duties that her mother had disliked. She had resigned herself to being an aunt to her brother's boisterous children, and she felt pleasure at being around them, as she felt pleasure at walking on the beach and spending the afternoon reading Hawthorne or George Eliot.

What other happiness should she have expected?

Their courtship had been brief, over the course of a single social season. They announced their engagement at a February ball, and had retired afterward, with a few close friends and her parents, to the apartment her parents kept in the city. The party lasted until dawn, and they had celebrated with more champagne and a breakfast of eggs and pheasant and oranges and her favorite tiny, sweet rolls that the cook had been making for her since she was a girl. Was that not happiness?

It was mid-November now, and she wondered what perversity had made Randolph insist that she come to Virginia at the beginning of the season. Though the truth was that she rarely accepted invitations in the city, not wanting to leave Tamora at the house with Harriet and the staff for longer than was strictly necessary.

He had promised her that there were plenty of good Virginia families around Old Gate that she would get to know. Douglas, his brother, who had settled in the next county with his wife, Mary, had promised that she wouldn't be too lonely.

Randolph had been in Virginia since late August and had told her he was too busy to come up to New York and escort them to Virginia. So it had just been her, Harriet, and Tamora that her parents had seen off at the station. Amelia had been ready for disaster, timing the arrival of their carriage so that they would be able to board the private car only thirty minutes before their departure. Her mother had been overly bright, going on about how nice it would be not to have to endure the brutal throes of the coming New York winter, and her father had stood, silent, glancing occasionally at Tamora as though she were a cannonball that might explode at any moment. Amelia couldn't blame him for it. Wasn't that how *she* always felt? But Tamora had been unusually calm despite the strange sounds and smells, and Harriet later told Amelia that she had given Tamora a little brandy in her milk and had molded some soft wax and tucked it into her ears. Amelia disapproved of giving children brandy, except for bad colds, and suspected that it had come from Harriet's own silver flask that she thought no one knew she kept in the large tapestry bag she always carried with her. But the proof was that Tamora stayed by Harriet's side, letting her hold her hand (and the black velvet ribbon that was tied to both of their wrists was almost unnoticeable against the black of Harriet's great wool coat), only occasionally poking a finger at her ear and making quiet *unh unh unh* sounds.

Yes, they would arrive in Virginia by ten o'clock in the evening, abandoning the unfamiliar train car for the even less familiar town of Old Gate. Randolph had promised to meet her at the station with a brand-new carriage that he'd had built just for her, so they could arrive at Bliss House in comfort and privacy. She had his most recent letter folded in the book she had brought along on the train.

I'm eager for you to see our new home, my dear Amelia. If only you could arrive to see the sun shining on its golden brick and to see it sparkling on the windows. Monsieur Hulot has made it a very special house, right down to the furnishings, with which I know you'll be pleased. This will be the home where our dream of being together without interruption will come true. Even now we are guarding the tender orchard saplings from early frost, and within two years you will have fresh peaches from our own land at our breakfast table, and as many apples as Tamora cares to eat in a day. There is a small amount of construction that will finish in the spring, but for the most part, the craftsmen and laborers are departed, and the house is ready for you and our daughter.

As I have promised, if you find yourself discontented with Bliss House, or find you cannot bear to be away from your parents, you may leave Virginia with my blessing, and I will follow you when I can.

Though I cannot imagine that you and Tamora will be unhappy here. Bliss House has all the privacy you could ever want. I would show you to the world, my dear wife, every day. But I know that your nature—and the health of our daughter— demands quieter surroundings. You will find them here, waiting for you, along with me.

Ever Your Devoted, Randolph

She couldn't recall having a conversation with Randolph about their being together without interruption, but her mother had told her often enough that a wife's place was at her husband's side. To his credit he very much understood her reluctance to be out in the world now that Tamora demanded so much care.

As the green and brown and gold countryside outside the window faded behind a curtain of gray, Amelia tried to imagine both the house and the happiness he had described. With a flutter of apprehension in her stomach, she realized that the countryside outside the window had disappeared and she was seeing only her own reflection in the glass.

Chapter 16

AMELIA

November 1878

Tamora sat squeezed into the corner of the brougham, her hazel eyes tightly closed, and her doll, Evangeline, pressed against her chest. The air inside the carriage was a tense mix of Randolph's jollity, Harriet's fluttering confusion as to whether she should flatter Randolph or tend solemnly to the silent Tamora, and Amelia's desire to get to Bliss House as quickly as possible. Randolph had met them at the station with the brand-new carriage, which smelled of leather and straw and sawdust from the stable and the spiced cologne that Randolph preferred. Sitting beside her husband, Amelia realized that she had missed that scent, a scent that both put her on edge and excited her. But at that moment she was far too worried that Tamora would suddenly explode in a screaming fit that would drive them all out of the carriage and onto the unfamiliar streets of Old Gate to feel anything but anxious.

"The photographs you sent to Missus Bliss of the house were most remarkable, but I confess that I can't wait to see the house in person, Mister Bliss." A smile spread over Harriet's rather homely, plump face. The road was not smooth, and Amelia could see the false brown curls Harriet wore bobbing near the back of her head, below her tiny, high-placed hat. The front of Harriet's hair was salted with gray, but somehow she had not thought to match the hairpiece to it.

"There's a good moon tonight, Harriet, but it won't do the house justice. I'm of a mind to have you all get out of the carriage with your eyes closed, lead you inside, and bring you back outside early in the morning for a proper look."

Harriet tittered. "But I would be sure to fall down, Mister Bliss. I can't see my way to walk with my eyes closed!"

"Don't you worry about a thing. You will see Bliss House from every vantage point at every time of day. And we won't let you fall down once." Randolph rested his palm on Amelia's leg. "Will we, my dear?"

Amelia gave a faint answering smile and wanted to suggest to Harriet that if she didn't want to fall down, she should stay out of the brandy she kept in her bag.

Most of the lights in the town were extinguished, and there appeared to be no streetlamps. The moon was, indeed, high. Randolph inquired about the trip and the acceptability of the private car. Harriet was enthusiastic, saying that it was quite the nicest way to travel.

"What did you think of the train, Tamora? Did you see any sights?" He reached out and was about to touch his daughter, but Amelia put her own hand on his arm to stop him.

"She's exhausted, and she's doing very well now. She slept most of the way. I think she found the train soothing."

Randolph nodded. "Well, then. That's good, isn't it? Wait until she gets to the house. Plenty of room for her. Plenty."

To Amelia he sounded as though he were talking about a house pet. A dog. There was no reaction from Tamora, whose blond locks had spilled from the hood of her cloak and hung in her face.

"We should be getting close." Randolph poked open the front window. "Where are we, Clayton?"

The driver's voice came down to them. "We're about to go up the drive, Mister Bliss. Mason is behind us with the wagon and the luggage. Right smart he's coming up."

"Look here, Amelia." Randolph closed the front window and leaned over to open the window nearest Amelia. "Look out there. Before we turn."

Knowing better than to try to dampen Randolph's excitement, Amelia looked out. The sky was cloudless and the moon shone down on a long row of bare trees that were so newly planted as to look like a short, broken fence. Beyond them, she could just make out the outline of the house she recognized from the photographs. Bliss House.

Amelia stood in the shadow of Bliss House.

Lonely.

Bliss House looked lonely. It loomed tall and singular against the night sky, rising over them like a temple in the wilderness. The land around it had been cleared, though there were woods to the west and east. In New York, and, to some extent, North Hempstead, where their Long Island house was, houses had neighbors. Certainly there were a few grand estates, but even they had carriage houses or porters' lodges nearby that were lighted at night. Here, there was nothing. Stars. The moon. Even the cold, still air felt empty.

Candlelight glowed behind all the windows of Bliss House's first two floors and the center windows of the third. Amelia wondered what was in the darkened rooms. Which rooms would be hers? How would they keep Tamora in sight with so many places to hide?

Though she knew the house was pale yellow brick, it looked white and stark in the moonlight, its mansard roof a pale gray. Where was the dome? Randolph had raved about the dome, but she could not see it. Despite the house's lonely aspect, it all looked surprisingly . . . ordinary. If Bliss House had been built on a park square in New York, with other houses flanking it, it would not be so remarkable at all. And what about the garden? She had anticipated that, Bliss House being a country house, its approach would be gracious and parklike. But there had only been the march of trees up the lane and a circular drive in front. On the left side of the house, there was what appeared to be a generous landing or patio with some plantings, and the walled garden was off to the right. Beyond the garden's ironwork entry, she could see a distant wall, but nothing of the maze or flowers in between.

She felt Randolph's eyes on her.

"What say you, Amelia?"

"It's very well done, Randolph. I look forward to seeing it in the morning light. You should be very proud."

It was enough. Randolph took her by the elbow and kissed her cheek. "Welcome home, my dear."

They turned at a sharp cry from the carriage, and they heard Harriet say, "We'll have some nice warm milk when we go inside, Tamora. It's time to come out."

Randolph let go of Amelia's arm. "I'll go inside and see that everything is ready."

Amelia nodded and went back to the carriage. "I'll tend to her, Harriet. Please see that her things are taken to wherever the nursery is."

Fifteen minutes passed before Amelia was able to bring Tamora into the house. The child's eyes were tightly shut, and her arms and legs were locked so tightly around her mother that Amelia could hardly breathe or walk. But they were out of the carriage. That was all that mattered.

"Come and meet everyone, Amelia."

Amelia felt as though she had walked out of the night and into a stage play in some grand theater. The ceiling rose three stories above her, and beyond the chandelier, which was lighted with what must have been a hundred candles within glass hurricanes, was the dome. While it wasn't nearly as grand as the domes she had seen in churches and various public buildings, it was truly beautiful and sparkled with the stars as they had looked the night Tamora was born. Just as Randolph had promised. As weary as she was, she knew that Randolph had reason to be proud of it.

From the outside, the house had shown two shallow wings on each side. Inside, there were long, railed galleries that went all around the two upper floors. The second floor gallery was broken only by the top of the hand-carved staircase. It was from these galleries she imagined people standing to watch them acting out their lives below. What had seemed a lonely place from the outside now felt like a public house that might hold hundreds of people. Watching. Judging.

Randolph, Harriet, and the servants watched her. She smiled.

"I knew you would like it," Randolph said. The gathered group made murmurs of pleasure and relief.

"But of course I like it, Randolph. It's just a bit overwhelming after the trip. And Tamora . . ." At the sound of her own name, Tamora clutched a handful of Amelia's hair, which was two shades darker than her own, and twisted it. Amelia gave a little gasp that she tried to cover with another smile. "I should take her upstairs."

But Randolph insisted that Amelia at least let the staff greet her, as they had waited so patiently, and Amelia acquiesced, all the while praying that Tamora would relax her grip. By the time she had met each person: a housemaid, a groom, a gardener, and the cook and driver—a married couple named Maud and Clayton Poole—she felt she might faint from pain, and knew she would forget their names as soon as she got to the nursery. She thanked them all and excused herself. Harriet went ahead of her, and the moment Amelia ascended the first stair, Tamora loosened her grip.

After she had finally settled Tamora and Harriet for the night, she went downstairs and wandered until she found Randolph in his library. It was a comfortable, masculine room, and she recognized his books on the shelves, and the paintings, including the portrait of himself as a young man.

"You look weary, my dear. Shall I take you up to your room? Or would you like to see more of the house?"

As much as she would have liked to see more of the house, her head ached where Tamora had pulled her hair, and she felt she might sleep where she stood.

"Tomorrow. I should like to see it all in the morning."

As they went up a nearby set of back stairs, he told her that there was a guest visiting for the winter, but that he wasn't in the house at that moment. Aaron Fauquier was staying at Missus Green's Inn and Boardinghouse for a couple of days, until Amelia and Tamora were settled, but he would be coming back.

"You'll like Aaron. He worked on the house, and we are planning some new projects for the spring. I think you will like him."

Amelia was too tired to think about having a semi-permanent resident in the house, but she said that she would be delighted to meet him.

They left the staircase at a second-floor hallway that led out to the gallery. "I had hoped to give you a room on the western side of the house with a view of the garden, but I suspected you would rather be close to the nursery and Tamora. There's a stairway near the nursery that leads down to the kitchen."

He showed her into a spacious bedroom that was softly lighted and decorated with sumptuous bouquets of hothouse flowers, despite the cold outside. The walls were covered in an ocean blue fabric with two different intricate mosaic borders of rust and green, and the curtains and bedclothes were embroidered with bouquets of peach, rust, and pale blue flowers nestled in delicate green leaves. A rich carpet that was of a color similar to the blue walls, with twining ribbons of green woven into it, covered most of the wood floor. Their home in North Hempstead was lovely, but it had been decorated some years earlier and was much simpler. Though she might have said she would have preferred the simplicity of that house, she was pleased with the room and with the thought he had put into it.

"Randolph, this is beautiful. It hardly seems like it's mine."

"I'm happy it pleases you." He came close and put his arms about her waist. "You're tired, I know, my dear. It has been maddening having you so far away for so long."

Shifting artfully out of his grasp, she laughed. "New York was not so far away after all. I feel as though we were there only this morning. Would it have been a terrible strain for you to have made the trip home a bit more often? Tamora and I have both missed you."

Randolph grunted. "Tamora has more interest in a broken spoon or that damnable stuffed squirrel your father gave her than in me. I had Clayton put all those creatures and dolls in the nursery as you requested, as I'm sure you noticed. Is she really no better?"

They had traveled this road so many times.

"Neither the doctor nor I are too hopeful of improvement, but I believe I have seen some. Yes. Harriet has her eating quite well at table. Though it was a long trip."

"But you only this moment said that it didn't seem so far." He shook his head with a rueful smile. "And you are one of the cleverer women I've known. Which is it?"

Amelia gave a small laugh to imply she had meant to tease him. "I'm just worn out. I must not be thinking clearly."

Sitting at the dressing table to take off her hat, she noticed that there were several beautifully crafted perfume bottles and jars for lotions and creams. There was an ivory-handled brush and hand mirror set as well. He had thought of everything. As she took off her hat, she caught his eye in the mirror. His face was more benign than she remembered it. Was it that they had been apart for so long? Or was there something about the house that had changed him?

At least the house was warm. Randolph had written to explain the unique steam radiator heating, which was much more modern than what they'd had in Long Island, and there was ostensibly a warming pan already in the bed.

But what was that reflected in the mirror just past him? She turned around on the bench's velvet cushion. There, beside the bed, was a tall vase full of peacock feathers. She got up to get a closer look. The feathers were particularly colorful and looked new.

"Who put these in here?"

"Why, they're one of the house's little themes, Amelia. Like the stars in the dome, and the garden paths that mimic the lines of the house."

"They bring the worst kind of luck. Of course you had to know that. Why would you put us at such risk?"

He came close to her.

"Amelia." His voice was low and reassuring. "When did you become so superstitious? Do you think I would really put you and Tamora at risk? Everything I do is to protect you both. I've told you that since the very beginning. It's my dearest wish to protect you from the ugly things of the world. People's unkind words, their vile glances."

He stroked her face, running his finger down her cheek and along the side of the nose he knew she hated. Was he reminding her? Certainly he was, but was it an intentional unkindness, or Randolph just being *honest*?

"Our poor daughter." He lightly kissed Amelia's forehead, and she could smell his scent. "Here, in this house, no one important will see her. In this part of the world they have a tolerance for the strange. For the unfortunate. They love beauty, but they do not shutter away the ugly." He turned her around so that she was staring at the peacock feathers, lush and menacing in their pretty vase, and began to unbutton her dress. When he reached the bottom, he helped her out of her overdress and crinolette skirt. Letting them fall to the floor, he pushed her firmly toward the bed.

She had, of course, been a virgin when they married. Their coupling had been painful for her, and Randolph had not been gentle. Her mother had hinted that men in business, ruthless men, could not be trusted to be kind in the bedroom.

"You will bear it, but see that he doesn't leave any marks on you. A gentleman never leaves marks. But I suppose it remains to be seen if Randolph is truly a gentleman." She had been looking frankly into Amelia's astonished eyes, but then she had turned to the morning room window. "Your father is a gentleman. He is rarely unkind."

Had there been a wistfulness in her mother's voice? Amelia had been deeply embarrassed to have such a glimpse into her parents' intimacy, but now she wasn't sure whether she should have envied or pitied her mother.

No, Randolph never left a visible mark on her. There were other marks, invisible marks, beginning the first month of their marriage, when he began to whisper things to her that at first made her redden and shrink away from him. He bade her do things that embarrassed her deeply. She told herself that if it became too much, if she were truly being degraded, she would make him stop. But she never did.

Now, knowing that to protest that she was tired would be of little use, Amelia quickly undid her corset. She had been without a personal maid since Tamora was born, and was used to doing and undoing the hooks and eyes that ran up the front of the corset herself. When she was free of it, she wavered a little and took a moment to get her breath. But Randolph took it as a sign of capitulation and he eased her onto the bed and quickly removed his jacket and pants and shoes. Rarely did he bother to remove his shirt. He had many and they were not precious to him. Neither did he appear to desire to press his skin against hers, except for the nether regions. It felt impersonal and strange, given the intimate and often vigorous nature of their coupling. How, she still wondered, did other husbands and wives act?

As he fiercely squeezed her breasts and her belly (somewhat larger than it had been at their marriage, but then she was forty now, a middle-aged woman), as though he were seeing what she was made of, he started the obscene patter that had so unnerved her as a younger bride.

He murmured of the strange and horrid things he made other women do. Made other women do to him. It excited him, and, over the years, disgusted as she was, she had found that it began to excite her, too. Whisperings of much younger women, some that he had overpowered or purchased or shared with other women. Young women with no teeth, or a missing limb. Women that he sometimes hurt, but no, never hurt so badly that they were killed.

Had she been waiting to hear these things? Boring into her, he told her how the girl had screamed in pain and began to cry, but begged him not to stop. She saw the girl in her mind, the fiery red hair, the garish makeup, the tawdry sheets, the other woman in the room. Watching.

Amelia felt her body approaching the edge of reason, the place that she suspected women like her mother had never gone. The image of Randolph hurting the girl burned in her mind; she felt the girl's pain, the waning of the girl's feigned excitement and the way it turned to fear.

As the orgasm rolled through her body, she could hear the screams, searing screams. But there was something not right about them. She opened her eyes, and the waves in her groin subsided, though Randolph continued, wordless.

The screams were her daughter's. Tamora had somehow escaped the nursery. Beyond Randolph's heated breathing, she could hear Tamora's quick footsteps running along the gallery. Harriet called after her, trying to keep her voice controlled as though not to disturb anyone.

They had come so far, yet nothing would be different.

Randolph finished, and she felt him spasm inside her. There would be no more children. If she were to become pregnant—unlikely at her age—she knew how to end the pregnancy quickly. Tamora had been some kind of punishment, probably for the way she had responded to the filthy words that Randolph had whispered in her ear as the child was conceived.

She had borne her punishment and would continue to as long as both she and Tamora lived.

Chapter 17

AMELIA

November 1878

"What a dear cottage that is. Whatever will you do with it?"

Mary Bliss, the *zaftig* wife of Randolph's brother, Douglas, stood at the window of one of the guest rooms that overlooked the garden. She and Douglas had traveled to spend Thanksgiving at Bliss House without their children. The window bore a film of steam and she had cleared the center with a towel from the bathroom. "I'm sure you couldn't see it if there were leaves on the trees. It looks almost like a fairy house."

Amelia, standing near the bed, smoothed a hand over the coverlet, which was embroidered with flowers that perfectly matched the wallpaper. It seemed very French to her, and was not at all what she might have chosen for the room. But Randolph and Monsieur Hulot had not consulted her.

Mary was nosy and often tiresome, but she was only twenty-five, the age Randolph had been when he and Amelia were married. She tried to be patient with her. There was only one house to be seen from that particular window.

"Randolph says it's to stay a tenant house." It didn't house Mason, who was Randolph's right hand on the estate, and his wife, Odette. Their house was closer to the orchards. But she had chanced to see a woman who she thought was Odette in the clearing in front of the cottage. There had been someone much shorter, and dark-haired, with fair skin, as well. Perhaps a boy? She hadn't been sure. Randolph had simply said, "A tenant," and had left it at that. She knew when to stop asking questions. It didn't mean she didn't continue to wonder.

Even before Randolph began whispering about his adventures with other women, her mother had hinted that younger men had stronger appetites. So while she knew that Randolph had been unfaithful to her from the first days of their marriage, she was certain that not even he would go so far as to bed a boy.

"What a shame. It would make an excellent place to take some solitude, yes? Or have tête-à-têtes with close friends." The exaggerated way Mary said *tête-à-têtes* sounded vaguely salacious, and for a moment Amelia wondered if every woman in the world besides her had a lover.

Mary's honey complexion and wetly brown doe eyes had worked their magic on Douglas Bliss, who had followed her like a puppy dog from the first day they met at Saratoga Springs. Amelia's parents considered the festive Saratoga Springs *gauche*, a word that might have described Mary's early manners. But Amelia had to concede that she'd developed a modicum of taste, at least in clothing, since giving birth to the first of their two sons, who had, thankfully, stayed behind with Mary's mother. Her yellow-and-gray suit was tailored to minimize her overly generous bust, though Amelia suspected it would be on full display at dinner.

"It's a shame the boys haven't had a chance to meet Tamora. Yet I haven't seen her since she was an infant, either!" She opened her arms in a luxurious stretch. "Am I a dreadful mother for not missing the boys? They are *so* exhausting. How lucky you are to have a girl. I hear they're so much easier."

Knowing Mary would see Tamora soon enough, Amelia tried to change the subject. "Randolph likes dinner at an appallingly early hour here in the country. I hope you won't mind if we dine at six-thirty."

But Mary wasn't to be dissuaded. She drew uncomfortably close to Amelia, so that Amelia could smell her gardenia scent. She was also close enough that Amelia noticed the grubby discoloration of the inside collar of Mary's suit blouse. Of course, silk was notoriously hard to clean.

"I'll bet you never have to take a switch to her, like Douglas does to our boys. He says it's the only way to make them men."

What is she saying? Beating a child is never helpful. Seeing Mary's serious eyes, she knew she wasn't joking. Randolph had only once suggested that they beat Tamora.

"She's too old to be such a savage. You spoil her, my love. If you didn't spoil her so, she wouldn't range about." He had unconsciously rubbed at the thumb of his left hand. "Or bite."

By the time Tamora was four, and had become aggressive, they had been to a number of doctors. Several had suggested old-fashioned bloodletting, one a ghastly transfusion that would have replaced half the child's blood with the blood of a goat. All agreed that she had a disease of the brain that might be cured by changing the amount and type of blood reaching it. All also strongly suggested that she be placed in a sanitarium where she might not hurt herself or others. Fortunately, she had not yet hurt herself beyond banging her head against the wall when she was overly tired.

"Did you know"—Mary's voice was a whisper—"that Douglas's father beat both the boys? Beat Randolph with a strap until he bled, when Randolph was only six years old."

Randolph rarely spoke about his parents, who had given up their New York City house and lived as recluses in East Quogue. They had only come to the church for Amelia and Randolph's wedding, rising and kneeling and sitting when required, but they had left right after the service, each shaking Amelia's hand, offering their best wishes. Randolph's mother had kissed her cheek with dry lips and smelled faintly of tobacco. They had arranged for a pair of coach horses as a wedding gift and had sent an enormous silver tureen in the shape of a turtle when Tamora was born. Randolph rarely saw them now that his business interests were not entwined with his father's, and they'd never invited Amelia to visit.

"Surely not." It was the only response Amelia thought she could give. Anything else would be simple gossip. She was familiar with the intimacies of her husband's body, yet had never noticed any scars.

But her voice must have been too sharp. Mary bristled.

"Well, you could ask him. He's *your* husband. Douglas and I have *very* frank discussions."

Amelia wondered about the truth of Douglas's frankness with his wife. No, she would not ask Randolph. That he had learned cruelty—subtle cruelty—somewhere was more than obvious, but her frankness with him didn't extend to things that she didn't really want to know more about. If he ever harmed Tamora in such a way, she didn't know what she would do. She hoped that she would have the strength to kill him.

⁓

Bliss House was large enough to accommodate at least a dozen guests, plus staff, but it bothered Amelia that Randolph had invited Douglas and Mary without telling her beforehand. She and Tamora had been at the house for only a week. Tamora had not calmed, and only that morning, before the couple had arrived, Harriet had spent an hour following her up and down the stairs when she wandered, making her excited *unh unh unh* sounds, as she sought out familiar rooms.

"It's good for her to get the exercise. We'll go outside later, but it hasn't warmed up enough yet," Harriet had told her.

How grateful Amelia was to Harriet. She nearly had as much control over Tamora as Amelia herself did.

Since they had arrived, Randolph was like a stranger to Tamora, and Tamora disliked strangers. Not only did she avoid his eyes, but she shied under his infrequent touch. If it wounded Randolph, he never said. When she was much younger she would sit near him and let him touch her hair if he was gentle. But here in Virginia there had been no such interaction, and Randolph didn't seem to be in a hurry for it. He never asked to have her brought to him nor entered the nursery.

Presenting Tamora to Douglas and Mary would be awkward at best. She doubted it would go as well as it had with Aaron Fauquier, the pleasant young man who was staying with them at Bliss House. Randolph had explained that he had been Monsieur Hulot's assistant who was now settling in Virginia, and that he hadn't had any time during the summer and fall to work on his own house in Old Gate because he had been so busy with Bliss House. So Randolph had invited him to be their guest until the spring. Aaron had politely made himself scarce to let Amelia settle in, but she quite liked him. He was far less serious than Randolph, and sometimes set up an easel to paint in the theater when the day was sunny. He had met Tamora but hadn't pressured her to be friendly.

At their home in North Hempstead, on Long Island, Amelia had furnished a small family dining room where they could accommodate themselves and four or five additional guests. Randolph had made no such accommodation for Bliss House. The five of them—Amelia, Randolph, Douglas, Mary, and Aaron Fauquier—sat in the formal dining room at a table that would comfortably seat sixteen, but at least Randolph hadn't insisted that she sit opposite him at the other end of the long table.

Mary sat at Randolph's right, with her husband beside her; Amelia was at his left, with Aaron Fauquier on her other side. Mary preened under Randolph's attentions, and he flattered her mercilessly until Amelia was certain that he was completely insincere.

Bliss House didn't feel like it belonged to her at all, and she had a strange feeling that it would never truly be her home. It was horrid, feeling like a guest in one of her own houses. She couldn't see herself growing old here, or entertaining her family. "Of course we'll come and see you!" her sister had said. Even as they had embraced at the station, she had known it wasn't true. Worse, Tamora was often bewildered and distressed, constantly in search of the sunny white room she'd had on Long Island. It had been a cruelty to bring her here, and Amelia wished she had never agreed to leave New York. But if the whole house felt strange and distant to her, the dining room repelled her.

Along with the mahogany-manteled fireplace, the furnishings were pleasant enough: There were two Chippendale sideboards and built-in, glass-fronted cupboards filled with the silver pieces Randolph had purchased in New York. The chairs were heavy and comfortable. But Randolph had carried—or let the architect carry—the peacock motif too far with the mural of hundreds, if not thousands, of feather eyes. Mary had exclaimed over it, saying she felt like a princess from the Orient, dining beneath the wondrous, watchful eyes, and that Randolph was *terribly clever* for thinking of such a thing. Douglas, always taciturn, hadn't commented, and Amelia suspected that he was of her mind about the eyes: No one should be made to feel like they were being watched while dining.

Emboldened by the wine, Amelia asked Aaron about the decoration of the dining room. Aaron's answer surprised her.

"It's funny you should ask. Monsieur Hulot had planned a more historical, idyllic mural. Mountains and forests, animals—stylized, of course, not terribly realistic. The colors were to be celadon and pale browns and blues. But then this summer, Randolph suddenly became obsessed with the idea of peacocks. Said he had dreamed of them. Hulot was outraged and almost quit over it. Said he had never heard of anything so ridiculous, that he was not a purveyor of the art of rug merchants." Aaron laughed.

"Rug merchants? What on earth did he mean?"

"Oh, I suppose he meant Middle Eastern art. Mosaics and such. Though there are many examples in French architecture of the last century with Eastern influences. It wasn't until I found the statue of Hera with her peacock that he gave in and extended the motif to the dining room."

Amelia glanced around the room. "It feels like they're watching."

"I have had that sense myself," Aaron said. "In fact, Bliss House has a certain feeling to it, don't you think? One has the sense of being never quite alone. It should be a comfort on a long winter night, out here away from town. I prefer having close neighbors, but I can see the attraction."

Amelia held her tongue. She, too, preferred to have friends and neighbors nearby. At least she had until Tamora was born.

"It's interesting how clients are influenced by the things they see when they travel. About the time Randolph inquired about the peacocks, he also came to Monsieur Hulot with a sample of the Oriental wallpaper he wanted in the ballroom."

She waited for him to continue, but he was suddenly silent. His face had gained a slight flush, and he quickly took a sip of wine. When he turned back to her, he changed the subject.

"That's an elegant necklace you're wearing. Is it a family heirloom?"

Amelia touched the ruby chandelier necklace at her throat. In fact, Randolph had given it to her that summer. She wondered if there were some connection between the red jewels and the red wallpaper. And why Aaron Fauquier had become so nervous.

Clayton Poole, the husband of the cook, Maud, was serving apple pie when they heard a commotion out in the hall and hurried footsteps on the stairs. Amelia blanched and rose from her chair.

"Will you please excuse me for a moment?"

Beside her, Aaron started and stood up. Douglas and Randolph quickly rose as well.

"Please do sit. I'll return in a few moments." Amelia's voice was strained.

It was too late. Tamora ran into the dining room, stopping only when she noticed all the people at the table. She was dressed in one of the thick flannel nightgowns that Amelia had had made for her out of particularly soft cotton. Her blond hair was loose and damp, but neatly brushed. It had been a good evening, then, if she had let Harriet brush her hair.

Harriet appeared behind her, looking stricken.

"Forgive me, Missus Bliss. I went to drain the bath, and she ran out. I should have known when she began to fret."

"Oh, what a precious love!" The men had resumed their chairs, but Mary rose, and with a swiftness that took everyone by surprise, was within a few feet of clasping Tamora to her generous bosom.

Amelia sucked in her breath. Tamora's face didn't change, but Amelia sensed her alarm in the way her achingly slender body tensed, the cords in her neck sharpened.

"What a sweet darling girl. Give your aunt Mary a hug."

Amelia found her voice. "Please, Mary. Not now."

When Mary turned to Amelia, confused, Tamora's head whipped to the French doors leading to the patio. One stood open a few inches because Mary had complained of the room's heat.

"Oh, no, you don't!" Harriet lunged at Tamora's back to keep her from the doorway, but Tamora was too fast, and was already disappearing into the November night before Harriet's words faded. Harriet fell onto Mary, her fingers hooking onto the fragile chiffon silk ruff standing like an inch-high wall along Mary's breasts. The chiffon and the silk beneath it tore, exposing Mary's expensive corset and partially dislodging one honey-cream breast.

Distressing as it was, to Amelia it was nothing compared to the idea of Tamora exposed to the cold November night, barefoot and in a nightgown, and she hurried around them. Stupid women! She wondered if Harriet was drunk.

Thank God there was no snow, but neither was there a visible moon. It astonished her how fast Tamora was. She was deliberate and often ponderous in her actions, but when she ran, she was like an agile cat, her feet seeming not to touch the ground. It was unseemly for a girl, but then there was so much that others might think unseemly about Tamora. Amelia's light slippers shushed softly on the brick of the patio as she ran. Tamora was already on the rough drive, as though headed for the road over a quarter mile distant.

The air froze Amelia's lungs. She was not someone who enjoyed brisk walks and exerting exercise, but somehow it was exhilarating, and she had a sense of her daughter's mad—*yes! Sadly mad!*—rush for freedom. And it would surely happen again because Randolph hadn't thought about keeping his daughter safe. Bliss House had no locks on the outer doors and windows.

When the ground beneath Amelia's slippers turned to gravel, she felt the unevenness of the rocks. How was Tamora even going on? The poor child's feet would be bruised and cut.

Amelia called after her, and it may have been her imagination, but she was sure the figure in white paused. If Tamora got too far away, she wouldn't be able to see her at all. The night was too dark.

There were loud, rushed footfalls in the gravel behind her, and she looked back to see shadows against the great lighted house. Two of the shadows were outlined in front of the dining room doors, but one was coming closer and closer. Finally, Aaron emerged from the darkness.

"Missus Bliss! Tell me where she is—I can't see her!"

Amelia had to pause and gather her breath so she could speak. She pointed. "There. The new trees planted along the lane. See how she weaves in and out?" Even in the darkness, Tamora was setting a pattern. Amelia knew if she accidentally missed a tree in her panic, she would retrace her steps to make sure she went between it and the next. It was as though by making patterns she was leaving a trace of herself wherever she went.

As Aaron ran toward the immature trees, Amelia followed at a jog, calling after him to take care and be gentle. *She will fight you like a cat.* This she did not say aloud. The important thing was that he stop Tamora and get her inside before she was injured or caught a deathly cold.

After a few moments, she heard her daughter howl with rage. It was a familiar sound that caused a hot flaring in Amelia's chest, but it meant that she had been captured.

◡

They re-entered the house through the dining room doors. Amelia carried Tamora, who pressed her face aggressively against Amelia's neck as though she were trying to burrow into it. Aaron walked close by, but out of Tamora's line of sight. Everyone else in the room stood, silent. Mary at least had the sense to look chagrined. Her bodice had been pulled up, and the torn chiffon artfully arranged to hide the damage.

"Harriet, bring up her milk. Just warm. And the sugar cubes and two dozen salted peanuts. Count them out. Tea for me, as well."

"I'm—"

Douglas put a hand on Mary's arm before she could say any more.

Randolph spoke. "Aaron, you seem to have things well in hand. Would you escort Amelia to the nursery, please? Amelia, I'll see to our guests."

It was like Randolph not to want to get involved when Tamora had embarrassed him. No one had even thought to get a blanket for the freezing child.

Aaron kept his voice low. "Of course, Randolph. I meant to."

⁓

To Amelia's surprise, Tamora didn't struggle when she put her down on a chair near the fireplace in the nursery. Aaron stood a dozen feet away, looking at the collection of animals and dolls arranged around the room in cases and on shelves. There were almost as many taxidermy animals as dolls.

"Here, darling, it's the softest blanket. Let's wrap you up." Amelia quickly wrapped the blanket around Tamora so that her feet were tucked inside but her arms were relatively free.

Tamora touched her mother's cheek with her thin white fingers. Amelia knew she could bear any unpleasantness when such a moment occurred.

"Of course you wanted to find me. Nobody is angry. Here's Evangeline." She set a doll that was grubbier and much better loved than any of the other dolls in the room on Tamora's lap. But Tamora didn't reach for it and simply let it roll onto the floor. She said a single word: "Brownkin." No inflection. She repeated it twice more.

Amelia sighed.

"Is something wrong? Can I help?" Aaron looked genuinely anxious to help, and not the least bit worried or puzzled, as another man might have when faced with a child who, under other circumstances, would be tied up like a captive animal in an expensive asylum. How was it that Randolph liked having him around so much? Randolph was nothing like him. At dinner Aaron had told her a bit of his own history: how he had been sent from Virginia to France to study when he came of age to fight in the war against the North, and that he had remained in Monsieur Hulot's architecture studio for more than a decade. He thought it was a kind of serendipity that the commission from Randolph had arrived just when he was planning to return to Virginia to set up his own studio.

So he was in his thirties, like Randolph. In the soft light of the nursery he looked younger. In that same light, Randolph did not look young. Randolph was "wearing life hard," as her father would say. As though his face were marking the occasional debauchery of his actions. This young man could be suspected of no debauch, she was certain.

What did Randolph admire in him? Probably his skill. Randolph was good at exploiting and using the skills of others.

"Tamora speaks?"

"Did Randolph tell you she did not?" She gave a little laugh and picked up the doll to put it back on a shelf. "She speaks when she wants to. Or at least she has a few words for the things she believes are very important. It started about a year ago."

"*Brownkin* is important?"

Tamora said the word again, more insistently.

"That squirrel on the table beside the big bed. Will you bring it to her?" Amelia knew it was a risk. Tamora could take exception to this man who had tackled her in the cold November grass only twenty minutes earlier and throw a fit. But sometimes the warm fire and her favorite blanket worked a kind of magic on her.

He carried the squirrel carefully, with a perplexed look on his usually placid face.

"That is Mister Brownkin. My father is a naturalist. He has rooms and rooms of butterflies and insects in boxes and drawers and in display cases. These last few years he's moved on to small mammals and birds." She laughed. "I can't say my mother approves.

She discourages him from sharing them with company, but he *is* awfully proud of his own work."

"Shall I give it to her?"

The squirrel was mounted on a small base, its back feet firmly planted and nailed onto the wood. The tail curved in an *S*, and its ears were turned outward slightly to show how white the fur inside was. Its tiny paws held an acorn in a death grip, and its mouth was open as though it were about to take a bite out of it.

Aaron held out the squirrel to Tamora. She did not look at him, but snatched the squirrel as though she were afraid he might take it away again at any moment. Tucking the squirrel's head beneath her small, pointed chin, she began to stroke its tail with one bony hand.

Amelia was ashamed of her daughter's thinness. She knew that anyone who saw her probably assumed that she was being starved for her bad behavior. It was not uncommon for people to think the insane did not care about food or even know when they were hungry. But Amelia understood very well that her daughter hungered, that she had feelings.

Harriet appeared at the door with a tray. "Here's the tea, and Tamora's food. I brought an extra cup in case Mister Aaron wanted some tea as well." She set the tea tray on the single full-size table in the room and removed the dish with the peanuts on it, along with a two-handled mug, to the child's table. When the tea was arranged, Harriet went to sit quietly in a chair and took up some knitting.

"Please sit down, Aaron."

They drank their tea in companionable quiet as Tamora stroked the squirrel. A bald spot the size of a shirt button had begun to form behind its left ear, and Amelia had no idea what would happen when all the hair was gone. At least there were no more brains in the poor squirrel's head.

She was grateful for the patient way Aaron sat, understanding without being told that Tamora would decide how the next little while would go. With the nursery door open, she could hear Mary laughing downstairs as they moved to the library for after-dinner wine. Mary was the kind of woman who, because Amelia had left the table, would go along with the men, and not retire to her own room while the men went into the library. But there was no real judgment in the observation. Amelia was not her mother, and they were in remotest Virginia. Not New York.

After a few minutes, Tamora unwound herself from the blanket and, still clutching the squirrel, went to the child's table and sat down in front of the food. The squirrel rested in her lap like a pet, its blank glass eyes staring over the plate.

Tamora arranged the peanuts as they watched. Harriet stopped knitting when Tamora put her hands back on the squirrel.

Instinctively, Amelia knew that there were either fewer or more than two dozen peanuts on the plate and braced herself for the tantrum. But the tantrum didn't come. Tamora got up, holding the squirrel in one hand, and picked up one of the peanuts from the plate. She crossed the room, and, without meeting his eye, held out the peanut to Aaron.

Chapter 18

LUCY

June 1899

Paris!

It had always been Lucy's dream to come to Paris, where her own parents and several of her Boston friends had taken their wedding trips. Only a dozen days earlier, she had walked in the moonlight down the path to the dock in front of the Archers' river house with Randolph, and had let him kiss her for the first time. He had held her so closely that for a moment her breath left her and she felt as though she were floating. No boy had ever kissed her so completely. After he kissed her a second time, he asked her to be his wife, to come and live with him at Bliss House. Now she was half a world away, out of reach of her parents and everything she had ever known, and she wasn't sure she ever wanted to return.

She stood at the window of their suite at the Hôtel Continental, looking down at the boulevard, watching the endless stream of small *fiacres* toting fashionable people through the city. They had visited the Musée du Louvre in the morning together and had arranged for a photographer to take their picture on the Rue de Rivoli, but now Randolph was lunching with an odd, intensely nearsighted man, Monsieur Philippe, whom he had introduced to her the day before. In the afternoon, she was to meet Randolph at the House of Paquin to order more dresses, and she was nervous. The women of Paris were dressed so smartly that she was terribly intimidated. In New York, Randolph had taken her to Lord & Taylor to buy some ready-made dresses for the crossing (and if the ones Randolph encouraged her to buy were more girlish than she and the rather opinionated saleswoman might have preferred, Lucy told herself it was because he felt the difference in their ages so strongly, and she loved him for it). The informal dresses she'd had at the river house had been barely suitable for traveling. They had fled Old Gate like thieves in the night, stopping at Bliss House only briefly to deposit Carrie (who, Randolph insisted, would surely be fired when the Searles discovered she'd been involved in the elopement, and so must now work at Bliss House) and to pick up Randolph's packed trunks.

To see the trunks secured and waiting in the front hallway had been a surprise. Had he been so certain of her? Was she so transparent? Her mother had cautioned her about appearing too eager and obvious with young men, telling her she was too lovely, too beautifully formed, and too wealthy to be desperate.

"Men can smell desperation on a girl. Neither you nor Juliet have anything to be ashamed of."

Lucy hadn't been desperate in that sense. Only desperate to see Randolph and to return to Bliss House. As soon as he kissed her, she felt her full strength returning and the anticipation of being at the house again made her return his kiss with an energy that alarmed and thrilled her.

Faye had wanted to accompany them as far as Charlottesville, but Josiah and Randolph had dissuaded her. She came to the bedroom to help Lucy pack while Carrie, stunned and excited herself, had gone to pack her own things.

"Mummy and I will deal with your mother. You're not to worry. How thrilling it all is. Now you really will be a scandal!"

"You say it like being a scandal is a good thing. What if they come after me?" The image of her father in the doorway of the theater burned in her mind. She still felt the shame of it. Mortified in front of so many people she knew.

Faye took her by the shoulders. "You'll be married. No one will be able to make you do a single thing that you don't want to do. Think of it. Mistress of one of the most beautiful houses in Virginia, married to a man who won't treat you like you're some decorated doll. You know his liberated views. He loves you because you're beautiful *and* smart. Do you know what a luxury that is?"

Was Faye right? She could only hope that Randolph felt that way. In truth, they had not spent much time talking. She would have to trust that Faye knew Randolph better than she.

Until *Walpurgisnacht*, he had had no presence in her life except as someone her parents avoided, and as a wealthy, local man who had lost his family through tragedy. She had heard that the little girl had been insane, and the wife, Amelia, had killed herself. There had been hints that he was involved in the deaths, but it appeared to be only gossip. She saw him so differently now, as though what she'd seen of him before was a false thing. A different man. Since he'd touched her at Bliss House, taken care of her so thoughtfully after she'd fallen in the nursery (what a ridiculous state she'd been in!), she *had* known a different man. The desire to truly know him had lodged in her like a wonderful and awful sickness.

She blushed to think of their wedding night and how he had been so careful of her at first. So gentle. After their marriage at the courthouse, with a cousin of Randolph's as a witness, they had returned to the Astoria Hotel. Randolph had had their belongings moved from their separate rooms and into a suite the size of three of the bedrooms in her parents' house.

On seeing the room, and the waiting champagne and the vases full of roses—all red, save one massive bunch of white, which he said was to honor her "superior innocence," a phrase that embarrassed but pleased her—she had kissed him passionately and not at all innocently.

She could hardly eat the extravagant dinner of lamb and sweetbreads, soup, and several different cheeses, each served with a different wine by a footman in livery who materialized from the suite's small kitchen at every right moment. The wine helped her forget how angry her mother would be that she had eloped, had not allowed her to orchestrate the kind of wedding she had always expected her daughter to have, indeed, helped Lucy forget that everyone in her family, especially Juliet, would feel betrayed and angry. It helped her forget that they were probably looking for her even as she and Randolph sat talking, over their soup, of the things they would do in Paris. It helped quell the tiny voice deep inside her that whispered that perhaps she'd done it all not because she loved Randolph, but to spite her mother and father.

That Randolph loved her, she was certain. In the suite's gold-lit bedroom, he had untied the satin ribbons of the white peignoir that the saleswoman had helped her select, and slid it from her shoulders, murmuring with pleasure at the fairness of her skin. Laying her down on the large, soft bed, he removed his clothes, and she saw him naked for the second time in her life. But this time was so different that she didn't even think to compare it to the first. She did, though, think of Josiah and his hurried, hungry fumblings.

When she responded to Randolph's careful touches with a passion of her own, he chuckled softly and called her his "wicked little bride."

The pain—not an unhappy pain—came quickly after. Then the blood. Far more than she had believed would emerge from her body. It was certain that the blood meant she was no longer a virgin, but she feared that so much of it was a sign that her old life had died, completely and forever.

~

The dresses she chose at the House of Paquin were much more to her liking than the ones they had bought in New York, and she could hardly bear to wait the two weeks it would take to have them made. After the two weeks, they would be fitted, and the dresses would follow her home. Randolph had been detained and sent a message that she should choose the dresses without him. Also, Monsieur Philippe would join them at the suite for dinner. Perhaps Madame Paquin's assistant had taken her too much in hand, telling her firmly what he believed flattered her most, but Lucy was happy with the choices, and returned with a thick portfolio of sketches for Randolph to see. Everything was the latest fashion: a fitted navy suit with large, intricately carved buttons, another suit with a black silk jacket and a vibrant ruby skirt, a number of day dresses in lovely pastels with the newer, thinner underskirts, and three evening dresses in silk and chiffon, one in a rich rose satin trimmed in pale blue with a square neckline that was just daring enough. She suspected that her mother would be pleased.

Except that her mother would probably never speak to her again. Lucy had written to her from the Astoria, asking her to write back to her in Paris, but there hadn't yet been time for a letter to arrive. If there were to be a letter. Which she doubted. Her father? They had been married by a judge, and she did not imagine for a moment that he would agree to solemnize the marriage.

~

That Monsieur Philippe was coming to the suite for dinner was disappointing. That they had dined out only one of the four nights they'd been in Paris puzzled her. Randolph, for his worldliness, seemed content to eat without company or music around him. After attending the opera (all in Italian, which she did not speak, but she was content to see the costumes and listen to the beautiful voices), she had thought they might go to Maxim's or another fashionable restaurant, but they had just returned to pheasant and soup and ice cream at the hotel. She did convince him to keep the windows open so she could hear the evening traffic and the voices in the street. The evenings were temperate and even seductive. They made love after dinner every night, and she felt a deep satisfaction with herself, with Randolph. The idea that her parents might have imagined that she would be unhappy in Randolph's presence made her smile. If only they could see them together. See their happiness.

Surely they would want to see me happy.

At five o'clock, a uniformed boy knocked on the door with a written message from Randolph. "Please order dinner at your leisure, my dear. My head is full of business. Have the steward select the wines. We will serve ourselves this evening."

It pleased her to order dinner, and, again, she selected ice cream for dessert. This time cream and strawberries. She missed the strawberries from home. There was a patch growing on the hillock below the stone wall at the back of her parents' property, and she and Juliet had spent many mornings as children eating as many as they could before the cook had a chance to come out and pick them for the family table.

At seven, Lucy dressed in a pale green silk gown with peach chiffon trim and short, open sleeves filled with layers of chiffon. If they were staying in, she wanted to at least look as lovely for Randolph and his guest as she would have if they'd gone out. Monsieur Philippe had the mien of a man who expected little from the world—an odd associate for Randolph, but then she knew nothing about his business—and she hoped to charm him for Randolph's sake.

～

Dinner was waiting beneath covered dishes when Randolph and Monsieur Philippe arrived. Monsieur Philippe squinted even harder behind his eyeglasses than she remembered, and the lenses themselves were smudged, as though he spent a lot of time handling them. He wore fawn-colored gloves that were also marked with ungentlemanly smudges of black and gray, and he didn't bother to remove them after coming inside. When he greeted her with a quick, airy kiss on each cheek, she caught a sharp scent of body odor that was little masked by his cologne. There was some other odor, too. Not quite tobacco, but sweeter, and it clung to Randolph as well.

Randolph was more composed, but as his lips lingered on her cheek in a more husbandly kiss, she felt a pinch on her left breast. Had Randolph dared to fondle her in front of Monsieur Philippe? Even at the Maypole he had been the perfect gentleman. Lucy decided she must have been mistaken.

"Ah, wine and water!" Monsieur Philippe fell upon the set table like a desperate man. His English was perfect, if heavily accented.

"Pour me some water, Philippe. I need sustenance to make it to my room to change my jacket." He turned to Lucy. "It stinks of the streets today. Some fool smoking a cigar—on the street, mind you!—ran into me and burned a hole in the cuff. I was very lucky he missed my hand." He held up his forearm so she could see the hole.

"Oh, no. We'll have that repaired. There must be someone close to here who can take care of it. It's too bad. I'm sure they would be very sorry if they knew."

Randolph laughed. "You have a very tender heart, my love. If only the world were as kind as you see it."

He took a water glass from Monsieur Philippe and drank deeply. "Paris water tastes like misery, Philippe. How can you people drink this stuff? I hear that when J. P. Morgan visits Paris, he brings casks of his own water melted from glaciers in the north."

"I hear he drinks the blood of North African infants on Thursdays, and that when he is cut, his own blood runs the color of American money."

They laughed again, thoroughly amused with themselves, and Lucy decided that, while they were not stumbling or slurring, they must be drunk.

Before Randolph entered the bedroom, which led to the dressing room, he turned back to Lucy. "We'll have no interruptions tonight? We are serving ourselves and they will take the things away in the morning, yes?"

"Of course. Isn't that what you asked me to arrange?" For one brief moment she couldn't recall if she'd confirmed with the maître d' to have the things taken in the morning, but she was almost certain that she had. It was a peculiar request. Her own mother was fastidious about making sure the kitchen had been cleaned before any staff person could either leave or retire for the night.

At least the champagne was cold, and by the time they finished the second bottle of red wine and the thinly sliced beef accented with tarragon and a sauce that was more of a blood gravy, she was laughing along with the two men.

To her surprise, Randolph helped her move the dishes to the kitchen.

"It's not too much work for you, my love, is it?" He touched the back of her neck as they passed down the hall.

"Of course not. I'm happy to do it."

When they reached the kitchen, they put the things down and he stopped her and kissed her, his mouth sweet with strawberry ice cream and wine. "Monsieur Philippe thinks you are quite the most beautiful woman he has ever seen."

Feeling puckish, she whispered, "Can he actually see me through those awful eyeglasses?"

Before returning to the table, she suggested that they have an early night, that perhaps they could meet Monsieur Philippe for dinner at a restaurant another evening. Randolph's eyes gleamed with affection, and he cupped a hand over her breast as he nipped lightly at her ear.

"You will wear this old man's body out with your voraciousness, my love."

⁓

As they played cards, the men drank port, while Lucy occasionally sipped a blackberry cordial. Monsieur Philippe won hand after hand of the German card game, Skat, despite appearing to not be able to see his cards very well. When she noted the stacks of francs in front of him, the much smaller one in front of her, and none at all in front of Randolph, she wondered if perhaps Randolph was letting him win. Still, the game made her pleasantly homesick for Juliet, with whom she had played game after game of twenty-one on rainy days and cold winter nights.

She hadn't yet written Juliet. Would their parents let her visit Bliss House? At sixteen, Juliet was not as bold as Lucy, and was her mother's favorite. That their mother played favorites was the worst-kept secret of the family. But because Juliet was sweet and loving in addition to being obedient, Lucy could not resent her for it. She resolved to write her a letter the next morning.

The noise from the streets had all but disappeared, and after stifling a yawn, Lucy quietly announced that, if they did not mind, she would go to bed.

As she rose, Monsieur Philippe nearly overturned his chair, so quickly did he also rise from the table.

"Of course! Randolph, we have kept your beautiful young wife up too late with our old men's games."

Lucy extended her hand and begged him to sit again.

He took her hand in one of his gloved hands and the skin of whatever animal the glove was made of was warm and slick on her fingers. She had the oddest sensation that she was touching human skin, and she had to keep the shudder from her voice.

"You're so kind Monsieur Philippe. Please join us again soon."

"Ah, yes, I most certainly will, beautiful Madame Lucy."

Behind his thick, smudged lenses, his irises and lashes seemed enormous and false, as though they belonged to a doll in a dirty shop window. He stared, his eyes so full of moist pleasure and want that she looked quickly away to Randolph. What did he think of the way Monsieur Philippe was looking at her? The man had been obsequious all evening, but the increasing amounts of liquor had loosened his tongue, and now his discretion. She couldn't wait to get out of the room, and for Monsieur Philippe to leave their suite.

~

Randolph kissed her neck, and she turned into him in a happy fog of half-sleep. Each night she reveled in the new habit of their lovemaking, wondering why no one had ever told her there were such pleasures in marriage, and now she sought his lips and let the rising tension of her body carry her to wakefulness. His breath came quickly, and while a part of her wanted the beginning of their lovemaking to be as languid as she liked it to be, she didn't attempt to slow him.

"Lucy, make me the happiest of men." His words were hot in her ear and he had untied the front of her gown and his hand massaged her breast. When he gently squeezed her nipple, she felt the twinge all the way to her foot. Her head was filled with the scent of him, and the weight of his body against hers made her feel safe.

In the next moment he took that safety away as surely as if he had abandoned her on a dark Paris street.

He pulled away slightly. Lucy looked up to see the reflection of the flame of the candle on the bedside table on two circles of glass.

"What is—Randolph?"

He put his hand to her lips and shushed her quietly.

"If you love me, Lucy. It will all be over in a few minutes." Whether Monsieur Philippe heard him or not, she neither noticed nor cared. Every sensuous feeling in her body fled, driven away by a flood of revulsion and fear. As soon as she had realized that Monsieur Philippe was also in their bedroom, she understood.

"I won't!"

"My Lucy. I beg you, my love. Please listen."

She could feel the other man watching, but he didn't speak.

Randolph closed the small distance between them and firmly gripped her shoulder when she tried to wriggle away. Now his whisper was fierce.

"He *knows* things about me. There is money involved. A lot of money. I'll be ruined, Lucy."

"Nothing is worth this. Dear God, Randolph. I'm your wife!"

"And that's why only you can help me. Please, Lucy."

There was emotion in Randolph's voice that she hadn't heard before.

"My parents."

"I don't want you to be shamed. No one will ever know. You will save me. Just tonight. Only tonight."

Still, Monsieur Philippe stood silently by. Now she was certain that she could smell him.

"And if I won't?" She had defied her father, and her mother. Only a few weeks earlier, every action she had taken was weighed against what they would say or do. But now here was Randolph, challenging her. No. Not challenging. Begging. Asking for the one thing she could give him.

He said nothing, but watched her.

She turned her face away, to the window.

⌒

Though her face was still turned away—her only defense, staring at that blank, blue velvet square of Parisian sky—Monsieur Philippe thanked her profusely when he had finished. He apologized for the use of the condom, but he would not, he said, want to interfere with the happy future of his good friend, Randolph.

It was an odd speech, and she heard it with the detachment of one who was dead. When she did not respond, he sighed and bid her good night.

Only when she heard him move across the room and the door open did she turn her head. Her neck ached along with much of the rest of her body, but she raised her head from the pillow as the light from the outer room sliced its way through the darkness.

It was Randolph who opened the door for the smaller man. Randolph who was standing just inside the door. Randolph who had watched his young wife being used by the odious little man who had not taken his gloves off since he arrived.

Chapter 19

LUCY

May 1900

Lucy held the baby close as she descended from the train car, looking for her sister, Juliet, on the nearly empty platform. But Terrance was the only familiar face. She was already disconcerted by the fact that she hadn't recognized a single passenger getting on the train in Charlottesville when they had stopped there, and she had the sense that she was returning home a stranger. They had been gone for eleven months, but it felt to her like as many years. She had left Old Gate as Lucy Searle, and returned as Lucy Bliss, the jaded wife of Randolph, and mother to two-month-old Michael Searle Bliss, the child she carried in her arms.

Even the carriage Terrance had brought to meet them was new to her, already bearing the Bliss coat of arms—blue and white, with three sheaves of wheat on the shield—which Randolph had researched when they arrived in London from Paris. The ostentatiousness of the coat of arms, even though its placement on the panel closest to the right front wheel was discreet by Randolph's standards, mortified her. Terrance, too, was different. She hadn't known him, really, but given the number of letters and telegrams that he and Randolph had exchanged while they traveled, she understood how Randolph relied on him. He had shaved his head and seemed even more reticent than before. As she crossed the station platform, he touched his hat deferentially. However it wasn't her face he was watching, but the bundled child in her arms. As his steady gaze moved to a point behind her, where their luggage was being unloaded, she felt her face grow warm. What did he know about her? About the child?

She ached to go straight to her parents' house, but she knew her mother would receive her coldly, if she received her at all. Faye had written that Selina would not talk about her in public, or even in private to her good friend, Pinky, Faye's mother. And if someone brought up Lucy's name to her, she would immediately change the subject to her younger daughter, Juliet. Lucy had written Juliet to tell her when they'd be arriving, but she knew that their mother and father sometimes intercepted her letters. Very occasionally a letter would get through, and Juliet would write back. But it was like two people having a conversation that could only be made sense of about a third of the time. Lucy suspected that her parents let a few letters get through on purpose so that Juliet could answer and Lucy would keep writing. Randolph had told her that it was the way spying worked: Enemies kept tabs on each other by sharing small amounts of information. That way the tension was slowly released. Lucy could feel the tension coming from her parents all the way across the Atlantic Ocean. Tension, or perhaps simply disgust. Both she and Randolph had written to her parents and had received no reply. Randolph complained that theirs was the worse kind of uncivilized behavior. Lucy bit her tongue at that remark. Randolph had no right to call anyone else's behavior uncivilized.

⁓

It seemed an ill omen to Lucy that it should begin to rain as the carriage made its way up the lane to Bliss House. Terrance had rolled down and secured the rain curtains on the sides of the carriage, but she could still see the house beyond the horses. The trees along the drive were swathed in clouds of wet, unearthly green. Randolph leaned forward hungrily as though he were about to greet a lover whom he hadn't seen in many years. The baby began to cry in his basket.

Odette and Mason, whom she hadn't yet met, stood with umbrellas at the edge of the drive. She was sad not to see Carrie, who had written that she could not get along with Terrance, and had found a position in another part of the state. Behind Odette and Mason, the rain had seemed to wash all color away from the enormous house. The yellow brick now looked jaundiced, and the windows reflected the gray sky like mirrors streaked with water. Why hadn't she ever noticed the iron works around the windows and surrounding the roof? Upright and wickedly sharp, they matched the length of iron fence standing at the front of the garden like a row of fierce soldiers.

When the carriage stopped and Randolph got out to help her down, she looked up at the second-story windows, remembering the woman and girl who had watched her from over the gallery railing. But she could see no one in the windows now, and she felt terribly relieved.

"Welcome, Missus Bliss. Shall I take Master Michael?" Odette reached with her free arm to take the basket containing the crying baby. He had been quiet for most of the train ride, unless his diaper had been wet or he was hungry. Lucy was grateful every day that he was a calm child.

Reflexively, Lucy pulled the basket to her. It had been her understanding with Randolph that she should be the only one to care for Michael Searle, but once they were on the train, he had begun talking about Odette as someone they might trust to care for him. She wondered at his change of heart. It was critical that no one handle their son whom they couldn't trust to be completely discreet. There were things about Michael Searle, about his birth and his delicate, imperfectly formed body, that, if widely known, would make pariahs of them all.

"His name is Michael Searle. Not just 'Michael.'" Lucy's tone was harsh, but Odette was unfazed.

Lucy had suggested to Randolph that her parents would have some mercy on her—on them both—if they named the baby after her father.

"Mercy for me from the Reverend Edward Michael Searle? Well, that's sure to get me into heaven, my dear." He was sarcastic, but still relented, though unpleasantly. "My next son, assuming *he* is fully capable of becoming a man, will be better named Randolph than this poor waif, I reckon."

He had looked down at the baby, whose mild features already were more like Lucy's than his own, with a mixture of pity and dislike.

Lucy was anxious. "Let's go inside. It's miserable out here, and no good for the baby."

"I say wait!" Randolph stopped at the front door of the house, barring anyone from entering.

The baby cried louder. In the woods, some bird also cried out as though in answer.

"I intend to carry my bride over the threshold. The last time she was here, she was not yet my bride."

"Randolph, please." Michael Searle's cries were agony for Lucy.

"Take that basket, Odette. In fact, take Michael Searle on into the house. All this damp can't be good for his lungs. I'm sure Missus Bliss will agree."

Reluctantly Lucy gave the basket to Odette, who hurried into the house. She disappeared with the baby into the shadowy hall.

"A little re-enactment of our arrival at our suite at the Astoria, my love. Except this is a place you'll never need to leave."

"Yes, yes, of course." Lucy tried a smile. The girl who had come to the *Walpurgisnacht* party, and to hear Hannah Tanner speak, would have thought of this moment as a happy dream. She willed herself to be that girl once again. "Mind your gloves, Randolph. The hem of my dress is certainly wet." It was one of her traveling dresses from Paris. One of her treasures. If Randolph's words were true, and she were to never leave, she might never have cause to wear it again.

Randolph lifted her effortlessly into his arms despite his fifty-plus years, and they stepped over the threshold and into the house. The chandelier above the great hall was lighted, along with all the lamps in the galleries. Every table held an elegant arrangement of flowers. There were more flowers than she had ever seen in one place, including their suite in Paris. The air was filled with the lazy scent of lilies and hyacinths.

Despite the presence of the servants, and Terrance, who was obviously not quite a servant, Randolph kissed her. She returned the kiss, slightly embarrassed, but with a sense of relief that the house was not nearly as grim as she had feared. It had surely been her own fears and worries that had made the idea of returning fraught with foreboding. No stranger awaited to share her bed or ruin her sleep. (Monsieur Philippe had returned one night, just before they had left Paris, and there had been no pretense of dinner. Knowing what would happen the moment Randolph had mentioned his name, Lucy had gotten quite drunk on champagne, so that the nightmare of his lovemaking would be somewhat dulled.)

When Randolph had had *his* moment—and it certainly was his moment—he set her down, and with a final kiss on her cheek, told Terrance to please show Missus Bliss to her room, and then to the nursery. For Odette had, indeed, disappeared with Michael Searle.

Randolph marched off to the library with the comment that he had nearly a year's business to take care of, and that Mason should please see to the rest of the luggage and the carriage.

"Mister Bliss has suggested that you take the floral bedroom overlooking the garden, and for you to also use the adjoining room as your morning room."

Mister Bliss. Lucy had never forgotten that her father had referred to Terrance as Randolph's *bastard* that day in the theater. It made sense that Terrance would be better trusted than any other servant if he was, indeed, Randolph's son.

"No. If Odette has gone to the nursery, I'll go there now. I know where it is."

"Very well." Terrance did not nod or bow, but turned from the staircase and went to help Mason with the baggage.

She would ask Odette where the floral bedroom was, after she'd gotten Michael Searle away from the awful nursery.

~

How she had dreamed of being chatelaine of Bliss House, imagining it to need a woman's touch again after Randolph's decades of absence. In France, he had suggested that she pick out some fabrics and furniture, and he had bought a number of paintings. There were things on their way for the nursery, as well, though she had kept the purchase of them to herself, as Randolph had made no comment about where the baby would sleep, except to say that children belonged in the nursery.

She remembered the nursery only too well. Josiah had protested that nothing had been thrown at them, that Lucy had suddenly ducked away from him, crying out, then seemed to dodge invisible things in the air. "It was pitch dark," he said. "Otherwise I would've known it was you right away. I didn't see anything." Perhaps he hadn't seen anything, after all. He was not a cruel man.

Lucy hurried up the staircase to the second floor, remembering how the galleries had been full of people. Now they belonged to her, and she could spend all the time she wished looking at the paintings or sitting in one of the quiet window nooks with a book. How Juliet would love the house, if only she were allowed to come.

One of the bedrooms she passed on the way to the nursery had its door open and she stopped to look inside. The room felt stale, as though the door had been shut for a very long time, and was only just opened in the past few minutes. Surely this would be Randolph's room, decorated in muted tones of blue and red and brown. A man's room. The headboard of the enormous bed was carved with people and animals and images of forgotten lands. Its brutal hunting scenes alarmed her, but not nearly as much as the idea that the house had sat, dormant and lonely, in their absence. She had the sense that Bliss House did not like to be lonely.

Lucy gasped. "Oh, dear Lord in heaven."

Odette sat in a painted rocking chair, Michael Searle swaddled in a blanket in her arms. She put a finger to her lips to hush Lucy, indicating that Michael Searle was asleep, or was close to it. Had she changed him before sitting down? Surely, Lucy thought, she would be registering some look of shock.

But Lucy's horror was at the state of the nursery. If it could even be called that anymore.

Odette whispered. "Before you say anything, you need to know that Terrance wouldn't let me change the room in any way. He said it was on Mister Bliss's orders, but I can't imagine such a thing."

In her arms, Michael Searle squirmed and yawned, punching one small hand free of the blanket. He gave a sigh and went back to sleep.

After a moment, Odette got up slowly, laid Michael Searle in a hand–hewn cradle resting near the rocker, and loosened the blanket around him, as the room was warm.

She came to stand near Lucy, still keeping her voice low.

"I got to know Carrie some before she left here, and she said that neither you nor your mother would put up with having a baby in this room, because it's more than just the furniture being old. And these . . ." She indicated the cases full of taxidermy animals, the dead butterflies, and the plethora of staring dolls.

Lucy shuddered. It was no different from the first time she'd seen it, and it was even more alarming during the day. What sort of mother would let her daughter play in such a place?

Mad, they'd said. The little girl had been mad.

"No. I didn't think you would want him in here. But I had no choice. I hope you understand."

Yes. Lucy understood. She wanted to think that Randolph—like so many men—had no feeling for the comfort and care of children. But she knew it was something far worse: that he was punishing her and Michael Searle. He blamed her for Michael Searle's deformity, and he had done from the moment the doctor, holding the baby, had called him into a corner, just out of Lucy's view.

"He'll stay in my room until this room is changed or we fix up another."

"You don't want him in this room, Missus Bliss. No child should ever sleep in this room again, no matter what changes you make to it. No, ma'am."

"We'll see." But even as she said the words, she thought of Randolph's daughter and Amelia. How they had stood outside this room, watching her.

The cradle wasn't heavy, and Odette followed with it easily as Lucy carried the sleeping Michael Searle down the gallery and across to her new bedroom. There she had Odette replace the long, upholstered bench at the foot of the bed with the cradle. In London, Randolph had insisted that the baby sleep in the second bedroom of their suite, so that Lucy might be a convenient wife, as she was no longer pregnant.

Now, in their own house, she had her own room, and she was not going to let Randolph get between her and her child. And Michael Searle certainly wasn't going to grow up in that hellish nursery.

～

A few days later, Lucy's first communication from her family came in the form of a note from Juliet. From its scrawled nature, Lucy understood that she had written it in haste. Their parents would not let her come to Bliss House under any circumstances. There was no mention of when they might see each other, though Juliet did not say she had been forbidden from seeing her sister completely. She wrote that she was desperate, too, to see her new nephew, and that she couldn't believe that she was already an aunt.

"It is my dearest wish that I see him before he has his first tooth. We shall make it very soon, I do hope."

Lucy folded the note and put it in the drawer of her writing desk, too dismayed to answer. At lunch she told Randolph about it.

"The good reverend is going to make you pay for your indiscretion. I'm sorry for you, my dear, but I have no interest in seeing either of your parents again."

"What if the rest of the town follows their lead? What if we are ostracized?"

Randolph smiled. "It is we who do the ostracizing. I will not be extending any more invitations to them. But it's a shame about Juliet. She is a sweet girl."

Juliet was chaste and faithful.

Wasn't I once chaste? What if Juliet were to know what I have become?
She pushed the thought from her mind. There were no Monsieur
Philippes in Old Gate.

Lucy toyed with her napkin, reluctant to mention the nursery,
but she felt she had to.

"Randolph, you know that I've put Michael Searle in my room
for now."

"He is young. If that seems good to you, that's acceptable."

"I was thinking that we should change the nursery into another
guest room. Perhaps paint it a nice, sunny yellow. Freshen it and get
some new furniture. You know, fewer cabinets and things, and perhaps add a pair of single beds and a small seating area near the front
windows. It has such a lovely view of the drive."

Randolph shook his head. "No. Change anything else you like,
but I prefer that the nursery remain as it is. Whether the boy uses
it or not is of no concern to me."

"But those animals! There are things in that room—" It wasn't
so much the animals, but the *presence* in the nursery. The girl,
Tamora, and Amelia. Lucy knew they were still there, though she
hadn't yet seen them again.

"I won't discuss it, Lucy. You have a dozen other rooms in this
house that you can alter to your liking. That one stays as it is."

"That's madness. Why would you want to keep those things?
They're hideous."

He put down his fork and looked at her with what could only
be described as amused malevolence. It was a look she had never
seen in his eyes and it frightened her.

"Perhaps when you are old and hideous, my dear, I should pitch
you on the trash heap. Or have you stuffed and kept in the room
with the other animals."

Lucy stood up from the table and would have stalked from the room
in disgust and anger if she hadn't noticed Terrance standing in the open
doorway to the kitchen. She took a deep breath, and said, "Excuse

me." As she left the room, she heard Randolph chuckle behind her, then ask Terrance to bring him a whiskey and his humidor.

At least, Lucy thought, he hadn't insisted that she move Michael Searle back into the nursery. A small mercy.

Randolph issued the first invitation of their new tenure in Bliss House the very next day, inviting a few of his favorites to dinner and to see the lantern slides he had purchased on their trip. Most were of Paris and the sites of the exposition, which had been about to open before they left for London.

Terrance had engaged two sisters, one as housemaid and the other as cook, to help now that Odette was spending more time with Michael Searle.

Lucy had approached Odette carefully, inviting her into the morning room for a cup of tea, with Michael Searle in his cradle nearby. She quietly impressed the dire need for confidentiality, and, perhaps, the idea that Randolph might mete out some punishment if she were to spread any tales or lies about Michael Searle.

"Missus Bliss, Mason and I have been at Bliss House a long time. I've had care of a child, and I've had care of secrets. And I have made sure to keep both most carefully. I have never truly liked Mister Bliss, but our employment has depended on it. But I do like you. What I see in that cradle is one of God's precious children. Nothing more. Nothing less."

That had been that. She treated Michael Searle with a firm tenderness that Lucy had never before seen in a servant.

Faye and Josiah were the first to arrive for the dinner party. Lucy had been nervous. She had hosted small soirées in London and

Paris (Monsieur Philippe notwithstanding) for acquaintances and business associates of Randolph's, but never in her own home. Bliss House *was* her home. It had to be because she had no other.

With the exception of Faye and Josiah, the crowd was older, but the women were particularly kind, and while they weren't of her parents' set, they were all from the county. Douglas, Randolph's brother, and his wife, Mary, had come to stay. Mary was a faded beauty who sat at Randolph's right hand. Faye whispered that she had once been something of a siren, but she'd grown enormously fat and now rarely left her house. They were at least as wealthy as Randolph. The rumor was that they were even wealthier, but such a thing didn't matter at all to Lucy. She was much more worried about what they would think of *her.*

After dinner, when the women had retired to the salon and the men were having cigars in the dining room, Faye took Lucy aside.

"I know it's telling tales out of school, Lucy-pie, but your mother looks dreadful. When I saw her at church on Sunday, she looked as though she'd been crying buckets. Juliet says she and your father are fighting all the time. He's worried that you and Randolph haven't baptized that precious little lamb of yours."

"If they're so worried, they should come here. They won't even let Juliet visit me." It was anguish to hear of her parents' upset. She had tried to think of them as cruel. They had certainly seemed so at an ocean's distance. But they were still her parents.

Faye arranged a stray bit of lace on Lucy's Paris gown. "I could kill you for this dress. Every man in the dining room was looking at you as though they wanted to bend you over the table and ravish you."

Lucy knew it was the champagne talking, but she was still amused.

"You used to dress like such a mouse. It's like you came back from Paris a libertine." Her face was very close now, and Lucy could see a gossamer line of perspiration along the baby curls at the top of Faye's forehead. "*Are* you a libertine, darling? What did you and Randolph get up to there in Paris? I bet you did naughty things."

Now Lucy was uncomfortable, and she remembered how Faye and Josiah had stayed long with the naked dancers beneath the Maypole. She looked away. "Oh, Missus Lovejoy's cordial glass is empty. Where has Terrance gone?"

"Fiddlesticks, Lucy. Don't be such a frump. I *saw* you, remember? I know the things that Randolph likes. Josiah and I were coming here long before you."

"Please, Faye. Not now. You're being silly."

"Why no May Day party this year? Are you spoiling the fun?"

Exasperated, Lucy excused herself without responding, leaving Faye to smile knowingly and take herself off to sit with a trio of women who had settled to a game of cards in the corner. Lucy tended to Missus Lovejoy's cordial herself, and then rang the bell for Terrance, who eventually arrived looking a bit bored.

"Will you please tell my husband that now would be a good time to begin the lantern show? Is everything ready?"

Terrance nodded and strode off in his steady, unhurried way.

Perhaps because the theater was the place where Randolph had first taken her hand for more than just a casual greeting, Lucy was pleased to have suggested that they use it for the showing of the lantern slides they'd bought on their trip. Terrance had set up the tightly woven silk screen and had Mason assist him in arranging the chairs.

This night, with the majesty of the freshly aired house, and the recent kindness of Randolph, Lucy was almost proud to be both mistress of the house and Randolph's wife. He took her arm to lead the party upstairs, and the sound of the guests' voices made her feel terribly gay. Michael Searle was already asleep with Odette watching over him. Lucy felt like a young woman again, and not at all like a drudge, as her mother had often complained that mother-hood had made *her*.

Lucy sat near the front, beside Faye. Randolph started with slides of London, of Buckingham Palace and the palace guards, and of the Tower of London. Then there was Paris: the Tuileries, the Eiffel Tower, shining new automobiles, the massive halls built for the exposition, images of foreigners in turbans and kimonos and cowboy garb. Randolph gave a running commentary, describing what the sites had truly been like. Several of the guests had never left Virginia, and Randolph was happy to show off his knowledge.

It was among the slides of people from far-flung lands that other, more vulgar slides suddenly showed up on the screen.

Lucy wanted to look away, but she found herself transfixed. The images seemed to have been shot in the secret club in Paris to which Randolph had taken her. Early in the evening at the club, there had been only live music, but after midnight the music moved offstage, into the wings. Onstage were couples and groups of people, their bodies oiled or even painted, writhing, some dancing. Many of the women were of other races, and alarmingly beautiful, and the men were white, with the exception of a few, and played at cruelly abusing the women. Their sex acts had been mostly simulated. "All smoke and mirrors and nothing real," Randolph had complained. Lucy, excited, and more than a little ashamed of her willingness to watch the shows, had worn a veil when they visited the club a second time.

But what was happening in these slides did not look simulated. The pleasure looked real. The violence looked real. The pain looked more than real.

Lucy gasped when she saw Monsieur Philippe's face—for surely it was him. And the woman—her pale body contorted beneath his whip—looked too much like Lucy herself. Beside her, Faye tittered. Surely everyone now thought that it *was* her. She wanted to sink into the polished floor of the half-dark room.

Around her, the other guests were restless. Occasionally one of the men made a low, appreciative sound in his throat. Each time the screen went blank for an upcoming slide, Lucy steeled herself for some new shock. What was Randolph thinking? Finally, one of the men groaned outright. Douglas, Randolph's brother, shouted, "Enough! Turn it off, Randolph."

There was a look of true fear on the face of the man now pictured on the screen. He'd been stripped of his clothes, and one of the women in the small group half surrounding him held the leash of some muscular hound who strained at the man, its teeth bared, its enormous hackles fanned along its neck. Somehow, Lucy knew that the next slide would show the man being savaged. Yet as she stared, she noticed that the faces of the three men in the slide—though different—all bore a remarkable resemblance to one another. The same broad forehead and strong nose. The same full lips and aggressive brow. They all looked like Randolph. But when she blinked, the men were no longer similar at all.

Abruptly, Randolph extinguished the lantern, and for a long moment the silence of the room was so deep that Lucy thought she might disappear forever inside of it.

~

The party ended quickly afterward, with Randolph uncharacteristically quiet. Lucy wasn't sure how he had expected the evening to end, but she suspected that he had thought to titillate them with the pornographic images. Everything she knew about him told her that he loved the attention, loved to shock people. How could she have thought that first May Day celebration so sophisticated? Since Paris and the clubs, and the vile Monsieur Philippe, she had come to see such things as tawdry, destructive fantasies. But she bore them for Randolph's sake. Even after all he'd made her bear in Paris, and his cruel joke about having her stuffed, she was still his wife, and had now borne his child.

After the guests were gone, and she had been to her room to give Michael Searle his late-night feeding, she knocked softly on Randolph's bedroom door. When he didn't answer, she turned the door handle to find it was unlocked. Randolph stood in the dark, looking out the window.

"Can you not sleep?"

"We shouldn't have come back here. We should have stayed in England, or settled somewhere else. I still have the house on Long Island. Would you like to live there?"

Lucy went to stand beside him. Despite the summer heat, his bedroom was much cooler than hers, and she shivered in her gown. It was almost as cool as a late fall night.

"People change, Randolph. Maybe the slides weren't to their taste."

He turned toward her. "They don't want me to be happy."

"Randolph, they're your friends. Of course they want you to be happy. Josiah wouldn't leave you alone until he saw you smile again tonight. Isn't that friendship?"

"You don't feel it, do you? It's your innocence. You won't let go of it. I think you deliberately misunderstand me. You're stubbornly young, Lucy."

She didn't argue further. Didn't he know that she had been trying to let go of her innocence for as long as she could remember? But this *it* of which he spoke. She wasn't sure she wanted to know what *it* might be. The strange element that had crept into his voice, and his face, exposed by the risen moon through the window, seemed a lot like suspicion. But what terrible thing could he possibly suspect of her?

Chapter 20

LUCY

May 1900

The message from her mother saying she would call the next day sent Lucy into a panic. Had she already heard gossip about the previous night's party? Lucy had wanted to go to church the previous Sunday to speak with her, but had been afraid that her father might condemn her, as well as Randolph, from the pulpit. She hoped that a blessing from her mother would ease their way, even though she knew that having her mother come to Bliss House was like asking a snake to bite her.

Selina Searle had been angry for an entire year. Anger piled on anger.

How could she make her mother love her again? It had come to her that, if she told her mother the truth about Michael Searle, she might gain her sympathy, and at the same time save herself. Randolph barely acknowledged the poor child. Lucy could not be mother, father, and loving grandparent to him. She needed someone to share the burden of her child's life.

From the first moment she had held him in her arms, she had loved him. He fitted perfectly against her and when she held him to her breast, he had suckled hungrily as she stroked the fine down on his delicate skull.

It was a skull that Randolph had suggested should be crushed into something formless. Crushed out of existence. How she had pleaded for the child's life behind the closed door of her bedroom of the London townhouse they had let. Randolph said he didn't trust the London hospitals and had engaged a private doctor and nurse to come when it was time.

Just after the birth, the doctor and Randolph had stood in the corner of the bedroom, whispering. Arguing. The hard-looking nurse had cleaned and swaddled the crying baby and was about to give him to Lucy when the doctor waved her away. Randolph looked over at Lucy, and then the baby, his face wearing a look of incomprehension. Randolph, who was always in command of himself and of everything around him. His fists were clenched, his eyes were wide. Thank God she had insisted on being awake during the birth. What might they have done if she had been asleep?

At last, her mother would know. A kind of insurance for Michael Searle's life.

She dressed herself carefully, putting on a day dress in her mother's favorite color of daffodil yellow. A feminine color. A color that made her mother smile. She dressed her hair in a proper bun, piling it full and round in the latest Gibson Girl style. Her mother, old as she was, always wore the latest of everything.

⌒

Standing in the shadow outside of her bedroom, she could hear Terrance's low, confiding voice and her mother's terse answers.

Selina was never concerned about being pleasant to servants, a fact that Lucy knew plagued her father, who was often kinder to servants than he was to his own family. Juliet had written that he had been so fond of sweet Carrie that he wondered aloud why she did not even try to return to the house after Lucy's elopement. He did not blame her. Lucy was surprised, too, that Carrie hadn't even tried to go back to her parents' house when she'd unexpectedly left Bliss House months before Lucy and Randolph returned to Old Gate.

"Hello, Mother." Lucy tried on a smile as she hurried down the stairs. Her mother liked it when people smiled at her. But when she saw her mother's frown, she slowed her step. The desire to have her mother's forgiveness dimmed.

Quickly, surprisingly, her mother's frown changed to a bright smile that lighted up her lovely face. It was always a kind of revelation to see how truly beautiful her mother was. In her pearl gray silk skirt and jacket—cinched fashionably at her waist, so that you would never know she had two grown children—she looked only about thirty-five years old, rather than almost fifty. The rich hues of her reddish-pink blouse and the roses on the hat that crowned her full, still-blond hair, put a bloom of health on her cheeks. Lucy had inherited the broader features of her father; she had always envied her mother's sculpted cheekbones, and slender nose with its neat tip and well-defined nostrils. Though one of Lucy's friends had confided that she thought Selina looked like she was always smelling something she didn't much care for.

Did her own mother like her? A part of her suspected that she did not, and she certainly didn't love her as much as she loved Juliet. It was a truth she knew she should try not to forget.

But now her mother was here. And she was smiling.

⌢

They drank tea in the salon, the air heavy with the scent of summer roses. Randolph had planted the roses for his first wife, Amelia, and while they had not been carefully tended in the decades he had been away from Bliss House, they still bloomed madly. Lucy had a plan to replant the entire garden and make it glorious again.

"This room is like a mausoleum with all this hideous dark furniture. I suppose Randolph won't let you change it? He *would* cling to the past. Amelia's things. Doesn't it bother you, Lucinda?"

Her mother hadn't spoken to her since her elopement, and now she was complaining about the furniture. Lucy might have laughed if she weren't already worried out of her mind. She didn't say so to her mother, but of course she had changes planned. Though she had no quarrel with Amelia.

She poured the tea, feeling the heavy ache in her breasts. If Michael Searle were to cry, the milk would come, and in front of her mother! Surely her mother hadn't breastfed her or her sister. There had always been nurses and a nanny.

Suddenly Lucy felt six years old again, afraid of the woman sitting in front of her.

"Your hands are shaking, Lucinda. You're spilling the tea."

Lucy set the pot on the tray and tried to breathe. She tried to formulate words in her head, to say the many things she desperately wanted to say, but she was overcome. Finally she put her face in her hands, and wept.

"Lucinda, what in the world is wrong with you? Compose yourself, please. The servants—that dreadful Terrance—will hear."

Selina sounded irritated, but there was a sharp edge of anguish in her voice.

"For heaven's sake." She stood up and came around the table to stand beside Lucy. Feeling her near, Lucy reached for the gray silk of her skirt and clutched it in her hand.

Selina started to brush her away, but then seemed to think better of it. She rested a hand on Lucy's shoulder.

"Bearing children makes a woman ridiculous. You've got to get control of yourself." She squeezed Lucy's shoulder lightly, and her voice softened. "You're obviously doing too much. I can't imagine what it must have been to travel so long with an infant. What was Randolph thinking? Where is he?"

Lucy wiped her eyes to try to stop the tears. Other girls had their mothers nearby when they gave birth. Mothers who came to stay to at least supervise the servants. But her mother had been an ocean away, and now she was here. Though her passages were full of tears, she could smell the lemon verbena from her mother's closet, where her dresses were stored. How she had loved to hide in that closet when her mother was out, burying herself in the beautiful dresses, pretending her mother was in them.

"Something's wrong with Michael Searle." She took her mother's hand. "I want you to see. Please come with me to see."

Selina tore her hand away. "Stop. Don't be excessive. I know you think I don't care, Lucinda, but I did ask after him. Faye told her mother that he looked very well."

When Lucy took her mother's hand again—and this time she did not pull away—she found it cold and trembling.

Lucy dropped her voice to a whisper. "Those first days, I think Randolph wanted to kill him. Our own son. He said he was a monster."

⌒

Michael Searle was sleeping. Odette got up from her chair and nodded to them as she went out.

"Why isn't he in a nursery of his own?" Selina leaned over the cradle to look at Michael Searle, but Lucy couldn't read her face. Was she pleased, or disappointed? At least she was whispering. She

191

said nothing about the way he looked, his mild, rounded features that looked so very like a Searle's.

"The furniture is too old. I'm having the room next to mine redone." Lucy didn't mention the animals or the sense she had that the room belonged to someone or something she couldn't see.

"Fine. Now, Lucy. I've seen him. He's a charming baby. May I go?"

Lucy bent to the cradle and lifted Michael Searle as gently as she could, not wanting to wake him. Though the cradle was lovely, it didn't suit their needs, and she had written cabinetmakers in Pennsylvania for a new, taller crib. She laid him on her bed and carefully adjusted his gown to expose the diaper.

"Lucy, this is unnatural. I don't understand." Selina began to pace, her voice louder. "I don't know why I agreed to come here. You wouldn't listen. In God's name why didn't you listen to me?"

Unnatural. The doctor had used the same word.

Lucy opened the diaper to find it was wet. She hadn't thought to lay out another, so consumed had she been with showing her mother. Michael Searle stirred.

"You must, Mother. You must. Please. I can't bear it alone anymore."

Though the afternoon had been beautifully clear, a cloud passed over the sun, darkening the room. She looked for shock on her mother's face, but found only sadness.

"I didn't understand at first. Then the doctor explained that Michael Searle is like a boy, but also a girl. He's not a monster. Randolph thinks he's a monster, but he's just a baby. Do you see?"

Michael Searle's face crumpled as he began to wake, unhappy.

"Cover him. Please."

Her mother stood at the window looking out at the garden.

"She was so proud of these gardens, as though she'd gone out there herself and planted them. I suppose when you don't know someone well, you talk about things like gardens. I never saw a woman so pale. The child, too. She had a strange name. Jewish. What was it?" She paused a moment, tapped on the window as though asking for an answer. "Tamora. That was it. Such a strange, un-Christian name for a little girl."

"You could at least say something, Mother."

Selina turned from the window. She looked sad, now. Not angry. "Randolph was right. It would've been a kindness to kill it."

Lucy's arms stiffened around her child.

"Why would you say such a thing? You're my mother. Look at him. He's a baby."

"He's your judgment for marrying that man. A judgment on all of us. You had to do the first thing that came into your foolish head. You never would listen to me. Sometimes I think you hated me." She gave an unpleasant laugh. "Even as a baby, you'd turn your head from me, preferring the nurse or your father. Why couldn't you be like Juliet? Why did you have to punish me every day just because you were born?"

Lucy crossed the room to where her mother stood, her head full of her mother's accusations.

"Hold him. Just take him. He needs you." Michael Searle felt unbearably warm in her arms. If only her mother would take him, she would love him.

"I've seen him. You have what you wanted. His life will be a misery, and you, his mother, are responsible. I won't be coming back here to this godforsaken house. I don't care what you convince your father to do." Her lip wore a sheen of perspiration, and a strand of hair hung in an untidy curl at her temple.

Lucy had a sudden image of bright green grass all around her, and her mother standing over a two-year-old Juliet, helping her hold a miniature croquet mallet. They laughed in the sunshine, their faces glowing with happiness. She remembered the desperate joy she had felt at seeing her mother's smile, the feeling of yearning for her. "I have never hated you. How could I hate you?"

"Don't make me stay here, Lucinda. I have nothing for you. I'm sorry, but I can't stay here."

"It was always Juliet. Father loves Juliet, and he loves me. But you won't."

Michael Searle began to fret again. The rubber teat Lucy had given him fell from his mouth and onto the floor, but neither of them noticed.

The air felt hot and thick to Lucy, and the ache in her breasts increased, tightening with Michael Searle's whimpers. Beads of sweat glistened on her mother's forehead. Her mother, her always careful, spotless mother. *If you could see yourself! How mortified you would be.* Was it the sun, beating through the windows? No. It was more than that. The very air seemed ready to ignite.

"I must go!" Selina was also breathless.

Lucy hardly knew what she was doing as she stepped in front of her mother. Her movements felt alarmingly slow and painful, as though she were trying to walk through boiling syrup.

"You won't stop me." Selina pushed at Lucy's shoulder, causing her to stumble. The blanket in which she'd wrapped Michael Searle unfurled, and before either of them knew what was happening, he lay, stunned and silent, on the carpet between them.

They stared at him for a moment that seemed to last a lifetime.

Lucy sank to the floor and quickly gathered Michael Searle into her arms. He stared up at her, his eyes wide and focused on her as though asking *why*, and it broke her heart.

"Lucy, what have you done?" Selina whispered.

Michael Searle squeezed his eyes shut and began to scream.

Selina dropped her gaze and turned to leave the room.

Holding Michael Searle close against her shoulder, the errant blanket laid over him, Lucy followed. Her own gown clung to her with perspiration, and Michael Searle burned against her. But she would not let him go again. No, she would not ever!

At the doorway to her room, she stopped. The wood floor was hot through the fine leather soles of her satin morning shoes. Across the gallery, Lucy saw two familiar shadows for the briefest of moments, but then they disappeared.

The vast hall trembled with waves of heat, like those off of a summer lake at noon. Overhead, the chandelier swayed like an uncertain pendulum. Selina gripped the gallery railing just outside the room and seemed to propel herself to the head of the stairs. Lucy couldn't hear the sound her mother's fashionable black boots made on the floor, but only Michael Searle's cries. She wanted to shout to her mother to stay off of the stairs, but she was inchoate. Why couldn't she speak?

Then she heard something else through the waves of heat. A voice that blended with Michael Searle's cries, like a whisper in a storm.

"Selina."

Where had she heard that voice before? It was feminine, commanding. It was a voice that frightened her, a voice that might come in the night to awaken you, unbidden, from a dream. She caressed the back of Michael Searle's head, touching him gently, wanting to give him all the comfort he needed.

Her mother started for the stairs, unsteady, holding tightly to the railing. She had just reached the top of the stairs when the voice came again, filling the hall.

"Selina!"

Now her mother heard, and she looked back at Lucy. The fear written on her face told Lucy that she knew it wasn't she who spoke. Lucy shook her head. This had nothing to do with her.

When Selina looked away, down at the front door, Lucy could see her mother's desperation, her need to reach that door to leave the house and never return. But her foot slipped as it reached for the step, and her mouth twisted with surprise and then pain. It was the slowness with which it all happened that let Lucy see, as though it were some kind of terrible gift.

Why had this thought come to her? That she should be celebrating what was happening in front of her, that she should consider it a gift? She would remember that thought. The shame of it.

In the seconds it took for her mother to tumble and slide her way down to the landing, Lucy felt the air clear. Michael Searle's tiny scream was pure and sharp in her ears, and her mother lay, unmoving, on the landing.

Somewhere above Lucy—or was it behind her or around her?— someone was laughing. There, above, on the landing outside the ballroom, a shadow without face or form quivered with what Lucy could only describe as delight.

Chapter 21

AMELIA

December 1878

Randolph was determined to have a party between Thanksgiving and Christmas that would formally introduce both Amelia and Bliss House to the neighborhood, and presented Amelia with a guest list so she could write out the invitations. There wouldn't be all that much more for her to do. He had set the household operations in motion long before she'd arrived.

He had hired Maud Poole as a cook, and her husband, Clayton, as a driver and houseman, a housemaid, and a groundskeeper who worked with Mason on the orchard operation when there wasn't much to do in the gardens. Maud had worked for a local judge who had died as Bliss House was being built, and had a heavy hand with sauces, but made excellent biscuits, which, Randolph said, was a skill highly prized in the neighborhood. When Amelia gave her the recipes she'd brought from Long Island, Maud had sniffed and said that she didn't like fish, and, besides, trout was about the only kind of fish they were likely to get when the weather warmed, and they certainly wouldn't be getting any crabs this far from an ocean. The way she said it made Amelia think that Maud didn't quite believe in oceans. Her husband, Clayton, shuffled audibly from room to room, coughing frequently from his former job in the mines. He was far less recalcitrant than his wife, who bullied him, though she was—to Amelia's shock—nearly twenty years younger than her fifty-year-old husband, despite the streaks of gray in her hair and the faded blue eyes in her plump face.

A laundress came to the house three times a week; she was the sister of the housemaid. Both were some kin to Maud and Clayton, but when Maud tried to tell her of the connection, Amelia listened politely for a few moments, then changed the subject back to the menu. Her own mother had long ago warned her about getting too involved in servants' lives.

"If you're so close that you know the names of their children, then you're too involved. They'll take advantage and you'll never be able to let them go unless they start stealing from you. Your heart is too tender, Amelia."

Because it was such a struggle to make the house her own, she was afraid that she was coming to despise it, despite its beauty. Or was it that she had begun to despise Randolph?

More than anything she missed their house on Long Island with its many smaller rooms, and stuffy but dear furniture she had inherited from her D'Jarnette grandmother. She missed having neighbors nearby. She missed walking to her dressmaker's shop, and her mother's house, and the quaint tearoom where she could meet her sister for lunch. At least she wasn't completely alone, though she hadn't made what anyone could call *friends*.

A few of the neighborhood women had called on her: heavily pregnant Selina Searle, the wife of the local priest, and Katharine

"Pinky" Archer, who seemed to consider herself the most important of the local gentry, dropping names that Amelia understood she was supposed to know and be impressed by. Reluctantly, Amelia had returned their calls, and had even been taken to a garden party at the house of Pinky Archer's mother-in-law. She, too, had been a name-dropper. There were several of those names on the list that Randolph had given her.

Parties filled her with dread. Yes, she knew well how to throw them. But Tamora was her Achilles' heel.

Randolph was pacing in the library.

"The first party, Amelia. We've waited so long. *I've* waited so long." His face held a longing that she hardly recognized. He looked young. Vulnerable. He had never in his life looked so vulnerable. Not even on the day their daughter was born.

"A hundred years from now, this will be the best-known house in the county. And it begins tonight. Just think!" He turned to Aaron. "It's the most remarkable house in the county, don't you agree?"

"Absolutely." Aaron also looked pleased, like an admiring brother.

Amelia had come to count on Aaron's calm presence. Randolph was always busy: planning, writing, walking the nascent orchards, giving Mason orders though there was little to do in these cold months. Aaron sat sometimes with her in her morning room when Tamora was calm. He read to them from *The Adventures of Tom Sawyer* and *Through the Looking Glass*, while Tamora would sit on her mother's lap, plucking at Brownkin's fur, or chewing on her thumb. But she was calm when Aaron was around. Always calm.

"Let's drink to the evening! Amelia, you, too." Randolph poured them each a glass of whiskey. The one he held out to Amelia had much less than the other two.

"Oh, I can't. It's whiskey. I've never had whiskey." Amelia made a face, and Aaron and Randolph both laughed.

"Go on. You can do it. There's no one here to see." It made her feel better that Aaron understood her hesitation. Randolph seemed to think it was a great joke.

"All at once, now." Randolph pressed the glass forward.

She sighed. "I suppose it won't hurt."

But it did hurt. Her tongue and throat felt scalded with the harsh, woody taste and it caught painfully going down. There seemed to be something hard in the whiskey. Not wanting to rudely spit something out with the men watching, she swallowed but then began to cough. She took out her handkerchief. The inside of her lips burned unlike anything she had felt before.

Finally, she was able to take her handkerchief away from her mouth.

"Amelia. Are you all right?" Aaron looked at the handkerchief and then at her face.

"What?" She looked down. The handkerchief and the bodice of her dress were spotted with blood.

"Good God, Amelia." Randolph grabbed her arm. "You might be injured internally. Cyrus Beard will be here soon. I'll have him look at you immediately." He shook his head, angry. "Clayton should be horsewhipped. I've put up with his shortcomings because I wanted someone who knew the area. But this is inexcusable."

"I'm sure I'll be fine." Her hand was shaking, and her tongue felt thick. It was her embarrassment that she felt even more keenly. "Clayton surely didn't do it on purpose. And it might have been the maid who was careless. Will you both excuse me?"

Aaron stayed close to her as she left the room, speaking softly. "Is there anything I can do?"

She shook her head, and hurried to the hall and up the stairs just as the first guest rang the bell.

Before Amelia started downstairs again, she looked in on Tamora and Harriet. The back of her tongue was sore where the piece of metal or glass had cut her, but the bleeding had stopped. As she spoke to Harriet, her words felt clumsy and too large for her mouth.

"Why isn't Tamora ready for bed? Has Maud brought up her milk?"

"Oh, how you startled me!" Harriet looked up from her knitting. Tamora sat on the floor surrounded by Brownkin and several of her dolls. She was wearing a dress, and her hair was combed. Her head lolled a bit, and her face was vacant. She rarely looked up when someone entered a room, but Amelia recognized a certain stillness about her that she only realized later should have been a warning. Stranger still, one of the dolls had a piece of cloth wrapped around its eyes.

"What's going on, Harriet? Why is she wearing a dress?"

Harriet seemed uncomfortable. "I thought I'd let her watch the carriages arrive. Doesn't she look pretty? She's been such a good girl today."

It was true that Tamora looked pretty in the dress. The pink color warmed her fair skin and the soft, long sleeves hid the thinness of her arms. And she *had* been good. Or at least calmer than she had been in many days. But it didn't explain why she was wearing the dress. Amelia decided that Harriet was perhaps being worn down, that she was amusing herself. Tamora wasn't suffering.

"She looks charming, but she should be in her nightclothes. Please take care of it. I don't have time to help. There are guests downstairs."

"Yes, Missus Bliss."

Amelia knelt down and kissed Tamora's cheek. Was that a hint of a smile on her daughter's face? No, of course it wasn't. Even when she laughed her strange, subdued laugh, she never quite smiled.

"Good night, sweetheart. Sleep well."

Tamora leaned away and moved the doll with the cloth over its face so that one of its bright glass eyes peeped out.

⌒

Perhaps it was the excellent wine that Randolph had selected, or the whiskey that had begun the evening—despite the piece of debris that had cut her—but Amelia found herself having a rather good time.

Everyone was enchanted with the house, exclaiming over its dome painted with perfect, glowing stars, and the artwork that Randolph had selected. (Though she knew he had a dealer who chose the works beyond the family portraits he had had sent from the house in Long Island.) Because the weather was snowy, Clayton had led the ladies upstairs to one of the bedrooms to refresh themselves so they could reappear relaxed and freshly powdered. Later in the evening, Pinky Archer, who had attached herself to Randolph, prettily asked if the ladies might be given a tour of the upper floors of the house, and he said, with no small amount of pride, that he had planned to show them all.

Seeing his pleasure, Amelia was reminded of how he had wooed *her*, how he had hung on her every word. Pinky Archer was young, perhaps twenty-nine or thirty. She was pretty in a classical sense, with upswept hair, and narrow shoulders and a waist much smaller than her own. She saw how Selina Searle, her closest friend, watched her out of the corner of her eye. Selina wore her pregnancy like a curse. Amelia had no doubt that she would put the child that was coming with a nurse and would have her own tiny waist restored in a matter of months or even weeks. She was obviously unhappy, and when she'd taken Amelia's hand, it was without warmth. But perhaps it was just the pregnancy. Amelia had found herself in tears nearly every day for the first six months of her pregnancy with Tamora. Surely Selina might be excused for being uncomfortable and a bit unpleasant.

"Are you pleased? Your husband has worked hard for this moment."

Doctor Cyrus Beard was at her elbow. His old-fashioned evening jacket squeezed his stout form as though it wanted to keep him from escaping it. Amelia admired his silver-white hair and mustache but didn't trust his diminutive, feminine mouth with its too-pink lips.

"I have nothing but praise for my husband. It's a remarkable house." Was her smile too big? Could he tell it was forced? She hadn't spent more than an hour with this man, but somehow she was certain she couldn't trust him. Not with herself, not with Tamora.

"I told him that any person in his right mind could be happy here."

There it was. The suggestion that someone in the house wasn't in their right mind. He knew about Tamora. Randolph had told her that he would be their doctor, but so far she had kept the child away from him.

"May we talk a moment?"

With a glance over her shoulder to see that Randolph was leading several women upstairs for the promised tour, she followed Cyrus Beard to the salon, where tables had been set up for whist. At home, it had been a game for mostly men, but somehow here there were men at one table and women at another. She wasn't at all surprised to see that the women's table was the louder.

She sat with Cyrus Beard in front of the fire. When they were settled, he leaned forward with a confiding air.

"Now you're not one of those women prone to taking ridiculous amounts of exercise, are you? Not wanting to walk all over the countryside or engage in lawn tennis for hours on end?"

Surprised by the personal nature of the question, Amelia leaned back further into her own chair. What a strange man he was.

"It's not healthy for women to take too much exercise. It develops muscle, and, I've found, often leads to the development of unsightly facial hair." He squinted at her from behind his thick spectacles, and she self-consciously touched her chin.

"I'm sure I haven't had any of—"

"My first wife, bless her soul, was fond of long walking holidays with her sisters, even after we were married. Couldn't talk her out of it. I'm convinced it's why we were only able to conceive one daughter. Her menses was never regular. Irregularity is a child killer."

Amelia blushed—something she couldn't remember having done in several years. "I'm so sorry you lost your wife. Such a tragedy."

"Oh, I have another. You'll remember her. She's playing whist. In the green dress. She's already produced a fine son. We're hopeful for a second."

The idea of having to perform wifely duties for the portly Doctor Beard vaguely sickened her, but she was careful not to let it show on her face. "I wish you the best of luck, of course."

"Lawn tennis is particularly dangerous. I have strictly forbidden her from lawn tennis. You don't engage in that, do you? At your age, you can't take many risks."

"Doctor Beard, why are you concerned about my age? Are you afraid I'll break a bone? I assure you that I'm from very hardy stock. Is Randolph concerned about something that he hasn't told me?" Randolph had a confidence in doctors that defied her own slim faith. After the myriad and absurd suggestions she had been given concerning Tamora's care, she would have been happy to never see another. The lumpish cut on the back of her tongue testified to that. What a relief it was that Randolph hadn't pressed Doctor Beard on her for that strange mishap.

It was a mishap that bothered her, though. Had it indeed been an accident? For a moment she wondered about Randolph. Could he wish to harm her? Or maybe she had irritated one of the servants. She hadn't known them long enough to be despised that much by them, surely.

As he started to answer, she became conscious of some commotion out in the hall. Not a shout or a scuffle; it was more subtle than that, as though there were some wave of unrest moving slowly through the house. She felt it in her chest, and she was suddenly afraid for Tamora.

Cyrus Beard leaned closer and put a hand on her arm to prevent her from rising. "You haven't conceived more children beyond your only daughter. Perhaps it's some defect in your womb that you're concerned about. Or perhaps there is a defect and you *have* conceived. And if that is the case, I can do nothing for you." He flustered a bit. "Yes, your age might be of some concern, but there's nothing one could do about that. I've told Randolph."

Now she stood, impatient. He had found the boundary of her tolerance, and she could hear the edge of cold in her voice. The one that her mother had told her that she needed to keep under control if she wanted to marry or have friends or be well thought of.

"Thank you for your concern, Doctor Beard. Again, I assure you that I'm in superior health. As we have no lawn tennis facilities here, I'm certain I can maintain that happy state."

He put up his hand, about to protest, but she was already turning away, conscious that the players at the nearest whist table were watching.

Randolph didn't know, and her mother didn't know. There had been two pregnancies after Tamora. One when Tamora was two and had already begun to cause Amelia concern. The second had been only the previous year. Both had been taken care of as soon as she had missed her second menses by the abortifacient provided by the pharmacist who had known her all her life, and who had no respect for the new wave of sentiment or even the laws that disallowed such things. After Tamora, there was nothing that could make her want another child. If Tamora—as much as she loved her—was a judgment for allowing Randolph to exploit her wifely duty in ways she knew were beyond the pale, and, worse, for sometimes enjoying it, she didn't need a second judgment. One that might have been more devastating than Tamora herself.

Chapter 22

AMELIA

December 1878

Amelia met Pinky Archer coming down the staircase from the third floor. The stairway was out of view of the front hall, and the candlelight from the sconce on the wall sharpened Pinky's already thin features and put a shadow across her cheek. Amelia met her eyes and wasn't sure how to interpret what she saw there. Was it pity? No, it was pity mixed with a note of scorn.

Yes, that is scorn I see. What have I done? What has Randolph done?

"I'm so sorry." Pinky stopped on the stair. She looked away from Amelia's eyes and adjusted her perfectly adjusted evening glove. "We must go. Thank you for a lovely evening."

Before Amelia could respond, Pinky had gone on, with another woman following close behind. Amelia couldn't remember the second woman's name, but she pressed close to the wall without speaking a word, only giving Amelia an embarrassed glance. Amelia wanted to grab her and shake her and ask her what awaited her up on the third floor. Continuing up, she felt as though she were in a terrible dream in which the staircase seemed to narrow and lengthen ahead of her.

When the scream came, it was no surprise. She ran up the final few stairs, heedless of decorum, and followed the sound to the ballroom, a room she had immediately found mysterious yet welcoming with its extravagant and red Oriental wallpaper and lacquered chairs and generous fireplace. But she had noticed that there were no windows (not such an unusual thing in ballrooms, but it always made her feel strangely imprisoned). And that there were two large, sturdy metal eyes hanging from the ceiling; eyes of the sort that seemed to await the addition of two large, sturdy metal hooks.

When Randolph had seen her staring up at them, he had told her that she would have to wait to learn what they were for. "I want it to be a surprise."

The ballroom was red as blood, but the timorous glow of the two dozen standing candelabra that Clayton had lighted gave it a look of romance. No one she knew had a red ballroom. It was at once lurid and fascinating.

Randolph stood in the center of the room, his face bathed in candlelight, a grin frozen on his face. He pushed the swing hanging from the eyes fixed to the ceiling by two lengths of velvet rope. No. Not rope. The metal hooks were attached to at least a dozen feet of chain that had been carefully covered by the velvet. Or not so carefully. The chain squeaked and groaned, the hooks scraped against the ugly metal eyes. Below it all, Tamora sat on the swing, gripping the chains so tightly that the tendons in her thin arms stood out in relief. Her eyelids were squeezed shut, her mouth open in terror.

Seeing Amelia in the doorway, Randolph spoke, shouting over Tamora's screams.

"Amelia! I was just introducing our friends to our darling daughter. A spectacular debut, don't you think?"

"Randolph, please, stop this now!" Running into the room, she reached out to stop the swing herself, but it was moving far too fast.

"Careful, my dear. I wanted you to see how well she did, but it's ruined now."

When the swing returned to him, he grabbed the seat with two sure hands, jerking it to a stop. Tamora was stunned into momentary silence, her eyes flying open.

Those eyes were not vacant, as they had been in the nursery. But Tamora—the Tamora she knew—was not in them. That Tamora had retreated somewhere far away from them all.

Amelia made soothing sounds that were possibly not even words as she gently pried her daughter's hands from the chains. Tamora's knuckles were blue with tension, and Amelia stroked the fragile fingers.

"Yes, darling. Mother's here. Let's go back to your room. Let's go find Brownkin." Finally, Tamora began to try to breathe deeply, gasping to fill her lungs. Amelia was certain she would begin screaming again, but she did not.

"Poor lamb." Harriet was there at her elbow. "She liked it the other day. We never would have put her on there if she hadn't liked it well enough." With the words had come the smell of brandy. "I'll take her back to her room, Missus Bliss."

Amelia turned to see Randolph looking wryly amused. He winked at her, and she realized he was either terribly drunk or out of his mind. Then he moved away, speaking to the gawping guests nearest him.

"Let's go down and see how the whist players are doing. I'm in need of a brandy. What about you, Aaron?"

Dear God, it *was* some kind of horrible dream.

Amelia saw Aaron then. His eyes were filled with sadness. Perhaps regret. He hadn't had the strength of character to stop Randolph from hurting Tamora. She felt another pang of anger in her chest.

When she spoke, her jaw clenched in anger, it was to Harriet. "You can sleep in the staff quarters tonight. Don't you dare come near the nursery."

Harriet stiffened. "I only did as I was required, Missus Bliss."

Amelia turned her attention back to Tamora, whose tense little body seemed as frozen as the statue of Hera in the garden.

"Mother's here," she whispered. "All the people are going away, and we will be all alone again. Don't worry, my darling. I won't let them hurt you anymore."

By the time she was able to coax Tamora from the swing, the ballroom was empty, and the candles had begun to stutter and smoke. She could hear laughter from far down on the first floor. So they hadn't abandoned the house. Hadn't abandoned Randolph. The fact that they had not sparked a feeling of betrayal inside her. Those who were left were Randolph's friends. Not hers.

She picked up Tamora to carry her to the nursery, and she felt the fluid softness of the child's pink dress flow over her skin. Staring wide, and speechless, Tamora was like a broken doll.

As they approached the nursery, Aaron stepped out of one of the open doorways, blocking her path.

"Please do not speak to me, Aaron." She moved to go around him, but he stopped her with a hand on her arm. Below them, a small group of guests stood in the hall, but Amelia didn't care what they heard.

"I'd only just gone into the room when you arrived. Please understand." He glanced at Tamora, eyes full of concern.

She held her trembling child closer. "You presume too much. Please take your hand away."

"I wouldn't have let him hurt her."

Now she wasn't able to keep the sarcasm from her voice. "Oh, good. I'm so glad that *this* doesn't mean she's hurt at all. Now, let me pass."

This time he let her go. She could feel him watching her as she continued to the nursery, and she hated herself because even in her current state of anger, she hadn't wanted him to take his hand away. She believed him when he said that he had only just gone into the room, and who was he to her or Tamora that he could have stopped Randolph? Randolph was his own law, and they both knew it. He had shamed Tamora, shamed them all. But Randolph had no shame, and so it would mean nothing to him. She almost envied him. Tamora was her curse and her blessing, but to him Tamora was simply another of his possessions, and tonight she had been a disappointing toy.

As she laid the dully responsive Tamora on her bed and took off the child's satin slippers and dress and undergarments (these wet with urine), she imagined what her life might be like if she were similarly able to divorce Tamora from her concern. There would have been no scene, no confrontation, no humiliation, because Tamora would be back in New York, constantly sedated under the care of nurses and doctors. The frontal portion of Tamora's brain would be gone, and Amelia might have the courage and humor to leave Randolph or take someone like Aaron as a lover.

She cleaned and redressed her and then kissed her daughter's damp forehead. Randolph might be so callous. She could not be. But she was tired of there being so little affection from Tamora. No comfort. No respite from Tamora's pain. No real affection in her own life.

When Tamora was settled, her arms locked around Brownkin and her head pressed into the pillow, Amelia could almost believe

Tamora was like any other little girl. Almost. She dimmed the lamps and went to stand at one of the windows that looked out toward the carriage house and horse barn. They were lighted and she could see the silhouettes of the waiting grooms and the remaining visiting horses and carriages.

At a movement in the shadows just below the window, she looked down. A man emerged, but she couldn't see his face. He stopped and tilted his head up. Was he watching her? Though the nursery window was dark, she stepped back, her heart quickening.

After a moment she made herself look again. Now there were two forms below, and as they came together, she was sure she recognized them both.

Chapter 23

AMELIA

December 1878

By the week before Christmas, everyone but Amelia seemed to have forgotten the incident with the swing in the ballroom. Invitations still arrived, even from Pinky Archer and the Beauforts, and Randolph had planned a big early New Year's Eve supper to take place before the Archers' late-night party.

If Tamora had forgotten the incident itself, she certainly hadn't forgotten how it had made her feel. How Randolph had made her feel. No longer was the ballroom on her frantic, barefoot circuits around the house, up and down the stairs. She had often stood at the ballroom doors until either Amelia or Harriet slid them open for her so she could go inside and run around the edges of the room. With her eyes half closed and her hair flying behind her,

her fingers traced the wallpaper, with its pattern of Oriental girls and strange old men. If Harriet tried to warn her about the chairs or fireplace, she would scowl and continue on. Now she ran along the gallery, passing by the ballroom doors as though they didn't exist, the expression on her face unchanging.

The other change was in the way she acted in Randolph's presence: She wanted nothing to do with him at all. He, like the ballroom, had ceased to exist for her. At dinner, if he passed by her chair and touched her hair, she would swat violently at the air as though brushing away a gnat, making Randolph laugh.

The first time it happened, Harriet admonished her. But Randolph replied with, "Leave her be. An animal doesn't know when it's being naughty."

He winked at Aaron who, to his credit, falteringly suggested that he was surely joking, that Tamora was a lovely little girl.

Amelia knew Randolph had meant to shock her, and so did not respond, but she was silently grateful to Aaron. Besides Harriet, he was the only one who had offered any sort of apology, boldly taking her hand in the front hall a few days later, saying that he admired her tenacity and dedication to her daughter. That he was certain that Randolph wasn't a bad man, but only a man who felt helpless in the face of his daughter's limitations.

Was he so naïve? If so, she liked him for it. But she found it a little difficult to understand why he hadn't helped Tamora that night. She had softened, though. Truly, she felt that he was her only friend in Bliss House.

"Please forgive me, Amelia. I want to be my better self when I am around you."

She had laughed then. Was he trying to win her good opinion by flattery? A woman who was years older and a generation wiser in experience?

He seemed to catch how she'd heard him, and he colored and gave her an abashed smile.

On impulse, she spoke more seriously. "Don't tell Randolph what you've said. Don't criticize him about Tamora. He doesn't like to be criticized, and he will surely trace it back to me. She is well, and I am here. All will be well."

"All *will* be well," he repeated. For a very awkward moment, she imagined he might kiss her. If he had, it would have seemed the most natural thing in the world. In the world inside Bliss House, that is. Outside—well, outside didn't matter because she felt more and more as though she had little or no business outside the house. Let Randolph travel. Let him spend his nights out of the house, away, or with whoever was in the cottage in the woods. A single night or a dozen. It didn't matter to her anymore. Or so she reminded herself whenever she suspected she was in danger of forgetting what he'd become to her.

Despite her constant preoccupation with Tamora, she refused to give up what she knew was her rather childish delight in the Christmas season. Her parents had always kept their celebrations religious and low-key, but she had loved to visit the homes of her friends who celebrated with parties and colorful decorations.

Randolph was not at the breakfast table, as he so often was not. Whether he'd gotten up early and left or had never come home, she wasn't certain and simply put the question out of her mind. Maud cleared away his unused dishes from the table with a little moue of disapproval as Aaron and Amelia discussed cutting greens for the house.

"We left a lot of beautiful evergreens standing in the woods, and there's rhododendron as well. It might be on the yellow-green side, but once we get it indoors and you put some ribbon and pinecones with it, it will look fine."

Amelia tried to imagine Randolph suggesting that he knew anything about how winter rhododendron might look, or where he might find some, and she smiled.

"Harriet and I will get Tamora ready for the weather, and we'll be right down. Will you get some baskets from Maud, and ask her to have some chocolate ready for us in an hour or so?"

Mason would be bringing a fresh-cut tree to the house on the weekend, and she had miles of gold satin ribbon and a large number of German glass ornaments: moons, stars, colorful balls. Also wax angels, crosses, and bells. So many bells in different colors. She had purchased them at Mister Schwarz's Toy Bazaar on Broadway and had them sent to Bliss House so they would be waiting for Christmas. There were toys, too, of course. New dolls. Always new dolls even if Tamora only glanced at them. One was sure to become her new favorite if it happened to be wearing the right color dress or had the correct color of hair. She had been in a ginger phase since she'd become so attached to Brownkin, though he was definitely a ruddy brown. Who knew what connection she'd made in her head between the brown, seedy squirrel and the ginger-haired dolls.

Christmas would, finally, offer some reason for cheer in Bliss House. Surely even Randolph's impulsive cruelties couldn't ruin such a happy time.

～

Gatchel's Ladies Fine Shoes in Lynchburg had sent her two pairs of boots on approval. They were thinner and less sturdy than the leather boots she'd always gotten up east, but there was no time to have the boots she'd left behind in New York sent down. She grabbed the black pair from her room and hurried to ready Tamora, who was not being cooperative.

"Tamora, darling. Your friend Aaron is waiting. We're going out in the snow. You love the snow!" Actually the day was warming, and the layer of white was melting quickly. They would have to hurry. Simply walking through the woods rarely amused Tamora. The out-of-doors was too unpredictable. Too alarming. How Amelia wished that the garden were more mature, its shining box-wood maze tall enough to hide in. The ridiculous statue of Hera with her peacock dominated the yard-high bushes.

Harriet, still contrite (and, Amelia was certain, sober), was more patient than usual, speaking to Tamora in the rhythmic singsong that appealed to her more than any other voice. Amelia heard it, saw how it worked, but she felt too ridiculous to use it herself.

"You go on, Missus Bliss." Harriet was working to get Tamora's second shoe on. "If I can get this one on her, she'll be fine. She likes her new coat very much."

For once, Amelia didn't hesitate or worry about helping Harriet. She kissed Tamora's clean blond hair and left the room, her thoughts already on the woods and the evergreens she would gather with Aaron. And, of course, on the chocolate that would come later. Feeling like a schoolgirl, she hurried down the stairs. Aaron emerged from the dining room wearing his overcoat and carrying two large baskets. A small saw was tucked inside one, and there was also a roll of twine. When he saw her, a smile broke across his face. She felt a pang at knowing that Aaron—a houseguest, almost a stranger—was the only one in the house with whom she could share her happy feelings about the coming holiday. Tamora had no sense of it. Everyone else but Randolph was a servant. Like her parents, Randolph had never done much to celebrate Christmas, though he usually made sure he stayed closer to home for the last two weeks of the year. She briefly considered going back upstairs to tap on his bedroom door, to see if he wanted to go with them. But her only motivation was duty. Propriety. Seeing Aaron's broad smile changed her mind. Randolph would probably mock them for doing something he considered servants' work.

This was not New York, and she didn't care what the servants thought about her going into the woods with Aaron. Besides, Harriet and Tamora would be with them.

If only they weren't.

The thought shocked her. Aaron was only being kind.

"Is something wrong? Is Tamora not well?"

She blushed. Was she so transparent? If he had somehow been able to read her mind, it would mortify them both. "Oh, she won't be hurried. That's how it is with her sometimes. Harriet is very good with her."

"But Harriet's not you, is she?"

⁓

The sun was even brighter than she'd feared, and the snow bloomed with circles of soggy, dormant grass and dirt. Tamora stepped carefully, anxious to walk only on the snow. Harriet stayed close by her, telling her not to worry, that her boots would keep her feet dry. Tamora liked warm baths, but she hated puddles and getting her shoes dirty.

When they'd first stepped into the drive and Aaron started around the garden and toward the woods west of the house, Amelia almost asked him if there wasn't somewhere else they might search. As though sensing her discomfort, he walked somewhat north, instead of due west, where the cottage was.

A part of her was deeply curious about the cottage. She had seen it from her window and had even once gone to the gate at the other side of the garden, imagining she might confront the girl living there. The girl was a mystery, though Randolph had begun to whisper when they were in bed together about the things he did with her. All she knew was that the girl was very young, and shameless. Did others in town know about her? She doubted whether someone like Pinky Archer or Cyrus Beard's gossipy wife, Sharon, would be able to keep from gossiping about the girl if they knew. Testing Amelia to see if she knew or cared that she was being so publicly shamed.

There might even be more than one woman living there.

"Two women are best. Two are miraculous." Randolph had told her, in the false sanctity of the bed they shared, how much he enjoyed being with more than one of his whores at a time. "Like succubi. Jealous of one another, each more daring than the other." Then the details would come. Details that made her sick and excited at the same time. Knowing he had betrayed her. But as she had never complained to him, but simply accepted, was it even a betrayal?

⁓

The baskets were nearly full. Most of the pine boughs they'd collected had long, fragrant needles and were sprinkled with sticky cones the size of the end of Amelia's thumb. She and Aaron worked together, laughing at the difficulty of cutting the flexible branches with the thin, equally flexible saw. Sometimes their gloved hands met, but Amelia pretended not to notice.

"Tamora!"

Amelia turned in time to see the back of Tamora's blue coat as she ran out of the little grove of pine trees and toward a cluster of oaks that still fluttered with dark gold leaves that the wind seemed to have forgotten. Harriet was running after her. Beyond the oaks, Amelia could just see the clearing with the cottage. She put her basket down to go after them, but Aaron touched her arm.

Before she could object, Aaron, too, was running behind Harriet, and now dodging past her. But Tamora was running quickly and soon disappeared from view.

What if she keeps running? What if she is never found?

Amelia shook off the treacherous thought and followed, hoping Tamora would eventually run for home. But they had spent little time in these woods, and Amelia was sure Tamora didn't know to look for the big house through the trees to find her way.

She found the other house, though. The cottage.

When Amelia reached the three of them, breathless, she found them standing at the edge of the clearing. Harriet leaned heavily against a tree, her bosom heaving beneath her serviceable black coat. Aaron had turned back toward Amelia and was waving her away. He looked a bit ridiculous in his panic—for it *was* panic on his face.

The woods were strangely quiet. A handful of melting snow fell from a tree branch and landed on the ground in front of Amelia, yet it made no sound.

Tamora was watching Randolph, who was walking carefully down the cottage's porch stairs. He wore his overcoat, but it was open and his waistcoat was unbuttoned. Beneath the waistcoat was a shirt, but no collar, and his hair was disheveled. His lip curled with either concentration or distaste as he descended. It was a strange sight: Randolph, always so self-possessed and careful of his appearance, of his actions, was definitely not at his best. He looked dissolute, like a rough man of the street who had borrowed a gentleman's fashionable coat and expensive suit. Yes, this was her husband. Not the husband he showed to her, but the husband he truly was. The husband who would keep a mistress within sight of his own home and whisper in the dark to his wife about the things he liked to do to her.

Aaron was obviously distressed, but it felt strangely normal to Amelia. That was the horror of it. Her training, her moral sense, her dignity all screamed for her to vehemently register her disgust—if not in defense of herself, then because of the presence of others. Yet she couldn't scare up even a whisper of indignation.

Aaron came to stand beside her, perhaps intending to offer her comfort or support. He at least had the sense not to speak.

Behind Randolph, the girl looked out of the door. Amelia caught a glimpse of a pale, terribly pale, oval face, a face that might have belonged to a dark-eyed ghost. The girl—for she was definitely a girl, and not a woman—was as small as Amelia's sister had been at ten years old, and her shapeless gown exposed her thin, smooth neck and collarbone. She seemed cold and anxious. Amelia's eyes were hungry for her and held her gaze for a moment. But she could not ignore the girl's bulging stomach.

Randolph hadn't told her about the pregnancy. What had he been waiting for?

Randolph, undeterred by the sudden appearance of an audience, adjusted his hat and walked toward Tamora and Harriet.

He sees me as well. I know he sees.

Before he reached Tamora, the door behind him closed.

"Let's go back to the house." Aaron spoke quietly, again touching Amelia's arm.

Amelia moved away. Not abruptly, but definitely.

Tamora started toward Randolph, and Randolph, obviously surprised and pleased, stopped and opened his arms to her. But she darted around him and ran with a shriek up the stairs of the cottage. Reaching the closed door, she began to pound for it to be opened. She pounded and pounded as they all watched, but it never did.

Chapter 24

KIKU

December 1878

It was a week before Christmas, and Odette finally pronounced Kiku's broken ribs healed. Still, when Kiku breathed too deeply, she felt a small pain that she was sure meant her child was still in danger.

"I never heard such nonsense. There's no way your tiny little rib is going to float down there and poke the baby. Have you never seen the inside of an animal? You're not a pig that's made mostly of ribs. The baby's way down here." Odette put a warm hand on Kiku's belly, cupping it just below her protruding belly button.

After Randolph had kicked her at the end of October, Kiku's pain had been excruciating, and Mason had wanted to call in a doctor. He and Odette had argued over which one to contact, because he didn't know if Doctor Beard would want to treat Kiku.

He didn't treat black folk, and Mason didn't know if Kiku would be considered white enough. "No doctor!" Kiku had called from the bedroom, even though it hurt to yell. Even though she knew it was rude to eavesdrop. They were her ribs, after all. In the end, they all agreed that Randolph would not want *any* doctor to know she was there, and Odette and Mason did their best to treat her themselves.

Randolph had finally come to visit her again in mid-November, and complained that the bandages were unnecessary, that she could not possibly be that badly injured. But he had not, to her surprise, made her remove them when he took her. Fortunately, his visits weren't frequent, though she knew it wasn't because he regretted what he had done to her. Amelia was installed in the house.

Kiki no longer bothered to attempt to diminish her pregnancy around him, and he did not speak directly of it again. Reluctantly, at Odette's request, he had provided Odette with more money to buy another pair of dresses that could encompass Kiku's growing belly. But he had told Odette that they would have to be fixed afterward to work as regular dresses. It was the only time he mentioned anything that might occur after the birth. On the future of the baby itself, he remained silent. Still, Kiku thought about that future. Every day, she prayed that the child inside her was a boy and not a girl. She would never forgive herself if she gave birth to a girl. Would death be worse than what Randolph might do to her girl child? She knew the answer. But would she be brave enough to kill it in order to save it? Again and again she prayed that she would not have to.

"Where are you? You're a million miles away." Odette folded the bandage and put it in the laundry to be washed.

"Randolph will be pleased."

Odette made an aggravated noise. "Maybe he shouldn't have kicked you in the first place, and then he wouldn't be so awfully *inconvenienced*."

At least Odette had never said *I told you so*. They both knew that she had been right to suggest the abortion, or to at least break the news to him earlier. Though there had been no guarantees that he wouldn't have acted exactly as he had.

"Did you bring the creeper vine? The reeds of the cat tails?"

"Mason bundled them and put them on the back porch. They're going to need to be soaked. You can use the laundry tub outside to boil them. Tell Mason when you're ready and I'll make sure he sets a fire under it. Be careful on the back stairs. They get slick, and there's snow coming."

Kiku thanked her.

"I wish you could get to church with us. At least for Christmas."

Kiku shook her head. "I would not know what to do there. And I would be seen."

"I guess it's too late to worry about that."

That morning she had seen Randolph to the door, something she rarely did as he often left while she was still abed. As she passed a window, she had seen some movement in the snowy woods and forgot to be cautious. There were always animals in the woods: a pair of horses earlier in the fall that Mason had had to lead back to the stable; night animals, like coyotes and raccoons; and squirrels that raced through the trees and disappeared into their shaggy nests. But no one aside from Odette, Mason, and Randolph ever came to the cottage. Mason had told her that Aaron was still at Bliss House, but she was certain that he had forgotten her.

Randolph stepped out onto the porch, and they both saw the little girl. "Well, what do we have here? It's my lovely, mad daughter." He didn't say it loudly enough for anyone else but Kiku to hear.

Tamora teetered at the edge of the clearing, directly opposite the cottage. Like Kiku herself, she was pale, and not very tall compared to Randolph. Her long neck, head, and hands protruded from her heavy woolen coat like the stark appendages of a wooden doll. Her untidy blond hair lay about her shoulders, a thick strand crossing her nose until she put up a hand to move it; if she had been wearing a hat in the cold, it was lost. Randolph had told Kiku that

Tamora was seven years old, but she looked younger. Even from the doorway, Kiku could see the redness of the girl's upper lip, and as though to demonstrate her runny nose, the child ran her sleeve across her face to clear it.

Randolph continued slowly down the stairs and began to cross the yard. He had worn a faint path through the trees, across the winter grass and to the garden of Bliss House, but it was invisible in the dusting of snow.

At first Kiku had thought Tamora was watching him. But no. It had been the cottage she was staring at, and Kiku herself.

So this was the broken child, the one whose distant screams Kiku heard when she was out walking most days in the woods. What a sad thing she was, like a spirit already. An angry little spirit.

An older, heavyset woman in a dark coat came close to Tamora, but didn't touch her. Kiku heard Tamora's name floating on the cold air, and there was Aaron trying to wave away another woman. From her height and expensive-looking clothes, Kiku guessed that this was Amelia. How strange to see the two people she was most curious about here at her front door. And Aaron. If only she could talk to him.

Kiku's eyes met Amelia's across the fading snow. She saw her hate. Saw her pain. When Amelia's eyes moved briefly to Kiku's belly, Kiku knew in that moment that they were linked together forever. How happy Randolph would be that they had finally seen each other. He liked nothing better than to put two people in opposite corners and wait for them to put on a show for him.

She would not give him the pleasure. Not now. Kiku shut the door and leaned against it, her heart hammering. The baby was excited, too, kicking and rolling. Kiku put her chin to her chest, surprised by the sadness that had welled up inside her. While she was still leaning against the door, wondering what was going on outside, she heard a violent shrieking and felt the door move against her back.

Tamora was throwing herself against the door. But Kiku would not open it.

Chapter 25

KIKU

December 1878

Kiku sat on the floor in front of the fire, with all the lamps she could find lighted nearby. The basket for the baby was going well. Mason had brought her a disk of soft cedar for the bottom, and she had already woven the cattails over and around it to secure it. As she worked, she hummed into the silence. When she was at Mason and Odette's house there was rarely silence, and tonight, Christmas night, had been no different. Odette had filled the house with evergreen branches and lighted every candle and had tried to teach Kiku the song "Silent Night." They had shared their dinner of ham and biscuits and oranges and a quince tart with her. Randolph had given Mason a bottle of plum port along with a gift of ten dollars for Christmas, and the three of them had each had a small glass of the strong wine before Mason took her back to the cottage.

Christmas seemed a nice thing to Kiku, and the story of the baby in the manger tugged at her heart. She had a home, of sorts, but she had no idea how or where her child might be born. The barn with the oxen and asses had, at least, been filled with life, unlike her lonely cottage. How she hoped that, like Mary, she would have a boy child.

Randolph had come back for only one night after Tamora had come to the cottage and said that he would probably not be returning until the New Year. He had given her a Christmas gift: a brown-paper-wrapped package that contained a silk robe with kimono-style sleeves. It was too large for her, but was decorated with peony flowers that reminded her of the peony trees planted near the temple closest to her village. He had not given her any gifts since she had left Madame Jewel's, and had told her not to open it until he was gone. When he did leave the next morning, she had not accompanied him to the door, but had stood on her toes to kiss his cheek.

He had harmed her so many times. But he was a sort of husband to her and had given her a home to live in and had kept her from the hands of strangers. Even if his hands were cruel and she feared him, he was now the constant in her life. And, she believed, he was the father of her child.

What if the child were like him? She had only imagined that the child—a boy—would resemble her, with black hair and fair skin and dark, small eyes. He would be strong, as her father was. When she pictured her child, she thought of her young brother, Shingen. Always into everything. Running, running, running even when he was supposed to be doing the few chores required of him.

Surely Shingen had not forgotten her yet. But would he recognize her? She still avoided the mirror on the vanity, but sometimes she couldn't help but see herself.

Her hair had grown several inches since Madame Jewel had cut it, and Odette had given it a slightly more feminine shape with a pair of shears made for haircutting. The face she saw in the mirror was much thinner than her face had been when the second mate had captured her. She had still had the look of a child then. It had been more than a year since she had seen her family.

Now she would have a child that her mother would never see. Her mother, who hadn't had a child until she was twenty-three years old. Quite old by the standards of the village. But her mother had told stories of how she had loved being married without children, even though her own mother and the ladies of the village chided her, saying that she wasn't doing her duty as a wife. When Kiku finally came, they had all stopped talking. The next daughter hadn't come until Kiku was four years old, old enough, everyone said, to be a help to her parents. How she had resented being the little mother to her siblings. How she would gladly take care of them all over again if she had the chance.

Her mother had woven reed and bamboo baskets for the family's fishing business, but also for all of her babies. When each one outgrew the basket, it became his or hers to keep their belongings in. The basket Kiku was weaving would be a copy of her own because she knew it so well.

When the knock came at the front door, Kiku startled. Mason and Odette usually came to the kitchen door. Randolph never knocked.

She rose and put her cheek against the door. No animal would knock, but a stranger would. But would a stranger that meant her harm bother to knock?

"Kiku, don't be afraid. It's Aaron."

For a moment Kiku thought that Randolph might be trying to trick her. He had told her to never let any strangers inside. Aaron was hardly a stranger, though Randolph could never know it.

"Please let me in. I won't stay very long. I just want to wish you a merry Christmas."

Kiku wondered if this was some Christmas tradition of which she was unaware: acquaintances coming to one's house long after one was supposed to be asleep, to bring Christmas greetings. If so, it was a very strange custom. She opened the door.

Aaron stepped quickly inside and, with a glance over his shoulder, shut the door. He wore the air of the frosty night about him. The lamplight showed his reddened cheeks and lips, and there was a dusting of snow on his hat and boots. He was smiling, obviously glad to see her, and though she was surprised, she found herself returning his smile.

She held out her hands for his hat, as she would have for Randolph's. He looked puzzled a moment, and she said, "Your hat?"

"Ah."

When his coat and hat and gloves were off, she asked him if he would like to remove his wet boots. He sat, and she knelt to assist him. There was an awkward, confused moment when he tried to stop her, and she felt a bit hurt when he finally said that he wished to do it himself.

She went to the kitchen to bank up the stove to heat water for tea, and when his boots were off, he followed her.

"I don't mean to put you to trouble. I only wanted to say merry Christmas, and to see how you're doing."

"Randolph knows you're here? Did he send you?" Her hope was that he had not, and she was not disappointed.

"I wanted to bring you a small gift. I know that you don't know many people here."

"Randolph would not have me know people. You are aware of that already."

"It was a surprise to everyone to see you the other day."

Kiku looked down at her burgeoning belly.

Aaron said, "I'm afraid that it has rather upset things at Bliss House."

"It is not my wish to upset Missus Bliss. I would do nothing to harm her. Or her daughter." The water in the pitcher was ice cold.

She poured it into the kettle, which she set on the burner, and then took teacups and saucers from the shelf.

"She's upset, but knows she can do nothing. I wouldn't worry. She feels threatened, but she is not a vindictive woman."

Kiku felt suddenly defensive for the baby inside her. "I guess we will know where her daughter's madness comes from, won't we, if my child is not also mad."

Taken aback, Aaron told her that he hadn't meant to insult her. "As with so many things, Randolph likes to play with people's lives. I'm sorry that he's put you in this position. Amelia won't harm you or the child. She really is a very kind woman. Patient."

"If you say that she is, I have no reason to doubt you. Of course she will worry for her child."

"Of course."

They were silent for a while as the water heated in the kettle. When it was ready, Kiku poured the water into the pot with the tea and Aaron carried the tray into the parlor.

As they drank it, warming by the fire, he asked her about the basket, and she told him that she was making it for the baby.

"It's extraordinary. You show such skill."

She blushed. "I made baskets for my father. As I told you, he was a fisherman."

They talked, then, for an hour or more, about their childhoods, their families. He said that he didn't want to make her sad, talking about Japan, but she said that it made her happy. Unlike Odette, he didn't pry into how she had come to leave her home, or what she had done in New York. She liked him for that. She liked how the firelight softened his face. Randolph never sat beside the fire to talk with her. He might read and fall asleep in his chair. But most often he would simply bed her when dinner was through.

"Wait. I almost forgot." Aaron stood up so suddenly that he nearly upset the tea things, and they both laughed nervously.

He took a package from his overcoat. It was not much bigger than his hand and wrapped in thick black velvet that was just about the softest thing she had ever touched.

"I have nothing for you." Her brow furrowed. She hadn't imagined that she would see him, and certainly hadn't thought that he would be giving her a gift.

"I wanted to surprise you. Are you surprised?" He was anxious, like a child, and she smiled.

"Very surprised."

She laid the package on the table and lifted away the folds of velvet.

"I saw many books and paintings of Japan when I was in Europe. There was a Dutch sailor who was also a painter. As I painted this, I remembered some of his works from his travels in the East."

The small picture still smelled sharply of paint. It was a garden scene, with a single, blossoming cherry tree, and green plants arranged around large, smooth stones. Watching over the garden was a temple with a curving, many-layered roof whose points reached for the sky. She had only been to one such temple when she was young, and it, too, had had a brown roof, trimmed in black. But it was the sight of the cherry blossoms that brought tears to her eyes. Her mother had loved cherry blossoms, and friends would bring them to her when they traveled in the spring, packing the ends of the branches in water to keep the branches blooming.

"Have I upset you? Kiku, please tell me."

Now the tears were coming quickly. Kiku, who rarely cried, could not stop crying.

He came to sit beside her on the sofa and took her hand. "My dearest Kiku. Tell me that your heart is not broken. That you're not angry with me. I couldn't come, but I thought of you every day."

She could not stop sobbing long enough to speak. Her heart was indeed broken. Not just for herself, but for the child who would never see her home in Japan. For the man beside her who had seen into her heart just as if she had cut it open and bared it there on the table for him. It was impossible to speak.

Seeing how it was for her, he drew her to him and held her against his chest while she cried. He stroked her loosened hair and repeated "hush, hush, my dear" and told her all would be well.

She did her best to let herself be calmed, but she knew that all would not be well. If Randolph came to her door, he might kill them both and feel justified. She knew that she should tell Aaron to leave but felt too weak to do so. They were doing nothing wrong. He had given her a gift, the way that Odette and Mason had given her gifts, and as she had given them a small basket woven of Virginia creeper vines. Gifts of kindness. Of affection. She knew that she wanted more than kindness from Aaron, but kindness was what she was desperate for.

"You deserve so much more than life has given you, Kiku. I want to help you."

She pulled back from him and took the handkerchief that he offered to dry her wet face.

"You must go. I cannot accept such a gift from you."

"Please, you must take it. I painted it for you. You can hide it from Randolph, can't you? Perhaps Odette can keep it for you. For now?"

Kiku saw the sense of the idea and nodded. "Perhaps. But you must not come here again. It's too dangerous."

Aaron collected their empty tea things onto the tray and rose to pick it up. "I know Randolph. I know his comings and goings. Neither of us will be in any danger, I promise you."

Mason was the only man she had ever seen gather dishes, and she would not have thought it possible from a gentleman like Aaron. The fact that he had done so made her like and trust him more. She badly wanted to believe that he would make sure that no harm would come to her. But both Randolph and Madame Jewel had pretended to be her protectors, and they had done her the most harm.

When he was ready to leave, the skies beyond the dark porch were even darker. Several inches of snow had fallen, and he told Kiku to go back inside before her feet, clad in the thick socks she preferred to wear in the house, got wet.

"I couldn't bear to see you ill." Aaron took both of her hands in his gloved hands. The gloves were warm from being near the fire, but she would rather have had the touch of his skin.

"You could never cause me to be ill."

Aaron laughed softly. The closeness of the dark seemed to beg them to whisper. "I am many things, but I am not the winter cold, nor am I melting snow."

"You have no lantern. How will you see your way back in the dark?"

"Someone might still be awake in the house. I would rather not draw attention to myself. Don't worry. I know the way."

She smiled. Of course he would know the way. He had built the cottage. But he looked at her so intently that she understood that he had been to the house many times, but simply had not come to her door. The thought made her heart beat faster in her chest.

No one had ever risked so much to be with her.

Later, lying in her bed, alone, she knew that he was also taking risks that might affect her. If Randolph found out, he might hurt the child. She didn't want to think about that. Christmas night, which was so special to so many people, was now special to her. She had rewrapped the painting and tucked it behind a loose wall panel behind her vanity. She could take it out and look at it any time she wished.

Before Aaron left, he had shown her how his initials were set far down in the corner of the picture, against the fronds of a palm plant. *A. F.* She could not read any English words, but Odette had started to help her learn her letters. Now she would know the letters A and F forever.

Chapter 26

AMELIA

December 1878

As Christmas came and went, Amelia could never have guessed that she could be so happy. How curious it was to her!

In the first days after seeing the girl in the cottage, she had been upset. Randolph had gloated noticeably, but hadn't once directly mentioned the encounter after the long walk back to Bliss House. She had felt humiliated in front of Aaron and Harriet and had felt badly for Tamora. But then that strange understanding of normalcy had reasserted itself inside her, and she felt sorrier for the girl in the cottage than she did for herself.

As soon as she stopped being angry, an odd thing happened: Randolph left her alone completely. He never came near except to fondly kiss her cheek if they met at breakfast or at dinner or after they returned home from an evening out. The only difference was that his lips seemed to linger a second longer if Aaron was particularly close by, as though he knew she was conscious of Aaron watching them.

How strange, and how strangely pleasant it was to her. They were engaged in a triangular game, and although she had never been a woman to care much for games, this one appealed to her.

Tamora had quieted. She slept longer in the cold winter mornings, and her circuits around the galleries were less frequent.

They had a letter from Amelia's mother, saying that she and Amelia's father were considering coming south in the spring, once the snow was gone. But only a week later, a letter accompanying the Christmas packages her mother had sent—a pair of woolen mittens and a stuffed screech owl for Tamora, a necklace that had belonged to Amelia's grandmother for Amelia, and an elaborate walking stick with a carved greyhound's head for Randolph—suggested that Amelia's father wasn't well and wished to stay home through the spring. Together the letters appeared nonsensical, but Amelia was just as glad that her parents would not come.

The house would impress them, but Amelia knew she would soon tire of her mother's constant criticisms. Everything had begun to run so well: Maud and Clayton seemed less resentful of her and had begun to follow her requests without question. Harriet was demonstrably sober, which helped Amelia worry somewhat less about Tamora. The rounds of Christmas teas and dinners had been lively, and she had almost come to like Pinky Archer. Less certain was she about Pinky's constant companion, Selina. But Selina was only a month or so from giving birth, and no woman was at her best when she was struggling with the demands of a pregnancy. It did surprise Amelia that Selina was so socially active, though she supposed that it was old-fashioned of her to expect that a woman would hide herself away for the last few months as she had with Tamora.

What if there had been something about her confinement that had affected Tamora in the womb? Maybe Tamora's *limitations* weren't so much about the filthy things that Randolph had whispered to her as she conceived, as they were about something that she, Amelia, had done.

Still, it couldn't matter. There was no fixing Tamora.

⁓

The New Year's Eve dinner at Bliss House ended with Randolph declaring that his head cold would keep him from going to Maplewood and the Archers' party with all their departing guests. Amelia suggested that she would remain with him, but he told her that Aaron would be a better, healthier escort.

It was a spectacular evening.

Maplewood was a grand, plantation-style house, fronted by a row of Grecian columns that had been wound with ropes of pine garland and wide red ribbon for the holidays. It was famous for having been built by a grandnephew of Thomas Jefferson, the fact of which no Archer would boast, but left to their sycophants. Amelia watched the older Archer children, who were only three and four, and their cousins gather around the enormous fir tree in the front hall that was lighted one last time for the holidays. They were in their sleeping clothes and robes, and their eyes were bright with wakefulness though it was long past their bedtimes. Two of the boys were poking each other, each trying to get the other in trouble, but the others were less restive. One of the girls had hair as blond as Tamora's that she wore in a blue velvet ribbon, and the wonder in the girl's gaze as she watched the lighted candles and glimmering tinsel made Amelia catch her breath. Tamora was afraid of their tree in the front hall and would not go near it.

"Did you have Christmas trees when you were a child?" Amelia and Aaron had ridden to the party alone in the carriage, and he now stood at her side.

Amelia laughed. "Oh, no. My father thinks they're pagan abominations foisted on us by the Germans." She became wistful. "I loved to see them, though. All my friends had Christmas trees."

"The tree at Bliss House is extraordinary. You have a good eye. Randolph should have let you help him furnish Bliss House. If I had only known—"

"But it wouldn't have made any difference. You know Randolph has very definite tastes."

"He has extraordinary taste in some things."

He didn't touch her arm, but he moved imperceptibly closer and now the sounds of the room receded from them. She knew it was just her imagination, but the hall was heady with the scents of candle smoke and pine. She felt her color rise, and it had nothing at all to do with the warmth generated by the candles or the number of people in the room.

"Why are you so kind to me, Aaron?"

"I'm not kind, Amelia. Randolph is my closest friend here in Old Gate. And I truly value your company."

Understanding that he certainly wanted to say more, she was afraid of betraying the inappropriate feelings that threatened to overwhelm her. If only she could speak plainly.

"You've no need to be modest. Of course you're kind."

The smile he gave her was rueful, but it changed instantly as their host, Robert Archer, joined them, patting Aaron on the back. "There's dancing upstairs. Amelia, I hope you'll save a round for me. We plan to keep you amused as Randolph seems to have given up on us this evening."

"Are you here to escort me upstairs?" Amelia kept her voice light. Flirtatious. It wasn't very natural to her, but she had to break the tension she had been feeling with Aaron. The distance that Randolph had given her had made her realize how much she needed Aaron.

"It would be a distinct honor to escort you. I'm sorry Randolph is under the weather, but I think it's rather a *coup* to have you to ourselves. I know that Randolph draws all of your feminine attention when he's extant."

Amelia heard the dig at Randolph. Randolph drew plenty of feminine attention, and not just her own. It occurred to her that Randolph had—in addition to bedding the girl in the cottage—bedded women that were in this very room. But as he was back at Bliss House, for just this evening she could pretend he didn't even exist. She intended to enjoy herself.

Laughing, she took Robert's arm.

"Will you come, Aaron?" Robert asked. "The countryside's best is here tonight, lovely young women ready to start the New Year with an eye to the future. I know one or two who were asking if you'd be here this evening."

"Of course. I'll follow along in a moment."

As Robert, with great flourish, guided her up one wing of the hall's grand staircase, she looked down to see that several young women in pastel dresses had settled around Aaron like a rabble of butterflies. She had never been part of a mindless group of girls. Or perhaps it wasn't fair to call them mindless. They were only doing what young women were supposed to be doing: looking their loveliest in order to get the attention of men like Aaron. Men from good families who had stable careers and could make them respected wives and mothers. It was how society worked. Aaron bowed slightly to the girls, and Amelia noticed how the candlelight illuminated the shades of red in his hair. She had to stop herself from thinking about touching his hair. Touching him. Robert was speaking and she caught that he was telling a joke in time to laugh with appreciation.

When Aaron finally came to the ballroom, firmly in the clutches of the young women, she found herself grateful that he did not overpay her attention. It would be unseemly, and she had already nearly given herself away.

She spent the evening answering questions about where Randolph might be and dancing with the most reputable husbands. Each time Aaron came into view, she quickly looked away, wanting to be careful.

They danced twice during the evening, but when the leader of the small orchestra counted down the last few seconds until midnight, she did not see him. There were kisses (none overly passionate, as befitted their class) and hands were vigorously shaken as though everyone were congratulating themselves on surviving to the New Year. After midnight, the scene felt anticlimactic, and she wanted more than anything to go home, to sit in the carriage with Aaron, alone and unseen, as Clayton drove them. Did she dare speak to him and tell him how she felt? That she was desperate to be with him?

The second time they danced was after midnight, and soon afterward it was time for the seated breakfast at the long tables the servants had set up downstairs while everyone was dancing. But her place card was far from his, and on the same side of the table, so she could not even see him.

By the time they left in the carriage, she was in such a state of nerves that she could hardly speak. Aaron talked of the coming year and his hopes for an early spring that would allow them to finish the outside projects that Randolph had planned. Amelia hardly heard him, but when he spoke of finishing his own house in town, she did listen. There would be no more seeing him every day. No more talks in the library after dinner if Randolph was gone, no making plans for adding to the garden, no listening to him read to Tamora.

By the time he helped her down from the carriage, her hand had gone cold in her glove, and she meant to bid him a quick good night. Bliss House was dark but for a single lamp in the hall and the sconces on the second-floor gallery. It felt empty. In lamplight, the distant dome always gave her the sense of being in some antique Italian church, and she could only just see the strange glow of the stars. Aaron had told her that Hulot, the architect, had used a formula of paint that he wouldn't share with anyone but the man who mixed the paints. Even Aaron, his closest assistant at the time, didn't know what the secret was.

She removed her gloves and turned to go upstairs.

"Amelia, is there anything wrong?"

She turned back. "Of course not. It's been a long evening—or I should say morning. I'm no longer used to balls lasting until three A.M. Sleep well." Her heart was agitated, making her footsteps unsteady, and she held onto the railing as she ascended. Was he watching her? He did not follow her immediately, and she was already in her room, her coat off and her ear pressed against the door, when she heard his footsteps on the stairs.

She could not sleep and felt she would never sleep again. That he had asked her if anything was wrong told her that she had left him with the impression that she might be angry or frustrated with him. She hadn't meant to seem cold when she was feeling exactly the opposite. Perhaps he thought she was jealous? The young girls had worried her. When she looked in her mirror, she knew she looked every one of her forty years. Practically an old woman! It was a miracle that she still had all of her teeth and that her hair had stayed blond, though in a harsh light, strands of gray had begun to peek through.

What was she compared to those girls? She had to know. She had to tell him that it wasn't that she was angry with him, but that she loved him. Loved him, as she had no other man.

Bliss House was well made, and her bare feet made no sound on the gallery floor. Aaron had thoughtfully turned out the sconces near his room, just as she had turned out the ones near hers. There was enough light from the front windows and the dome to make her way, but she could see no details on the faces of the portraits she passed or the patterns of fabrics on the furniture. It was as though she had come out of her room into an alternate world.

Am I not leaving my own world behind? No longer daughter, wife, mother, but now a mistress? If he will have me!

If she had not driven him away with her uncertainty and, yes, jealousy. She would be no better than the woman-child who was about to bear Randolph's bastard. Would the child even be able to speak English? Or would it only speak her heathen tongue? That the girl in the cottage might bear Randolph a son hadn't before occurred to her. He hadn't given *her* a son.

But Aaron might.

No light shone beneath Aaron's bedroom door, but as soon as she was inside and closed the door behind her, she sensed he was awake. Waiting for her. She was certain then that if she had only waited in her room a few minutes more, he might have come to her.

He didn't speak as she slowly crossed the Aubusson rug that Monsieur Hulot had acquired in France for the pleasure of Randolph Bliss's treasured wife.

Amelia's whole body was shaking with cold and anticipation. She wore one of the several fine, nearly transparent gowns that Randolph had sent her as part of her trousseau almost nine years earlier. Her mother had thought it scandalous, but was too grateful for Randolph's money to object. Amelia had kept the two she had never worn wrapped in their silken envelopes and had religiously replaced the lavender when it was no longer fresh. Had she, perhaps, been saving one for this night without understanding why?

Standing over the bed, she looked down at him, certain she would burst into either tears or laughter from happiness. When she reached out her hand to touch him, he grabbed it and pulled her sharply toward him.

"Why did you come, Amelia? What do you think you're doing?" His voice was loud and vehement. It was nothing like she had imagined it would be: tender, even grateful.

"But I thought—"

"I didn't imagine you'd be so foolish. Don't you see that this is exactly what you *shouldn't* be doing?"

There was genuine concern on his face, and she wanted to touch that face, to tell him that she knew what she was doing—no, perhaps she didn't quite know what she was doing, but whatever it was she *had* to be doing it. She couldn't bear not to be close to him—but he held her hand, her forearm so tightly that he hurt her.

"When I saw you dancing, when I danced with you—" What did she want to say? The words wouldn't come. If only she could touch him. Show him. She had imagined them coming together in perfect communion. Not the shameful coupling she had with Randolph. Yes, he had taught her to please him, and she had not gone unsatisfied, but there was always the ugliness of it. His vile words. The spoken presence of others in their bed. With Aaron, it would be only the two of them, their deep admiration and affection for each other purifying their union.

"Don't you see that this is what Randolph wants? He's made you weak, Amelia. Get out. Get out now."

"I don't understand. In the woods—every evening we've spent together. You want to be with me. I know you want to be with me."

He shook his head. "No. Don't make me say it. Go back to your room. You have to forget about this."

Now she pulled away and he let her go. She was still shaking. A low fire burned in the fireplace, and the room was chilly. She was supposed to be in bed with him, warm and cherished. Beloved.

"God, Amelia. I didn't want to do it. He *made* me do it." Aaron swung his legs over the edge of the bed and sat up, naked to the waist, looking muscular but also vulnerable. He pushed his hands through his thick hair, and she remembered wanting so badly to touch it herself only a few hours earlier. But the memory felt like it was coming to her from a different life.

"We could go away together. I have money, Aaron. Money that Randolph doesn't know I have. We could leave here, and you could work for yourself. It will be enough." The begging words came out of her mouth, and she was stunned by them but found she couldn't stop. Until that moment she hadn't even considered leaving Bliss House. Leaving Tamora. But she knew she would if he said he wanted her. She had never begged anyone like this in her life.

He got off the bed and took her by the shoulders. "You have to stop this. Someone will hear. Don't say any more, Amelia."

"Is it because I'm old? I can please you. I promise that I can please you." She was still begging, but in the back of her mind were the words *he made me do it*. "Why can't we be together? He won't know, and if he did he wouldn't care. He doesn't care, Aaron! He doesn't care if I live or die. Why should I be faithful to him when he hasn't been faithful since the first month of our marriage?"

"You have to calm down, Amelia. Breathe. You're going to faint if you don't breathe."

It was all coming apart. She was coming apart. She tried to breathe but even when she calmed slightly, she was still shaking. "What did Randolph tell you? What did he make you do?"

Aaron looked away and dropped his hands from her shoulders.

"Why can't you tell me?"

"I should have stopped it. Seeing you like this—I was wrong, Amelia. You don't deserve this."

Now she was silent.

"It was money. I cheated Randolph. I did the billing for the final costs of Bliss House, but I made a second set of bills and charged Randolph more than Hulot told me to. Randolph caught me. Hulot fired me, but Randolph told me that if I stayed here in Old Gate, that if I worked for him, did what he told me to do, he wouldn't prosecute, and would talk Hulot out of prosecuting."

He wasn't looking at her now, but at the fire. He looked young. So young and pitiable.

"I don't even know why I did it. Never before in my life had I thought of stealing anything from anyone, Amelia. It's not like I didn't have enough money. It was something about being here

242

every day, seeing the house come together, brick by brick. It made me want things—things I had never even thought about having before. And then when Randolph told me I had to stay, had to help him finish the spring projects, do whatever he told me to do, I couldn't leave."

"I see."

"I don't know why he wanted me to do this to you. I'm your friend. I swear I'm your friend, Amelia. I was going to tell you. But I had to have a plan to get away from here. He said if I made you fall in love with me, if we—" He looked away again. "Then I was supposed to humiliate you."

She understood.

Looking down at her gown, she again realized her own near-nakedness, but this time felt real embarrassment and gathered the sides of the full gown to hide herself.

"You and Randolph will be happy to know, then, that you've succeeded. Please forgive me. I'm the one who was weak."

They stood there in silence, the fire casting its dim light on their flushed and troubled faces.

Amelia wanted to be angry, wanted to scream and hit him, but all of the energy, the force that her elation and anticipation had brought her, had gone. When she left, she closed the door behind her, firmly, for that moment not thinking that she might be heard. He didn't follow.

Before she reached the staircase, Randolph stepped out of the shadows.

"I liked that gown when I bought it, yet you never wore it for me. I wonder why."

Amelia stopped. Of course he had been waiting. He had probably been waiting since begging off the party at Maplewood.

"What's wrong? You look unhappy."

Knowing she was taking a chance, she tried to pass him, but he pulled her back into the shadows, almost causing her to fall.

Shoving her against the wall, he pressed against her. The odor of brandy mixed with cigar smoke and something else, something fetid, was on his breath.

"Didn't he want you, Amelia? Did he look at your sagging breasts and your slack jaw and turn away?"

"You know what he did, because you made him do it."

There was enough light that she could see his teeth when he smiled.

"All in good fun, though, wasn't it? Did thinking that he wanted you thrill you? I'm sure it felt very exciting. Very dangerous."

"You're a criminal, Randolph. I've known it for a long time. But most criminals wouldn't sink this low with their own wives."

He pressed her shoulder, hard, against the wall. "Such a compliment, my dear. I've always thought of myself as a man with a taste for adventure. I hadn't thought of myself as a criminal. A mastermind, would you say?"

With that, he used his other hand to rip the neck of her gown, jerking her so that her head slammed back against the wall. Both her breasts were exposed, and he squeezed one so that she had to force her jaws together to keep from crying out. "Did he go so far as to do this to you before he threw you out? Or was he more of a gentleman?"

She tried to move away, to the side, but he held her tighter. "No, no, my love. I've gone to a lot of trouble over you, and you're not going to take my pleasure."

He had taken her before when she had refused him, but never against a wall or where someone else might hear. He kissed her neck, devouring her, talking to her. "Did you beg him? Did you tell him all the things I've taught you that you might do for him? Did you get on your knees for him?"

She knew what he wanted. If she told him what he wanted to hear, maybe it would be over quickly.

"Yes."

"Did you take him in your mouth?"

"Yes."

He opened his robe and she realized he was naked beneath it. As he fumbled to rip the rest of her gown he grunted, and she thought of Aaron, just a room away. Surely he could hear them. Surely he would come.

"You must have been so hungry for him. Did you beg him to take you on your hands and knees so that you could rut like beasts on the floor? Beside the fire?"

God, please let this end!

"Yes. Yes, I did. Please, Randolph. Don't. Someone will hear."

Without warning, he backed away from her and wiped his mouth with the sleeve of his robe. "You're a liar. I watched you from the moment you went into his room. I watched you grovel, but he wouldn't even touch you, you disgusted him so."

She looked away. Some women considered him handsome, and she herself had almost believed him handsome once. But his cruelty was etched all over his face.

"I would tell you that you're no better than a whore, Amelia, but that would be an insult to a whore. A whore at least knows how to lie effectively. Knows how to flatter. You have a long way to go before you reach a whore's level."

He tied his robe and pushed back the hair that had loosened around his face. "You'll want to clean yourself up, my dear. Lust has an odor all its own, and it no longer becomes you." He started down the stairs.

When she was sure he had reached the bottom, she wrapped the shredded gown around herself and walked slowly across the gallery to her own room. As she turned to close the door, she noticed that Aaron's door was open a few inches. She watched as it closed altogether, and heard the key turn in the lock.

Chapter 27

AMELIA

January 1879

There was nothing like a child to drag one back to the reality of life. Amelia woke to the sound of Tamora howling as she ran past her door. Harriet's slower, more measured footsteps came after. She guessed that Harriet must have done something out of order at breakfast. But when she saw the quality of the light coming in the windows and looked at the clock, she realized that she had slept until almost noon. She closed her eyes again, not wanting to move.

For hours she had cried into her pillow, her sobs like those of a child who desperately wants her mother to hear and come and comfort her. Her own mother would have come, but would have told her to stop being ridiculous. She had married Randolph for the very best reasons, and they had a child together. It was her duty to remain married to him. Her mother would have no understanding of a man who squeezed his wife's tender breast until he left bruises or demanded to hear the details of her tryst with another man. It would be as though Amelia were speaking Hindustani or Russian to her mother. She would look away, puzzled, rejecting such strange words.

That Aaron had heard, that he had done nothing as Randolph assaulted and mocked her made her sick to her stomach. He was not any kind of man. He was weak and as untrustworthy as Randolph himself. But even as she thought these things she pitied him almost as much as she pitied herself.

She considered leaving with Tamora, taking her and Harriet up east, back to the house in Long Island. As he had planned and built Bliss House, Randolph had told her that Virginia could become their winter home. There was the letter that said she could go back to New York at any time, but she knew now he hadn't meant it. Would she dare to leave him? If she did, he might stop their funds. The money she had would not last more than a year, and she certainly couldn't support her parents. Or he might demand that Tamora be put in the care of doctors.

A part of her—a small part that was growing—was coming to think that it might be best for them all if she gave up trying to be a mother to Tamora. Randolph had the money to have Tamora kept in comfort and safety.

She touched her injured breast. Without Tamora, she might travel. As Randolph's wife, she would have credit anywhere she chose to go, if he would let her. No longer did she desire affection or compassion or, God forbid, any kind of physical relationship with Randolph or any other man on earth. Her body had been violated enough. Her heart had been cheaply given and she had paid the price for it: her husband's triumph and her humiliation.

If she couldn't be quit of Randolph and their daughter, what was left for her?

Randolph might die.

Was she so desperate as to kill Randolph? They would surely hang her, even if she ran back to New York. No one would believe how she had suffered at his hands. She hardly believed it herself. Randolph was more than a criminal. He was a monster. A monster who was about to have another child in the world. With an innocent but heathen mother, and Randolph for a father, it was surely cursed.

She had no plan, no reason to move except that she could not stay in her bed all day. Harriet would need to be relieved. Perhaps it would be one of Tamora's sweet days, and she would let Amelia brush her hair and read her a story. Perhaps there would be no tantrums. There were those days. Those were days when she could pretend, just for a while, that Tamora was not like the children she had seen at the private asylum, children so drugged that they slept most of the day and were wakened just long enough to eat and occasionally be bathed. That she was not a child who might be kept in one of those horrific face masks or straitjackets. The doctors had told her that those children—children like Tamora—didn't really know any differently. That they were animal-like in their *limitations*. No, no, they insisted. It wasn't that they actually *were* animals, but that their understanding was animal-like. They needed care and needed help keeping themselves from harm.

Wasn't that what she and Harriet, and to some small extent, Randolph, Maud, and the odious Clayton had tried to do? They kept a constant suicide watch. She had heard of a family in a nearby county who had a disturbed maiden aunt who was free to roam the town. Everyone knew her and knew her to be harmless. She sang, they said, songs from her childhood, and was returned home every evening by any resident who happened to see her around the dinner hour. But she had a habit of picking up stray objects and eating them: bolts and screws or bits of fabric or ribbons or even small seashells. Everyone knew to watch out for her putting things in her mouth as though she were an infant. (Even Amelia had once swallowed a button, to the chagrin of her mother.) Finally the woman had swallowed a nail, and she had died a slow, painful death. But she hadn't meant anyone harm. Had not meant herself any harm.

Tamora was like that woman. They had to be vigilant. They had to keep watch so she would not die before—before when? Before she became an old woman? Amelia had no idea what would happen to Tamora when she, Amelia, died. If Randolph outlived her—which, given the vileness of his soul, seemed likely, because it was well known that the meanest people live longest—she would certainly be institutionalized.

Amelia knew all these things, but she could not face them this morning. She wanted to die herself. She certainly didn't want to see Aaron or Randolph or any other human being. She wanted out of her life.

There was no sign of either man when she emerged from her room. It was the first day of the New Year, and she had put on a loose day dress and kept the stays of her corset lightly fastened so her breast would not be injured further. She found Clayton in the kitchen bent over some sort of puzzle that had been fashioned from two horseshoes and a bit of wire.

"Have you seen anything like it, Missus Bliss? Maud gave it to me as a gift for the New Year, but I can't make heads nor tails of it." At the stove, Maud chuckled.

"I've made black-eyed peas for the New Year, ma'am. You'll want to eat them for good luck before you go off calling."

"Thank you, I'm not hungry, Maud." She turned to Clayton. "Please take this note to Maplewood, Clayton. I won't need you the rest of the day. I won't be making any calls."

"But Mister Bliss said—"

"If Mister Bliss requires you, then you should certainly take him where he wishes. I'm asking you to take this note for me. If you are unable to perform that duty, you may go and ask Mason or one of the other hands to do it, and I will tell Mister Bliss that you have been uncooperative."

He took the note from her hand and gave her a quick nod and a "yes, ma'am." When she left the room she heard him mumble under his breath and Maud laugh in response.

She went upstairs to find Tamora having a tea party with Brownkin and her dolls. Harriet was knitting, but she looked exhausted. Strangely, she had looked less well since she had stopped drinking so much.

"I'll stay with Tamora this afternoon, Harriet. If you'll come up and ready her for dinner and then take her for the evening, I'll deal with her now."

"That would be a blessing, ma'am. She was a hellion this morning, but I didn't want to bother you as you'd been out celebrating the New Year and all. Mister Bliss made sure that Maud and Clayton and me had a bottle of that lovely champagne that was served at dinner last night, after Maud and Clayton and the girls from in town cleaned up. Did you have a good time at the party?"

After assuring Harriet that yes, she'd had a pleasant time at the party, and no, she hadn't checked on Mister Bliss this morning, but that she was sure he was fine, Amelia closed the nursery door on Harriet and took her place in the rocking chair. As though to prove to her that she might be the daughter Amelia hoped her to be, Tamora brought Brownkin over to her for her to kiss and then went back to her tea party. Tamora did all the actions for each doll, lifting the teacups to their lips, and then also touching their mouths with the wax fruit and cakes that Amelia had bought the previous year at Mister Schwarz's Toy Bazaar. To her surprise, Tamora had never once tried to eat the wax food herself, though Amelia's father had told her that it was surely a risk. How little her parents understood about Tamora. How little they wanted to understand.

Maud brought lunch to the nursery. Tamora counted her food and arranged it the way she preferred on the plate before eating. Amelia told her all about the children at the party at Maplewood and how the Christmas tree had shone. She didn't mention the girl in the blue velvet ribbon because she knew she could not keep the emotion out of her voice, and any strong emotion distressed Tamora. It was best, anyway, because the thought of the little girl led to thoughts of Aaron.

She had walked down the gallery outside Aaron's empty room before coming up to the nursery, and, as any proper hostess might, looked into his room to make sure all was well, and nothing needed cleaning or arranging. She had thought he might have gone for good, but his things were all still there. For a moment, she had stood in front of the fireplace, remembering how unhappy he had looked. How vulnerable and young.

But he was not vulnerable. He was weak. And she had been—as he had told her—also weak.

It was fatal to be weak around Randolph. Why hadn't she understood that before? From Aaron's window she saw the cottage in the distance. Gray wisps of smoke rose from the chimney. The girl would be warm in such a cozy place. What did she do all day? Soon the girl would have a child, just as Amelia had. What would Randolph do about the child? It had been on her mind. It was one thing to hide a mistress in the woods, but quite another to hide both a mistress and a child and whatever children there would be in the future.

After lunch, Tamora did not struggle at all when it was time for her nap. At Amelia's urging she climbed onto her bed and let Amelia tuck the hideous Brownkin into the crook of her arm.

"Rest well, my love." Amelia kissed her daughter on the forehead. Tamora did not give kisses in return.

She found she didn't want to leave the nursery, which felt as safe as the nursery she had spent her own childhood in. It had had five tall windows through which she could watch the street and the changing seasons, and some long-ago inhabitant had painted the walls with sky blue and yellow stripes. The furniture had been beautifully shaped, but sized for children. She would have liked to have had that furniture for Tamora, but her parents had sold it long before Tamora's birth.

When she had made inquiries about it to her mother, her mother had been dismissive. "It was ancient furniture, Amelia. We had no use for it, and we got a very good price. Some of the pieces were quite valuable. Every bit makes a difference." Like the nursery furniture and much of the family silver, Amelia had also been sold for a very good price.

Confirming that Tamora was asleep, she went to her morning room and retrieved the small lap desk she used for correspondence. The Christmas holiday and the decorating and the parties had put her behind on everything but the most timely pieces of mail. Back in the nursery, she got to work. She had to thank her mother for the Christmas gifts and let her know that she understood that her father's health certainly took precedence over any travel they had thought of doing. It did not take much imagination to hear in her mind the growling tone her father had surely used to inform her mother that he didn't want to make the trip. In truth, Amelia knew he disliked travel. There were letters from three school friends, two, in fact, from just one of them. Samantha Brown, whose family was less prestigious than the others—or so Amelia's mother had judged—had written first to wish her happy Christmas. The second letter was dated a week later and had only just arrived. Samantha's maternal grandmother in North Carolina was very ill, and while she had to rush down to help nurse her and could not stop in Old Gate, perhaps Amelia would come to her grandmother's house for a brief visit? Her grandmother had a retinue of nurses and servants and only asked that Samantha come and read to the old woman for an hour or so each day, as she had a pleasing voice, and she missed her.

Amelia's first reply was written quickly. Of course she was terribly sorry to hear that Samantha's grandmother was ill, but the demands of setting up a new household and her care of Tamora meant that she couldn't leave Virginia at present. The other two notes were dispatched just as easily. Neither of the women demanded much. Their notes were polite and mentioned their children and husbands and had a bit of gossip about mutual friends. She replied in kind, describing the extravagant holiday celebrations she'd attended since arriving in Virginia, celebrations that were so different than the ones she'd known as a girl.

After sealing the letters, she looked up to see Tamora still sleeping. For the most part, she favored Amelia's side of the family. But her forehead and nose were decidedly Bliss family features.

Could she leave Tamora for just a few days? God, she wanted to run out of the room and put on traveling clothes and leave that afternoon. There were surely trains out of Lynchburg that would take her to North Carolina. Samantha's grandmother lived in one of the larger cities.

It was evident that Randolph meant to keep Aaron there to torture her. They were both puppets to him. How foolish she had been, half listening to all Aaron had told her about the upcoming projects Randolph had planned. She had been thinking of *him*. Of being with *him*. But in the end, she had been thinking of herself and her own unhappiness. Or rather she had been thinking of desperate alternatives to her own unhappiness.

Hadn't Randolph urged her to travel a bit, to familiarize herself with the neighboring areas? It was true that North Carolina wasn't exactly in their neighborhood, but she had never once traveled without him or Tamora or her parents since she had been married. And did she really need his permission? No.

What about you, my child? My Tamora?

A week. She would be gone a week at most. A day's travel on the train either way, and a few days in between, visiting with Samantha and keeping her company when she wasn't with her grandmother.

It was as though God had moved his hand over her life to ease the pain of the last twenty-four hours. A sign that He believed she deserved better than she had recently been given. That her (brief) respite also must have entailed the sickness of an elderly lady and the long-distance travel of her friend occurred to her, but she didn't think about it too deeply.

She took out another sheet of paper and wrote to Doctor Cyrus Beard. She had no love for the man as he was extremely close to Randolph and, she suspected, had some hand in Randolph's infidelities. (She had no proof of this, but something about the confidences the two men appeared to share made her suspicious.) He was always calling himself her "servant" and saying how he wished to be helpful. If there were anything a doctor should be helpful about it should be the acquisition of a woman with nursing skills who could help Harriet if Amelia were to go away.

Chapter 28

LUCY

May 1908

"I want to ride Julius to school, Mother. Why can't I ride Julius?" Michael Searle's voice was dangerously close to being a whine.

"Because you're only eight years old and Julius is unreliable on the roads. Terrance will take you in the car." Randolph spoke from behind his New York newspaper, which he received by mail.

Michael Searle looked down at his plate, mumbling. "It's embarrassing driving in the car. And sometimes Terrance pinches me."

Now Randolph closed and folded his paper. "If he pinches you, it's because you deserve it. Don't be such a sissy."

Michael Searle looked to Lucy, who shook her head, warning him not to talk back. "I'll speak to Terrance."

"No! Please don't tell him I said anything. Please, Mother. You'll only make it worse."

Seeing his anguish, Lucy was prepared to let it drop. She would take Michael Searle to school herself in the car.

"Don't be ridiculous." Randolph stepped on the kitchen bell set into the floor beneath the dining table. It was not quite eight-thirty in the morning, and they sat in the dining room at breakfast, watched by the unblinking peacock-feather eyes on the walls. No one moved again until Terrance came in from the kitchen.

"Have you been pinching Michael Searle, Terrance?" Randolph didn't bother to look up from his plate but speared a forkful of sausage and put it in his mouth. In the past two years, he had become clumsy about his eating, yet peculiarly shrewd about the money that was being spent on food. Too, he had become less fastidious about his clothing. The collar he had put on that morning was stained with cigar ash and Brilliantine.

Terrance cleared his throat. "I'm afraid young Michael Searle has been making up stories again. He's quite the storyteller." He cast a side-eye at Michael Searle, who stared down at his full plate.

Lucy worried that Michael Searle was not eating enough. He was too thin, with anxious, tapered hands and bony arms that he kept covered with shirts that stayed carefully cuffed, their sleeves never rolled up. Odette tried to tempt him with sweets and puddings and plenty of milk and cheese, but he was often too nervous to eat. At eight years old, he already had secrets, which was a horrible shame. But she could do nothing to change it.

"Terrance, you are not to touch him. I'm telling you now, in front of Randolph. Your job is to take him to school, and bring him home, and that's all."

"You won't address Terrance that way, Lucy."

Lucy never knew what Randolph might take sideways these days. *He* had become more secretive than anyone else in the house, disappearing for hours at a time. She had seen strange women making their way around the side of the house from the servants' quarters and was certain he was bedding them. Sometimes she heard voices in the night and laughter. She only prayed that Michael Searle didn't hear it in the room beside hers, near the front of the house. Randolph's room was still on the other side of the gallery, the hall a gulf between them.

"Of course, *Missus* Bliss." Terrance gave a little bow and took Randolph's empty plate. He stopped in front of hers, and she nodded.

Her heartbeat had quickened. Terrance sometimes disappeared with Randolph. It made her uncomfortable, and she wondered what they were up to. But, on the other hand, she was just as happy not to see Terrance around the house.

She and Randolph had two different sets of friends, and she had, over the years, excused herself from Randolph's now less frequent evenings of more ribald entertainments.

"I'll ride with you to school today, darling." Lucy touched her son's hair. "Terrance can drive us both."

Michael Searle ducked away, even more embarrassed, but he did not protest.

There was no private primary school closer than Lynchburg, and Randolph had judged the local schoolhouse, which sat at the western edge of Old Gate, good enough for Michael Searle. Lucy hadn't been sure if the phrase *good enough* was meant to be sarcastic or serious. Faye's six-year-old twin girls had started at the school this year, and between Faye and herself, the school was well outfitted with books and supplies and a decently paid teacher.

Lucy noted the jealous glances of some of the other boys—boys who arrived on foot—as Michael Searle got out of the car. They didn't dare harass him while his mother was looking on, but she knew it was different inside the schoolroom. He seemed miserable and, giving her an I-can't-believe-you're-making-me-do-this-again look, took his lunch pail and turned for the school's front door.

"The boys don't like him. But he gets along fine with the girls, I hear." Terrance's voice was loud enough that the other children surely heard over the rumble of the Packard Model 30's engine.

"That's enough." Lucy leaned back in the car's rear seat. The front passenger seat was more comfortable, but she didn't like sitting next to Terrance. "Let's go home. I'll drive in and pick him up myself this afternoon." Driving the car still intimidated her, but she would do it.

There were now twenty or thirty cars regularly on the streets around Old Gate, and the Packard 30 was one of the most distinctive. Her father still refused to ride in a car, preferring horseback or the small trap her mother had used to drive.

Her father lived alone, now that Juliet had moved to France. She had been dutiful, tending him and being his hostess in the years after Selina's death, a death for which he still blamed Lucy and Randolph. As Lucy blamed herself. Her mother's fall had stunned everyone, including Randolph, though in the aftermath he had told her that it was probably for the best, which had upset her. Now she wasn't so sure. From her mother's attitude on meeting Michael Searle, she knew that she and Randolph would never have been forgiven.

Her father hadn't wanted either of them to come to the funeral, so Lucy went alone and was ignored by him. There was to be no graveside reconciliation, but Lucy held onto Juliet and counted herself lucky that her father hadn't driven her away or treated her cruelly in front of the other mourners.

She had loved her mother, though her mother had made it awfully difficult. For the rest of her life Lucy would feel her mother's absence. Feel responsible. At least Juliet didn't blame her. And Juliet had been the better daughter to their widowed father, until, five years later, she married a French count after meeting him at the Grange, the resort hotel near Charlottesville. It had made her father doubly sad to lose the last woman in his life. Though, within

Lucy's hearing, he said to a parishioner, "At least I saw *one* of my daughters into a decent Christian marriage."

Lucy tried very hard not to be angry. Randolph, however, refused to even go to church, so anxious was he to avoid him.

Though Michael Searle was already eight years old, he only saw his grandfather officiating in church. Edward Michael Searle never sought out his grandson, or Lucy, in any other capacity.

Lucy tapped Terrance lightly on the shoulder. "Please stop at the butcher's. I want to have them deliver some lamb for Easter."

"I'll order it on Tuesday." His response was terse, disrespectful. She and he were about the same age, and sometimes she thought he tried to take advantage of that fact. Also, the more dependent Randolph was on him, the less respectful he was of her.

"Stop at the butcher's."

He parked in front of the butcher shop and got out to help her from the car, but then returned to his seat to wait. When she glanced back at him as she went inside, she noticed he had taken out a pocketknife and was cleaning his nails.

The bells hanging on the inside of the door gave a cheerful jingle as she passed through. Despite the thorough whitewashing of the shop's walls, sawdust on the floor behind the counter, and neat, hand-lettered signs with prices and the meat on offer, the air inside the shop bore the sickeningly sweet stench of newly let blood.

"What can I do for you, Missus Bliss? Terrance was in here for some chops and a roast on Saturday. Need something else?"

"The chops were delicious, Mister Crocker. I've just come in to order a lamb roast for Easter." She had it in her mind to invite her father for Easter lunch, though she was certain he wouldn't come or even acknowledge the invitation. Randolph had just shaken his head when she suggested it. "How is Missus Crocker? Is she recovering well from her abdominal surgery?"

"Slowly. She can't get around very well, so I'm running the shop by myself for a while. We have some help, though. The doctor says she'll be better in a few weeks."

They discussed the amount and the price of the lamb, and when it would be picked up. Finished, she turned to go, but the sound of footsteps on the stairs and a familiar voice stopped her.

"Uncle Carl? Auntie wants some marrow bone soup."

Seeing Lucy at the counter, Carrie turned away quickly and started back up the stairs. Lucy called after her.

"Carrie Crocker! You're here."

"Oh, yes, she's been here these two weeks. Did you not know she was my niece? She's been a great help. Carrie, come say hello to Missus Bliss." Mister Crocker smiled. "Carrie used to work for your mother and father. That's right. And maybe for you out at the big house for a while? I think that's right. Carrie?"

Lucy was shocked at the change in Carrie. Her once lovely red hair was faded with age, even though she was, Lucy recalled, not much older than thirty. Her shoulders were slightly hunched in her loose blouse. Most shocking was the long, dark pink scar on the right side of her neck. It felt impossible to hide her shock, but Lucy quickly smiled.

"Carrie, it's been such a long time. You didn't leave word where you'd gone, and even Mother and Father wondered. Though I expect you know that Mother died soon after I returned. I've missed seeing you."

Throughout this speech, Carrie watched her cautiously, fingering the silver cross on a chain around her neck. Her uncle upbraided her.

"Cat got your tongue? Why, anyone would think you were a twelve-year-old girl with no sense, Carrie Crocker. You could at least say *hello* to Missus Bliss." He looked back at Lucy. "She talks a blue streak to my wife. Quite wears her out."

After another moment's hesitation, Carrie came around the meat counter to greet Lucy. One of her charms had been a friendly openness, which seemed to have disappeared.

"I'm sorry I didn't write. I took a position with a family in Norfolk County. I'm still there, but they gave me leave to come and help my aunt and uncle." Her voice was so quiet that Lucy had to lean forward a bit to hear her.

"I know we were gone a long time. I had so hoped that you would come back. You wrote that Terrance was difficult to work with, and I can see that now that I know him. It must have been very hard for you."

At Terrance's name, Carrie froze. She looked past Lucy to the Packard, and Terrance, who was still looking down at his hands.

"I have to go upstairs back to my aunt. I'm so sorry." Carrie held out her hand to shake, but Lucy took the chill hand in both her warm, gloved hands.

"Call on me at the house before you go back, won't you? I want to hear all that you've been doing, and you should meet Michael Searle. What would you think about coming back to work for me?"

"Oh, no. I couldn't do that."

Lucy could see that the butcher was eavesdropping, and she wished that she might have a moment alone with Carrie.

"Then let me take you for tea this afternoon before I pick up Michael Searle. The new little tearoom on the next block is so dear."

Carrie took a step backward, bumping into the meat case. "I can't. I won't. Please just go away and leave me alone!" She turned and hurried around the counter, and past her uncle, who reached out to try to stop her.

"Carrie Ann, come back here!"

Lucy was puzzled, yet not insulted, as Carrie's uncle obviously thought she might be.

"I'm so sorry to have upset her." Lucy hated scenes, and she had certainly been the cause of this one. "Please offer Carrie and your wife my apologies."

The butcher was embarrassed. "No. We are sorry, Missus Bliss. I don't know what got into her."

Lucy waited until she and Terrance had returned to the house to say something to him about seeing Carrie. As he took her hand to help her out of the car, she asked him if he remembered her.

"I do. She was unhappy here. She said she wanted to work somewhere else. You asked me about it when you returned."

Lucy nodded. "I just saw her at her uncle's butcher shop. She looked more than unhappy. I think her new situation must not be a good one."

Terrance shrugged. "That has nothing to do with you, Missus Bliss. I'm sure that if she had stayed a little longer, or waited for your return, she would have found life very pleasant here."

When Randolph did not appear for lunch, Lucy asked Odette to prepare her a tray so she could eat in the garden. It was a beautiful afternoon, and she had a new book of poems to read. Before she was through eating, Randolph came to stand in the doorway of the salon. He stood watching her until she asked him what it was that he wanted.

"I wanted to see what a whore does in the light of day."

Lucy sighed. His jibes and criticisms were rarely so direct.

"Randolph, what in the world have I done to offend you?" He had become so erratic of late, sometimes gazing at her as though she were a stranger. He complained of voices trailing him through the house, chasing him to his room or the library.

She had come to think of these times as his *spells*. Both she and Michael Searle and even Odette knew to avoid him when he was acting so strangely. Only Terrance stayed close to him. Always Terrance.

Lucy's own experiences with the ghosts were more benign. Since her mother's death, they only seemed to sigh mournfully. It was strange to live in a place with ghosts, but not nearly as frightening as she would have thought it would be. When Michael Searle was a boy of three or four, she would sometimes hear him in his room, talking to someone. When she asked him, he would simply say, "The girl." But it had been a long time since he had mentioned her.

"You were out with Terrance all morning. I saw his face when you returned. He looked troubled. I asked him if you had propositioned him, and he tried to deny it, but I know the truth. I know your secret affinity for each other, and it disgusts me."

She closed her book and looked out to the maze with its lovely nude statue of Hera. Surely Hera had some wisdom she could use right then. Zeus had been a true pain to live with as well.

"I'm afraid you mistake your perfidy for my own, Randolph. I've seen the women who have been coming here, into the servants' quarters. You're the one who should be ashamed. I've done nothing. And really. Terrance? Surely I would have better taste than to sleep with your valet." She almost added, "And certainly not your son." But she held her tongue.

He charged over and stopped just short of her chair, breathing heavily. She recoiled as he leaned close, a dozen inches from her face. He was unshaven, and his breath smelled of coffee and tobacco. "It's an affinity, I tell you. You should be ashamed. Your good father would see you burned at the stake."

At that moment Odette came out of the salon and stood by, waiting. Feeling her watching him, Randolph turned slowly around.

"Negress, you're involved in this, too. I never should have brought you into this house."

"Perhaps you are right, Mister Bliss. I have seen too much."

"Insolence," Randolph snapped. "Both of you." He pushed past Odette and strode into the house.

Odette walked slowly over to collect the tray. "You all right, Missus Bliss?"

"I'm sorry he was so rude to you, Odette. Josiah fears it's a kind of dementia."

Odette shrugged. "He's no different than he ever was at his worst. They're plaguing him."

"Who's plaguing him?"

"Missus Amelia Bliss. Maybe his daughter."

Lucy was silent.

"I know you know what I mean, Missus Bliss. You hear them, too. Michael Searle hears them, and he has since he was a little one."

Yes, the voices. The ghosts had called Selina's name, had caused the dreadful heat, and the shaking of the house that made her mother fall. But why had they caused it? Why did they hate her mother so when they hadn't done anyone else real harm?

"Poor Michael Searle." Lucy sighed. "His life is made of secrets. Did he tell you? I wondered if you knew."

"He's a good boy, and a better son than Mister Randolph deserves."

A butterfly came to rest on the arm of Lucy's chair, its yellow wings closing like hands in prayer. She put a fingertip close to it to see if it would move, but it stayed where it was.

"The voices are loudest inside Mister Bliss's head. They will drive him mad one day. It's already started. If you will beg my presuming on our friendship, ma'am, he has earned it."

Chapter 29

LUCY

May 1908

Lucy parked the Packard well down the street from the butcher's shop and got out to walk. One day she had chanced to exit out the back door of the flower shop and saw that there was a small courtyard onto which many of the shops opened. It was pleasant there, with a well pump and a few small benches. Almost like a park. The Crockers and several other shopkeepers lived above their shops or rented out the living quarters, so it wasn't unusual to see laundry hanging from post to post. In all, the courtyard had an appealing, European look about it. And she knew exactly where the gate was where she could gain entry without being noticed on the street.

No one stopped or appeared to see her take the stairs up to the apartment above the butcher's shop. In her hands she carried a bouquet of flowers and a small basket of cakes the cook had hurriedly made for her earlier in the day. She rang the bell.

Carrie's face appeared at the curtain behind the glass, and Lucy saw how she bit her lip, anxious, before she opened the door.

"I've brought some things for Missus Crocker. I'm sure she's not well enough to see me."

Carrie let her into the apartment's roomy kitchen. Up here, there were the smells of liniment and marrow broth, instead of blood. At least now, she thought, it might smell of flowers, too.

"Thank you. I'm sure she'll like them very much." Carrie took the flowers and cakes and laid them on the scarred wooden table that held crumbs of bread and a curled cheese rind. Perhaps the remnants of her own lunch.

"I was hoping we could talk for a few minutes, Carrie. Do you mind?"

"Not in here. Let's go down to the courtyard."

Neither of them was under any mistaken impression about the nature of Lucy's visit. Carrie left for a moment to check on her aunt.

⌒

"What happened to you, Carrie? Why did you leave?"

Carrie's hands were restive in her lap, her fingers plucking at the edges of her apron pocket.

"I didn't want to worry you, you being on your honeymoon, and all. Your parents were already so angry. The cook came to see me, and I explained, and she said your mother was in a perfect rage, and that your father was worried. I tried to tell her that all would be well, and that Mister Randolph had improved my salary. I told the cook you were happy, Miss Lucy. That she should tell them that."

Lucy reached out to squeeze the other woman's hand. "Thank you for that. It's their fault they wouldn't listen. Nobody ever blamed you. I think my father would even have taken you back."

She regretted the last part immediately when she saw Carrie's face fall. "Oh, do you think he would have?"

Lucy nodded, but continued quickly, "I'm sorry you were unhappy at Bliss House. It meant so much to me to know that you were there, waiting. I had no idea Randolph and I would be gone so long."

Carrie sighed. "I should have written you again before I left." She touched the scar tissue on her neck. It seemed an unconscious gesture, as it had seemed when she did it in her uncle's shop.

"Who did that to you?" To Lucy's surprise, Carrie didn't hesitate to speak, and the words came in a flood.

"Terrance wouldn't leave me alone. He followed me every-where. Every time he caught me alone, he stood over me. Staring. Asking me questions, telling me I was—telling me I was pretty, and that I should leave my door unlocked at night so he might come and visit me." She shook her head. "You hear of women doing such things, it's true. But I never gave him any leave, or even so much as a look, I swear to you. I swore to Odette, but she wouldn't listen and said that I should just ignore him, that he was lonely and only wanted to be my friend."

That Odette would take such a position did not sound like the Odette that she knew, but Lucy did not say.

"I locked my door, and even pushed the little dresser against it at night, and he caught me in one of the upstairs rooms as I was dusting, and told me he had seen the marks on the floor, and that he'd heard me pushing it, and that it didn't matter because he could make me let him in."

"But he couldn't. There were others in the house, yes? Surely Mason wouldn't have let him hurt you."

The look that Carrie gave her told her she was being naïve. And of course she was. Carrie had had no friends at Bliss House, just as Lucy herself had had no friends in Paris.

"That's when I wrote you."

"But you were vague, Carrie. You didn't tell me he was threatening you. How was I to know?"

The way Randolph had laughed and shaken his head when she had told him Carrie had written that she and Terrance weren't getting along. "When the master's away, oh, how they'll play!" He had brushed it off, and so had she because of her own turmoil. Yes, she should have known. Should have taken better care.

"He said the first day he saw me with you, the day we saw the preacher woman, that I looked at him. He said he knew that I was meant to come to him. That Mister Bliss had agreed."

So, the truth. Arranged between them. *Mister Bliss had agreed.*

Two weeks later, after many sleepless nights with the dresser against her door, she had decided to go to Lucy's father's church, to beg him, after the service, to let her return to her job. She said she wanted to make herself look especially nice, as the Episcopal church was where the richer families went, and she didn't want the Reverend Searle to think her disrespectful. So she had taken her curling iron to heat it in the stove, and was alone in the kitchen when Terrance came in. At first she thought he would let her by, but then he tried to grab her, and she held him at bay with the heated curling iron. But he was too fast for her and took it from her and held it against her neck.

"The smell was awful. Like pig's flesh over a fire." Carrie looked away, sickened by the memory.

They sat, silent, Lucy imagining the iron burning Carrie's skin. The cruelty on Terrance's face. She had never known him to be so wicked, but she didn't doubt Carrie's words. She was heartsick.

"My aunt and uncle had told me my position at Bliss House was a good one, and I needed to make it work. I *couldn't* tell them that I was afraid."

"Did you tell them what Terrance did? Did you tell Odette?"

"Odette gave me enough money to get to my mother and another job in Norfolk County, and told me I should have left long

before. That I was a plague to Terrance because he wasn't used to
having pretty girls in the house."

"Dear God."

"I don't think she meant to be mean. I don't know if it was that
she cared for him like family or was afraid of him, too. He said that
if I told anyone what he did, he would tell the police that I was a
thief, and that I would go to jail. Even if I didn't go to jail, he said
I'd never find work again."

~

Lucy waited until she knew that both Randolph and Michael Searle
were asleep before she confronted Terrance. What else could she
have done but offer Carrie money? The tears she had fought as
she apologized weren't enough. Carrie hadn't wanted the money,
but Lucy had begged her to take it as some kind of reparation.
She urged her to go back to Norfolk County as soon as she could
possibly leave her aunt, and Carrie had told her not to worry. She
had not wanted to return to Old Gate at all, but her mother had
pressured her. Her aunt was finally almost well, so it wouldn't be
long. Lucy had embraced Carrie when they parted, but it was an
awkward moment.

Terrance sat at the big table in the butler's pantry, smoking his
last cigarette of the day. He didn't bother to get up when Lucy
came into the kitchen.

"What did you do to that poor woman, Terrance?"

"Poor woman?"

"You terrorized Carrie. She could hardly bear the thought of
coming back to Old Gate to take care of her aunt because she would
be too near you."

Terrance ground the remains of his cigarette out on a china
saucer. When he saw her notice, a shadow of a grin came to his
face. She had never once seen him smile fully.

"Whatever she told you, she didn't come here a virgin, *Missus* Bliss."

"I'm not interested in her virginity. You scarred her. You threatened her."

"She misunderstood me. Ask Odette."

Lucy's heart beat wildly in her chest. Although it distressed her that Odette hadn't helped Carrie when she was first told about Terrance's unwanted attentions, she didn't want to have to confront Odette. She liked Odette. Depended on Odette to take care of Michael Searle. To keep their secrets.

Terrance pushed back his chair. "We could wake her now. I'm sure she'd be happy to talk to both of us."

"What do you think Randolph will say when he knows what you did?"

Now he stood, a look of mock perplexity on his face. "What do *you* think he will say?"

"I will do everything in my power to get you out of this house. I don't like you near me. I don't like you near my son."

"Do you mean your son? Or your daughter? I'm confused sometimes. I'm sure his friends at school would be equally confused. Don't you agree?"

More than once in the following days, her complaints against Terrance rose to her lips when she was with Randolph. But when she thought of her son's sweet, mild face, she bit back the words, knowing Terrance would not hesitate to ruin his life. A life that had hardly yet begun.

Carrie's letter arrived less than a week later, saying that she had returned to Norfolk County, and that she was sorry to leave without having seen "sweet little Michael Searle." Lucy was not disappointed, finally believing that it had all worked out for the best.

Chapter 30

KIKU

January 1879

Kiku secured her robe more tightly around her and took one of the blankets from the bed to wrap around her shoulders. It had begun to snow in the night, but the surrounding trees had kept the snow from piling too deeply around the cottage. The third-hand, wool child's coat that Odette had found for her back in September had never fit her well, and now the sleeves rode above her wrists and the front wouldn't meet, leaving a gap the width of one of Randolph's books when opened.

Randolph had not come to see her in several weeks, finally repulsed by her growing stomach, and so she was nearly always alone. Once again, she felt too cold to make her way out to the woodpile and eyed the two shelves stuffed with books that she could not read.

All of the books were bound in the same wine-colored leather that Randolph had told her was called *Moroccan*. She stood on her toes and snuck a hand from beneath the blanket to take one from the shelf.

The leather might not burn, but when she opened the book and fingered the thickness of the creamy white pages she knew that the paper would crackle and burn cleanly in the fire, and that she might spend hours tearing the pages out, one by one, and laying them on the now-smoldering logs. All those words! They flowed over the yellowed pages like endless schools of fish, taking peculiar shapes, stopping in one place, only to flare off and continue farther down the paper.

Inside her the baby rolled, as though to encourage her. She put the book on a nearby table and touched her belly, looking for the bump of the foot that sometimes revealed itself as an outline beneath her skin, but today the child was nestled far inside her.

Surely he is cold, like me.

The thought made her angry.

Letting the blanket fall, she held the book in the air by its tooled front cover and tried to tear out a hunk of pages, but they resisted and she only bent them. With a grunt, she tried again, and again. Finally realizing that she could only do a few pages at a time, she worked quickly, ripping out three, four, five, but no more than that at once.

On the fire, the pages quickly flamed, and they smelled just like seasoned wood. But though they burned and burned they gave off little heat. She ripped them out faster, nearly burning her fingers. What right did Randolph Bliss have to keep her freezing here?

Where else would I go? I have no home. This is my only home.

What would happen when the child was born? Randolph had refused to speak of it except to say that the world didn't need another bastard.

With a great cry, she threw the book's empty cover onto the fire, where it lay for a moment before beginning to smoke and curl. The little chimney was drawing and the smoke didn't come into the room, but the smell still sickened her. She retched and grabbed the blanket to hurry out the kitchen door.

Her boots slid on the snow-slick steps and she fell onto her elbows and back, banging her head and shoulders against a stair. Her fall was nearly soundless, reverberating only through her body.

She opened her eyes and lay motionless, staring up at the tops of the leafless trees against the sky.

What if I die here?

No, she would not. Her hands and arms could move. She turned her head from right to left. Pressed her hands against her belly. If anything had happened to the child, how would she know? There was no question of a doctor. Randolph had said she had no need of one, though Odette had told her he was wrong and had wanted to engage a midwife. But she was too afraid of Randolph.

Indeed, what if it died inside her?

Will I live with the corpse inside me forever?

Rather than alarming her, she found the idea comforting. She would be the living and the dead at once. A creature unknown to the world. Unless the ghost of her child escaped, and, unhappy, blamed her for its death.

Better to blame Randolph, my child.

She carefully turned onto her side to raise herself and stood. When she was moving again, with only some stiffness in her back, she gently shook out the blanket to rid it of the snow from the stairs. The terrible smell and her nausea forgotten, she retrieved the wood basket from the porch and walked hesitantly to the woodpile. Though she considered herself strong, she could only carry four or five of the split logs at once in the basket. Barely enough to feed the fireplace through the night.

When the baby comes, we will sleep together in blankets by the fire, and if he wakes crying, I will calm his cries with kisses. But the image of Randolph arose, unbidden, in her waking dream. He would want her again when her body no longer repulsed him. Or perhaps he would abandon her altogether. Force her and his child out of the cottage.

Arranging the blanket again around her shoulders, she bent to fill the basket with wood. Her lips and fingers were stiff, and she realized she should have put on the gloves that Odette had given her for Christmas. She could picture them sitting on the kitchen table, waiting.

With the wood basket full, she grunted as she lifted it, feeling the stretch in her groin muscles. Inside her, the baby suddenly rolled, which made her smile. Her fall on the stairs hadn't hurt it.

As she turned to go back to the cottage, she saw something black on the unbroken snow.

It was a boot. A child's boot.

Setting the basket on the snow, she picked up the boot. It was still pliable, not completely frozen, and—strangely—not covered in snow. She looked about her. The only footprints in the snow were her own. Looking up into the trees, she wondered if some bird might have dropped the thing there. Above, she saw only twisting branches and squirrels' nests. She put the boot into the basket, oddly leery of leaving it on the ground.

But cold as she was, she knew she had to look further. It had to be Tamora's boot. Tamora, who, according to Odette and Mason, wasn't allowed to go anywhere by herself.

"Touched," they had said. Always screaming because she didn't speak.

Kiku said the girl's name, her breath forming the word in the air.

There was no response.

She looked toward the deeper woods and now saw the other boot a dozen yards away. Cold gripped her heart. She ran toward the second boot, and, yes, perhaps there were footprints now. Faint footprints even smaller than her own.

She called for Tamora again, her voice louder. Stronger. There was no echo, but the sound seemed to grow, expand in the spaces between the trees.

Now there were stockings. Thick black stockings lying in a tangled knot. She picked them up, hardly able to feel them with her stiff fingers. The child was losing her clothes! Where was she going?

She bent to look for more footprints, cursing the white brightness of the day. Bright and frigid. She almost wept with frustration. The footprints had disappeared.

Her own boots were little protection against the frozen, snowy ground, and she could no longer feel her toes. There were beggar children in New York whose toes froze off during the relentless winter, so that they were left with gray, hideous stubs at the ends of their feet. In summer, their deformed feet were exposed on the steaming summer sidewalks. She had tried to give one the pennies in her ditty bag, but Emerald had pulled her away, saying that their parents or keepers often maimed them just to get pity.

Her body told her to return to the cottage. No one would ever know that she'd found the clothes. Looking down at the stockings in her hand, she dropped them onto the snow and stared at them. Wondering.

No one would ever know.

Could she be so cruel?

But as she was about to turn back to the cottage, she saw the clump of dark green wool hanging on a distant bush. When she reached it, she also saw the dead squirrel with its feet mounted on a piece of wood, and a nut clasped between its front paws.

⁓

Kiku knew the tree in which she found the dead girl, and had once imagined the arch-shaped, peaked hole in its side to be the home of a *kodama*, a tree spirit. She did not know for certain if this tree contained a *kodama*, because there was no one to tell her so. But in the fall, the tree had dropped sweet black walnuts that she had gathered, and she had been sure to thank the tree. Back at the cottage, she had cracked and eaten nuts, even though they sometimes hurt her teeth. She had hidden them from Randolph, her own treasure.

Tamora was curled in the hole, her bare legs folded against her, her head resting on her knees, her face looking out to the woods. The wind played with the blond hair that just covered her face, hair that was not much longer than Kiku's own. Her arms were clasped around her legs. She might have been trying to make herself as small as possible against the cold, but to Kiku she looked like a half-dressed doll that some child had tried to hide.

On the ground just outside the tree were the torn remains of a dress or gown that might have been rent by an animal. Or had the child herself ripped away the dress and discarded it, the way she had left behind her other clothes?

Kiku knelt before the girl and half covered her own face with the blanket to feel the warmth of her own breath. The wind picked up, and the girl's hair moved again; through the strands, Kiku could see that her eyes were tightly shut, her lips a shocking blue line in her delicate face. She was so thin that her arm seemed that it might break if Kiku touched it.

She knew she should do something. Find someone. But she could only stare. Was the child's ghost still nearby? Kiku felt no presence but the cold's. She touched the girl's hair, calming it. In her belly, her own child kicked.

They are brother and sister. My child knows this child.

That grief should touch her child even before he was born seemed a horrible omen. But it was done. She couldn't protect him from what had already happened.

Where was the mother, that her child should be discovered, dead, by a stranger? No, not a stranger. Kiku knew it had surely been the child in her belly that led her here.

The girl was not even as heavy as the basket of wood seemed on Kiku's weariest days. The most difficult part was getting her up the cottage stairs because her legs and arms were still stiff and awkwardly bent. Once inside, Kiku knelt to lay her on the rug in front of the dying fire. When the fire was warmer, surely she would unbend.

No mother should have to see her daughter frozen inside a tree like a cast-off doll.

Outside, the day was even brighter, and when Kiku went back out for the wood basket, she saw two red cardinals watching her from a rhododendron. She had brought the dead squirrel back to the cottage, too, but left it on the ground near the steps. It must have been important to Tamora if she had been carrying it with her.

Her own hands were still stiff as she rebuilt the fire with the cold logs, but she was intent. Searching around, she found two small sticks of fatwood that she had earlier missed. Carefully, she used the poker to bury the leather cover of the book farther back in the piled logs.

When the fire was blazing, she stayed close to it for a few moments so that its heat drew the blood back into her face and hands. The baby rolled, no doubt hungry. She was hungry, too, but she felt the presence of the dead child too strongly and knew it would be wrong to eat with her nearby. She touched her belly, urging the child to be patient, and got up to get another blanket from the bed.

Moving the girl had become more difficult. Either Kiku was wearier or the warmth of the cottage had increased the girl's heaviness. As she worked, she hummed a quiet song about a pair of quarrelsome birds that her sister, Hanako, had particularly liked. As she placed the girl onto the blanket, she looked more closely at her chalk-white face with its circles of blue around the eyes and blue mouth. Like the rest of her body, it was so thin that the bones might have been trying to escape from her taut skin. Had the child's face changed? Was the mouth different in some way?

Kiku's heart jumped to think that Tamora might not be dead after all. "Tamora?"

There was no movement, no answering breath. The cottage was silent except for the cracking of the fire. But in the distance, she heard raised voices like the ones she had sometimes heard before the house was finished and Randolph's wife had come.

She wrapped Tamora in the second blanket, thinking that she should have also gathered the clothes from the woods. Now she was only wearing her bloomers (which, Kiku gathered, were probably soiled, as there was a smell of feces about them that was getting stronger) and undergarments, including a clean, soft chemise without lace or any sort of decoration, as a baby might have worn. The child had removed her clothes as she wandered to her death. Had she wanted to return to the earth as she had been born—naked and innocent?

Warmer now herself, Kiku hurried to her bedroom and returned with the hairbrush. Kneeling again, she saw that the girl's face was still chalk-white. So the fire did not warm the faces of the dead. Picking up Hanako's song again, she began to brush the child's hair. Hanako had disliked having her hair brushed or arranged, but of course this girl did not complain.

How is my Hanako? So much older now. You will be doing all my chores. Complaining, no doubt.

She was still brushing the girl's wind-knotted hair when she heard pounding footsteps on the cottage porch. Men's footsteps.

Chapter 31

KIKU

January 1879

Kiku gripped the hairbrush tightly as Aaron knelt over Tamora's body. He was dressed for the cold in a great, rough coat, but had taken off his hat and heavy leather gloves and laid them on the floor beside the girl. Crystals of ice and snow melted from his boots onto the rug.

He looked up at Kiku.

"When did she come to you? How long has she been dead?" His voice was calm but concerned. "They've been searching for her these last two hours."

"I found her when I went outside to get wood. She was in a tree. Like an animal. Without her clothes."

He hesitated before pulling back the edge of the blanket from Tamora's shoulder. His eyes did not linger on the girl, and he soon covered her again. The girl's jaw suddenly slackened and her mouth emitted a gassy sigh. Aaron recoiled, and looked up at Kiku, who spoke quietly.

"Her ghost is free now." Inside her, the baby gave a violent kick that made her flinch.

"Please don't say that to Amelia, Kiku."

"I shall not see Amelia."

"Well, you may, at that. The sheriff is sure to investigate. There will be questions. I'm sorry."

"What do you mean?" The policemen who came to Madame Jewel's house were always friendly because, Emerald had told her, Madame Jewel gave them envelopes of money and sometimes reduced rates with the less expensive girls. She hadn't thought about police here in Virginia.

Aaron stood up and went to her. "Ah, my poor darling. I didn't even think of you. Are you all right?"

Kiku let him embrace her, and she suddenly felt very tired. He stroked her hair. "Were you frightened?"

"She was a very sad girl. She was never quiet. Now she is quiet."

"Yes. She was very sad."

They stayed like that for a few moments. Behind him, the fire burned, unable to warm the poor girl in the blanket.

"We must open the door." Without waiting for Aaron to respond, Kiku opened the front door again, and the icy breeze rushed inside, sweeping into the fireplace, bending the flames. On the porch, it played at the set of bells on a chain that Mason had made for her, and she knew that the girl's soul was free. Kiku waited, standing a bit behind the door in her blanket to stay warm. When the breeze calmed, she closed the door again.

"Kiku, that's just an old wives' tale. Her soul is with God."

"If you don't believe, then what harm can it cause? She will not be colder."

Aaron sighed and looked down at Tamora.

"Randolph needs to know she's been found. I don't want him to know that you found her. I'm afraid of what he'll do—or more what Amelia will want to do. She's away but she'll return soon." He closed his eyes for a moment. "God, this might kill her."

"How could they lose her in a house full of servants?"

"Sometimes it's easier for a person to be lost when there are a lot of people around. Everyone thinks someone else is watching."

"Should I gather her clothes?" The thought of going back into the cold now that she had warmed some was unappealing, but she wanted to do the things that were right. Now that Tamora's ghost had left her body, it was nearly over.

"I don't think that's a good idea."

"Why not?"

"Kiku, you need to stay inside. Think of your own child. I can get the clothes. Or Mason will."

She knelt beside Tamora and touched her hair.

Aaron got down on one knee. "Tell me. I need to know. Why did you bring her in here?"

Anger rose up inside Kiku like some ugly living thing. "You would have left her out there to be eaten by some wild animal, some night creature? She tore her clothes off in the cold and hid in the tree. Can you not see that? She must have been afraid!"

"They're not going to understand. You have to be prepared. You don't understand the way things work."

"I understand the truth, and I did my best for her. We shouldn't be arguing like this. Not with her here. Go and find Randolph." She didn't like being angry, and especially not with Aaron. "Please. She can't stay here."

Aaron took her hand and helped her to her feet again.

"My dearest, I'll have to bring them back with me." He looked down into her face. "Don't be angry. I'm only trying to protect you. I'm sure they'll be kind."

She gave a grim laugh. "Randolph? Do you think Randolph will be kind to me when he learns that his daughter is dead on my cottage floor? Maybe you are correct that I should have left her in the tree." But as she said it, the words turned to ash in her mouth. She was not cruel.

"I'm sorry." Aaron stood in the doorway, his face full of regret. He pulled her close to him, kissing her hard on the mouth. Then he was gone, hurrying down the front steps and into the woods.

Kiku watched him go, touching her fingers to her lips, which still pulsed with the feel of him. He would return with Randolph, and Randolph would see her with Aaron, and he would know. Now neither she nor Aaron nor her child would be safe. Shaking with cold and fear, she closed the door and went to stand over the girl.

"Tamora. Why have you brought this on us? What shall happen now?"

Chapter 32

KIKU

January 1879

The three men stood around the body. Now there were three pairs of boots melting onto the rug.

"Amelia mustn't know she was found here." Randolph didn't look at Kiku, but she knew that his admonition was because of her. He had looked right through her as he had come in the house, and she knew better than to try to speak to him. Was her own life in danger? It was possible that they would find her in some way responsible for the child's death.

The doctor, who had introduced himself as Cyrus Beard, had moved Tamora's body to the sofa. Kiku had thought it a small sofa until she saw how tiny and lost the girl's body looked on the coral velvet. The doctor bent over her and carefully forced her jaw open and lifted the lids of her closed eyes. When he did this, Kiku looked away, saddened by the violation of the girl's delicate body.

He looked closely at her hands and her ears as well. Then he turned to Kiku.

"You said you found her in a tree?"

Kiku glanced at Randolph before speaking. "In a little house in the tree. A walnut tree." She pointed vaguely to the west.

The doctor knitted his brows. Surely he thought her crazy.

"Not really a house. Just a little place where animals or spirits can hide."

Now Aaron spoke. "A hollow. It's called a hollow."

Kiku nodded. "She was hiding there. Without her clothes."

Randolph seemed to study her.

"They are still outside. Like a trail of breadcrumbs for birds." She spoke more boldly. "I found her boot first. And the other, and the sweater. And the squirrel."

"Stop!" Randolph put up his hand. "My ward obviously has some strange ideas, Cyrus. Why is my daughter dead?"

The doctor took off his eyeglasses to wipe them clean with his handkerchief. They had steamed on entry to the now-warm parlor of the cottage and wouldn't stay clear.

"Removing her clothes has been one of the girl's frequent afflictions, yes? You've told me this."

Randolph cleared his throat, but it was the doctor who continued.

"The child has frozen to death. Not long ago by the look of her skin and her eyes."

"Should we be talking about this, Doctor? With a young lady present?" Aaron indicated Kiku with a nod of his head.

The doctor looked at Randolph.

"I don't see that she should not hear what we say." Randolph sighed. "It appears that she brought the child in here on her own. She's obviously not afraid of the dead."

"It would be helpful if I knew when she'd been found. How long has she been in front of this fire?"

"I went out soon after I woke."

"Was anyone else here to see you?" The doctor left the other part of his question unspoken. *Was the child here with you?*

Kiku shook her head. Why were they asking such foolish questions? Odette had told her that Tamora acted like she had demons in her head, and Kiku herself had heard the girl's frequent screams. But she had done nothing to her, and had only seen her the one time, when the girl had banged on her door. She had no reason to harm her.

Perhaps Aaron had been right. Randolph was not going to believe her. Not going to protect her. Even though the room was warm, she again pulled the blanket close around her.

"Kiku, did Tamora come to the house? Was she alive when you first saw her?" Randolph's voice was just the slightest bit cajoling, but held a warning. It was the voice he used when he was about to accuse her of something. Of moving his things in the cottage, or taking money from his wallet, or, as he had that fall, accusing her of seducing the workmen, enticing them to the cottage to have sex with them. That was one of his theories about how she became pregnant, when, of course, she had already been pregnant when they first arrived.

"She was not. I have already told you."

"Where is the clothing?" The doctor had put on his glasses again and was peering at her. Behind him, the dead girl still lay, as though forgotten.

"Her clothes are outside. I have done nothing!" Frustrated, angry about the accusations that Aaron had told her to expect, angry that he had been correct, she started away from the group of men. But Randolph grabbed a handful of the blanket, and when she moved, it fell away.

Without the blanket, the rise of her pregnant belly was obvious. The doctor stared, but Aaron's eyes shifted to the fire. Kiku put a protective hand on her stomach, not very much caring what the doctor thought. With a smile tugging at the corners of his mouth, Randolph gathered the blanket and replaced it on her shoulders.

"You're no longer needed, Kiku. Go into your bedroom and rest. Odette will come over to tend to your needs today."

The doctor had finally looked away, but now Kiku could feel Aaron's eyes on her back.

Please don't watch me. Don't let Randolph see you watching me.

She closed the bedroom door behind her. It was cold in the room. The fire was spent.

Please let them leave soon.

She was hungry, and the baby was hungry. It felt like hours had passed since she had gotten up and gone outside. Climbing onto the bed, she hugged her knees as close as she could to her belly.

The voices outside the room continued at a murmur, but she did not try to make them out. Would she be taken away? Would she be killed quickly, or would they wait to hang her until after the child was born? In New York, Emerald had read a story out of the newspaper to her about a pregnant woman who had killed a man, but her execution had been postponed until the birth of her daughter. If they were to do that to her, what would happen to *her* child?

The answer was Randolph.

Randolph's only other child was lying dead just outside her bedroom door. Of course he would want another.

Still chilled, but suddenly overcome with weariness, she lay down on her side and fell asleep within minutes.

Her sleep was deep and fretful, and in her colorful dreams, she felt herself trying to reach the bedroom's door to open it. Her body felt so heavy that she had a difficult time even leaving the bed, but she was certain that she must get to the door. When she was finally sure she was free of the bed, she still couldn't feel the floor beneath her feet. The door loomed and bent in front of her, as though alive, but as she reached for the knob, it moved farther away.

What is this madness? Am I no longer in my home? Have I been tricked?

Even in her sleep, she was certain that she hadn't left her house, and this was some other house within her house. Outside the door she couldn't touch, she heard a woman's angry cry, then a high, tortured wail. Kiku drew her hand back. The door was solid again. Someone was shaking it, and the sound was like thunder, filling the room, shaking the floor and ceiling. The iron feet of the bed clattered as they danced on the floor.

Kiku shrank away. There was some monster on the other side of the door, and it was a monster that was not Randolph. This monster was female, and it meant her harm. She knew she must hide. She tried to slide under the jostling bed, but her belly had become as enormous as a great glass globe she had once seen in the window of a shop while walking in the city. Its ungainly shape made her unsteady as she tried to rise to her feet, and she had to hold onto the foot of the bed. Tottering for the window, she managed to stay upright, but knew at any time she might fall. She pushed back the curtains. While the room was still daytime-bright, the window itself had disappeared; bricks filled the frame where the glass had once been. Alarmed, she pounded on the brick until she was sure her hands were raw, but her fists made no sound on the coarse brick. The bed had stopped moving and now there were no other sounds except the woman's plaintive wailing and Kiku's own sobs.

Exhausted, and unable to form even a single word in response to the woman's cries, she sank onto the bed and lay down, spent. The thick feather mattress collapsed and folded around her so that she could not turn one way or the other. The effect was suffocating, and her belly grew and grew, cutting off the air to her lungs. Her own child was killing her.

Unable to breathe in the dream, Kiku forced herself awake and opened her eyes. The light in the room had changed little, but the air was as thick and as oppressive as the silence. The blanket and robe had entangled each other, and she struggled to free herself. Her flannel gown was soaked with sweat, and her hair lay plastered against her forehead and neck. She threw the blanket and robe aside and jumped from the bed as though it were on fire.

Putting her hands to her belly, she found that it hadn't changed in size at all, and tears of relief filled her eyes. The baby was still, though, which worried her. Her dream had been so tormented that she could not imagine that the child had not experienced it as well.

Will my own child mean my death? Such a thing cannot be possible.

But the thought took root inside her.

Pressing her ear against the door, she listened. There were no voices. No crying women. But there was something.

At her feet, the key lay on the floor, fallen out of the keyhole. When she tried the handle, it turned easily, and the door opened.

Chapter 33

LUCY

May 1914

Sometime after midnight, Randolph stood at Michael Searle's door, pounding on it, telling him to come out and stop hiding. Lucy threw on a robe and went out to the hall to confront him.

Randolph now existed in a state of perpetual wakefulness, which meant that the rest of the house suffered as well. Long ago, she had told Michael Searle to lock his bedroom door at night so Randolph would not wake him. Previously, Randolph had come to him in the night to compel him to perform strange errands, like taking a lantern into the orchard to find the withered apples that Randolph believed were "soiling the ground," or to muck out the stalls because he had, that morning, fired the groomer. Randolph was nearly seventy years old, and in the past five years, he

289

had aged more quickly. He had lost considerable weight, and the very infrequent times he demanded that Lucy come to his bed to perform her wifely duties, she had been surprised that he was not more fragile. The very act of sex seemed to flood him with some of his old vigor, though the appearance of strange women at the back of the house had become far less frequent.

"Randolph! Let the boy sleep. He's done nothing wrong. Please, please go back to bed."

The hall blazed with light from the newly electrified chandelier. The rest of the house had been electrified two years earlier, in 1912, but the chandelier had had to be taken down and wired. The electric light gave everything in its glow a harsh look that Lucy didn't like. It made her feel too exposed.

"He's in there plotting with Aaron. I can hear them all the way down in the library. They're plotting to take over everything that belongs to me, and they must be stopped. Just because that creature is my child doesn't mean he will inherit everything. There are others, Amelia. There are others, as you well know!"

It wasn't the first time he had called her Amelia. During the day, he rarely confused her with his long-dead wife. But at night he was obsessed with Amelia. Obsessed with either believing Lucy was she, or that she was walking the halls of Bliss House, her footsteps pounding in his head.

"Let's go downstairs and I'll warm you some milk. Listen. You can't hear them now, can you?"

Randolph turned his head slightly, listening. "Aaron is crafty. I never should have had him stay here. He infected this house with his perfidy. You, too, Amelia. He infected *you*."

Odette had told her about handsome Aaron Fauquier, who had been involved in the building of Bliss House and was staying with the family when Amelia Bliss had killed herself. There had been a small scandal because, after Amelia's death, Randolph had accused him of burning down an empty cottage in the woods where

Randolph had once kept a mistress. Fortunately, it had been winter and the fire had not spread, and Aaron had never been prosecuted. Soon after, he had moved to Lynchburg to work as an architect, selling his unfinished house in town. Lucy wondered if he were even still alive.

Knowing Randolph as she did, and the regretful tone Odette's voice took on when Amelia Bliss's name was mentioned, Lucy immediately sympathized with Amelia. Had something really happened between her and Aaron Fauquier? Lucy knew that if there were an Aaron Fauquier living in Bliss House right now, she too might seek solace from Randolph's capriciousness in his arms.

"Please. Let's go downstairs."

"You tell Aaron that I won't stand for his turning Michael Searle against me."

"Of course, Randolph."

He followed her to the head of the stairs and maneuvered around her. "No, I won't stand for it."

Lucy! Push him, Lucy! Suffer him no more. Send him to us, Lucy!

Did Randolph hear the voices, too? They were loud in her ears, not quiet or aimless as they so often were. Lucy took another step toward Randolph. It would not be difficult. All it would take was a firm shove, and he would be gone.

Now, Lucy! Do not wait.

Could she? The house had taken her mother. Why was it demanding that she push Randolph? Why would it not please itself, as it had with her mother, Selina? The answer came quickly:

Free yourself, Lucy. Free your child!

I can. I will!

She was not hypnotized, nor was there a fog of enchantment in her head. Her head was clear as she lifted her hand to Randolph's back, but before she made contact with it, he spoke. Lucy looked down to see Terrance standing at the bottom of the stairs.

"What do you think, Terrance? Fauquier is up there impor-
tuning that young man to cheat me. I heard them from down in
the library. This must stop. If they don't stop, I'll kill them both!"

Despite the unholy hour, Terrance was dressed. Always he was
dressed as though he slept in his plain white shirt and black pants and
trim black jacket. Dressed and spotless, so different from the silent
young man who had opened the door of Bliss House to her almost
fifteen years earlier. It seemed to her that the more careless Randolph
got with his appearance, the more careful Terrance became of his own.

Lucy halted her step on the stair, lowered her hand.

"Mister Fauquier is a duplicitous individual. I can understand
your distress." Terrance was always calm and affirming with his
employer. *His father?*

Randolph nodded vigorously. "We should talk about what needs
to be done. This can't continue, and Amelia is too compromised."

"I'm going to make him some milk. You can go back to bed,
Terrance." Lucy tried to keep her voice from shaking. There had
been a tone in Randolph's words that alarmed her. He had never
suggested that he would kill Michael Searle, or anyone else, but
now she feared he was considering it.

Terrance looked skeptical. The harsh light from the chandelier
highlighted the sharp bones of his cheeks and his small, dark eyes.
He looked to Lucy like an animated cadaver. "Shall I return to
my room, sir?"

"Leave us, Amelia. I've no time for your ministrations. You
have treated me shabbily for too many years to try to make it up
to me now. And how do I know that you won't poison my drink?
I'm sure that's what Fauquier would have you do."

Lucy had no answer. How, indeed? She could hardly believe
how easily the idea of murdering Randolph rested in her mind.

"Very well."

Terrance gave her a grim, satisfied nod and held out his arm for
Randolph to grasp as he took the last stair, but Randolph rebuffed him.

"Stop treating me like a child, Terrance. Know your place."

It was with her own grim smile of satisfaction that Lucy turned and went slowly back up the stairs to speak to her son.

⌣

"He doesn't frighten me anymore. He's mad, Mother. He should be locked up. Do you think he really sees the ghosts as well?"

Lucy sat beside him on the bed and lightly stroked his hair. *Yes, he sees them.*

"In the day, he's almost normal," she said. "Who knows what he sees at night. I don't know that there's anything we can do, my darling. Not right now." *Not now. Not yet.*

"I'm big enough that if he tries to do something to me, I can defend myself. I've done it at school."

Both his delicate features and his wealth had made him a kind of target at school in earlier years. But now that he was fourteen most of the bullies his age had quit or been taken out of school to work on their families' farms, so the past two years had been easier. Michael Searle was not big, but he had a lean strength that he had cultivated by riding his horse, Julius, and working in the orchards under the elderly Mason. Michael Searle took a great deal of pride in working with Mason, and his hands were not nearly as soft as those of other boys of his class.

"You've done wonderfully. I'm so proud of you."

After a few moments of quiet, in which they could hear Randolph's loud complaints to Terrance, Michael Searle said the words she had known she would eventually hear, but hadn't wanted to.

"It's time for me to go away to school, but I don't want to leave you here with him."

Lucy rallied, unwilling to show her distress. The child hid enough pain of his own. "Darling, it is definitely time. And while I know you'll worry, I promise that I can take care of myself. He's deranged, but not dangerous, and much of the business is in the hands of lawyers now. I've been making inquiries and I think not a military academy as your father suggested. The Episcopal academy near Washington is a good one, and you could come home for holidays."

"Could you come and visit me there?"

"Of course. If that's what you want." She covered his hand with her own. "We'll have to talk about the summers. There's too much going on in Europe right now, and they say there will be a war. It's not a good time for summer holidays there."

What went unspoken was his reason for not wanting to come home. They both knew all too well.

"What if I have to live with another boy at school?"

It was a worry she had shared since he was a small child. There had been no swimming with the other children during the summers after he was nine or ten years old, lest he be required to undress, and someone note the insufficiency of his male member; no visiting at other children's houses overnight as some were fond of doing. She and Odette had kept his hair short and masculine even as some of the other boys had worn their hair around their collars and cheeks like young Byrons.

"We'll arrange for you to have a private room, and if the school disagrees, we will find you another school, or have Josiah write some explanation. He won't ask questions. He will do what I ask."

Josiah Beard had stepped into his father's medical practice soon after he and Faye had married. If Randolph had told him about Michael Searle's affliction, he had remained discreet, and he would happily indulge her request for the sake of their families' relationship. Randolph was a very private man, and it would have made sense to Josiah that his son would be private as well. Plus, he and Faye were both fond of Michael Searle, and their twin daughters were his friends, celebrating birthdays and holidays together. They had been partners at dancing lessons as well.

"What about—?" Lucy hesitated. A year earlier, Michael Searle had come to her in her room, shamefaced and fearful, and lifted his shirt to show her that his breasts had begun to bud. She and Odette had been frank with him about his differences from other children before he went to school, and she had told him it might happen. But she had held him as he cried, and his tears had mixed with hers on her cheek.

When they were done crying, she and Odette had given him the softest cotton bandages they could find and had shown him how to bind himself so that the breasts would not show.

With a confidence she did not quite feel, she told him, "Perhaps they will stop growing. That is what we hope." But there was no expert they could safely ask. She wouldn't even know where to find an expert in such things and would die before telling a stranger her son's secret.

Aside from Randolph and Odette (and possibly Mason, though she did not worry about him), only Terrance knew. She would never be free of Terrance for that reason.

"I'm good at wrapping myself now, Mother. No one will find out. I promise."

He looked at her with such trust and confidence that it almost broke her heart.

A week before the fall school term began, Michael Searle shook hands with his father on the platform at the train station. Faye, Josiah, and their girls looked on, the girls' pretty faces dewy and pink with heat. Terrance had stayed with the car out on the street. He had given Michael Searle a leather letter folder embossed with his initials before they had left the house, an act that both touched and puzzled Lucy. Was he trying to gain the boy's trust? Randolph showed no emotion, but gave Michael Searle a brief lecture on the hiring of cabs.

"Yes, Father."

Faye's girls giggled behind their hands. A soft breeze ruffled their demure pastel blue-and-pink dresses. They reminded Lucy so much of when she and Faye had been their age. Their dresses were slightly longer and more sophisticated than the ones Lucy and Faye had worn, and they looked almost like young women. Lucy and Faye were now also less burdened with layers and layers of ruffles and adornment. Faye's nautical-style dress was loose through the waist, accommodating her more generous bosom, and Lucy wore a mauve linen and cotton two-piece dress with a straight skirt and long, belted jacket that buttoned on the diagonal. As the day was fine, she had worn shoes, rather than boots, and had made the bold choice to go without stockings because of the heat.

When Randolph stepped away, one of the twins impulsively approached Michael Searle and put her arms around him.

"Don't be afraid," Lucy heard her whisper. "You will be so much happier there." When she pulled away, she glanced briefly at Lucy with her eyes the muted green of winter grass and went back to her mother.

"We must go." Lucy kissed Faye, whose own brown eyes were glazed with unshed tears, and was grateful that she had a friend who cared so much for her son.

As the train pulled away, relief crept over her son's face, and she knew that they had made the right choice. What she did not know then was that he wouldn't return to Old Gate for nearly four years, or that their circumstances would be so changed.

Chapter 34

AMELIA

January 1879

The moment she stepped off the train back in Old Gate, Amelia knew something was very wrong. She liked to think of herself as a woman who didn't give in to strong emotion, but the feeling had started as a sharp twinge at the back of her head when she arrived at the station to find that neither Randolph nor Clayton Poole was there to meet her. It was not simply a matter of their having forgotten, she was certain. The platform, indeed the entire street had been deserted, and she had been the only person to come off the train. After waiting for thirty minutes, cold and angry, she had dragged her valises to the empty stationmaster's office and set them inside. It wasn't her fault that they had forgotten her—she had planned the hour of her return with Randolph even before leaving—but still she felt frustrated and embarrassed. It had been uncomfortably chilly on the train, but the sharp wind cutting across the platform was far worse. She began to walk, thinking she would eventually run into Clayton Poole and the carriage. Her fine leather boots were useless against the thick snow and her feet along with the bottom inches of her skirt were soon soaked. She walked, uncertain of where to stop. There were no cabs in Old Gate, as there were in the city, no line of carriages outside the station. In fact, the thought of the differences between New York and Old Gate drew an involuntary sneer on her cold-stiffened upper lip. Old Gate was nothing like the city, nor even as convenient as North Hempstead. It didn't help that she still felt like a stranger here.

Old Gate was laid out in a strange confusion of concentric circles, but the road on which the station sat—just outside of town—ran straight through. But Bliss House was more than a mile outside the town on the other side, and she worried she might freeze to death before she reached it. She passed the road that led to Maplewood, as well as the Baptist church and town hall. It was Sunday, but services had either ended for the day or they hadn't yet resumed.

Was everyone dead? Was she dreaming?

The stores were unlighted, some even shuttered, because it was Sunday. At the farthest edge of town, where there were a few houses set well back from the road, there were signs of life: candlelight flickering in a window, footprints and hoofprints in the snow as though someone were leading a horse up ahead. But she could see no people.

Damn Randolph! Damn the good-for-nothing Clayton Poole!

Her anger heated her as she walked, lifting her feet and her skirt as high as she could above the snow. Fortunately, her wool cape of green and gold windowpane plaid was lined with fur and covered most of her body. Hiding her hands within, she felt like a clumsy wraith billowing through the streets. Surely there were people watching her from windows, either not knowing who she was or laughing at her inconvenience because she was Randolph's wife.

Beneath the anger and the growing pressure in her head was the certainty that she should be at home, with Tamora, this very moment.

Above her, layers of clouds the color of coal ash scudded over the treetops, racing her home. If only she could reach up and grab the tail of a cloud and let it deposit her there. She might fly like the witch Randolph had once, in supposed jest, accused her of being.

Finally the road flattened and she could see the entrance to their lane a quarter mile away. The entrance with its ridiculous gates, as though it were one of New York's great estates. As though anyone here would bother to arrive unannounced. Randolph's pretensions refused to end and had worsened now that they lived among these Southern heathens. Thank God her parents had refused to visit. Her mother's criticisms would be her undoing.

Her spirits lifted when she saw a pair of horses pulling the brown carriage emerge and make the turn onto the road. Her boots were like sodden stockings on her feet now, and she couldn't wait to get out of the snow. She removed a gloved hand from her cape and waved to flag the carriage down. So happy was she that she resolved not to immediately send the shiftless Clayton Poole packing with his impertinent wife, Maud.

But despite her frantic waving—waving that grew more frantic as the carriage approached at a dangerously fast pace, the horses' hooves spraying up arcs of glittering snow—she might well have been invisible. The carriage passed her seconds after she jumped to the barely defined edge of the road, slipping on a feathery patch that laid her on her side, the horses' quickening hooves missing her by a half dozen feet.

Her horses. Her own carriage nearly killing her!

Clayton Poole, his stupidity frozen on his face like a gruesome holiday mask, had been the driver. But there was another face in the carriage. A red-cheeked, often sly face. A face that she had trusted. The *only* face she had trusted when she had left Old Gate for a short visit to see Samantha in North Carolina.

Harriet. Harriet's face was all fear, and pushed forward as though she would make the horses run even faster.

The front door of Bliss House was open, like an invitation to a bad dream. The house felt more alive than it ever had before: welcoming and repelling her at once.

Now that you are back, you will never leave again and I will punish you.

Guilty implication hit her like a wave. Her soul answered: *I will be punished.*

As a child she had had a pet rabbit. But she had gone away to Boston with her parents for a month, and no one had thought to make provisions for the rabbit. Not one servant had stayed behind, and so the rabbit, Sir Hopkins, was forgotten in its gilt wooden cage.

No one had punished her; her mother blamed the servants.

But a week after they had returned to the dead and moldering rabbit in its hutch in the garden, Amelia used paper shears to cut off her own hair in jagged hanks and hid the damage beneath a linen-and-lace mob cap that had belonged to her grandmother. When her mother jerked the cap off her head, Amelia refused to tell her why she had done it. The reasons weren't even clear to Amelia herself. She felt the same sense of guilt now. The same desire for punishment.

The trip to North Carolina hadn't really been necessary. It had been pure selfishness that had made her leave Tamora alone with Randolph and Harriet and the nurse that Doctor Beard had engaged for them.

If only Tamora were all right.

Perhaps Randolph had fired Harriet, sick of her, and hadn't hesitated because he knew Amelia was on her way home.

"Randolph!"

There was no answer. Only her own voice traveling to the top of the house.

"Tamora! Darling, come to Mother!"

The house was empty, the cold from the doorway beaten back with heat and a sense of something living, breathing, but empty. Amelia was filled with regret for a thousand little things, each one tied to the life she had had before she had come to this house. Now they could never be forgotten or forgiven.

At that moment, she would even have been glad to see Aaron. They had been awkward and cool with each other, and he had managed to make sure he was away during dinners for the time she was there after the debacle of the small hours of New Year's Day.

The chandelier was lighted, an extravagance that she didn't understand. *All* the lamps were lighted. Had Bliss House caused them all to come on by itself? Clayton Poole was gone, but where was Maud?

"Tamora!"

"I'm here, Mother."

She looked up. Tamora had never spoken those words before.

Tamora stood outside the nursery, leaning on the railing, her tangled hair hanging about her face in blond ropes. No one had brushed her hair in days, it seemed. What had that slag, Harriet, been doing? She had probably stolen as much silver as she could get her hands on on her way out.

"Mother, watch."

Amelia couldn't help but stare at this new, disheveled, calm, loquacious Tamora. Of course she would stare! Had Tamora grown in the six days she had been gone? The doctors hadn't been hopeful about her reaching a normal stature, but there she was looking as straight and tall as any seven-year-old.

"Yes, my darling. I'm here." Despite the wetness of her boots, her ruined dress, and the snow melting on the hall rug, Amelia kept her face upturned. Let her lose both of her feet and her hands, if necessary, if her daughter was speaking to her. It was a miracle!

Happiness melted to terror as Tamora, now peculiarly agile and bold, climbed onto the railing with a happy bounce and sat with her bare feet dangling into the air.

"Look, Mother! Look at me!" She raised her arms in a victorious V, her hands outstretched to heaven, so that she was only attached to the gallery railing via the thin, grubby nightgown that covered her down to her knees.

Amelia held back her scream, not wanting to startle her daughter.

But is this my daughter, my one Tamora?

Should she stand beneath the railing to catch her if she fell, or should she run to the stairway, in hope of distracting her from her game?

All these stairs, Randolph, the dangerous openness. You know she can be uncontrollable. How he had smiled, so patronizingly, reminding her that he or Harriet or the nurse would be there every moment, and certainly he would make sure she came to no harm.

Where are you now, Randolph?

She chose to stand beneath those small, kicking feet.

"Mother would like you to get off the railing. Please do what Mother asks, Tamora."

"Say 'pretty please,' Mother. If you say 'pretty please,' I might."

Tamora's was an oddly adult voice now. But Amelia obeyed, at the same time praying that Aaron or Randolph, or even Maud, might appear to help her.

"Pretty please with sugar on it, darling." She tried to keep the shaking out of her voice. "And cinnamon if you want. You know how you like cinnamon."

Tamora laughed like a girl a dozen years older.

"Why are you such a dirty little slut, Mother?"

Amelia was speechless, her breath gone.

"Where did you ever—?" She couldn't finish.

"Daddy taught me all the words, Mother. Words that you won't even say because your mouth is too pure. What's it like to have the mouth of a virgin whore? That's what he called you, Mother. His stick of a virgin whore."

Now Amelia was sure she was hallucinating. Perhaps she hadn't risen from where she had fallen in the road, and her brain was slowly freezing, shutting down. This talking abomination could not be her daughter, but was the bitter mix of her growing hatred for Randolph and his heathen whore, and her worry about Tamora. The real Tamora was surely safe in her bed, tucked in for a nap and maybe even medicated to sleep by the fleeing Harriet.

Perhaps Randolph hadn't fired her, but she had fled because of something terrible Randolph had done to her. Or to Tamora.

She bit the top of her knuckles, hard, to make sure she was awake. Not dead or dreaming.

"Tamora, come down. Right this minute. I've had enough of this game."

Am I shaking from cold, or from fright?

Surely this Tamora would get off of the railing and disappear, and Amelia would go to the nursery and find her true daughter asleep in her own comfortable bed. Only then would she find Randolph and discover the truth of why she hadn't been met at the train, and why Clayton Poole had carried Harriet away from the house as though she were a criminal being pursued.

"I'm coming, Mother."

Tamora's victorious expression disappeared, and her face turned as violent as the clouds visible in the windows around the dome above their heads. She was perfectly still for a moment before stiffening like a wooden doll, and leaning forward, forward, forward, until her body left the railing.

Amelia's mouth opened but no sound came out. She opened her arms to catch Tamora, straining to keep her eyes on her angry face. She would be her daughter's target. If she were to die saving her, it didn't matter.

But the impact never came. One moment she was looking into that purple-gray face, those eyes that had turned hellish and strange, and in the next she was staring up at the balcony to see Tamora standing safely behind the railing. Laughing.

Her laughter filled the hall, growing louder and louder, until Amelia had to cover her ears. Tamora laughed, and then she began to run, her footsteps thundering through the house. Amelia watched as Tamora—*but oh! This is surely not my daughter, my own daughter, but some demon child*—ran to the stairs and began to descend as though she would run into Amelia's arms. When she was halfway down, she began to fade like a shadow disappearing in a slowly growing light, and then she was gone.

Amelia felt her heart drop inside her from a great height.

A sound from the back of the hallway startled her and she cried out.

"Amelia, how are you here? How did you know?"

Randolph came out of the shadowed entry to the library and crossed the room, holding out his hands to her. She found she could not move.

Chapter 35

KIKU

January 1879

Mason pounded on the cottage door, startling Kiku and Odette, who had just awakened.

"You've got to get out. Odette!" His words were muffled as though his face were pressed against the wood.

"Sweet Jesus, what is wrong with you?" Odette opened the door, and Mason stumbled in.

"She wants her dead."

He stopped speaking when he heard the bedroom door open and saw Kiku standing there.

"You've scared us both to death." Odette pushed at his chest, irritated, but Kiku could see worry in both their faces.

Despite his hurry, Mason propelled Odette gently away.

"Maud sent Clayton to tell me Missus Bliss is screaming about Kiku and Mister Randolph. She said she was going to come here."

So it wasn't the police who were going to hurt her or take her away. It was Amelia. Hers would be a rougher justice than even that of the police. Kiku had worried all the previous day and through much of the night, imagining the pain that Amelia was feeling, knowing that her child was dead. Kiku's own child kicked inside her, a constant reminder that it was still alive, even as Tamora lay cold and dead in some room in the big house.

"I will see her."

"Oh, no, you're not going to be here." Odette was in motion, putting on her boots. "We're getting your things now."

"I will talk to her. She will understand." Kiku put her hand on her belly as though to reassure herself that she was saying, doing the right thing.

"Clayton said she looks like a wild woman and hasn't slept all night. She knows the little girl was here."

"We'll take her to our place," Odette said from Kiku's bedroom.

They weren't listening to her. Kiku could not make them listen. For a long time she had wanted to speak with Amelia Bliss, to tell her that she meant her no harm. That she was only Randolph's concubine and made no claims on him.

Why would I claim such a man, a man who hurts me? Does he hurt Amelia so?

"I must stay here. She has seen that I'm with child. She will trust me."

"She's talking like a fool. You're going to have to carry her out of here." Odette turned to Kiku, pointed at her belly. "There is such a thing, little girl, as being too foolish to live. And I know you want to live long enough to bring that baby into the world."

"You had best listen to her, Kiku." Mason's voice was low and serious.

Nodding, she withdrew into the bedroom to dress.

When everything was gathered, Mason carried out her bag, and Odette held onto Kiku's arm as they went down the porch stairs.

"You couldn't have brought a trap or the carriage?" Both she and Mason had to help the ungainly Kiku up onto the broad seat of the wagon. "How is she supposed to ride on this bumpy old thing? You want the baby born in the road?"

"No time."

A distant, hoarse keening shuttled through the trees between the cottage and the gardens of Bliss House.

"Dear God. That poor woman." Odette looked through the trees, but they were too far away to know if Amelia was any closer to them than the house.

Kiku's heart ached for Amelia. There was nothing she could do for her now. But a day would come, she was certain, that she could somehow help her. None of them knew why the girl, Tamora, had been wandering in the snow, but Kiku was as certain as she could be that it was Randolph's fault.

Odette was called to the big house the afternoon of the second day to help with preparations for the funeral. She didn't want to go, didn't like the unpleasant way the people who worked at the house sometimes treated her. Kiku knew this, but Odette didn't complain when she returned, exhausted, her hands aching from scrubbing all afternoon.

Kiku woke from a late nap to find Mason sitting at the kitchen table with his wife, rubbing her fingers with the minty salve that Odette kept to keep her skin from drying in the winter cold. But when Kiku entered the room, Odette pulled her hands away from her husband and rested them in her lap.

"Go on and put it away," she said quietly.

Odette puzzled Kiku with the way she never wanted to be seen asking for comfort. There were times when she wanted to sit with Odette and rest against her shoulder in the way that her own baby sister had done when she was very tired.

"Did you see Amelia?"

Odette nodded. "She's white as that snow outside. Didn't speak much."

"And Randolph?"

Odette shuddered. "He's there. She won't let him near her. I don't blame her."

Kiku heard the hesitation in her voice. Odette rarely hesitated.

"Don't." Mason put the lid back on the jar of salve. Kiku could smell the mint, and it made her hungry. Since she had arrived at their house, she had been hungrier than she had been since she arrived in Old Gate back in the summer. "It's gossip. We don't engage in gossip."

Kiku wanted to know more, but she had become practiced in navigating the vagaries of Odette and Mason's relationship.

She went to the shelves and took down the flour and fat for biscuits. Odette didn't stop her as she often did. Mason retired to the small parlor in the front of the house. Kiku knew she'd find him reading by lamplight when she came to get him for dinner. They had passed the equinox, but the days still felt short, and it was already getting dark outside. When the biscuits were shaped and cooking, she put the beans and ham she had made that afternoon on the top of the stove to heat. The baby kicked when she breathed deeply of the smell of baking biscuits, and she realized she didn't want to leave this pleasant house where she had friends.

Friends. Had she ever before had good friends? Not since the village. On the boat, Christiana had slept beside her and taught her English, but they were desperate friends by circumstance. Madame Jewel had called herself her friend, but it was the girls who looked out for one another.

They ate in silence. When dinner was over and cleared, Mason went to bed, but Kiku and Odette stayed by the fire and sewed by lamplight. Odette had brought her linen and cotton and the softest wool she could find for the baby. She wanted Odette to talk about Randolph and what he had done to his daughter, but she knew she needed to be careful.

"What do you think Randolph will do with us when our baby comes?"

"You go away, is what you do. You don't think he wants a child running around here, do you? I think he'd just as soon kill it." She paused, obviously thinking she'd been too frank. "I know that's not what you want to hear. He's not a man made for children, though it might be different if you have a boy. Rich people don't care so much about bastards. He might even bring it to the house to raise."

It hadn't been difficult to hear, because Kiku knew it was the truth. Randolph had no use for a baby. In the darkest hours of the dark night she had thoughts—terrifying thoughts—of what he might do to the child that would be worse than murdering it.

Was it possible that he would give the child to Amelia? What might Amelia do to it in her grief?

Mason had made a cradle for the baby and she had been rocking it, empty, for practice, with her stockinged foot. Now she stopped.

"Where would we go?"

Odette was silent.

"Not to New York. Not back to—" Kiku was about to say "Madame Jewel's." She felt herself redden with horror at the thought.

"Maybe you won't have to worry, Kiku. Maybe he'll let Mason and me take it."

Kiku knew it was one of Odette's sadnesses that they had had no children in all the years they'd been married. It was, perhaps, one of the reasons she was so harsh with Mason. Did she blame him? That she loved him, Kiku understood. When he had presented the cradle, Odette had been unable to keep the pride from her face. Mason looked as though he wanted to disappear into the floor.

"I would see him then."

"Yes, you would."

Kiku had been so relieved when Randolph stopped coming around her because of her pregnancy that she had almost *almost* forgotten the real circumstances of her life. Why she was there, living in a cottage in the woods like a girl in a story. But she wasn't a girl in a story. When Randolph had arrived at the cottage with Aaron, it became real once again.

They sat, silent, each thinking of the fantasy of Kiku being there to see her child grow, each knowing that it was unlikely to be, but afraid to think of all the things that were more likely to happen.

Kiku woke to faint morning light and sounds in the kitchen. Normal sounds, low voices. Odette and Mason were to attend the funeral and go immediately back to the house to help with all the guests who were expected. Mason had said that Randolph had invited the entire town, though Amelia had wanted only family and their closest friends.

Mason had told them how, at that first big party after Amelia arrived, Randolph had tried to show off his poor, addled daughter by putting her on a swing in the ballroom, and everyone in town had been scandalized. But Mister Bliss had had no shame and had laughed when his wife discovered it.

"He just kept right on, inviting people back to parties and such. Missus Bliss tried to keep to her room, but he made her come out and be with them." Mason had shaken his head. "He's not a kind man, Mister Bliss."

Now their poor daughter was dead, and Kiku suspected the same fate for her child.

But my child will be perfect. Randolph will not be ashamed.

She fell back asleep, warm in the bed, and when she woke again, the house was empty.

There was no *butsudan* in the house, so she could not offer traditional prayers for the little girl. Odette and Mason often prayed to their god together, standing in the kitchen, and she hoped that the gods of her home would understand when she prayed with them.

When she had dressed and prayed and eaten, she put on her warmest clothes and borrowed Mason's second coat, one that had belonged to Randolph and did not fit Mason very well. It was enormously big on her, but it covered her belly.

The baby was still today. It had shifted greatly in the night, waking her for a few moments, but now its movements were subtle, as though it had gotten itself comfortable. Kiku, though, had to remove the coat again so she could relieve her tortured bladder before she went into the woods.

It had been weeks since she had watched the big house from the woods, because the cold had kept her inside. She had to walk for ten minutes to make her way from the orchards to the woods near the cottage. Beneath her feet, the brown dirt peeked through the sun-melted snow. The bare trees were punctuated with bright red cardinals and their mates. Odette had said that cardinals were souls visiting from heaven, and she put out breadcrumbs to attract them to her yard, though more often the crows came and chased the cardinals away and ate the bread.

The drive in front of the big house was filled with carriages and their drivers, and a few individual horses, which stood tethered to a pair of posts. She guessed that she was late, because she only saw two sets of guests arrive, all swathed in black. No one looked her way. Everyone was focused on the house.

Her hands were cold, and her feet were numb in her boots. There was no coffin or corpse for her to see. She had already seen it. By now Tamora was buried in the graveyard of a church in town. It was Amelia she had wanted to see, but of course she would be inside the house, not outside in the cold.

But what was there, in front of the garden wall? Something had moved, catching her eye. Unlike a human or animal it seemed to drift, like smoke. As it took shape, becoming real in color and form, she sucked in the frigid air. It saw her. It watched her.

Kiku felt her belly contract. Was the baby afraid? A child in the womb, so close to the world of spirits, might be able to sense their presence.

The figure near the garden stayed where it was.

Kiku turned to go back to Odette and Mason's house, feeling the eyes of the dead girl watching her back as she walked.

Chapter 36

AMELIA

January 1879

After seeing Randolph in the hall, Amelia had run past him, up to the nursery, and found Tamora—the real Tamora—laid out on her nursery bed. The ghost or demon or whatever it was had been a shock, but that shock was nothing compared to the brutal ache that rose in her when she put her arm beneath her limp child's shoulders and held her to her.

When Randolph came to the door, she screamed for him to get out. They left her there, alone, for the rest of the day and night. It was the kindest thing he had ever done for her.

She emerged at seven the next morning, closing the door calmly behind her.

It was Clayton Poole who let it slip where Tamora had been found. She had dragged herself down to the kitchen, thirsty, and he hadn't known she was behind him, listening. It was as though everyone had thought that *she* had been the one who died, the one who could not hear or see or talk. Randolph and Terrance and Aaron were nowhere in sight.

"Poor little bugger was in a tree, half naked and curled up like some animal. It was a terrible thing, Mister Aaron said. It was the girl, the squinty-eyed one, who found her," he said, talking to the man who delivered milk to the house. The man had shaken his head vigorously to try to warn him that Amelia was behind him, but Clayton kept talking, enamored with the strange story. "They brought her back here, but it was the girl who found her. Took her into that cottage."

The deliveryman coughed, and Clayton finally turned around.

"Missus. I didn't see you there." He faltered. "Can I do something for you, ma'am?"

She left the kitchen without answering.

Tamora/not-Tamora was standing on the stairs. "What will you do, Mother? Will you kill the little Japanese whore, Mother?"

Amelia was no longer startled to see her, but now she ignored her. She went to the library.

"Do you want that girl in my place, Randolph? Did you kill our daughter so you can start over with that girl and her bastard?" Her voice was loud and angry. She didn't care who heard her.

Randolph stood up and came around the front of his desk. "I've made the arrangements with the church and sent a telegram to your parents. You're distraught. Let me get some of the medicine that Cyrus left for you."

"Did you plan it with her? Did you send our daughter to that cottage so she would die?"

"You don't know what you're saying, Amelia. Please let me take you upstairs."

"Stop it! Tell me the truth!"

Randolph dropped his air of concern and assumed his usual cool, patronizing tone. "You give me too much credit. I would not take such a woman for my wife even if you were dead, Amelia. And my bastard? This is not England or Europe where bastards are recognized so easily. Our puritanical friends are not forgiving, and even I wish to live in society."

His words were almost a relief. Randolph had no need for murder and subterfuge. If he had wanted to have the girl in Bliss House, he would simply have sent her and Tamora back to North Hempstead and done as he wished in Virginia. She would have gone, happily, especially after her humiliation in front of Aaron.

Tamora had no doubt gone in search of the cottage, and, indeed, had found it. It was certainly the girl who had killed her, jealous of her birthright and anxious to be the mistress of Bliss House. She imagined the Japanese girl—if she were Japanese, as Tamora/not-Tamora had said—walking through the halls, her tiny, slippered feet silent on the well-joined wood.

"*She's* the one who should be dead. Not my daughter! I will kill her, Randolph."

When she saw the alarm in his eyes, she knew he had lied to her. He actually cared for the girl. It struck her as a remarkable thing. She had never known Randolph to truly care about anyone but himself. She thought of the wallpaper in the ballroom. All the pretty Oriental girls, reminding him of his whore.

He approached her and tried to grab her by the shoulders, but she slipped away. "Now you're being ridiculous, Amelia. Kiku has done nothing to you. Listen to yourself. You don't know what you're saying."

"Oh, I very much know what I'm saying." They faced each other and for once she saw him as she suspected he truly was: a vulnerable, ugly bully. Not so much evil as manipulative and weak-minded. Cruel because he didn't really understand how to be anything else.

"We'll get you away from here, Amelia. Cyrus will help. I'll take care of you."

She left before he could say any more.

Tamora/not-Tamora stood at the gallery railing, silent and watchful, as Amelia ascended the stairs, but Amelia said nothing to her. If she were to be a murderess, she wanted to say a final good-bye to the child lying dead inside the nursery, and ask God's forgiveness.

Amelia carried nothing with her when she left for the cottage, creeping up to the third-floor theater first to get to the outer door unseen. There was snow, but she didn't notice the cold. She could only see the girl—Kiku—before her, could only feel rage.

No longer would the girl live in her charming cottage in the woods like a fairy-tale princess.

The woods seemed empty and silent, too, though she knew that they were as full of winter life as they had been on the day that Aaron and she had been in the woods gathering evergreens for the house. The day that Tamora had pounded on the door of the cottage, wanting it to open.

Tamora/not-Tamora was somewhere behind her. At the edge of the woods, Amelia turned and saw her by the garden wall. A chill wind was shaking melted snow from the branches of the pine trees, but the wraith's untamed hair did not move.

Amelia didn't pound on the cottage door as Tamora had, but put her hand on the doorknob and turned it.

The normalcy of the place struck her like a blow. She had had an idea of gambling room decadence, with tawdry satins and flocking on the walls and crude furniture of the sort one might see in a cheap restaurant in New York. Such was the image she had of a mistress's lair. But it might have been a parlor in any small Virginia house, with a sofa and two chairs, and a smoking stand that contained the remains of a cigar. There were books on the shelves, books that she recognized from Randolph's library on Long Island. Did this woman read? She had no idea if she even spoke English.

A fire was dying in the grate. The girl had not been gone long.

In the bedroom she found the large bed neatly made with blankets and quilts. She walked quietly, almost reverently. This was where Randolph did the things with his mistress that he had begun whispering to Amelia in the dark not long after Thanksgiving. He had told her of the suppleness of the girl's young body, her submissiveness.

"She is utterly mine. She has no will but to please me. You are incapable of such submission, Amelia. You are not made for that."

No. She was not made for that sort of submission. But submitted she had. Submitted in ways that a modern wife must submit to her husband: in things financial and geographical. He held the strings of the family purse, and if she did not want to live in penury, alone, or with her disagreeable parents, she had to submit to his will. It was not slavery, but a contract.

Randolph had always been free to break that contract, but she had not. She had tried with Aaron, but he had betrayed her. God, how she had wanted him. If only she had been able to have him for a day, it would have been some confirmation that she was alive, and not some automaton who was bought to be a set piece for a house and life she understood but did not care for.

She touched the bed and felt the strength of the girl's presence, felt her power. Her very presence had stolen Tamora and left behind the mocking *thing* that now pretended to be her daughter.

There were clothes in the wardrobe. Summer clothes that were simpler than she had imagined the girl might wear. But also two dresses that confirmed her occupation: a bright green dress trimmed in black with tiers and tiers of machine-made lace. The second dress was purple. Not a royal purple, but the vulgar purple of the theater. The purple of shop girls out for a night of fun, a night of drinking too much and attracting men. Not fine wine, but ale. She took the dress from the hanger and inspected it as though she were going to wear it herself. It was tiny—almost as small as a dress that Tamora might have worn. (Though not purple, never purple.) The shabby fabric was badly soiled, particularly around the hem and neck, and there were artless seams indicating that it had been quickly altered for the girl to wear. She held the dress to her nose. It smelled of body odor and layers of faded perfume. Leaving the wardrobe open, she let the dress drop to the floor.

On the dresser sat two pathetic hats on cheap stands. She tried to imagine the delicate girl—yes, Kiku was delicate, she had seen that—wearing such atrocities. She suspected that the simpler clothes in the wardrobe were ones she had acquired since coming to the cottage. The hats, and the hideous dresses, were the wares of a true whore, and did not seem to suit the girl she had seen in the doorway.

There was murder in Amelia's heart, but the reality of the girl was that she was just a girl who was not that much older than Tamora. She told herself that it didn't matter. Even the youngest women were capable of deceit, and anyone that Randolph had taken as a lover—a lover who had full knowledge that he had a wife and daughter—was probably capable of even worse. The sort of person who didn't care whom she hurt.

She had come into the cottage with rage. If the girl had been there, would she truly have been able to murder her with her own hands? She had no gun, no knife, no other weapon. The goal had been to face her, to make her pay for what she had done. Her life for Tamora's life. But now that she was here, in the girl's very bedroom, she knew she would have hesitated. Aaron had been right when he had told her she was weak. The thought deflated her.

Randolph was everywhere: a shirt over the back of a chair, the books, the cigar stub in the front room. Soon, Randolph himself would surely come in search of her.

"Tamora, were you here?" There was no answer.

But as she started from the room, something fell to the floor with a *thump*. Nothing was immediately evident, and she bent to look beneath the bed.

There. Beside the oak dresser. The shabby tail of some animal protruded from a corner near the dresser's leg. At first she thought it might be a cheap fur piece of the kind that low women wore with their evening clothes. But it was no fur piece. It was a squirrel's tail.

She snatched Brownkin from the floor. One side of his fur was matted and flattened. Tamora had kept him well brushed. In fact so well brushed that what was left of his fur was quickly falling out.

Brownkin.

Not only had Tamora been in the house, but she had had Brownkin with her. There could be no other explanation but that the woman had lured her here and then killed her by stripping her and putting her out in the snow to die.

Amelia lost all reason. Cradling Brownkin in one arm, she used the other to sweep the ugly hats and jewelry and hairbrush and mirror to the floor, screaming with rage. The only things that remained were a peacock feather and a grubby rag doll. Holding the doll by its legs, she tried to tear it in two, but it would not rip. Dropping it to the floor, she crushed it beneath her shoe and left the room. In the parlor, Randolph's books were first, and the ones she didn't throw across the room she piled into the fireplace willy-nilly like some strange fuel. She jerked down the simple curtains and picked up the smoking stand and swung it at one of the front windows, shattering it. After pitching the cigar stand onto the porch, she found a knife in the kitchen and returned to the parlor to slice the cushions of the furniture. As the fabric tore, she pulled out the horsehair and wool stuffing, strewing it on the floor like the entrails of a gutted animal.

Aaron found her on the freezing porch, holding Brownkin and weeping. Her rage had all been spent, and she didn't pull away when he said softly, "Amelia," and helped her up from where she sat on the step. They walked through the same woods through which they had passed together only a few weeks earlier. She saw nothing but her feet moving through the melting snow, heard nothing but the crack of twigs as they crunched underfoot.

"Kiku didn't kill her. I swear she didn't kill her. She tried to help her."

Her heart and mind resisted his words, but she knew they were true. The girl who lived in the cottage was not who had killed Tamora. She herself was responsible. *She* had left Tamora in the house with a father who didn't love her. With her father, a drunken nurse, and a stranger named Missus Williams. If Amelia had put Tamora out in the snow and locked the door behind her, she couldn't have done more to kill her.

"She must have gone out in the very early morning when everyone was asleep. I wasn't here. I'm so sorry I wasn't here, Amelia."

Weeks earlier she would have thrilled to the tenderness in his voice, but now she only heard the words. Everyone was so sorry.

They would all be sorry for a long, long time.

At the wake, mourners clustered around Amelia like so many black-feathered turkey vultures. The soft noises they made might have been words, but Amelia couldn't make them out. She nodded and let them take her hands, noted that some of the faces around her were tearful. She saw Pinky Archer in her ostentatiously unadorned black hat and wondered who might make such a hideous thing. She herself wore no hat and couldn't even recall if she had worn one inside the church, though she knew she must have, because women were required to cover their heads in church, and she had been, in her life, obedient.

The mourners whispered among themselves. They ate. Maud had covered the tables in food and Odette and the hired girls, also in black, hurried back and forth from the kitchen. Amelia could not eat. Could not remember eating.

Tamora/not-Tamora watched from the third floor, her unkempt hair around her face, grinning like she was watching a very funny play. Amelia had never seen such a look on her true daughter's face in life. This was Tamora reborn. The winter had stolen away her sweet, inchoate girl and replaced her with a devil-child. Tamora/not-Tamora was a cruel imp who leapt about the railings of the gallery and disappeared through closed doors. She moved things: lamps and pieces of furniture. She stole Maud's spoons in the kitchen. Amelia saw Randolph in her then. Amelia knew she had sometimes been thoughtless, but—with the exception of what she had done at the cottage—she had never been intentionally cruel.

Except to Randolph. But her words could not touch him. Randolph wore his own cruelty like medieval armor, and he was well covered.

She watched him on the other side of the room. His face was mockingly somber.

False face! Liar! Look at your new daughter! Do you see her, Randolph?

He hadn't believed her when she told him about Tamora/not-Tamora. He claimed not to have noticed that things had been moved or the running footsteps in the night. Tamora's footsteps. Tamora's laughter.

Sitting in the salon, with the vultures clustered around her, she could not make out their words, but she could hear Tamora/not-Tamora taunting her from the hall.

"Mother! Mother! Look how funny they all look. Look how funny you look. Like a crow, Mother. You look like a crow that's been drowned in a lake. Your feathers are all droopy. Are you sad,

Mother? Are you sad that I am dead? Sad that you left me behind to die?"

The night before, when Tamora/not-Tamora had come into her room, Amelia had told her that she had not meant for her to die. She had cried and begged Tamora/not-Tamora for forgiveness. But the thing pretending to be her daughter only stared at her and laughed.

Doctor Beard had finally come at Randolph's insistence and had given her some medicine to calm her. She had quieted, letting them think that the medicine had worked, but Tamora/not-Tamora remained in the corner of her bedroom, waiting until they left to begin torturing her again.

Amelia knew she would live with the torment until she could bear it no more, and then she would die.

"I'm tired," she announced to no one in particular. A sympathetic clucking spread through the cluster of men and women gathered around her, and as she rose, the group parted to let her through.

She didn't look back though, she could feel them watching her. Tamora/not-Tamora stood waiting at the foot of the stairs, also watching. There was no sympathy in her face, but only mocking.

No, this wasn't her daughter. This was her own demon. Her Tamora was somewhere else. Perhaps somewhere else in Bliss House, hiding. She would only come out when Amelia was able to tell her it was safe. There was only one way that Amelia could think of to be able to do that.

Chapter 37

KIKU

February 1879

Kiku answered the door to find Doctor Beard standing on her porch looking vaguely irritated, as though he didn't want to be there.

"Mister Bliss has asked me to do an examination. Please disrobe and lie on the bed with a blanket to cover yourself. Do you understand?"

She didn't even think of refusing, and there was no one to whom she might appeal. If she had refused, Randolph would have been displeased. Odette had told her several times that it was about time she was examined by a doctor or midwife. The only western doctor she had ever seen was at Madame Jewel's, and he had inspected her for syphilis, a malady of which Madame Jewel was particularly wary.

When she had arranged herself on the bed, he came in and took her pulse and listened to her heart, and palpated her abdomen. Then he shifted the blanket, instructed her to spread her legs, and inserted a viciously cold metal instrument into her vagina.

He was just as brusque and unpleasant as he had been when he had come to see Tamora's body.

When he was finished with the examination, he asked her if she knew when she had become pregnant. Kiku held the blanket to her body, feeling far more exposed than she had felt when undressed in front of the men at Madame Jewel's. "June?"

"Ah. I would say that is about right. This baby should come in the next six to eight weeks." Then he was gone.

Six weeks. She felt as though she had been pregnant forever, and yet also that it had only been a few months. Odette would be happy to know that it wouldn't be much longer. She supposed that Randolph would be pleased as well.

With the doctor gone, Kiku dressed and went back to arranging the baby's wrappings and diapers and gowns in the drawer she had set aside in the dresser. Everything was soft, though not quite as soft as the velvet that held Aaron's painting. Fortunately, most of the baby's clothes had still been at Odette and Mason's house when Amelia had come and destroyed all that she could in the cottage.

Randolph had not apologized for Amelia's behavior. When he arrived to look things over after Mason told him what Amelia had done, Kiku did not speak or weep, but only waited to hear what he would say. She had come to feel that the things that Amelia had destroyed were hers, but so often Randolph, when he was feeling particularly cruel, reminded her that everything she had belonged to him, and that she could be replaced by any other woman at any time.

"Only the size of the clothing would matter. But there are plenty of small young women like you. Not quite as exotic, but you have proved to me that women from other places are not so different, my dear. I might as well have a Negress from Richmond or Cuba if I hunger again for something strange."

So Kiku did not complain to him, though she later told Odette her real feelings. It was not for herself or her things that she was worried. She feared that Amelia might come after the child. Odette had told her of the war and of soldiers who had cut babies from their mothers' wombs. Amelia was no soldier, but she was mad from grief. Kiku had sympathy for her grief, but she'd had nothing to do with Tamora's death, no matter what Amelia believed.

Randolph had not stayed long that day. "You may reside with Odette and Mason until the furniture is replaced." He had closed the door behind him, leaving Kiku standing near the scattered pieces of broken window.

At his request, Aaron had replaced the upholstered furniture, the mattress, and all the shattered dishes. Mason had seen to the broken window quickly, covering the opening with boards until the new glass could be delivered the following week.

⁓

With the baby's clothes arranged, Kiku saw to her own toilette. Her hair seemed to have grown two inches since Christmas, and if it had not been so fine, she might have been able to style it into a high bun, the way Odette was now styling hers. At least she could get it back into a ribbon now. Aaron had said that she had hair as soft and dark as a summer night, and he liked to press it to his lips. He had only kissed her, though she had told him that she would like to be his lover after the baby came.

"I want you to be so much more than my lover, Kiku. We must be patient." She was hopeful that he would soon return.

But it was Randolph's boots she heard on the porch that evening.

Once inside, he embraced her with uncharacteristic affection. "I've brought you a little present from Doctor Beard, my dear."

"Doctor Beard does not seem the sort of man to give presents. What could he want to give to me?" The mention of Doctor Beard made her uncomfortable again. The metal device he had put between her legs had been colder and more distressing than any item that Randolph had taken pleasure in putting inside her.

Randolph smiled. "He's a doctor. Not all doctors have pleasant bedside manners, but he knows his job."

"I'm sure you're right." Kiku went to the stove to put the root and chicken stew that she had made on their plates. It was Odette who kept the chickens. She had told Kiku that she should ask Randolph for her own chickens, but Kiku had no interest in chasing chickens around a yard or wringing their necks. She had no trouble with fish, which panicked for a few moments out of the water before dying on their own. It was not a way in which she wished to die, gasping for air, but it would be preferable to having her head squeezed from her body.

"He's sent you some tea. You should only eat lightly with it. Not a full meal."

"I have plenty of tea, Randolph. You are very generous."

"Ah. Chicken stew. Another one of Odette's recipes? It occurs to me that I should have her in the house as a cook. Maud Poole has her strengths, but her skills are limited, and Clayton is a far better driver than he is a houseman."

Kiku regretfully scraped half of her serving of stew back into the pot. She was hungry, but she knew that Randolph would be watching how much was on her plate. She suspected that the doctor's tea would be as distasteful as he. Not once had she had tea here in America that tasted like anything she drank at home in Japan.

Odette would not approve of her drinking the tea that Randolph had brought, she was certain. She made sure Kiku had plenty of dried peppermint tea to settle her stomach, but there were no other medicines that she thought Kiku needed. Odette had little trust of doctors and preferred to use local remedies from a woman she knew. Kiku thought she might also be the woman Odette had suggested she go see to get rid of the baby.

"I won't be staying tonight. Amelia is still in a bad way."

Kiku looked up. He rarely spoke of Amelia.

"I am sorry for her. Will she not eat?"

"Maud leaves a tray for her. Sometimes she'll eat a little at night, but I cannot press her. She's been in the nursery for weeks, and won't open the door when we knock. Doctor Beard says she may need to go to an asylum. Her grief has overcome her."

Kiku poured the steeped tea through a strainer and into a cup.

"Doctor Beard says you should have three cups of the tea."

Kiku smiled, careful not to show her teeth, as Madame Jewel had instructed, a habit she saw no reason to break. "Three cups? But I shall be awake all night."

When he complained that he had gone to the cost and trouble of having the doctor see her, and wished that he had not as she was ungrateful, she quickly apologized and said that she would do as he asked. She knew that if Randolph left, she would not have to drink the second and third cups.

He patted her hand across the table and told her that he was only concerned for her health. It was an uncharacteristically gentle thing for him to do.

When he resumed eating, she lifted the cup and, pleasantly surprised by the minty smell of the stuff, took a sip.

Randolph held up a hand. "Wait! Oh, my dear, I almost forgot." He took a small corked jar from his pocket, removed the cork, and spilled some of its contents into a spoon. "He said to put two good-sized spoonfuls of this into the tea. I had forgotten."

The stuff foamed as he stirred it in, changing the smell from something minty and pleasing to a smell like the breath of a man who has drunk too much beer.

Kiku made a face.

"Just drink it along with your dinner. It will taste better."

She drank, finishing the cup under his steady, benign gaze.

⌒

He had said that he would not be staying the night, but he changed his mind, and when dinner was over he told her to clear the table and then come to sit with him in the parlor.

The tea did not settle well in her stomach, and she was only too happy to get up and have something to do. When she finally came into the parlor, Randolph was in the middle of his cigar and had a book open.

"Sit down. I want to read something to you."

Another astonishing surprise. She had long ago come to the conclusion that Randolph might never surprise her again. She had been in Old Gate for nearly six months and had gotten used to his routines. He no longer even surprised her with new degradations in the bedroom. But this evening something was different. Perhaps, she thought, the plight of Amelia had softened his heart. And who would not be touched by the loss of a child? Tamora had been dead for more than three weeks, and Amelia hadn't been seen out of the nursery since the funeral. Was it possible that Randolph had become lonely?

She took her place on the sofa and covered herself with a wool lap rug that Aaron had brought along with the furniture. All hope that she might see Aaron that night was gone. He would not come near the cottage if he knew Randolph was in residence, and because of Amelia's illness—if that was what it could be called—Randolph was frequently at home, and Aaron could not take the chance of visiting.

"It would be bad enough for him to know that I was calling on you, and even more distressing for Amelia."

Kiku understood his position, but what she did not understand was why he did not leave Bliss House. Yes, Randolph was his employer, but he was not a captive, as she was. He was a man who could take care of himself, and not a woman without resources. She reminded herself to ask him why he did not leave.

Randolph adjusted the lamp.

"It's a book that I had always hoped to read to our Tamora. But she would not sit, would not listen to me for more than a few minutes at a time. I don't know if she even knew that I was speaking to her."

There had been evenings when he had read a bit of a book to her, and then questioned her about it. If she could not answer the questions, he teased her, saying that she had so little understanding that he might well be reading to a housecat. They were not happy memories. But she smiled and nodded, ready to listen.

He read to her of a girl named Alice who followed a rabbit into a hole and found herself in a strange room where she drank a potion from a bottle labeled "Drink Me." It was an odd sort of story. The idea of talking animals was not an unfamiliar one, but together with her uneasy stomach, she found the story unsettling. Inside her the child was still, which was unusual because it was often very busy after she ate a meal. As she listened, she relaxed: The fire was warm, and the wool rug was comfortable on her legs and belly, and Randolph's usually booming voice was calming. Soon, unease was overtaken by comfort and she felt her eyes get heavy and close. Her chin nodded onto her chest.

⁓

"Let's get this next cup of tea into you."

Kiku woke to see Randolph bent over the small tea table where, not so long ago, on Christmas night, she had shared tea with Aaron. For the briefest of moments she imagined that Aaron was in the parlor as well, but when her eyes adjusted to the dim light (Randolph had extinguished his reading lamp), she saw that they were alone.

"I want no more tea. I want to go to bed." Her voice was petulant and childish, and Randolph tut-tutted.

"No one likes to take their medicine. That is a universal truth. After this cup you should have to take no more, and I'll give you a few sips of brandy as a reward."

Kiku shook her head vehemently and cast off the wool rug, nearly upsetting the fragile table.

"My dear, it's on orders of the doctor. He's concerned that you haven't taken good care of yourself, and this will help you feel much better."

Kiku wanted to tell him that she hadn't felt badly at all until she had drunk the tea, but only managed to mumble that her stomach had taken ill and she wished to go to her bed.

"You shall go straight to your bed like the good girl that you are. Right after you have your medicine. Would it help you if I put a label on it that read, 'Drink Me'?" He smiled, pleased with a joke, but Kiku couldn't quite make out why. The memory of the words "Drink Me" came to her, but it was a fuzzy memory. Had she heard a story, or had it all come from a dream she'd had? She recalled a mouse, and a sea of tears, but then it became confused with walking in the woods with Aaron as they collected pinecones together, and someone was watching them, and she had no baby in her belly, and the snow melted wherever they stepped.

"I've put some sugar in it. That will make it all the better. Only don't tell Doctor Beard if he questions you about it. He is a stickler for the rules."

Rules. Kiku knew she had broken some rule, but she wasn't sure which one. Her belly ached, but the thought of some tea with sugar sounded good. Still, what she most wanted was to go to bed.

Randolph picked up the cup and came to sit beside her. He looked stern, but kinder than she had ever seen him look before. She thought of the girl in the book and the rabbit, and for a moment she imagined Randolph as a rabbit and the thought cheered her.

She took the cup and saucer from him and sipped the tea. Perhaps there wasn't quite as much of the foaming stuff in this cup, and Randolph had been generous with the sugar as well. It was the perfect temperature for drinking, and as she sipped he talked to her of springtime in Virginia. Of the dogwoods whose white blossoms among the leafless trees seemed to float in the air.

"*Kodama*." She rarely interrupted Randolph, but tonight she felt somehow free.

"What is *kodama*?"

"*Kodama* are the spirits of the trees. Maybe here they show themselves in the spring." She wanted to add that Tamora might now find a home among the *kodama*.

He nodded, but she knew he did not believe in spirits or gods. Though he sometimes went to church, he would then come to her and mock the people he saw there, calling them "pious Pollys." That he acknowledged her words with even a nod was almost as unusual as her contributing to the conversation.

He continued on, talking about the small frogs, called peepers, which emerged as soon as the night air warmed a few degrees, and the lengthening of the days. It was as though the doctor's visit had made a new man of Randolph. He didn't mention the child, but surely he was thinking of it. It would be born so soon, and would no doubt be able to recognize his father by the time the dogwood blossoms on the trees turned to leaves.

Would Aaron have gone away by then? If only she could believe that they could escape together. Or that Randolph might tire of her and simply give her to Aaron.

She finished the tea, and he offered her the promised brandy, telling her she had been a good little patient. But she took one sip and shook her head. It was no better than the tea, certainly, and not at all a treat.

He waited on the back porch as she went to the privy with the rug around her shoulders and a muffler around her neck.

In the privy, she struggled to make water. Everything between her legs felt oddly numb. She felt she had to go badly, but could make little happen. Randolph was patient and did not call after her to hurry, though he must have been cold and uncomfortable on the porch. When she came out, apologetic for taking so long, he said it was of no matter and helped her up the slick porch stairs so she would not fall.

"What is the bell for? I don't remember having it put there." He touched the large dinner bell that Mason had mounted on the porch's railing.

"When the baby starts to come, I'm to ring it for Odette. She says that she will be able to hear it, even in the night."

"Ah. That is very sensible."

Inside, Kiku made a move toward the dirty dinner dishes. Before Randolph had arrived, she had brought water in to wash them, and had warmed it on the stove. Randolph waved her away.

"To bed. Those can wait."

She did not argue.

~

The pains woke her from a dreamless sleep, and she opened her eyes to a muted dawn. Randolph was not in the room, but she heard sounds from the parlor. Odette had told her that she might have a few contractions in the last month, but that they would not be real contractions. This pain, though, was strong. It felt very real.

She lay there in a sweat, knowing it was not time for the baby to come, but also that there was no way to stop it.

"Randolph!"

He opened the bedroom door immediately.

"What is it?" He had certainly not slept. The shadows beneath his eyes were as murky as the dawn, and his eyes were bleary as though he'd been drinking, or perhaps reading too long.

She begged him to ring the bell for Odette to come, and told him that she thought the baby was coming too quickly.

"I cannot stop it. I can do nothing!" Another pain, stronger this time, pulled a deep groan from her throat. She closed her eyes, and when she opened them again, she saw that Randolph was not the only other person in the room.

⌒

"Can't you give her some morphine? This is agony."

Kiku heard the impatience in Randolph's voice, and in the doctor's answer as well.

"It's a damned dangerous way to birth a child, Randolph. When they come early, their lungs aren't necessarily developed. And bleeding occurs with the mother."

With the mother. She was the mother, and the baby might be born unable to breathe.

"She doesn't even know how long she's been pregnant. You could be wrong."

They talked as though she weren't there, and in a way, she was not.

"Where is Odette? Please ring the bell. Please bring Odette!"

The doctor looked at Randolph.

"The wife of my orchard keeper. Though I have been thinking to bring her to the house to work."

"Please, Randolph. Please bring Odette. She will help with the baby."

Randolph shook his head. "There's a doctor here. You are not some servant who should do with a woman who has no medical experience. Who knows what harm she's done already. The fact that you're having the child now may indicate how poorly she's taken care of you."

Kiku wanted to scream that this doctor had not been sent to her until that morning, that Odette was the only woman she had ever spoken to outside of New York.

Another spasm shook her and she didn't bother to restrain her voice, but cried out, long and loud. Randolph covered his ears, but the doctor appeared unperturbed.

"Perhaps you should leave the room, Randolph."

"Make sure the child lives."

Kiku heard the unspoken words, "The mother doesn't matter." In truth, it was the same thing she was thinking and feeling, though the idea that Randolph wanted the child frightened her. If it were a son, as she hoped, what would he do with it?

She had been old enough to help her mother when her brother was born, carrying in the fresh wrappings her mother had made certain were ready and dabbing her mother's dry lips with a wet sponge. The women of the village had gathered at the house, telling her father to go away until they called him back, and the women had laughed and told stories as they sat, waiting, in between her mother's pains. It was like a party. A party without men or boys. Being there had made her feel special.

The doctor was still brusque, but not unkind. He stacked pillows, a blanket, and her folded coat behind her so that she was not lying flat on her back. In between the pains, which came at irregular intervals, he sat in a chair by the window and consulted a large black book. As he read, or stared out the window, Kiku lay there thinking of her child fighting to get out. When the pains came, it seemed to her that he was making his way out with very sharp knives.

"Will my baby die?"

The doctor took off his glasses, closed his eyes for a moment, and squeezed the bridge of his large nose with two fingers. She thought that he would not answer her, but he finally sighed and put his glasses back on.

"Many do. Doesn't matter if they're early or late. It's in God's hands."

Another pain came, and he got up to look beneath the sheet that was draped over her legs, then he went to the door.

"Would you be so kind as to bring me a goddamn brandy? It's almost time, and if I'm to do without a nurse, I need some fortification. A cup with a small amount of water for the girl, as well."

Randolph did not look at her as he handed the drinks to the doctor. He quickly closed the door and was gone again.

"A sip or two only. You'll vomit if you drink too much."

Kiku drank as much as she dared, gasping when she was done.

A moment later the baby started to come in earnest, and she screamed in her mother tongue, using every curse she had ever heard her father use, and cursing Randolph, calling down the names of every god and goddess she'd known as a child, and cursing the vile god of Randolph and the doctor, the god who had treated her so cruelly and had her child's life in his filthy white hands.

Chapter 38

KIKU

February 1879

The sound of the baby's first cries was still in her ears when Kiku awoke, though the windows were now dark, and she sensed she was alone. Had she dreamed of the baby? Her mouth was dry, her tongue molded to the roof of her mouth.

Water. I must have water.

The memories returned slowly as she made out the shapes of her bedroom. The door was open now, but had been closed all afternoon because the doctor had been with her. She remembered screaming, and the doctor telling her to stop her hysterics. The terrible pressure between her legs, and the doctor telling her to keep her hands away, and the final expelling of the baby from her body. Then the screams of her child and her own cries of relief. How weak she had been, but she had begged to hold her child, and the doctor hadn't answered, but came to the head of the bed without the child, who was screaming, screaming out of her sight. The doctor's mustache quivered on his lip as he held her shoulder with one strong hand, and put a foul-smelling cloth over her mouth with the other. As Kiku fought for air, her child's screams had faded.

She sat up in bed, the sheets beneath her wet, and her legs freezing cold despite the blankets piled over her. She called out for Randolph, already knowing she would get no answer. Perhaps it was the knowledge that Randolph had most likely taken the child that kept her from screaming. To hear her own screams would make it all the more real.

Someone had left a pitcher of water and a cup on the bedside table. She drank deeply from the pitcher, not caring that the water ran over her chin and onto her ruined nightgown. There was enough light in the room to see that someone had also gone through her dresser. The drawer where she had kept the baby's things was open, and she knew without looking that it was empty. It had been a poor layette. She had seen prams in New York with lace and fine woolen blankets peeking out, and babes in arms in caps that were far finer than anything Madame Jewel owned. Randolph would make certain that even his bastard child had fine things, as long as that child was not with its mother.

Her body was slow to move, and when she stood, shaking, she felt a rush of blood between her legs.

They have left me alone to die.

The blood was not constant, and in the darkness she found the things she needed and cleaned herself up the best that she could. The ache, though, did not abate and was stronger in her heart than in her belly. For a moment she sat on the bed to gather her strength. The meaty smell of blood filled the room and her nostrils, and she immediately felt ill.

In that moment she remembered the tea, and she understood that Randolph and the doctor had made sure the baby would be born that night. The tea had been some kind of terrible medicine of the kind Odette had feared. It would have been a great mercy, she thought, for the tea to have killed them both. Not only had they taken her child from her, but they had robbed her child of the last days that it would be safe from the world outside.

Surely even Randolph wouldn't be foolish enough to take a newborn any farther than the big house. She tried to tell herself that the baby was safe, but she knew that the house was the last place that a child of hers would be safe. She had known from the moment she had seen the house from the woods, months ago, that the place that Randolph called Bliss House was safe for no one at all.

It took her the better part of an hour to prepare to go outside. When she was able to finally leave the bedroom, she found that the fire in the parlor had nearly burned out. Randolph had sent no one to tend it. No one to tend her. Wrapping the blanket around her still-shivering shoulders, she shuffled to the back porch and rang the bell for Odette. It was late—nearly ten o'clock—but Odette had told her that she should ring the bell at any hour. As she stood on the porch, the moonlight sparkled on the frosted remnants of the footprints she had left on the uncleared steps. It had only been the night before. It seemed like a lifetime.

She rang the bell again, just in case Odette hadn't heard it the first time. Randolph would hear it as well.

Let him hear. Let him know that I am still alive.

Inside, Kiku drank more water and took some cornbread from the cupboard where she kept it covered in a large bowl. She attacked it hungrily, so that much of it crumbled from her hand and onto the floor.

Exhausted, she sat in the parlor to wait for Odette. Perhaps Mason would come with her. When she felt herself begin to bleed again, overflowing her monthly rags, she did not rise. The new sofa might be ruined, but she did not care.

An hour passed, and Odette did not come.

Knowing she was not yet strong enough to go anywhere, Kiku got up and walked a little, fretting that something had happened to Odette, that she had been attacked by an animal in the woods as she made her way to the cottage. The woods had not been kind, and Kiku was beginning to be afraid of them. Her living here had disturbed them too much, and now Tamora's spirit was roaming nearby.

Had Aaron heard the bell? He had no doubt known Randolph was at the cottage, but now that it was night, wouldn't he come?

The fire had faded again, and as she carefully bent to revive it, she heard the call of an owl outside, and was less afraid. With the fire blazing, she put the poker aside and, leaving the door open behind her, went to stand on the front porch.

Beyond the trees, she could see that Bliss House was alive with light. Her child was somewhere in that house.

The night was cold, but she did not feel it.

I will come to you. I will find you in that terrible place.

There was movement in the house. No one was sleeping. Was it that a baby was crying, keeping them awake? She listened with her whole body, but could hear nothing but the sounds of the woods.

Where was Odette? Why hadn't she come?

She was about to go back inside when she caught sight of someone or something moving high up on the big house's third floor. Moonlight flashed on a window as someone opened it.

A figure—Kiku was certain that it was a woman—stood framed in the window with a faint light behind her. She stepped outside the window and fell down, down into the darkness.

Chapter 39

AMELIA

February 1879

"Amelia. I have a surprise for you."

Randolph was outside the nursery door, calling for her. He was using his persuasive voice. The voice that had convinced her to bring Tamora to Virginia and leave her life on Long Island far behind.

She pretended that she didn't hear him. She had been sleeping in the nursery all these days and nights since the funeral. Her clothes were dirty and hung loosely on her, but she did not think of how she looked to others because she saw no one. Tamora/not-Tamora came to her in the night and let her brush her hair as much as she wanted. Tamora/not-Tamora whispered to her that something was going to happen, and she couldn't wait for Amelia to find out what it was.

"You have to eat something or you will die before it happens." Tamora/not-Tamora often made her open the nursery door after everyone had gone to bed and eat the soup (always cold in the dark of night) and bread and sometimes cake that Maud left on the table outside the door.

One night, Amelia had pushed the cake toward Tamora/not-Tamora. "You eat. You're too thin."

"Don't be silly, Mother. I can't eat because I'm already dead."

"I wish you wouldn't talk like that, Tamora. You know it upsets me."

"You are my dear mother, and I only upset you because you are so dear to me." She gave Amelia a grin that could only be described as wicked.

It made a bizarre kind of sense to Amelia. What happened between them were the only things that were real to her. Sometimes she looked out the windows in the daytime and saw Clayton bring the carriage around, and Aaron or Randolph get into it. No one came to the house except Doctor Cyrus Beard, a man who was her mortal enemy. He wanted to take her away from Tamora/not-Tamora, but she would not go. She would never leave Bliss House.

"Daddy dearest is at the door, Mother."

Tamora/not-Tamora sat where Tamora had always sat, at the tea party table. But Tamora/not-Tamora had dug the eyes out of several of the dolls and when she pretended that they were eating, she made them spill the tea—which was actually water from the bathroom—all over themselves and then laughed at them, telling them that they were filthy little pig children who needed to be punished.

"I hear him."

"He's not going to go away this time. It's time for the things that I told you were about to happen. Do you remember, dear Mother?"

Tamora/not-Tamora got up from the floor and came to where Amelia sat in the rocking chair. She yanked on a lock of Amelia's hair that was hanging in her face. "Pay attention, Mother! Why won't you pay attention? I'm getting angry with you."

"I'm sorry, my love. What is it?"

"I told you that you haven't eaten enough. You aren't thinking clearly, and I will have to hurt you if you don't pay attention. But you don't have to eat anymore if you don't want to, because it's almost time."

Amelia didn't ask her what it was time for. She announced so frequently that the time was coming that Amelia had lost all sense of anticipation.

"Don't bother telling Father that I'm here. He won't believe you, just like he didn't believe you all those other times."

"Yes, darling." Amelia rested her hand on Tamora/not-Tamora's hair, which remained tangled no matter how much she brushed and brushed.

"You must answer the door."

Amelia pulled her hand back.

"You *must*!" Tamora/not-Tamora slapped her cheek. "Pay attention, Mother! You must answer the door."

Amelia felt tears rise to her eyes. She hadn't cried in so very long, but the idea of opening the door to Randolph made her remember the last time she had cried, on the steps of the cottage in the woods, the tears warm on her numb cheeks. Aaron had been there. She remembered Aaron, remembered it all. All of the memories came back to her, and as the tears spilled, the room changed in front of her. Tamora/not-Tamora was gone. The chairs from Tamora's tea table were upended, the dolls scattered about the floor. Their eyes had not been gouged out, but stared up at her with vapid curiosity. Brownkin was in her lap, his tail bare of fur and revealed to be ragged, half-rotted skin, black in patches and gray in others. He was hideous, and she threw him to the floor with the scattered dolls.

"Amelia. Please come out. I won't beg you. You can leave, Amelia. Go anywhere you want if you like. But after I've shown you the surprise, I think you won't want to go."

Still, she didn't answer. Yes, sometime she would come out. But it wouldn't be today, no matter what Tamora/not-Tamora had said. And where had the child gone? She disliked the way she came and went. Amelia never saw her enter a room. She was always just suddenly there, speaking or playing or tumbling around the open part of the floor like a Chinese acrobat. Where had she learned such things?

Amelia got out of her chair and went to the window. There was no carriage this evening. Doctor Beard was not there. No one had come to visit. The sky was dark above the trees. Night. She had come to like the nights best of all.

She could smell food through the door. Had Randolph brought her evening tray? Maud was the one who usually came, tapping lightly and saying, "Please eat, Missus Bliss. We're that worried about you."

Food did not tempt her. If Tamora/not-Tamora were to return, she might eat something to please her, or at least to stop her from scolding. But she was not hungry and was certain that if she tried to eat she would not keep it down. It was as though her body saw food as poison. In a way, it *was* poison because it kept her alive.

She turned from the window at a sound from the door. The sound of a key turning in the lock. Looking down, she saw the nursery key hanging from a ribbon at her waist. It had been Harriet's key, and she had found it on the dresser of Harriet's bedroom after Harriet was gone. She had a second key that was on the nursery's fireplace mantel.

"You didn't think I couldn't get in here, did you, Amelia? That would've been very naïve of you. Surely you aren't that naïve."

Randolph had peeked around the door at first, but now opened it wide. The gallery blazed with light from the chandelier. She could smell the food that Maud had left, but that was not what he had revealed at the door.

"I've indulged you in your petulant hiding up to now, my dear, but I couldn't wait any longer to show you my surprise. Doctor Beard agreed that it would cause an instant change in your deplorable condition. I told him that we could not go on this way, with you locked in the nursery like a madwoman in a penny novel." He shook his head ruefully. "Though, I must say, Amelia, that you are rather looking the part. You're going to want a bath."

"Leave me alone. Leave me alone to die, Randolph. You've taken everything away from me. Let me have this room. Let me have a peaceful death." She touched her hair, and finding it loose from its bun (in fact the bun had disassembled itself completely many days earlier), she pushed it back from her face so that she could see him as clearly as she dared. Surprisingly, she felt as though she might dare much. He had invaded her territory. The territory that she had claimed for herself and Tamora/not-Tamora. "Just go. Bring your Japanese whore into the house if you like. I'll not bother either of you. You can start your new life any time you wish."

Randolph laughed. "What an imagination you have! Do you recall that I told you that I would not debase this house by bringing her to live here? I have kept my word on that and will continue to keep my word."

"Then why are you bothering me?" Amelia wrung her hands, suddenly uncertain.

"I have changed my mind on another front. That is the surprise I'm anxious to share with you." He looked down at the basket sitting beside him on the floor. It was a simple basket, a Moses basket of light reeds that looked carefully crafted. She had seen that basket before. She had touched that basket.

"No! I don't want to see it. Go away!" Amelia rushed the door to slam it shut, but Randolph was too fast and shoved it back at her.

"You're acting like a madwoman again, Amelia. Don't force my hand with this. I don't want to have to send you away."

She retreated to the back of the room, to the window that looked out over the eastern side of the property and the carriage house beyond the drive. "I won't see it. You can't make me see it!"

Randolph picked up the basket. "Stop being foolish. He can't hurt you, and you're acting like he can. He's tiny, Amelia. He's hardly even a baby, he's so tiny. Look. Look at him." He strode across the nursery, kicking one of the upended tea table chairs out of his way so that it landed on top of one of the staring dolls. "He can't hurt you. When has a baby ever hurt anyone?"

She would not look! As Randolph came closer, she pressed herself into the corner beside the window and put a hand on the cold glass. If only she could push the window open and escape. But the window was fastened, and she was caught.

"Just think, Amelia. We can raise him as our own. We will say that he is the child from some distant part of your family whose parents have died. No one will question it. You're a woman of integrity. No one will dare question you."

"Get it away from me."

In the basket, the baby began to writhe and fuss. Its mouth worked, its tiny lips stretching in its distress.

"He needs a mother. You will be his mother."

"He has a mother. Take it away. Why are you doing this to me?" Amelia began to sob. She was not heartless. It was an infant like any other infant. Hungry like any other infant. The way Tamora had been as a child until she stopped wanting to eat.

"He is my child. He can be our child. Tamora was imperfect, and God called her back to Him. But this child can save you. Listen to me. This child can *save* you, Amelia."

Hearing Tamora's name, she took a breath, and her sobbing subsided.

"How dare you. How dare you talk about Tamora that way when you're holding that son of a filthy pagan. Tamora was *my* child!"

"Your child is dead because you left her, isn't she?" Randolph spoke over the baby's pathetic cries. The baby was so tiny that its loudest wail didn't reach the level of his speaking voice.

There. He had said it. Said what she had been thinking since Tamora had died. Her fault. Wasn't every child's death the fault of the mother because she had neglected her duty of protecting it?

"Get away from me. You don't have the right to speak her name. You're a monster. Raise your bastard. But you'll do it without me." Finally, here was her courage. She didn't need to remain behind a locked door any longer. She saw Randolph as a weak, vulnerable man, finally the weaker of the two of them. He had suggested the inexcusable thing. The impossible thing. He had swept all regard or concern for her out of the house, out of his life, as though they were so much trash.

Where had this courage come from? This courage that propelled her past him and through the disheveled nursery, a place that she no longer needed. Tamora/not-Tamora was beckoning at her from the doorway, looking excited.

"Mother! Mother! I will help you. Come with me!"

Amelia followed as Tamora/not-Tamora ran down the gallery, and she laughed with the freedom of it. She felt light, lighter than air. This was how Tamora must have felt as she ran, evading the strong, warm hands of Harriet or her mother's tender grasp. How difficult it had been for Tamora to simply *be*. No wonder she ran. Amelia felt closer to Tamora in those moments than she ever had before.

Randolph was calling after her, telling her to stop, that Doctor Beard would be there soon. "Don't be foolish, Amelia. This is madness. You are mad!"

Yes, perhaps she was mad, but it did not matter. If this was how *mad* felt, then she would have more of it! As they reached the staircase to the third floor, Tamora/not-Tamora stopped and reached for her hand. But even as Tamora/not-Tamora took her hand, Amelia could see that the child was fading. Her hand felt ice-cold, even colder than it had the first time she had touched her, and that moment had been shocking. Tamora/not-Tamora was leading her to the place where she would find the real Tamora. The child that she had known her daughter could be. The child she would have been if she had not been blighted with the sickness that she had surely inherited from her father. For Randolph was ill. Of that she was certain. He had been mad from before the first day that they met. If only she had been honest enough with herself to ask his brother, Douglas, if Randolph had always been mad. Surely Douglas would have told her. He had always seemed like an honest man.

No one was coming after them. When she and Tamora/not-Tamora reached the third-floor gallery, she paused, breathless, and Tamora/not-Tamora stopped as well.

"Come on!" Tamora/not-Tamora pinched her to get her attention, but Amelia wanted to see where Randolph was. It seemed Randolph had not crossed the gallery, and neither was he coming behind them.

Amelia called out, taunting him even though she couldn't see him. He was carrying a baby in a basket. "Your baby, Randolph! He's your baby now. I'm sure you'll be a *wonderful* father." Then she laughed, knowing she sounded like the madwoman he had accused her of being.

Tamora/not-Tamora tugged at her hand, but she was not so strong now. She had faded even more in the hallway's bright light.

"I'm coming, darling. Don't pull so." Yes. She would follow her daughter/not-daughter because she knew that the real Tamora was at the end of their journey. Far down below, the front door opened.

Randolph called out, "Aaron, she's gone to the third floor. Will you go after her?"

For all his agitation, Randolph did not sound frantic. How hard he worked to prove that he was in command of everything around him. His wife was a problem for someone else to handle. Amelia heard Aaron answer, but she didn't care about Aaron, either.

"This way, Mother." Tamora/not-Tamora led her past the theater to the small bedroom at the very front of the house. It was lightly furnished, and she had only visited it once, to make sure it had been dusted properly before their party so that anyone who might wander into it looking for quiet would find it hospitable. Hospitality. For all her mother's shortcomings, she had at least known to teach Amelia to be hospitable.

There was no one in the room, but one of the windows at the far end of the room was open.

"Mother, I told you I would help you. You must go quickly, before they find us."

This was surely the surprise that Tamora/not-Tamora had meant. Somewhere behind them, she could hear Aaron calling her name. He *did* sound frantic, and she knew that he would take what she was about to do very personally. She smiled to think of it. It was vengeful and mean, and she hadn't thought of herself that way. But it was his own fault. He had let himself be Randolph's pawn, because *he* was weak.

She was no longer weak.

"Help me, darling," she said to the fading child beside her.

For once, Tamora/not-Tamora was not irritable or capricious or crude. She nodded and let go of Amelia's hand, and stepped up onto the low sill of the open window.

"Hurry, Mother!"

Amelia watched the creature-child that had been both a torment and a comfort to her spread her arms and fall into the cold night air. She had faded so much that Amelia could see, through her small body, the carefully laid-out beginnings of the maze that Aaron had planned and planted below. But she disappeared completely before she reached the ground, as Amelia had known she would.

She stepped up onto the sill. When she looked far afield, she could see the stars above the ragged line where the dark sky met the even darker mountain ridge. It was a majestic sight, the sort of thing a person might want to see just before they died. If only she hadn't glanced down at the woods beyond her own garden, it would have all been perfect.

Smoke drifted from the chimney of the little cottage, and light spilled from the open front door. It did look like something out of one of the fairy tales her father's German mother had told her when she was small. Tales of wolves, and talking birds, and witches in the woods who were always trying to trick children and eat them. The stories had frightened her as a child, but she wasn't afraid now.

There was a figure on the porch of the cottage, and Amelia knew it was the woman-child watching the house, waiting to see if Randolph would return her baby to her.

Hearing Aaron's running footsteps in the gallery behind her, she stepped out the window, watching the woman watching her, until the cold air took her breath away, and she closed her eyes.

Chapter 40

LUCY

January 1919

Randolph was dead.

A long line of mourners waited in the thin, winter light of the hall to express their condolences to Lucy and Michael Searle, who stood by her side. Douglas was there, too, with Mary, who was fashionably under-attired in one of the French jersey dresses that had emerged in wake of the war. The faces of Old Gate society were suitably arranged for grief, but Lucy knew they were also there because they were curious. They had seen Lucy in their homes, but she was in the habit of sending them elaborate gifts rather than reciprocating their hospitality, because Randolph had long ago stopped allowing guests in the house. His death must have seemed sudden and mysterious to them.

He had become a further recluse these last two years, rarely leaving Bliss House, or even his bedroom. The previous October, Lucy had brought their lawyers to see him so they could witness his diminished state, and from that point they had brought all questions about his businesses and investments to her. Those times when Randolph did come out of his room, she found his appearance shocking: He had stopped bathing, and his hair was carelessly trimmed, though Terrance still shaved his face frequently. He shuffled through the halls in soft slippers and a series of baroque-looking robes that might have been made for a king. When she asked him where they had come from, he replied, "Terrance." Though how Terrance had managed to get them, she didn't know. He rarely left his master's side.

Immediately after Randolph's death, he had set about readying the house for the funeral. Lucy saw no grief on his face as he moved among the mourners.

"Darling, I can't believe we weren't here." Faye embraced Lucy and kissed her warmly on both cheeks. "Josiah is heartbroken."

Indeed, Josiah had dark circles beneath his eyes, and those eyes had an inward, pained gaze. Randolph hadn't wanted to see him very often, either, and news of Randolph's death had come while he and Faye were in New York on a month-long vacation. There had been no time for a good-bye or even an examination of his good friend's body.

Lucy embraced Josiah. "Dear Josiah, I don't know what to say." In fact, she felt far sorrier for him than she did for herself. She knew she should feel bad, but the truth was that she was relieved Randolph was dead. She might begin to live again. Except for Terrance. Always Terrance.

"I wish I had an explanation for what Randolph suffered, Lucy. I'm only glad that you were able to care for him the way you did."

Lucy nodded, and thanked him, and said that she was glad that he and Faye had been able to come home so quickly. When they moved on, she glanced at Michael Searle. Almost nineteen, he was taller than she, and while his face was smooth, his jaw had sharpened and hardened. In his black suit he looked every inch the grieving young man. Did he grieve? They hadn't talked, but had only had time to go through the actions of grief. She suspected that he was not terribly sorry, either, for the death of this man who had treated him with so much disdain. A man he hadn't even seen in four long years. She wanted to hang onto Michael Searle and never let him go again.

⌒

Lucy knocked on Odette's door, and after a long moment the door opened a couple of inches. Seeing that it was Lucy, Odette let the door swing open and made her way back to her rocking chair in front of the window overlooking the herb garden. She sat down carefully, her thin sweater hanging loose over her diminished frame, hands tightly grasping the arms of the chair. When she was resettled, she gave a gusty sigh of relief.

"You're a pretty sight in your widow's weeds. Is everybody gone? I have something I want to give you before you go."

"I brought you some angel food cake. How are you feeling?"

Odette had come down with a fever the same morning that Terrance had found Randolph dead in his bed, and Lucy had told her that she would bring in a couple of girls from town to help serve at the wake so Odette could stay in her room and rest. The Lynchburg doctor Lucy had taken her to the previous summer had diagnosed her with lung cancer, but Odette worked as much as she was able. "I won't stop earning my keep," she had said on the drive home. "You can depend on that. Like strong medicine, I don't go down easy. That's what Mason used to say."

At Odette's nod, Lucy put the plate with the cake and a fork in the elderly woman's lap.

"Angel's food at the Devil's party." Odette chuckled to herself.

Lucy pulled the room's other seat, a cane-bottom hassock, near to Odette's chair. She sighed less vehemently as she sat. "I'm glad it's over."

"It won't ever be over. Not in this house. They're all still here."

"I meant all the fuss of the funeral. But Randolph is gone. It's already been strange not to hear him at night. Talking to God knows who."

"You think that's going to stop? I hear it. I hear it every night."

Lucy touched Odette's wrinkled forearm. Her physical decline had seemed to coincide with Mason's death three years earlier. He had been older than both Odette and Randolph. Lucy had paid for a grave attached to the church where he and Odette had worshipped all their married life, and she had bought one for Odette beside it.

"How sure are you that Mister Randolph is dead? He's not just trying to fool you?"

"I saw him, Odette. I saw him dead in his bedroom, and I saw the coffin lowered into the ground."

Odette gave a grunt of disbelief. "The body may die, but souls that mean don't die. Just like the souls of the wronged. They live on." The corners of her mouth twitched. "I may just live on myself, I'm that mean."

Lucy smiled. The last thing that Odette was was mean. "What about heaven?"

"Mason's in heaven." Odette sat up straighter. "Mason deserved heaven. One of the only people I know who deserved heaven."

"He was a good man. He was very good to me."

"He was good to everybody. He didn't look at a single person different from another. He did his job and loved everyone like the Lord tells us all to do. I didn't love him nearly the way he should've been loved, though Lord knows I tried."

They sat in silence for a moment.

"I loved Randolph. Once. I think I even loved him a little when he died. After Michael Searle went away to school, it was like he lost much of his desire to be cruel. There was no one left. Just me. And he was afraid I might leave if he pushed me too far."

"What will you do now? You and Michael Searle going away?"

Lucy laughed. "Where would I go? That was what was so funny about Randolph thinking I would leave. My sister, Juliet, and her husband left France for Norway when the war came, and are still there. My father long ago sold my family's house and moved into a small house near the church. We could hardly move in with him. In fact, I should probably bring him here. This is my home. Michael Searle's home. I want him to have Bliss House when I'm gone."

"Even though he won't have a family then? What's he going to do in this place alone? You should make him go away from here. There's nothing for him."

"What makes you think there's anything for him out there? Randolph's gone. No one here will hurt Michael Searle anymore."

What could Odette be thinking? If Michael Searle were to have any chance at happiness, it was here, in the house he knew best. Together, they could make Bliss House a better, happier place. She wouldn't live forever, it was true. But they would find him someone. She knew he worried that he might never marry, never have the love of another person. A woman. Before he went off to school, she had sometimes heard him weeping in his room, and she, more than anyone, had understood why.

"You look out, Miss Lucy. Don't be a stupid woman. Don't be blind, like he wanted you to be. Like you have pretended to be sometimes. I'll be gone, and there will be no one to remind you."

"I don't think—" She and Lucy were necessarily close, but Odette's words were disrespectful, if not downright rude.

"You don't have to pretend with me. I've seen everything in this house. I'm not going to see much more because I'll be dead soon. Probably before the end of the week. I bet I don't even make it to church on Sunday." She pursed her pink lips in irritation and turned her face again to the window.

"Why do you say that, Odette? You don't want to die, do you?" There had been times that Lucy had wanted to die. She thought of the hideous man in Paris. The smell of Brilliantine on his hair and the image of his clouded spectacles were burned in her mind. But it was the moment she had noticed that Randolph was still in the room, watching, that she had wanted to die.

"Can't say I particularly want to. But when I do, I won't stay around. There's plenty of dead here already. Not everyone stays, though I don't know if it's a choice or it just happens that way. I don't believe your mama's here, do you? Mason didn't stay. Mason's waiting for me with the Lord."

Lucy let Odette's words linger and dissipate in the close air of the tidy bedroom. So much talk of death.

"I'll have one of the girls bring you dinner. Would you like some soup? People brought a blue million pies and cakes, but not much in the way of meat."

"I don't want any meat. It troubles my teeth, and I can't swallow it."

Was this what it was like to be an old woman? Lucy could not see herself sitting and staring out a window, unable to eat meat. Then, she had't really been able to imagine herself turning forty years old, either. There were new lines on her face, and she had put on weight in her hips. Some of her dresses had had to be let out, but there hadn't been a man in many years for whom she had cared to keep her figure. There had been Randolph, and that was all. And that had been a very, very long time ago.

⌣

In her bedroom, Lucy slipped the envelope that Odette had given her into the lower drawer of her bedside table. She had careful instructions not to open it until after Odette was dead, and though Lucy had thought the whole thing very macabre, she had agreed, and kissed Odette's withered cheek. As she left the room, Odette had called after her.

"Push the button so the door locks, please."

Lucy disagreed that the door should be locked, but didn't argue. If Odette were to be ill in the night, or—heaven forbid—were to die, it would be trouble to get to her. Lucy had the set of master keys, and Terrance had another set. Who was Odette trying to keep out? Ghosts?

Exhausted, Lucy told Michael Searle that she wanted to lie down before dinner and went back to her room.

Lying on her bed, curtains closed against the late afternoon sunlight, Lucy stared up at the ceiling. The house was silent. Michael Searle was in the library, looking through his father's papers. There was a will with various bequests that they would have to handle, but it was in the hands of the lawyers. Randolph had long ago hinted that there were other children, and, of course, that had long been rumored. Had he acknowledged them? How many lives would be ruined with his death?

The biggest question was what he had left to Terrance. If Randolph had truly believed Terrance was his son, did the will mention him? She closed her eyes. No. It wasn't possible. Michael Searle was his only son, she his only real wife.

Sleeping, she dreamed of a laughing little girl, of chasing her through the garden the way she had chased Michael Searle when he was young. The girl was blond, her hair shining in the sun, but her clothes were rags and her skin unwashed. Was this Tamora? They had a portrait of Tamora, with her strange, fixed gaze, and this girl was something like her.

When she ran into the maze, which was far taller in the dream than it had ever been, Lucy opened her mouth to call after her, but she had no name to call.

She tried to say, *Wait!*, but her mouth felt full of something, and she had to stop running. Now both her mouth and throat were full and she began to choke. Inside the tall, leafy maze walls, the little girl's laughter continued like an endless happy song. But Lucy couldn't breathe and she tried to cough out whatever was in her throat. It wouldn't come, and so she put her fingers into her mouth, not finding her tongue, but a tangle of something that felt like petals and pliable stems. Tugging, she felt whatever it was move, far down her throat. Something came loose: Her hand was full of red heart-shaped petals, flowers with delicate white and blue stamens that had bent with her violence. Alarmed—terrified!— she pulled and pulled and the flowers tumbled from her mouth, attached to their long, plum-colored stems. The harder she pulled, the more painful it was. Still, she had to breathe, and her breath wouldn't come.

The knot of stems seemed endless, but finally they began to change and the stems were no longer plum-colored, but tinged with brown. The taste in her mouth was gritty and base. The dirt that followed was harder to remove and hurt ever so much more than the stems. Not just dirt, but pebbles and rocks and the occasional piece of metal. Even a small tool that made her want to scream in fright, and nail after nail after nail.

When the nails stopped, and the narrow planks of wood began working their way up her throat, she was paralyzed with fear. They twisted their way out and her breath came in bursts with their twisting. One, two, three, four planks, each one longer and broader than the last, and she knew that she was giving a strange kind of birth to the house looming behind her. It had to stop! She thought of the stairs and the dome and the sharp, sharp bits of iron that would pierce her throat and make her bleed to death. But she could not wake!

The little girl's laughter continued on. Laughter that by its very existence mocked her. Mocked her plight.

Finally, finally, the last plank worked its way out and she cast it to the ground with a loud clatter, and for a moment she could breathe again. But only for a moment. Her throat filled with something that tickled, like water coming up instead of washing down into her stomach. It grew larger. Larger. She opened her mouth as wide as she could and put her fingers inside to pull out whatever it was, and other fingers gripped hers in a violent grip, and she knew, *she knew*, that *someone* was coming out of her and she wanted to scream, but there was no air to scream. So she pulled, not letting go of the fingers that held hers, and she brought the hand and forearm out, and in the bright sunshine she saw the stout, wrinkled fingers and the liver spots and her husband's firm fist, and she knew, *she knew*, that the growing pain in her gut was her husband, Randolph, and he *would* come out.

She woke on her side, her own fist pressed against her mouth, desperate to breathe.

It was after midnight, but several bulbs along the gallery outside her room burned in their sconces. Michael Searle's door was closed, and no sliver of light showed beneath. Across the expanse of hall, Randolph's open bedroom door revealed a landscape of dense black shadows.

Desperately thirsty, she might have drunk cool water from her bathroom tap, but she couldn't bear to remain in her bedroom even with all the lights turned on. Randolph's presence consumed her, and she still couldn't shake the notion that he existed somewhere inside her. Bliss House had presented itself to her that first day as a place where ghosts might live beside the living. Had she forgotten? It made a strange kind of sense that Randolph would still be here. *But inside of me?* The thought made her stomach roil.

At a sound above her she looked up to see Terrance on the third-floor gallery.

"What are you doing up there?"

"Are you not well, Missus Bliss? Michael Searle said you had gone to lie down, but that he couldn't wake you for dinner." Concern from Terrance made her suspicious. She wasn't quite sure what their roles would be now. He had been Randolph's man since he was only a boy.

"I'm going to the kitchen for something to drink." She suddenly realized her feet were cold on the floor; her black silk funeral dress was creased, the thick lace trim flattened. Though she wasn't old-fashioned, she was acutely aware that her feet were bare and her ankles exposed, in front of Terrance. But she would not run away like a silly, backward girl. Bliss House was hers now. Terrance was little more than a servant.

He didn't respond and went out of sight. She could hear his footsteps on one of the back stairways.

They met again in the kitchen. For the first time, Terrance looked tired to her. Older. They were the same age, but Terrance's closeness to Randolph had kept him indoors for the most part, and so his skin was relatively unlined.

She told herself that she should have no sympathy for him. Randolph's cruelty had been like mother's milk to Terrance. In a way Randolph continued to live through him.

Inside me, as well. Randolph is still here.

But for once, she and Terrance were almost companionable in the kitchen. In truth, Lucy didn't want to be alone, yet she hadn't wanted to wake Michael Searle. Odette needed her rest, and she was not friendly with the housekeeper or housemaid. After drinking a glass of cold well water from the kitchen tap, she realized she was hungry and made a plate of roasted chicken for herself from the icebox. There was cornbread, as well, in one of the larder cabinets.

"Would you like something to eat?" It may have been the first time Lucy had asked the question of Terrance, but he showed no surprise and only said, "No, I don't care to." She knew he didn't like to eat in front of others. Randolph had joked about how he had neglected Terrance's table manners when they traveled together.

"How he eats doesn't matter a whit. It's how he serves that's important. He's trained well to serve."

Terrance made them tea, and they sat at the big table in the butler's pantry with him as host. As Lucy ate, he smoked a cigarette without apology, and she did not complain. It was as if the true reason for their previous enmity had evaporated. They were like Civil War generals from opposite sides after Lincoln was dead and the war was ended. She and he had lived in the same house almost half of their adult lives.

"Odette is dying. Did you know?"

Terrance nodded. "It won't be much longer. I hear her wheezing in her sleep. Sometimes early in the morning. I think it would be a kindness for someone to put a pillow over her face." He watched Lucy, his eyes unwavering from hers. She knew he had meant to shock her.

"God will take her soon enough."

Terrance smiled his mirthless smile. "Of course, you're right."

Lucy sipped her tea. "This house needs her. There's no one else like her here. I think she's been the only one with any sense. Randolph was right to trust her and Mason."

"She wanted to be my mother. I didn't want her to be my mother. But she was always very kind to me." He stubbed out his cigarette into a china ashtray.

"Tell me, Terrance. Will you leave here? I'm sure Randolph has left you plenty of money. If not, I would give it to you. You could go anywhere. Anywhere in the world, now that the war is over."

"Will *you* leave?"

"There's nothing for me anywhere else. I have Michael Searle. I'm not interested in remarrying. No. I think I will stay here." She touched her napkin to her mouth and rose from the table. "There's more angel food cake, I believe."

Terrance did not respond right away, and she felt his eyes at her back as she opened the cupboard and took out the cake. Uncertain where the girl had put the cake slicer she had used earlier in the day, Lucy gently pried a hunk of the cake from its body with her fingers and laid it on the plate. She took it back to the table and sat down.

"Randolph assured me that I might live here the rest of my life, if I choose to. I see no reason to leave. He was my father, you know."

Lucy put down her fork. "How long have you known?"

"I lived with Odette and Mason until I was eight, and then he sent for me. For more than ten years he dragged me all over the northeast, and Europe, training me to be his valet. His butler. His messenger." In his silence, Lucy wondered what horrors he had seen as a boy, but he didn't go into any more detail.

"Odette told me he was my father when he brought me back here. By then it didn't matter. I did what I was told."

"Are you sorry he's dead?" The words were out of her mouth before Lucy realized how very rude they were.

Terrance looked at her. The overhead light made his deep-set eyes look hooded. Almost black.

"Are you?"

Chapter 41

KIKU

February 1879

So Amelia was dead. Kiku waited for someone to come and tell her that what she had seen was real, but no one came. She took Odette's and Mason's silence as her answer and did not ring the bell again. They had chosen, or had been forced by Randolph to choose, between her and their livelihood. Aaron, too, had abandoned her.

For another day, there was little strength in her legs, and she moved slowly, gathering herself. She would go to the house and find her child. There was no guard at her door. No one to stop her. Whether anyone at the house saw her didn't matter to her anymore. The threat had come from Randolph, and he could only hold her life over her now. That life mattered not at all.

"Kiku. Kiku."

She opened her eyes. She had made a nest of the only clean blankets left in the cottage and lay on some cushions near the fire. Her sleep had been fitful, and she had awakened alternately chilled and sweating in the night.

Seeing her eyes opened, Aaron knelt and held her gently to him. She thought that she might be dreaming, but he was touching her, and his skin was cool against hers.

"Did you think that I had died?"

"I was certain you were alive, though Randolph told me you had died. But I couldn't get away from the house."

"Tell me."

Aaron laid her down again. "Let me get you some water. You're burning up."

She grabbed his arm with both hands to keep him from going. "Tell me."

"He's at the house. Odette is caring for him, and a wet nurse has come."

Kiku stared back at him. The gods had listened. They had not given her a girl child. It was a small mercy in the hell of her existence. She felt the tears start then, and she couldn't hold them back.

Aaron, moved by her reaction, sat back on his heels and stroked her head. He let her cry without interruption, and when she was spent, he told her that he was going for a doctor. Not Doctor Beard, but another that he thought he could trust.

"No. Take me to the house. I have to see him. It's my right to see him."

"Randolph."

"Randolph doesn't matter." Kiku saw that Aaron was still afraid of Randolph. She saw that he was not brave, and knowing it made her sadder still.

"When you're better."

She saw, too, that this was a lie, and that he was hoping he might change her mind. He looked away from her gaze, ashamed.

So much shame. To these people—even Aaron—her life was all shame. She had borne her child in shame. She had been hidden away for shame. She had been stolen from her home for shame. Strangely, it was everyone else who was marked by that shame. All she had done was survive.

"You are all so afraid of him. I could never tell you the things he has done to me because you would never be able to look at me again. Why don't you all see that there is nothing to be afraid of? What can he take from you? Look at me, Aaron."

He turned his face to her.

"Are you so afraid of losing your reputation? Your living? You abase yourself as a slave who welcomes his whip. I will not do that anymore. Are you less than I am? I don't want to believe that's true. Would it not be better to die? Randolph has no reason to kill you. Me, he will kill if I do not escape him first."

"Then let me take you away from here. This moment. Let me show you."

He was vehement. Rash. But he would not understand her.

"If you won't take me to the house, tell Odette to bring him here. I won't try to steal him. I only want to see him. Then I can go."

"We'll go away. We'll have all the children you want to have."

"Yes, of course. But I must see him first. What has he called him?"

"Terrance."

There was little to do but wait. She knew that if she tried to walk to the big house alone, she would collapse in the cold. In spite of the haze it cast over her, the fever helped her to understand everything more clearly. She moved the books from the shelf nearest the fireplace and made a small shrine to the goddess Harati. In a metal bowl she burned scraps she had torn from the useless, bloody sheets, offering up the birth of her only child. She kept candles burning and prayed constantly. Harati would make certain that she would see her son. Hold her son. Never before in her life had she been so focused on a single image: her son's face. It didn't matter that she had not seen it after he had left her body. She had seen it when she closed her eyes each time she laid her hand on her belly, she had seen it in her dreams, and she would see it for eternity. She would be with him for eternity.

And Randolph. She would never leave Randolph. He had kept her so jealously that he deserved to have her forever, did he not?

The fever came in waves. When it was at its hottest, sometime in the late afternoon, she made her way to the front door and opened it.

There was something on the air, some damp scent that made her think of spring. The day was warmer than it had been in weeks, and the icicles hanging from the edge of the porch roof were melting, and she believed she could hear the water sliding into the ground. Below the ground, each drop found the others and together they became a stream that might cool her, and bear her away, far underground, where she might be safe.

Kiku!

Kiku looked past the trees to the far garden wall. The sky opened and rain began to fall. It was a warm rain that turned to mist as it hit the hard ground that was now bare of snow. She held onto the stair railing as she stepped down off the porch, and the raindrops softened her sweat-stiffened black hair.

Far ahead, she saw the woman and the girl through the trees. The girl raised her hand in greeting, and Kiku lifted hers in return.

Odette was coming with the baby. Watching the girl, the words had come into her mind.

Be ready. He comes.

On the Sunday before Christmas, Mason had read from the Bible about the prophets who had foretold the coming of their Jesus. *Be ready!* All were warned to be ready. An angel had come to the girl, Mary, as well. *Be ready, O Blessed One!*

With great effort, Kiku had gone to the pump and brought water inside, a little at a time, to warm it. She bathed as best she could and dressed in one of her old dresses—the purple one with the layers trimmed with black lace. It was tight in the bust because her breasts were numb with milk her son would never have, and at the waist and hips because she still had the shape of pregnancy. But get it on she did, and she dressed her hair in the vanity mirror. She brushed her teeth with the brush and paste that Randolph insisted that she use, and the taste of sleep and fever was gone for at least a while.

The ruined sheets went onto the back porch in a pile. What did it matter? Their scent might draw animals, but someone would eventually come and burn them. Perhaps the next girl that Randolph brought to live there.

Aaron had brought some bread and cheese and milk with him, but she had only eaten a bit of the bread. The fever had stolen her appetite. She drank only water, grateful that the well pump had not frozen as Mason had once said it might.

She slept curled on the sofa, exhausted.

⁓

The door opened with a gust of wind that stirred the fire and cooled Kiku's burning skin. She gasped, overwhelmed with such joy that she could not speak. Morning had come while she slept, and Odette stood framed in sunlight, holding Kiku's son in her strong arms.

"I'm here as soon as I could get here." Kiku had never seen Odette looking so worried. Aaron ushered her inside and closed the door.

When Kiku tried to stand, she felt lightheaded, as though she would fall, and sank back onto the sofa.

"Stay there. Let me get him out of this wrap. It's colder than yesterday, and I was almost afraid to bring him out." She cast a glance at Aaron, who was trying to help her with the small bundle.

"I knew you would come, Odette. They told me you would come."

If Odette wondered who "they" might be, she chose not to ask. She demurred when Aaron tried to take the unwrapped baby from her and bent slightly to put the baby in Kiku's arms.

Kiku's arms were weak, and she had been almost afraid to hold him, but once he was against her, she felt new strength surge into her body.

She murmured to him, words that neither Aaron nor Odette could understand, putting her warm lips against his warm forehead. He opened his eyes at her touch. He could not focus easily, as all newborn babies cannot, but she saw the depths of his dark eyes, and recognized him, and knew he recognized her. She memorized the shape of his tiny nose, and his delicate brow, and kissed his hair again and again, breathing against his skin, wanting to be sure he was warm and that he would know her scent.

How proud her mother would be. He was a tiny but strong baby. Now that she had seen him, she knew he would live.

He opened his mouth, and Kiku thought he was going to cry, but he only yawned and blinked and worked his mouth a bit. The fingers of one of his hands were wrapped tightly around her finger. She had never felt such happiness. When he turned his face to her chest as though looking to nurse, she felt the numbness in her breasts increase, and then the milk started to come. The baby began to fidget, as though he could sense it through the thick bodice of her dress. There was nothing she could do for him but hold him tighter and begin to rock him in her arms.

Odette sat at the other end of the sofa. Aaron paced, stopping every so often to look out the window. They all knew Randolph might show up at any moment, though Aaron had said he was in Lynchburg, making special arrangements for Amelia's funeral, which was to be held two days hence. Many people were coming from New York and other states to attend.

"When he came to our house, he had the baby wrapped up in a quilt. He didn't even give me time to pack a bag, but said I was to come and stay at the big house and take care of the baby." Odette sighed. "I couldn't say no, Kiku. I didn't want to say no. Not when I saw how fragile he looked. He didn't look like a baby who was ready to come out, and Randolph was running him around here like he was the fittest baby ever to be born. I just wanted to get him inside, and so I grabbed my coat and got in the carriage. I didn't even get to talk to Mason about it the next day. Mister Bliss has him moving into the house, too."

Kiku kissed the baby's head again. He had calmed and seemed to be falling asleep.

"My son was not ready. After I drank the tea that the doctor sent with him, and it made me ill, I feared that Randolph meant something terrible to happen. Please do not worry, Odette. You did what was right. I am happy that he will live, and I will watch over him."

Aaron, who had been pacing between the windows, came to the sofa.

"Odette and I must take him back. Randolph can't be trusted. He may have been waiting to see if we would take this chance. I'm sorry, Kiku. I promise I'll come back."

There would be no more holding her son. This she knew. Brushing her lips against his hair one final time, she whispered in his tiny ear and he turned his face to meet her cheek in his sleep as though he might kiss her good-bye. Odette made a sound that she might have claimed was a cough, but it was full of emotion.

"Keep him warm. Keep him safe. Tell him every day how much I loved him."

"I'll bring him. Every day that I can." Odette lifted him gently from Kiku's arms, and she and Aaron put the warm blankets back around him.

Kiku nodded, confident that Odette believed her own words.

"Let Aaron bring the woman I know to help you. She will make your fever go, and you'll be strong again. I'll tell her about the tea, but I'm madder than hell at you, Kiku, for drinking it. That was the stupidest thing you could have done."

"I will talk to Aaron when he returns. I'm too tired to see anyone right now."

"I *will* bring this child back to you. You get strong, do you hear me? If you don't, I'll come feed you myself."

Aaron opened the door. "We need to hurry." But in spite of his words, he strode over to Kiku and kissed her too-warm cheek. "I'm coming back. Sleep if you can."

As the door began to close, Kiku heard her son's tiny voice calling to her, but there were no words. Only a lonely cry.

⌐

Aaron returned within the hour, and after assuring her that the baby was well settled and nursing with the wet nurse, a woman whom Odette knew well from church, he made her some peppermint tea and heated some broth he had brought from Bliss House's kitchen. He had also brought more blankets.

"There are already several people who've come for the funeral. Did you know Amelia was dead? Did Randolph tell you?"

"I have not seen Randolph, but I knew she was dead. I saw her fall from the window."

"That's not possible."

Kiku nodded. The fog of the fever had returned and she was weary. "I saw her with Tamora. By the garden. She will not leave Randolph's house because her child will always be there."

"No, Kiku. She's gone, and Tamora's gone. Perhaps Randolph will want to bring *you* to the house now. He's already taken in the child. I would understand if that's what you wanted. It would mean leaving the child behind if you come away with me. Randolph says it will not leave the house without him, and I believe he means it."

Kiku touched his face, but did not speak for a moment. He was trying to be brave, she knew. But he would need to be even more brave. "I would like some broth. Would you help me drink it?"

Afterward, he fortified the fires in both the parlor and the bedroom and put another blanket around her when she began to shiver violently. "Tonight I'll bring Odette's friend. She'll help the fever go so you can be strong. We will leave here, Kiku, and you will be my wife."

When her shivering subsided, she held out her arms to Aaron, and he caressed her.

"If I am to be your wife, you must take me to bed now."

He gave her a weary smile. "There will be time for that. Right now you must recover."

Kiku shook her head. "We must hurry. You'll have to carry me. I think I will not be too heavy for you."

Aaron picked her up in his arms as though she were a child, and of course she was still much of a child, so fine-limbed and slender even after the birth of the boy. It was with some difficulty that she convinced him to remove his clothes and come to her beneath the blankets. He seemed shy to stand naked before her, but his desire for her, even in her fragile state, was clear.

"My love."

He kissed her then, and held her, and they listened to the fire in the grate and the silence from the woods. She lay pressed against his chest and spoke to him softly of what she needed him to do. Only then did she pull away a bit to look into his eyes.

When she saw the disbelief there, the horror, she was sorry for him. But not sorry enough to take back the words.

"I won't do it."

His handsome face was now so dear to her. It was a kind face. Though she knew he was almost two decades older than she, she felt very old. Old, old, old. He had refused what she asked, but she knew he would eventually agree. If only he could look through her eyes and see the future as she saw it. Then he would know that there *was* no other future but the one she could see. It was a future filled with people, with the house. He was afraid that she would be alone in the dark, but she would never be alone again. Her son was there. She would watch him grow. She touched the prickly curve of Aaron's jaw and stroked his cheek with her forefinger.

"There is no other way. I am dying and I cannot leave here. He will not let me have my son."

She had never seen such pain in a man's face before. Every man she had known—who had known *her*—had worn either a mask of self-assurance or a look of childlike vulnerability. In Randolph's face she had sometimes seen momentary tenderness, but it had been the fleeting tenderness of the butcher for a favorite lamb. She had been the continual sacrifice, and nothing more.

"I wish it could be different. I wish that we had met on the shore near my home. I wish that we could have had many children together, with bright green eyes and perfect teeth."

At this she saw a flickering of pleasure in his eyes, but it quickly melted into a glaze of tears.

She put an arm around his neck and again rested her head against his chest. She began to sob, pressing her face to his skin, wishing with her whole being that she could make herself leave with him that very night. But she hadn't the strength and never would again. Even if she were strong, she knew she couldn't leave her son, couldn't leave this hot countryside with its bitter winters and sun-soaked, humid summer days, and torpid nights. She couldn't leave her son alone with Randolph, unprotected and unloved.

For so long *she* had lived unprotected, but now she knew that she was loved. Her son would be loved. If he was to have to live in that terrible yellow house, she would fill it with her love. But everyone else who lived there would feel her rage. Kiku's eyes squeezed tightly against her own hot tears.

Tears are for children and the weakest of women. Her uncle, her father's brother who had never married, had said that to her when she cried because a baby turtle she had captured and put in a small enclosure in the garden had been eaten by one of the village cats. She hadn't cried more than a tiny dish of tears since she had last seen her home, and she had long ago ceased to be a child, no matter that Randolph and sometimes Odette treated her like one. It would never matter that she had been weak at this moment. Her son would never know. He would grow up strong and protected and only know her strength.

Aaron shook with his own grief, and Kiku was humbled by his emotion.

She touched his brow.

"Husband."

He touched her wet cheek, wiping some of the tears away, then wiped his own, and their tears mingled together.

"Wife."

Aaron's kiss was tender. So tender, yet as certain as his footsteps on the cottage floor, as certain as the firm lines of brick that formed the yellow house. He was like a man who had found a rare and great treasure, and wanted to explore it, celebrate it. Cherish it. There were no more tears, even when they later opened their eyes to the encroaching darkness of the winter evening that meant they would never lie together again.

Chapter 42

LUCY

May 1922

"Lucy, I hope you're not thinking of getting back on a horse once you heal. You always were a dreadful jumper. You try to control the horse too much." It was Faye's first visit to the house since Lucy had come home from the hospital, and she had promised Michael Searle that she would come every day until Lucy was able to get out of bed.

It was 1922, and Randolph had been dead more than three years. They had been a good two years. Lucy had gotten back out into Old Gate society, had even had a few small parties of her own at the house, and had traveled to Boston to see old friends. The ghosts had been quiet. Michael Searle had been happier at the university than either of them had thought he might be. She and Terrance

373

had come to a functional understanding: He preferred to keep his role as manager of the house, yet sometimes sat down with her at lunch so they could discuss servants and other things that came up, but otherwise he kept to himself. If the kitchen servants thought it odd, they didn't say, and Lucy was enough of her own woman not to care about their gossip. They were a long way from the last century. Then came the accident.

Lucy tried to make a joke about Faye's own horsemanship because Faye hadn't ridden a horse since the twins were in diapers, but it felt as though time had slowed, and her tongue was heavy in her mouth. Her leg was broken in two places, her knee shattered. The horse had gotten right up—she remembered that much—and galloped back to the gate to wait to be led into the stable. She had been practicing the jumps alone, which she knew was foolish. But the groom had been within shouting distance, and had come running when he heard her cries. Terrance had called Josiah Beard, and he had arrived just before the ambulance from Lynchburg. Old Gate had no hospital, and the doctors in Lynchburg had kept her there for two weeks, but Michael Searle had finally been allowed to bring her home.

It was high summer. Michael Searle was home from the university at Charlottesville, and up to the day of the accident they had enjoyed a pleasant routine. He worked in the orchard operation for the cooler part of the day, one sleeve of his chambray shirt punctuated by the black mourning armband that he had sworn to wear for five years, as though to prove to the world that he loved his father, as though to prove to himself that his father had loved him. Lucy practiced in the expansive riding ring she'd had installed the year after Randolph died. Later, they would have iced tea and cake together and read before it was time for dinner. If it wasn't too hot, they ate on the patio while the sun set around them. After the accident, Michael Searle went back to the orchards only after they had hired a qualified nurse, who, along with Terrance, took care of Lucy. A part of Lucy felt helpless and deeply foolish, but the morphine drops that Josiah had prescribed made her worry less about it.

Faye had protested that she could certainly do the day nurse's job, but Josiah and Michael Searle had convinced her that an hour or two in the late afternoon, after the nurse was off duty, would be perfect.

"There's a new doctor in Lynchburg, Lucy. His last name is Collins. First name Frederick. He's a widower, and, oh, is he handsome! As soon as you're healed, I'm going to throw you a party, and he'll be invited. I don't know what he'd make of this place." She waved a hand, indicating all of Bliss House. "But maybe he likes houses with history. Have you seen any ghosts since you've been taking that medicine? Josiah says it puts some people right out of their heads."

Faye chatted on, and Lucy simply nodded. Faye had gotten sillier as she'd gotten older: perpetually girlish. Even her two teenaged daughters seemed slightly more mature and conservative than she.

The ghosts of the house had left Lucy alone, for the most part. There were sounds in the night, sometimes on the third floor, but Terrance said that the theater door had sometimes been found opened. He suspected boys from town coming up the stairs on a dare, or even inside, and suggested that they put a lock on the door.

How strange to think of locks on the outer doors of Bliss House.

The housemaid had complained of seeing lights in the orchard at night and figures out near the springhouse, but there was no evidence of vandalism or tampering in the daylight.

"Unreliable," Terrance had said. He let the housemaid go, saying he believed she was a secret drinker. Randolph had indeed left him a considerable amount of money, which Lucy did not begrudge him, and had put in his will that it was his wish that she provide Terrance a home at Bliss House for as long as he wanted. (There had been no other bequests to errant children, as Randolph had hinted. Surely the will had been made before the madness took hold.)

"I am *hopeless* with this." Faye held up a piece of finished satin about two inches wide and a foot long. Even Faye, who had been very adventurous as a teenager—it had been she, after all, who had insisted that they go to Randolph's *Walpurgisnacht* ball—bemoaned her daughters' fondness for all things modern. *Flapper* was a word she used with distaste, though Lucy had noticed that she had had her hair cut in a curly bob, despite being well over forty years old. "You are so lucky not to have a daughter to drive you mad with begging you to do ridiculous things like sewing tiny beads on headbands. And I've left my embroidery scissors at home. Do you have any?"

Lucy caught the question about scissors but little else.

"I keep all my stitching things down in the salon now. The light is better. But I think I have some scissors in the bedside drawer."

Faye opened the top drawer and rummaged. "Who would think you were so untidy behind closed drawers?" She giggled at her joke. "Behind closed *doors*?"

Lucy smiled.

"No scissors there." She opened the lower drawer. "Wait. Here they are." She set the scissors on the table. "Here's an envelope, too, with your name on it. Look at the tiny writing! Why didn't you ever open this?"

Lucy turned her head to see the envelope Faye was fluttering at her. The envelope had yellowed, but she recognized Odette's perfect, tiny script.

"Odette."

"Odette? The woman who was so scary?"

When she was younger, Faye had considered anyone who didn't respond immediately to her charms as scary or mean.

Lucy had raised her head on the bank of pillows, but let it fall back. "I'll look at it later. Just leave it on the table. I'm too tired." The mention of Odette made her sad. She found so many things sad now. Just when she and Michael Searle had begun to feel happy. Even Terrance had begun to look slightly less grim. Josiah had said the medicine might make her emotional, and he had been right. But it did help so very much with the pain.

Faye put the letter down and made Lucy sit up a little again so she could fluff her pillows.

"Poor Lucy. Poor, dear Lucy. It will all be better soon."

When Lucy woke the sun was setting. Michael Searle had replaced Faye and was sitting beside the bed reading a book. Foggy as her head was, she remembered the envelope and asked for it after she had a drink of water.

"Shall I read it to you? I don't mind."

He looked tired himself. She didn't know what was in the letter, but something told her that he should not be the one to read it.

"Maybe you could bring me a bit of supper? Some toasted bread with bacon, and some soup. Soup always cheers me up." She wasn't very hungry, but knew he would be glad to have something to do.

"Of course. Iced tea, too. I'll bring some dinner up for myself, as well, if you don't mind."

When he was out of the room, she carefully slid her finger under the lip of the envelope.

You look out, Miss Lucy. Don't be a stupid woman. Don't be blind, like he wanted you to be. Like you have pretended to be sometimes.

It had been those words that made her reluctant to look in the envelope right after Odette died. The envelope had been in that drawer, but she hadn't seen it, hadn't *wanted* to see it the dozen times she'd opened the drawer in the previous three years. She had made it invisible.

"I'm sorry, Odette," she whispered.

She opened the envelope and pulled out several crisp, yellowed sheets. One sheet was slightly smaller than the others, and it was covered with Odette's hand.

> *Dear Missus Lucy Bliss,*
> *It was wrong of me to keep this letter for so long, but I did what I felt was right. Mason agreed with me.*
> *It bears some hard truths that you will have to endure. Now that Mister Bliss is dead, and I am dead, you can know them.*
> *This letter arrived in the days after Missus Amelia Bliss jumped out the window and died. They say that Mister Bliss was not near her when it happened, but you and I both know that he drove people to do things that were surely against their nature. He did not have to have his hand on her to kill her.*
> *Harriet Rinehart was the woman who took care of Tamora. As you will read, she ran away on the day that poor child was found dead in the woods. When I saw the letter in the mail, and who it was from, I stole it. Missus Amelia Bliss was dead, and it didn't seem right that whatever it said should be told to that evil, evil man. I ask for no forgiveness.*
> *Please do not worry for me. I pray that I am with Mason and Jesus now. I need nothing more.*
> *Your friend,*
> *Odette Goodbody*

As Lucy read the other, longer letter, she learned that everything she thought she knew about her own life was most likely a lie.

Chapter 43

February 1879

Chesapeake, February 6th 1879

Dear Missus Bliss,

    I tried to write this letter before I left, but I had to depart in haste. Yes, I saw you on the road as you returned, but I begged Clayton Poole to drive on because I could not bear to speak to you. I am sorry that your poor daughter has died. You will want to find fault with someone, and I pray that you will not decide that I must be that person.

    The events of my last night at Bliss House are burned forever in my mind. I know you were reluctant to accept the services of the night nurse, Missus Williams, that Doctor Cyrus Beard acquired for Tamora. It is not my business to know what drove you from this house in such haste, but I could see that it was an urgent thing, and that you were determined to go. I saw no

379

immediate fault in Missus Williams, or I would certainly have warned you. You have been generous to me despite my many and varied sins. If you are willing, I would be grateful for a good reference from you because I'm certain that I will not get one from Mister Bliss.

I did hate to leave you, Missus Bliss, as you have been so kind to me. Now that Tamora, bless her dear soul, has been taken from us, I would be of no more use to you. But I must tell you what I have seen and heard or I will die an unconfessed woman. Please know that I <u>could not stop</u> what I saw. May you and God forgive me.

In your absence, Doctor Cyrus Beard advised a kind of treatment for Tamora. Mister Bliss told me not to ready Tamora for bed two nights ago, but to leave her dressed for when Missus Williams came on duty. In the first two days after you left, Tamora was much better behaved in your absence than either you or I anticipated. She was a good girl, Missus Bliss. I do believe she loved you more than anyone else. She still could not bear to be around Mister Bliss, though. If he chanced to come into the nursery, she would begin to scream. He treated it as a great joke, as he does so many things. It worsened with each day that you were gone, with each night that she spent with Missus Williams. I do not believe that Tamora slept much during those nights. In the morning, she was dead asleep on her bed, with circles under her eyes.

I must confess to you, Missus Bliss, that Mister Bliss encouraged me to engage with evil drink while you were away. He was like Satan himself in the garden, bringing me brandy each night. He sat with me and we drank and I was much flattered at first. I have tried so hard to stay away from evil drink. You know how I have tried.

The drink made me tired. I confess it was a relief to feel the comfort of the brandy. I have often thought that a small drink in the evening might help you, Missus Bliss, to forget the difficulty of the day. It is a mission from God what you tried to do for your poor child, and I was happy to try to help you in that. I swear to you.

I slept too heavily. One night I woke to evil sounds coming from somewhere in the house, but they frightened me. Now I know that those sounds were the sounds of your beloved child screaming. But they were like sounds from Hell, and I was afraid to leave my bed. I'm sure I heard an animal roaring, though I now believe that it was Mister Bliss, trying to frighten the child to death.

I was weak. God will please forgive me. I pray that you will forgive me. I knew I could not leave the child there alone with Mister Bliss and Missus Williams, but neither could I do anything to stop them. After the first night I heard the screams, I drank until I could drink no more. Mister Bliss put a new bottle on the table outside my door each night. It was like a gift from Hell Itself. There was nothing on earth that could make me reject it.

Then Missus Williams came to see me. She was afraid, as I had been afraid. Or I thought she was afraid, but now I believe that she wanted to show off. She was that sort of woman.

I had not yet drunk enough to fall asleep, and she came into my room. I'm certain that she had been given drink as well, though I know she told you that she didn't believe in drink. Never believe a person who tells you that, Missus Bliss. For those who appear resolute are often the weakest. They draw a line and dare themselves to cross it. Once they cross the line, they know no limits. They are the most dangerous people.

What she told me and what she showed me made me cross myself like a Papist.

According to Missus Williams, Doctor Beard advised that the child should be restrained in ways that I know you would have prevented. She told me that he had given Mister Bliss a strait-jacket to keep her attention, and advised that she be struck, but not in ways to leave marks. Doctor Beard said that in order for her to be forced to pay attention to what Mister Bliss was saying to her, that she might be restrained in the ballroom by means of ropes hanging from the ceiling. The ropes would keep her from lying down, or kneeling, or running away.

I tried to stop them. I begged Mister Bliss to let the child go. It will not do you any good for me to describe her unhappy state. She was, indeed, like a little animal. A pitiful little animal. It was the saddest thing I have ever seen, and I pray I never see the like.

Mister Bliss was angry that she had brought me to see him, and when she threatened to go to the police, he struck her. The little one was looking away when Missus Williams fell to the ground. He told me to untie Tamora and take her away back to the nursery. She was a pitiful thing, and did not weigh any more than a dog.

If Doctor Beard's advice was to make her more compliant, I am ashamed to say that in some ways it worked. She was not the child you knew, Missus Bliss. In a few short days she had a look in her eyes that was as distant as the moon.

I don't know what happened to Missus Williams. She surely left, but I did not see her again after Mister Bliss struck her that terrible night.

You will forgive me, I hope, for giving Tamora her medicine to help her sleep without dreams. God help me, I thought to give her enough to make her sleep and never wake up until the Lord Jesus brings us all to him on the Glory Day. Mister Bliss will not be there on that day. Of that I am certain. Not Doctor Beard either. They are evil, evil men, and <u>God Will Punish Them.</u>

My distress was such that I laid Tamora down in bed in her clothes after I gave her the medicine. There was no heart in me for undressing her.

I do not know how or when she left the house. When I woke in the morning, her bed was empty. I was certain that I had given her enough medicine to keep her asleep until the late morning. God knows she needed the respite that sleep might bring.

It was Mister Aaron who brought her back with Mister Bliss. No one would tell me where they found her, but I saw them carry her out of the woods on the other side of the garden. Mason walked behind them. Mister Bliss would not let me see Tamora. He told me that if I was not gone before you returned home that he would make sure that I was held responsible for her death.

Please forgive me, Missus Bliss. I did the best that I could in the face of evil. I understand that you had to go away. I know that Mister Bliss is not the man that he appears to be. You have done the best that you could as well.

You have lost your angel, but she is with God now. She no longer knows pain or unhappiness. I pray that you will find peace on earth without her.

Yours, Most Sincerely,
Harriet Rinehart

Post Script: I would not bring you more pain, but I think you must know. Missus Searle, the Reverend Searle's wife, was here several times when you were not at home, soon after we came from New York. I don't want to be a gossip, but as she came here also the very afternoon that you left for North Carolina, I cannot stay silent. It is well known in Old Gate—please forgive me because it is gossip, which I know is a sin—that Mister Bliss has been known to pay a certain kind of attention to women who are not his wife. Women besides the poor child in the cottage in the woods. I chanced to be in the hallway outside the library when Missus Searle was with him, and I heard her weeping. He was very angry with her, and I felt almost as though I should go inside, but I was afraid I might *lose my position if he knew I was there. Missus Searle said that the Reverend Searle suspected that the child of which she was soon to be delivered was not his child at all. She said he did not know who the father might be, but that he was determined to find out, and would Mister Bliss protect her because she knew it might be <u>his</u> child, and did he not care for her any longer. It was a tragic, but evil state of affairs, and I confess I felt sorry for Missus Searle even though she had done wrong. Mister Bliss laughed, and accused her of being a woman of loose morals, and said that the child could be anyone's. He said he did not believe it was possible that it was his, and that she should go back to her husband and never bother him again. I had to hide when she soon ran out of the library in a terrible state, and if Mister Bliss had come right after her, he might have seen me. It wasn't to be, thank goodness. I was able to escape into the kitchen. And so I write to tell you this in my constant sorrow. I wish you only good things, Missus Bliss, and pray you find some comfort in this knowledge of your husband and faithless friend. —H. R.*

Chapter 44

KIKU

February 1879

"Please tell me you've changed your mind."

Aaron returned late the next day, as he had promised he would, but Kiku could not have told him what she had been doing. The fever had stolen all sense of time passing.

She recognized him and knew she had charged him with something terribly important that concerned her son. It meant that she would soon be with her son, and that was all that mattered.

Sometime in the night her son had come to her, grown now, and looking like a tall, Americanized version of her father. He wore riding clothes, a wedding ring on his finger, and eyeglasses. She wondered at the eyeglasses, and would have asked about them, but when she held out her hand to take his, he was no longer there.

She had sunk back onto the pillow, her heart filled with a sense of cruel loss.

"The fire has died. Will you take me away now?"

Aaron cast a look at the low fire, which had not quite truly died, and could not understand how she had kept it going since he had built it up the previous afternoon. She looked as though lifting only two fingers might pain her grievously.

"It's all ready for you."

Kiku smiled. "You are my husband. You are a good man."

⁓

Aaron brought the horse to a stop behind the springhouse. It was dark enough now that they couldn't be seen from Bliss House, but he wanted to be certain. He slid off the horse, careful to keep one hand on Kiku, who had ridden slumped in front of him on the saddle. Even bundled in her coat and boots and another quilt, she was as small as a child.

As she leaned into him, her feet nominally on the ground, he used his free hand to untie the bag he'd roped to the saddle, and let the bag fall. Slapping the horse on the rump, it galloped off, back toward the warm stable. The house was full of people, but none of the visiting footmen or grooms had remarked on him taking the horse. He had ridden into the woods behind the stables and made his way well south, into the orchards, before crossing over to the woods that surrounded Kiku's cottage.

Sliding the bag onto one arm, he picked up Kiku, whose eyes were glassy with fever. She weighed almost nothing. She turned her head to watch the horse disappear into the darkness.

"I have ridden a horse. I must tell my mother. She will not believe me."

"You did well on the horse. I'm very proud of you." Aaron kissed her hair. "Are you cold, my darling?"

Kiku responded at length in Japanese, which he did not understand, but he did not think she was suffering.

Earlier in the day, he had lighted a few of the lanterns along the passage leading from the springhouse to the underground rooms. Randolph was too busy with his guests to notice his comings and goings, and Aaron had been careful. It pained him to see Randolph as the center of attention, feigning grief for his "dear Amelia." Aaron knew the truth of Randolph's deep betrayal of his wife, while understanding that he had not treated her much better. But now that Amelia was at peace, perhaps she knew how horribly sorry he was.

What kind of person had he become? What he was doing now was tantamount to murder. The woman in his arms was dying. Left in the cottage, she would have died, alone, before morning, and he would have remained blameless. He should have gone for the doctor, as Odette had wanted, but it had not been what Kiku wanted. For once in her short life she would have what *she* wanted, and he would be with her, in the place she was so desperate to be.

When they reached the first room, the one just beyond the enormous door at the end of the passage, Aaron laid Kiku on a long cushion that he'd placed against a bare wall, and she was able to unwind slowly from the blanket.

"You've made this room bright for me. Will you stay?" Her eyes shone. Her fever was coming in waves that grew hotter and hotter.

Aaron smiled. He had done nothing but light the lamp in the passage. Its weak glow barely reached to the far end of the room and the partially built brick wall he had constructed the previous night. A bucket of mortar covered with a wet cloth sat opposite them, along with the stacks of bricks that he would use to close the hole he had left. All Randolph would know was that the room's crumbling outer wall had been repaired and shorn up with the brick.

The space behind the wall was just shy of three feet deep. Big enough. It was Kiku's wish to be placed behind it when she was dead, so she could be a part of the house, a part of her son's life forever.

"Will you stay with me for a while?"

"I won't leave you. Here." He brought the bag close and sat down on the cushion beside her. "Lie down, my love." He lifted her head to his lap and stroked her hair. "Are you thirsty?"

She was weak from the fever, but nodded. He picked up the cup of water he had poured from the canteen and held her so she could sip. When she turned her head away slightly, he put the cup down. Her breathing had changed to a shallow rasp.

He rested his head against the cold wall and closed his eyes. Her skin burned beneath his fingertips. He could do nothing more.

If he had been brave, and had taken her away while she was still pregnant, she would have delivered the child without incident. There was no proof that it belonged to Randolph, but they also had no defense against him. They had no proof that he had bought Kiku from a brothel and kept her prisoner for months. If they had run, Randolph might have sent the police after him, and Kiku would have been once again at his mercy.

Always, Randolph won.

With her eyes closed, Kiku floated.

Tamora and Amelia were in the garden. Amelia sat on a bench watching her daughter, who sat beneath a tall statue of a woman holding a peacock that struggled to fly away. Kiku's son sat beside Tamora, playing in the broken white shells spread over the ground. The girl was dropping daisy petals into his hair, and as they bounced from his hair to his face and onto his pudgy little arms, he giggled as only a small child can giggle, delighted. Tamora giggled as well, and Amelia smiled to hear them.

But another, larger shadow cast itself over the whole garden, and Kiku looked up to see Randolph standing in the window from which she had seen Amelia fall. His presence made her angrier than she had ever felt before, and she flew to the window, certain she would break it, but, no, she melted through it, and through Randolph. When she turned back to find Randolph, he had run away into the darkest reaches of the house. She searched and searched the big house for him, spreading herself through it so that she could feel every grain of every wood panel, every satin surface of paint on the portraits. She couldn't find him, couldn't feel him, anywhere.

In frustration, she gripped the very foundations of the house, shaking it, making the enormous chandelier shudder and swing, and rattling the windows in their panes. But the house would not fall. Not yet. The time would come.

Kiku rested. Waiting. The air in the house thinned and filled with light, but despite the thinning of the air, she found that she could breathe more freely than she had ever before.

She had held her baby in her arms, felt the soft down of his hair against her lips. He was here, and so was she.

His name—which she had whispered in his ear when he was with her—emerged like a last sigh from her lips: *Iwao*. Without her, he would have to be strong, like stone.

◠

Aaron held Kiku close against him for a long time before wrapping her stilled body comfortably, securely, in the quilt and placing it inside the wall. Remembering the bag, he retrieved the velvet-wrapped painting he had made for her and tucked it inside so it rested against the quilt.

He brought some bricks and the mortar from the corner of the room and began to fill in the hole. Little by little, the quilt was consumed by shadow, until it disappeared forever.

Chapter 45

LUCY

Walpurgisnacht 1924

Lucy ran barefoot into the woods.

How long had it been since she had left the confines of Bliss House after the moon had risen? Perhaps a year, maybe longer.

As the woods swallowed her, she thought of Tamora, Randolph's daughter, dead in the hollow of a tree more than four decades earlier, and now a constant presence in the house. But Tamora had run into a bitter January night, and now it was almost May. May Day.

Minutes before, Lucy had been lying in her bed, floating and calm, her bedside light on because she had learned to hate the dark and its shadows. Terrance had just given her the medicine, the shot of morphine that helped her forget—for just a while each day—that her husband might have been her true father. But when she slept, her dreams were gray and flat, like newsreels, the people in them lifeless and distant. The medicine saved her, saved her dreams from plunging her into hell.

That Randolph's figure was not distant had been her first clue that she was not dreaming. His face, framed against her own blank ceiling, loomed over her. At first he only stared, but when she screamed, his mouth broke into a partially toothless smile, and he lunged at her, unsteady on his feet.

Rolling away from him, she had clambered off the other side of the bed. Randolph was no ghost. The stench about him might have been death, or only uncleanliness, but he had surely come from the grave. She had seen the coffin lowered into the ground five years earlier. Five years!

He had stretched one arm after her, beseeching her, his voice gravelly with age and disuse. "Lucy! Lucy, don't leave me!"

No ghost.

So many times she had thought back to the afternoon that Hannah Tanner had come to Bliss House, and the look on her father's face when Randolph spoke quietly to him. Her father had looked suddenly ill, and had stalked from the room as though he might at any moment break into a run. That had surely been the day that Edward Searle had come to believe that she was Randolph's daughter, and not his. And that Randolph would have her. Yet neither of her parents had worked very hard to prevent her from being with him. Had their fear of Randolph been so great that they had risked their daughter losing her very soul? Or was it simply the seed of doubt? Perhaps her mother had argued the lesser of two evils, that she had been wrong to accuse Randolph.

Although Randolph was frail enough that Lucy knew she might knock him over to escape him, she couldn't bear the thought of touching him. To touch him would have been to touch death itself. But he moved so slowly that she had been able to run past him and out of her bedroom.

As she ran for the stairs, Terrance had shouted to her from the third-floor gallery, telling her not to run, that she should not be afraid.

He knows about Randolph. He knows that Randolph is alive.

She did not stop but kept running down the stairs, nearly falling in her panic. In the salon, she pulled open the doors to escape through the garden.

The woods would hide her.

In the distance there was a light where there was not supposed to be a light. Stairs leading to a cottage that wasn't supposed to exist.

Lucy opened the door.

It was the kind of room she had only seen in books about the Far East. At first glance it had appeared almost completely empty, but now she could make out the pale *tatami* mats spread across the floor, and the highly polished wooden cabinet against one wall. The light came from a pair of slender lanterns set atop either end of the cabinet. The room smelled of damp grass, reminding her of the long walks she had taken with Michael Searle before her accident.

"Is someone here?"

Still holding onto the polished doorframe, she took a tentative step inside. The woven mats were gentle on her bruised feet. What was this place, and why hadn't she found it before? From the outside, it had looked like any other cottage, with a deep front porch, a pair of windows on each wall adjoining the front door, and a large transom over the door to keep air flowing in summer. This was not Odette and Mason's old house, but was somehow built on the crumbled foundation of another place. Perhaps the cottage burned down by Aaron Fauquier?

She felt such an overwhelming sense of peace that she collapsed to her knees, covering her face with her hands to weep. Here was safety. Here was a promise of comfort she had never known. All thoughts of warning Michael Searle, of the horror that waited for her in the place that had been her home for most of her life, of the monster that was her (*living!*) husband, fled. She wept in great, heaving sobs that released the ache in her chest and covered her hands and face with mucus and tears. Her very life seemed to be flowing from her—*how shocking that she had so much life left!*—and she thought of her mother, who had so thoroughly disdained weeping and anyone who indulged in it. The thought of her mother made her cry harder. Not from love, but from recognition of Selina Searle's weakness, her inability to love her. She wept for herself, and for who she was, and was not. She wept for the woman who had wasted so many months, years of freedom—*yes, it had been freedom*—not seeing it for what it was because she was living in a haze of half-life.

Finally, she lifted her face from her hands and breathed deeply of the room's scent, letting it fill her lungs with warmth. If she, who had spent so much time in these woods, had not known of this place, then surely no one else would. She couldn't stay here forever, but perhaps for just a while, until she could gather herself.

Across the room, something new rested between the candles on the cabinet. The flames wavered in the still spring air as though someone had just walked through the room, but when she looked around, she saw only her own shadow on the wall. It occurred to her to be afraid, but, strangely, she understood that nothing in the house would hurt her.

Too weak to stand, she crawled over to the cabinet and touched the small bundle of fabric. At her touch, it cascaded over the edge of the cabinet and slipped to the floor.

It was the most beautiful robe she had ever seen. Taking the length of silk in her arms, she let her hand play over the kimono-style sleeves, and the delicately stitched placket that had been carefully matched to the pattern of peonies embroidered onto the silk.

In the pale flame of the lamps, the silk glowed ivory, but the flowers themselves were the purest white, trimmed in a vibrant rose.

Kneeling, Lucy slipped her arms into the robe and let the silk settle over her. She had so many beautiful clothes of her own, but nothing felt like this, like warm rainwater pouring over her skin. The pain from the scratches and cuts she had suffered disappeared as she closed the robe and tied it carefully with the sash.

Was it the scent of the flowers on the robe that she smelled? No. There was a small ceramic cup on the cabinet, and she leaned forward to take it. It was warm, filled with some drink. Unafraid and very thirsty, she held it to her lips.

The tea was sweet with honey, and she drank greedily, so that a bit dribbled down her chin.

She laughed as she wiped it away with her fingertips, a little embarrassed, even though she was alone.

Yes, she was truly alone. So unlike Bliss House, which felt full to her. Full of people, of movement, of a kind of constant hum of *being*. She closed her eyes with a sigh and, setting the cup down, lay on her side, letting her cheek rest against the woven mat.

Whenever she lay down in Bliss House, she felt its vastness. There was no corner that didn't feel distant, unconnected to the rest of the world. Only the morphine made her feel small and protected within herself. But now she felt no worry. The cottage was like a cocoon. When she woke again, would she have wings?

She smiled, falling into a dream.

～

Alone, yet not alone. Someone watched Lucy from the shadowed corner of the room with pity in her dark eyes. The smile on Lucy's face faltered. She whimpered in her sleep, murmured her child's name.

～

Lucy heard the crunching of leaves, the snap of a fallen twig underfoot, but they were the sounds of her dream: a tea party in Bliss
House where she served Faye and her mother poppy seed cakes
from the rigid body of a large, flat fish whose single eye had been
replaced by a vortex of molten red that threatened to erupt all over
the cakes.

"Careful. Take them all." She pushed the fish at her mother,
whose face kept turning into a man's. He was someone Lucy had
met, but she couldn't remember where it had been.

Faye complained that she was cold, and worried her pocket
handkerchief, which made crackling noises that Lucy thought
sounded like dry leaves. Lucy's mother snapped her jaws at the
cakes, her changeable lips slathering.

"We must be warm! We must go to France, Lucy. Take me to
France!"

Lucy wanted to tell her that France was impossible, that it was
the scene of the first degradation, but Faye couldn't know, and Lucy
was anxious that her mother shouldn't bite her hand.

Now Lucy herself was cold, colder than she had ever been
before, and her hands shook as she retreated from her ravening
mother, whose teeth had grown in her mouth and were now protruding slightly from her lips. Her tongue emerged, grotesquely
lengthened, and probed the air lasciviously for the poppy seed cakes.

When Lucy retreated from her mother, she fell onto the settee,
and it broke under her. She collapsed onto the floor.

But it was not the floor of Bliss House.

⌒

Lucy looked up to see Terrance standing over her. The leather
medicine case whose appearance filled her simultaneously with
euphoria and dread was open in his hands. The case was black in
the darkness, which was disturbed only by the soft glow of a lantern

a few feet away, but she knew it was red, red, red, the color of the drops of blood that sometimes came out of her arm as the needle went in.

"Get away from me! Get away!" She dug her bare heels into the dirt and leaves, but she was caught in a tangle of ivy and brush. The cottage had disappeared as mysteriously as it had appeared, and she was in the woods again, surrounded by ruins.

I was never in the cottage. I was never safe. Tricked!

"Where is he?" She screamed Randolph's name, her voice ringing through the woods. Screaming made her feel warm. The sound made her feel powerful. Why hadn't she screamed more? Would the other servants hear her? Randolph would not have come out of the house. Something was keeping him there. She was certain he hadn't left Bliss House since the day he had been found *dead*. She screamed again.

Terrance leaned forward and slapped her face. "You have to calm down. I won't let him hurt you. I promise. He got out, but it won't happen again." Behind him, the lantern flickered, and a shadow darker than the shadows of the trees rose up behind him. Lucy watched it take shape, brighten.

"What is it?" Terrance glanced over his shoulder.

There was something—*someone*—there. Lucy saw the long, dark hair first, then the oval face and small eyes, black at their center. Where the eyes were supposed to be white, they were a fiery red. As red as the vortex of the fish's eye. "Dear God."

The girl's gaze rested on Lucy, but then turned to Terrance. Even though her eyes were terrifying, Lucy saw something in them soften.

"Stop it!" Terrance took her chin in his hand. "Look at me."

"She's watching you. She knows you."

The girl—a ghost, surely, because she definitely wasn't real—reached out for Terrance, but her small hand didn't quite reach him. Still, he shuddered, then quickly recovered himself.

Lucy had never heard him speak so sharply to her. They had almost become friends. He had been the one to help her when she needed more and more of the medicine. He hadn't even asked why, he didn't even know their true connection: that he might be her half-brother. When she looked at the girl's face and back to Terrance, she suddenly saw the resemblance.

Was she a sister? The ghost—why use another name for it, for that's what she was—was so young. Not more than a teenager, younger even than Lucy herself had been when she married Randolph. Her simple gown was not any style that Lucy had ever seen, and she could not make out much detail or color because the ghost was as insubstantial as steam from a boiling kettle.

No. That wasn't a sister's love in her burning eyes, and neither was it a lover's. Lucy had caught that look in her own eyes in a mirror once, when she was with Michael Searle.

It was Randolph's mistress. Terrance's mother.

When the leather strap jerked tight around her left arm, Lucy cried out. So hypnotized had she been, staring at the girl, that she hadn't realized what Terrance was doing.

"This will help you. If I give you more, it will help you forget."

Distressed as she was, she didn't struggle. More morphine was a good thing, yes? Then she could face the knowledge, listen to Terrance. So many questions. But she was in the woods, not her bedroom. She couldn't go back there. Randolph was there.

"Why, Terrance? Why isn't he dead? I saw him. Why isn't he dead?"

Terrance turned back slightly so the light shone on the syringe as he filled it. "I've kept him from you these past five years. The rooms underground. I've kept him down there. He's my prisoner. *Our* prisoner."

"What do you mean? Tell me."

Behind him, the ghost watched Terrance, a look of hunger on her face.

397

"Everything he did. To me, to you, to everyone who knew him. He deserved worse than death. Did you know he built this house on the scene of a vicious murder? He *chose* evil. He *chose* it. Odette told me he killed my mother, and they never even found her body."

Lucy was silent. She was freezing cold. She prayed the morphine would warm her. Nothing Terrance could say now could surprise her. She felt she had gone mad.

"He built rooms underneath the house. He was going to keep women there, just to see what it was like to use them and watch them die. Now he has to live there with his own insanity. I never meant for him to escape."

You are as mad as he is. Mad. Poor Terrance. What did he do to you?

"The funeral?"

"A drug. Like this one. The undertaker is a friend."

"Terrance, she's watching us." Lucy fixed on the ghost—whose hair and dress moved with a breeze that Lucy couldn't feel.

Terrance lifted her banded arm. She couldn't wait to be warm again. "You will feel much better in a minute. I have put more than usual in the syringe." Drawing the lantern closer, he prodded her arm gently until he found a vein, and asked if she was ready.

Lucy nodded, holding her breath as he inserted the needle. "Thank you, Terrance." She closed her eyes.

He let her fall back slightly onto the brush.

"She's here. Your mother is here."

Startled, Terrance looked behind him. "There's no one here."

The night wood was at rest around them. When Lucy opened her eyes again, the ghost had dropped back and was now watching them both.

"She looks like you."

"You're dreaming. You can sleep now. I will take care of you."

The lantern light illuminated one side of his bald head. Lucy remembered getting off the train when they'd returned from Paris to see that he had shaved all his hair off. Randolph had lost much of *his* hair after they married, but he was vain and had added powders and pomades that he thought no one knew about to make it look thicker. She forced the most recent image of him out of her mind: the sagging skin, the fine, lank strands of icy white hair. His mottled cheeks and neck. A monster.

"When you wake up, he will be gone. I can control him. I promise I'll help you forget."

Lucy didn't know how much later it was—a few seconds, maybe. Or hours. The memory of something unpleasant pricked her. In her mind she could see it, and knew it existed, but it had little or nothing to do with her. She heard the rustle of leaves. She smelled the leaves. Woodsmoke.

"Michael Searle?"

When she opened her eyes again, she could hardly breathe. She might have been submerged in deep water, struggling frantically upward, looking for the light. There was darkness above her, a tangle of tree branches. Thrashing to one side, she saw the girl-ghost, her bloodied eyes searching Lucy's own. Was that pity in them? Lucy tried desperately to form a thought. But beyond the girl, *through her,* a bright orb of white light bobbed through the trees, moving away from them, leaving her behind. When full darkness came, it closed neatly, and finally, like the shutter of the camera of the man on the Rue de Rivoli.

"Lucy! Lucy!"

Lucy heard Terrance's voice, but it came from far away. She was floating, floating above herself. Above Terrance. He was shaking her but she could no longer feel anything.

She was free of her body. Free.

Chapter 46

LUCY

There is no pain anymore.

There is no color. Only the silver of not-day, not-night.

There is loss.

There is desire.

There is no peace.

There is the Oriental girl, in her sad little dress. The want is naked in her clear, young eyes, and I would take her in my arms and comfort her, but there is no comfort here. No comfort anywhere.

There is no time for rest. As she turns her back on me, and moves through the silvered trees, I follow, not questioning how I am able.

There is Bliss House, standing straight and tall like a journey's end. But it is not restful. It is silver against the silver sky, and shimmers before my eyes, its movement constant, like a breathing thing. Are we its breath?

There is the garden. The girl and I pass through its wall.

There is Randolph in the window above, and I feel nothing, but only see him staring into the darkness. He cannot see us. But, oh, he feels us. Oh, he feels us. His desire is black as tar. Black as the soil of hell. As black as my own.

There you are, Randolph.

There, behind the doors leading to the salon, are Amelia and Tamora. Mother and child, together. As the girl and I pass through its doors, Bliss House shudders. Above us, Randolph swallows, his ancient throat parched and weak, and he breathes on the glass. He is still watching, but we are all four inside the house.

There are others here, too. We are many. We are one.

There is no satisfaction for us here.

We only know desire, sense desire.

We are here, Randolph. We are all home.